THE TIME OPENER

1692

Tara —
HAve a safe trip to 1692!

First Edition

THE TIME OPENER
1692

J L Tracy, Jr

TATE PUBLISHING
AND **ENTERPRISES**, LLC

Published by Tate Publishing & Enterprises, LLC
127 E. Trade Center Terrace | Mustang, Oklahoma 73064 USA
1.888.361.9473 | www.tatepublishing.com

Tate Publishing is committed to excellence in the publishing industry. The company reflects the philosophy established by the founders, based on Psalm 68:11,
"The Lord gave the word and great was the company of those who published it."

Published in the United States of America

ISBN: 978-1-68142-350-0
1. Fiction / Historical
2. Fiction / Science Fiction / Time Travel
15.05.27

Tuesday, August 19, 1692

PROLOGUE

Late Afternoon
Country Highway, Essex County Common Lands
Massachusetts colony

"Thank you for carrying the feed, Humphrey," Charlotte Whittemore said to the store owner, Humphrey Case Senior, as she finished settling items firmly in place. He had followed her out of the store with bags on his shoulders, and now was helping her load her purchases into the wagon. "I cannot say that I would have the strength to load the grain."

"It is my pleasure," Humphrey said, grunting through the effort of lifting the second sack of milled corn onto the wagon. "May I say, I cannot help but take notice that you have purchased more from my shop in this summer than last?" He turned and gave an appreciative smile to her.

"I have indeed," she replied, waving away a couple of flies that were buzzing around her face. "I fear for my safety if I tread into the boundary of either Salem or Salem Village."

"Why do you say that?" he asked, pausing to look at her with one squinted eye blocking the late afternoon sun.

Charlotte harrumphed irritably. Humphrey's general store was as close to the towns of Salem Village and Salem Town as she was comfortable being in the last several months.

"You know quite well what madness has taken North Massachusetts."

"Ah, yes, of course," Humphrey said, realizing that she was talking about the many witches that had been discovered since early April. He hoisted the final sack onto the wagon.

"Do not believe me a fool or blind to the things that happen," Charlotte warned him. She used her fingers to count her points as she made them. "I attend church regularly, I sit with the town in Salem Town during the town meetings, and I pay what I am able to give to the crown and the parish in tax and tithe. Yet, because I am an old woman and widow, and I own land between the two towns, I should be in danger of being accused." She cast a mistrusting glance eastward down the road, where beyond the trees, about two miles to the east and north, lay Salem Town. Several women whom she had known for years now sat in the town jail, perfectly innocent of the crimes attributed them, and awaiting their fates from the town justices.

Humphrey could not see any justification for her alarm; he himself was in his sixty-second year, and so did not agree with her conclusions.

"My lady," he said with confidence, "I do not think you should have things to be afraid for. Those who have been accus-ed have also been try-ed in front of a court and jury, appointed by the servants of King William. You are a good woman, who does no evil deeds, and should not have fear."

"Yes, well," Charlotte responded politely, "I tell you now, whether witches are real or fraud, the danger from either truth is as real as the other."

He paused for a brief lull, and then offered a bemused and friendly smile as he returned to his point. "In truth, I am delighted that you have taken to patronize my shoppe, as is Mary."

She relaxed in his geniality to return her own genuine smile of appreciation. "And I thank you for your help with my goods and groceries."

He opened his mouth to reply when several sharp cracks echoed out of the trees, and startled both Humphrey and Charlotte.

"Musket fire?" Humphrey knit his brow, trying to identify the sounds.

"It certainly sounds like it to me." Charlotte's mouth tightened into a thin line. She had travelled over two miles to reach this outpost, isolated between those two settlements, to get some supplies. This fact, along with the cursed heat, already had agitated her fussiness. The musket shot now brought about a sharp pain in her back when she startled. Indeed, much of her day had already been spent working the daily chores of the small farm she had kept after Wallace's death.

"It is rather late for a hunting party," Humphrey noted as they both continued to look around to find the source of the shot, listening for more.

"I would have thought that the hangings had already

completed this morning. Regardless, they are a bit closer to the store than I should like."

Charlotte reflected for a moment on his remark; disdain mixed with her anxiety, and brought a frown to her face. This very morning, five witches had been sent to hang by their necks. Even the renowned Reverend Cotton Mather himself was in town from Boston to give witness to the final day of the accus-ed, and had led the congregation during Sunday services to pray for their souls.

A few moments later, they heard another report of a musket, followed quickly by two more. They could now hear faint sounds of shouting. It had come from the southwest, along the highway towards Boston. It was also the direction of her farm; now Charlotte would need to navigate through an active hunt in order to return home.

"Ah, so it is indeed a hunting party," Humphrey smiled broadly in realization. "Perhaps a deer."

"Well, it is much too close to my way for me to feel safe to drive home," she allowed her mild amount of displeasure in her voice.

Humphrey considered her fatigue and discomfort, and, reminded of his just-brewed tea that was cooling in the anteroom of his shoppe, turned to face his customer and friend more directly. "It has been a warm day; may we offer you some refreshment as you wait for the hunt to end?" He finished his proposal with a slight bow.

Charlotte's face softened a bit as she looked over at her horse, and then at the sky. Daubing the sweat from her brow with her handkercher, she resolved that having some company with Humphrey Case and his wife and children would actually be a nice way to spend the next hour. "Very well, I accept your invitation. Besides, I think my horse would also like a little more time to rest before he has to pull an old woman and a heavy load back to the farm."

Humphrey offered his elbow for escort. Mrs. Whittemore accepted his arm, and the two walked back into the store, leaving the distant hunt and its fading sounds to the hunters.

The fear of being shot threatened to seize Andrew Wells as he ran, leaping over a fallen tree. He glanced back to make sure his friends were still racing through the woods as well. Brent was only a couple steps behind him and to his right, while David was struggling to keep up from almost ten yards back. They were trying to escape from Salem, and now from the unsuspecting hunting party that had discovered their true identities.

"David, come on!" Andrew shouted over his shoulders, ducking around low-hanging branches.

"Don't…slow down…for me," David shouted between wheezes. "I'll catch up…don't worry!"

Andrew vaulted a felled trunk; his lungs stung as he pushed himself to keep sprinting as fast as he could. His tunic, drenched with sweat, hung just loose enough to keep snatching on low-hanging twigs. He hadn't expected to find his life in danger when he joined the team just two weeks ago. One simple error and an oversight later, he now found himself running nearly recklessly through unfamiliar woods, trying to dodge musket bullets in seventeenth-century Massachusetts.

Another crack of gunshot interrupted his thoughts.

"Andrew! How much further do we have to go?" Brent shouted breathlessly, following Andrew between gnarled trees.

Andrew looked down at what he was holding as he ran, and concluded that the trees and bushes were still too thick and close. He had lived in the nearby area once for a few years; he desperately hoped the pond he'd fished in recently wasn't a manmade pond, and was here now.

"There's too many trees! Hopefully only a few hundred yards!" he shouted back. His focus was equally sharpened and interrupted by his dread of tripping on this rocky and root-tangled ground. "We need to make it to Cedar Pond!"

"Halt, you sinful warlocks!" the gravelly voice of one of their pursuers yelled out. Another musket fired, and the bark on the trees to Andrew's left splintered. He was close enough to feel that one.

"Warlocks? *You* halt!" Brent yelled back. He ducked past a low branch as two more shots rang out.

"If you cannot get them with your shot, try to catch them, fools!" shouted another voice, full of frustration, far behind them.

Andrew stole a glance back again. David jumped between the trunks of a forked tree, while the sounds of musket fire mixed with shattering bark met his ears.

"Ha! He missed me!" David wheezed with exhilarated relief and some amusement.

Andrew finally saw the clearing and water up ahead through the trees; it was a real pond after all. It should also give plenty of space to allow them to get home. He dodged some more brush as he began to poke furiously at the tool in his hand. Sparing one more glance back at David and the Puritans chasing them, he estimated that they had given themselves a good hundred-yard lead. *That should give us just enough time to get through*, he estimated.

He emerged from the thicket surrounding the pond and broke into a full sprint towards its muddy beach. He heard Brent following closely. As they reached the water's edge, Andrew stopped himself awkwardly, and making the final adjustments to the metal-clad item, squatting low as he did. Brent skidded to a stop in the mud-grass next to him, and Andrew saw that David had just entered the clearing.

"Come on, David!" Brent called out impatiently. David simply waved back, running awkwardly and now visibly struggling to breathe.

Andrew poked once more on the tool and it burst into life. He quickly but deliberately lifted the hammer-sized apparatus upward from near the ground to just above the height of his own head. A yellow-blue glow appeared along a line he seemed to be tracing in thin air. As he was finishing the top of the line, the bottom of the glowing line began to separate, revealing an opening with darkness inside and widening more and more as the line extended. It continued to open in the same way a rip in tight pants would split, and made a sound like ripping fabric and static electricity.

"They have ceased running!" declared a hunter now at the edge of the woods. "Make haste!"

Andrew looked back as he stowed the tool in his pocket. David had nearly caught up them; the townsmen however had stopped near the edge of the clearing to begin reloading their muskets. One man paused when he looked towards Andrew's black hole. The man's face shone with fright and bewilderment. He tried to continue reloading, but his fears left him fumbling with the musket components.

"Don't slow down, just jump!" Andrew ordered as David reached them. The rift finished popping open into a nearly perfect circle, and he lunged through it into the darkness. Andrew heard an "oof!" and a sequence of splashes.

"Go!" Andrew urged Brent. Musket fire rang out over the quiet water; the Salem hunters were apparently unwilling to leave the protection of the trees. Brent stepped through, his feet shifting awkwardly as he entered the darkness. Again, Andrew heard him cry out with an accompanying splash. Andrew gave one last look to his pursuers before anxiously stepping through; he, too, stumbled as he found his foot fall several inches before splashing into water. He regained his balance without falling completely, and looked back into the daylight from the rift. All three hunters remained hiding at the thicket's edge, yielding to the terrifying vision they now saw. The Puritan with the gravelly voice spat on the ground.

"Back to your fiery Master, evil witches!" he yelled with disgust. "Never bring your poison to our village again!"

Beside him, the other hunter did the sign of the cross. It was then that the opening began to heal itself, closing from the bottom up. It had nearly closed when Andrew could hear one of the men ask, "My God, what sort of evil magic have we witnessed this day?"

The opening finished closing. A gentle orange glow from the injured night air faded as it finished healing; and then it was gone, leaving them lit only by the bright moon. The steady summer noise of crickets chirping, combined with faint hums from the highway, was one of the most comforting sounds Andrew had ever heard. Their week of Hell was over. His heartbeat pounded in his ears, and he could hear each of his silhouetted companions pant heavily, exhausted from the thrill of their escape. He savored the gentle breeze on his drenched clothes and the cool foot of water in which he sat, near the shore of Cedar Pond. Andrew then looked up at the moon in the dark sky, and breathed a great sigh. They were finally back when they belonged.

Wednesday, August 20, 1692

CHAPTER I

8 A.M.
Falmouth, Barnstable County
Province of Massachusetts Bay Colony

Daniel Aaron Quincy, who was known by his middle name, Aaron, squinted in the morning sunlight as he entered the center of town. He took in a deep breath of the strangely warm-but-cool air. The day seemed to be off to a good start, and he felt great, excited for the journey ahead. He pulled lightly and skillfully on the reins, indicating to his horses to slow down some and to turn the corner they were approaching.

"Good morn, Aaron!" called out an older man who was tending his own horse as Aaron passed.

"Good morn to you, Mister Wright," Aaron respond-ed, nodding back with a pleasant smile. He guided the horses along the street, aiming for the general store down the street, exchanging greetings and brief pleasantries with several of his fellow town folk as he drove towards his destination.

The morning sun caught his eye as it glinted off the trees at about the height of the town buildings to his right. Aaron guided his horses to a stop, taking care to set the back end of the wagon to be nearest to the store entrance. He dismounted from the carriage and took the front steps with a sprightly bounce.

Inside, he noticed the storeowner was at the counter

talking to a customer who appeared to be buying meal, while a young boy was sitting on a stool against the side wall whittling a piece of wood.

"Pleasant morning, Mister Bentley!" he offered in salutation to the merchant, and swinging a small sack onto one of the stacked wooden crates that stood next to the entryway.

Obadiah Bentley offered a smile to Aaron. "I will be free to help you in a moment, Aaron!" Aaron nodded politely, placed a few apples into his sack, and then moved on to the next items. Aaron glanced at the boy nearby on the stool.

"Hello, young Mister Trent," he said to the youth. "How is your father this day?"

"He is good, Mister Aaron, sir," Trent replied with a shrug, digging at his fingernail before returning his whittling project.

Aaron looked curiously at Trent as he shifted items in the sack. "And pray tell, what has you here this morning, and so early?"

Before Trent could answer, the other customer passed between them as Bentley escorted him out. The morning daylight reached through the door seemed to bring a touch of youth to his middle-aged graying features. "Mother and Father needed a day to themselves, so Trent will be with Grandfather instead," he said, tousling Trent's hair; the boy wiggled his head out of his grandfather's hand without looking up from his handiwork. Bentley chuckled at his grandson before turning back to Aaron. "I assume you are here to get some supplies for your trip to Salem?"

Aaron was a bit surprised that Bentley knew of his trip. While it was known that he did go to Salem every year before the autumn, he had been so busy this season with preparing for the baby that he had not discussed his plans with very many people.

"How did you learn that I am travelling to Salem?"

"Aaron my boy, you go every autumn," Bentley answered with a mild expression of feigned dismay before adding, "Also, Anna told me, as she was heading to her parent's house yesterday."

He watched Aaron add some wagon rivets to his sack. "I was surprised you did not escort her, considering how far along she is."

Aaron often found Bentley's gravelly voice to be unexpectedly friendly and soothing, and so did not feel put off by his remark.

"I promise I have not been neglectful; it was only that I still had a lot to arrange with Cyrus," Aaron walked over to the counter and set his sack on it for Bentley to begin to tally. "And then there was the situation with Tomas and his flock that I had to deal with," he sighed as memories of frustration appeared briefly. He then dropped his voice so that Trent would not hear.

"Besides the fact, she insisted anyways. She seems much quicker to anger lately."

Bentley snorted in amusement as he sifted through Aaron's purchase. "My boy, that will pass, I give my word. How much longer before the baby arrives?"

"Within the fortnight, we do expect. Cyrus and I will have to return quickly, and we should be able to. Last year only took four total days. I am as prepared as I can be so that I am here in time for the birth, I hope. We shall see," Aaron said as he glanced between Bentley and Trent. The boy had continued his whittling but was now listening closely to the conversation.

Bentley told Aaron the tally of his purchase, and Aaron dug into his pocket for his money purse. He pulled out the necessary pence coins and handed the payment to Bentley, who thanked him politely for his business.

Aaron walked down the steps outside and secured his newly bought sack of things in the back of his wagon. When he finished, he walked up and petted the horses as he untied them from the post, and then mounted the wagon.

He paused momentarily as he thought back to the day before, when he helped his wife to prepare and leave to her family plantation. He had felt unsettled and still wanted to accompany her, to ensure her safe arrival, but he also had much to do with loading the wagon for the Salem trip. Her parents' land was east of Falmouth, a distance of about seven miles from their own land; to accompany her would have meant to lose nearly three hours of day for travel. Anna had wanted him to come with her, but agreed that it would be an unneeded loss of time. "Besides," Anna had said warmly, "an early beginning to your trip would bring an early end to it!" And so it was that they had wished good-byes to each other; he had watched as she rode off on the old family carriage before he went to the stables to tend to the horses that remained.

Returning his focus to the present, he drove a short distance further down the street, towards the smithy. Aaron looked at the stone chimney that he knew rose from the forge inside the smith's shop, admiring the hardiness of the structure built to contain and focus the extremes of heat and fire. To-day, no smoke rose from the chimney, an indication of its blacksmith's holiday.

Aaron slowed the wagon and pulled them close to the entrance. Just as he stopped, his best of friends, Cyrus Bartle, walked out from the smithy, carrying his own travel items over shoulder.

"How goes this morn for you?" Aaron called out as the wagon gently lurched to a stop.

Cyrus tossed his satchel into the back of the wagon just behind the seat, and climbed up to take his place next to Aaron. He and Cyrus had been close friends as long as he could remember, in spite of those occasional periods of time when Cyrus' bachelor's ways had made it difficult to get along, particularly after Aaron and Anna had married.

"Greetings, Aaron!" His accented voice betrayed his excitement for the trip; it was an excitement that Aaron shared. "It is a very fine morning to start a sojourn, my old friend!"

"Excellent. Let us begin, then," Aaron replied, and gave a solid tug on the reins, clicking his tongue at the same time. The wagon gently lurched again, this time responding to the horses' start. Since the smithy was located near the edge of town, the road took them on their way, and

Falmouth quickly gave way to forest.

"Have you heard of any reports of highwaymen?" Aaron asked again; he'd asked Cyrus this several times over the past few days. He realized that his anxiety had grown over the summer, perhaps due to his wife's waning pregnancy. He wanted as few surprises as possible.

"I have told you as much as I know," Cyrus said with a measure of deliberate patience. "And I have heard not a whisper in a month."

The warm morning soon became a hot, dry day, and the sun continued its trek across the sky as the two friends traveled north. They had traveled this path every year since Aaron had been seventeen, when his father had taught him the business side of tanning and selling his wares. Their well-practiced drive would take them north to Sandwich until just after noon, then northwest towards Plymouth; they would then continue to Boston, and then on to Salem by evening. The roads for the first half of the travel would be sparse and rough, considering the limited number of merchants who traveled overland between townships in the Old South Colony. However, Aaron and Cyrus both expected the second half to go by faster since the roads in the Upper Colony would be much more smooth and clear of heavy traffic. Because of the pending birth, they agreed to forgo the usual weeklong jaunt and make this year's visit conclude quickly. Their agenda was to take one day to, and then one day fro, with only a day to make their barter and transaction with the pelt merchant Walter Britson.

As they approached Plymouth, Cyrus reached back to

the supplies sack that Aaron had purchased, and pulled out an apple. He offered one to Aaron, who declined.

"I say, Aaron, I think I would like to meet one of these bewitched folk while we are in Salem," Cyrus took a big bite out of his snack. "I wonder if they have the power to enchant this apple, and make it bigger!"

Aaron smiled at the thought of a giant apple, as fat as a pig.

"Whatever would you do with a bigger apple?" he asked. He already guessed what his friend might answer.

"Bigger apples yield more cider, of course," Cyrus said with a juice-filled crunch.

"As if you need more cider," Aaron chided. "You fell asleep just this Saturday, drunk from cider. Poor Mabel had not a clue what to do about such a first evening."

"I promise you, she had a clue. It was my misfortune to not stay awake long enough to escort her to her home!" Cyrus said with a playful hint of debauchery, while chewing another bite of apple.

"I am certain that escorting her was not your true plan," Aaron said. "If Reverend Wentworth knew of your adventures with the unmarried women of our town, we might not be permitted to be friends."

"Regardless, how much cider I need may not be my point; there are times *you* could indulge more," Cyrus offered casually.

"Perhaps you forget I do not much care for the drink," Aaron replied. "I bought the apples for you, anyway."

"Ah, so that was your intention," Cyrus waved his apple

core at Aaron's conspiracy. "However, I am still unconvinced that you would refuse full swig of any hard drink."

"Be convinced of what you wish, my friend," Aaron replied as he tipped his hat to a passing carriage driver.

"I know what it is!" Cyrus snapped his fingers, sounding both inspired and suspicious at the same time. "You do like wine, this I know. It is not the cider, it is the child. You either do not want to or are not permitted to have a drink until the baby is born. Tell me now, which is the truth?"

"I do enjoy wine, and I do like cider," Aaron responded. "I just do not care much for it lately. But Anna and I decided on this several weeks ago. Besides, it was no secret; I told you of this the next day." He looked at Cyrus, saying, "I think you were distracted by Sara Brookes when she came to the forge with her father. There are times I wonder what I should write down to make sure you remember, distracted as your mind can be at times."

"Ah, yes, Sara I remember; your denouncement of spirits I do not," Cyrus said airily; even now Aaron could see he was clearly more interested in Sara than in this current conversation. Aaron frowned, knowing that he would not be able to get Cyrus to agree with anything on this point, and decided to let the topic rest.

They traveled on, and the two friends took turns at the reins every few hours. They succeeded in reaching their expected milestones, and took breaks regularly as the horses needed them. Aaron was pleased to find the horses were handling the drive much better than he initially expected. One of the horses was still very green and had a lot of fight, but had behaved quite well so far.

The men arrived to Boston by the middle afternoon, pausing long enough for Aaron to buy two particular items. At one of the shops he purchased a tin of fine Virginia tobacco for his father-in-law, and at the other he bought some woven fabrics per Anna's request. She always enjoyed their annual visit to Boston, and Aaron had promised to get linens in her absence. They got back under way within a half hour and were now travelling with the sun to their backs, with Aaron again at the reins. Over the next two hours, they watched their shadows slowly grow longer ahead of them on the road, until they finally passed a familiar farm.

"There is the old farmhouse. I believe we are just outside of Salem now," Cyrus observed. It would not be far before they passed the general store belonging to Humphrey. His store stood at the crossroad which would offer the choice between Salem Village to the west and Salem Town to the east. They would take the east road.

"This is nice country." Aaron commented. "However, if Anna and I ever do decide to leave Falmouth, I think I would prefer Braintree, south of Boston."

"You like Braintree?" Cyrus asked with disdain.

"Every year we pass through it, somehow I feel like it is another home," Aaron answered, yawning. "For this day, however, I cannot wait to get to the inn."

Cyrus opened his mouth to respond when a rather loud

crack exploded from under the wagon, causing the horses to start. Both men were jerked with a lurch. Without warning, a flock of birds suddenly emerged from the foliage surrounding them, swarming as they took flight to escape the noise. The horses, already agitated, now were upset ino a mad gallop; the wagon jumped and jostled its riders and cargo wildly.

"What the –?" was all that Cyrus or Aaron could get out. Both men were now flipped backwards, with Aaron nearly losing his grip on the horses' reins. Just as he was getting his footing back to calm and slow the horses, the wagon twisted as the horses dodged a sunken spot in the road. Unfortunately, the wagon wheel slammed into the very sink the horses had evaded. The sound of wood bursting into splinters was followed by the wagon tilting awkwardly, causing the reins to slip from Aaron's fingers. The wagon, damaged and in danger of coming apart, was racing out of control.

CHAPTER II

Aaron was twisted backwards over the seat of the wagon, battling the items in the back to gain his footing. A sharp pain from a box corner jabbed his back; his arm was dangling over the side, and his left foot was caught under the wagon bench. Aaron caught a glimpse of Cyrus having similar trouble, but the world was tumbling and shaking all around, preventing Aaron from freeing his foot and regain his balance.

"Cyrus! The reigns!"

"Damn the flock of birds!" Cyrus grunted as he was jostled. He was in a better position to regain his balance. Finally he set his foot and lunged forward. His hand closed around the reigns, and he gave a powerful tug on the horses' bits.

"Whoa!"

Now that he had good balance and a firm handle of the reins, Cyrus climbed over the bench. He gave the reins another firm tug, and both of the horses loudly whinnied their dismay.

Aaron ignored the pain in his ankle and managed to get his arm back inside the wagon. This allowed him to work his foot free from under the bench. He climbed to join Cyrus on the bench.

The horses were starting to slow down, obeying Cyrus' commands to stop. After a few moments, the sloping wagon slowed to an uneven stop. Aaron breathed a sigh of relief, and heard Cyrus do the same.

"I will see to the horses," Aaron said, still breathing fast. Cyrus nodded and both men stepped down from the carriage. Aaron headed over to check and sooth the horses; Cyrus dismounted from the other side, and took a few steps to the back of the wagon to inspect the axle that had held the now-absent wheel.

"Hello boys," Aaron cooed, letting his voice resonate in his lower range. "All is right now," He patted both of the horses, shushing and continuing to speak in soft, low tones. The horses were still agitated, whipping their large heads and stepping impatiently in place, but they began to respond to Aaron's calming efforts.

"The whole wheel has been destroyed," Cyrus announced from the rear of the wagon. "Did you bring your spare wheel and mending tools?"

"Yes. I suppose we have no choice except to replace it?" Aaron had walked back towards Cyrus, pausing briefly to reach in and sift through the disarrayed items in the back corner of the wagon and pulling out horse treats.

"The rim is gone, most of the spokes are ruined, and the core is cracked. There is no repairing it."

Aaron reviewed the damage with dismay

"The wheel is in the undercarriage So long as they were not thrown, the tool set is under the bench. I say, never leave your home without it!" he said.

He gave the horses treats, and then led them from the wagon and tied them to a tree. The two friends then walked down the road for several hundred yards, collecting all the pieces of the wheel that had been strewn by their wild careen.

"Well, this must be what started that adventure," Aaron said, picking up pieces to a shattered stick.

"I daresay it was the birds that really set the fate of the wheel," Cyrus remarked with a frown. The two men began their walk back to the wagon.

"I find myself blessed to have a smith along with me, skilled with the hammer that will repair my lost wheel," Aaron said, finishing with a poetic drama. He waited for Cyrus to catch his eye to see the intended humor.

"I am skilled," Cyrus replied with a touch of pride, nodding to acknowledge Aaron's remark, "but still a journeyman. Besides the fact, you know quite well how to replace the wheel. We have done such things since we were boys."

"'Tis true, my friend. Perhaps you can arrange with your apple-witch to magic the wheel into repair if you feel unequal to the job." Aaron laughed heartily.

Cyrus rolled his eyes in mock suffering. "I will do the job, but I may choose to leave you here to walk the rest of the way when I have finished it," he replied.

They returned to the wagon, set the broken wood and torn metal in the back, and began working to replace the wheel.

Within half an hour, they had successfully mounted the

new wheel on the wagon. Cyrus tightened the clamp in place on the axle as Aaron stood up.

"If you'll excuse me, I shall leave the remaining task solely to your capable hands," he said, brushing the dirt and dust off his trousers." Nature beckons me."

"Do not take too long, for I may yet still leave you as I promised earlier," Cyrus teased, speaking to Aaron's receding back. He paused for the briefest of moments as a prank crossed his mind; he then dismissed the idea and returned to his work.

Aaron walked a few yards past the brush, near a couple of trees. He felt the wind that was rocking the treetops also blow his hair slightly. He found a suitable spot and began to relieve himself. Glancing about in the meantime, he took in the view of the woods around him. A glint of light flashed briefly from the grass about a hundred yards away, snatching his attention. He watched steadily as he finished, and a few moments later, another flash appeared, lasting longer than before. The contrast and brightness of the flashes of light reminded him of the shimmering sea in the morning sun near his home. Redressing himself, he finally saw where the light was coming from; it would burst in light briefly from moment to moment, as if the sun shone on something metal.

Aaron walked towards the shifting, twinkling sunlight. As he got closer, he noticed it seemed to be some kind of metal; iron perhaps, or maybe silver, but polished finer than any metal he had seen before. It could have been the hilt of a sword, but it lacked nearly every other detail would have made it such a thing. He gazed at this item that lay in the grass, admiring its pure colors but feeling unsettled by the objects' truly unfamiliar appearance.

For several long moments he stood there, seemingly seized into a trance by it. He heard Cyrus' voice call to him faintly. It took another half minute to realize that Cyrus had spoken, and, shaken from his daydream, Aaron bent over to pick up the item that was not a sword hilt.

"Humph!" Aaron grunted with curiosity. This silver item with colored circles, green-black rectangles, and strange, short copper-red prongs (which looked sharp) was definitely not heavy enough to be a sword hilt.

"Aaron! I have finished," Cyrus repeated. "Put yourself away and let us continue on to Salem!"

Aaron took a quick pace back. Ducking through the low branches, he returned quickly. He found Cyrus setting the tools into the wagon.

"Cyrus, you must look at this!" Aaron said, extending his discovery to his friend. Cyrus took the thing from him, turning it over in his own hands.

"What is this you have found?" Cyrus ran his fingers over the contours. "Are these precious stones of some kind? They do not sparkle," he said, more to himself.

"Can you make sense of it?" Aaron asked, "Of what do you think it is made?"

Cyrus unconsciously shook his head slowly, his understanding hindered but not his fascination. He held it in a beam of sunlight that had defied the trees. "This metal may be steel, but it lacks heft; perhaps it is hollow. It has a polish smoother than my own eyes have seen before. These stones have a feel that is unlike any stone I have held, and I do not recognize the cut." Cyrus paused as he continued to examine its details.

"The prongs are definitely made of some metal I have never seen; perhaps with copper or brass, but not only those metals." He looked into the woods from where Aaron had emerged. He looked back at Aaron. "You found this out there?"

"Yes. The sun shone off of it and helped me to see it lying in the grass." He paused in reflection of his finding the mysterious object. "I first thought it might be the hilt of some kind of sword, but it is quite clearly no such thing."

"No, this is no sword hilt," Cyrus said, handing the object back to Aaron. "I have no ideas." Aaron took it back and looked to the sky. He then produced a small, pocket-sized sundial from another pocket; it had been a gift several years before from Cyrus on Aaron's birthday. Cyrus had built it as a combination compass and sundial, so that Aaron would be able to orient it wherever he was. He studied the rudimentary clock for a few moments.

"We have lost an hour and are behind our schedule," he began with a sigh. "Let us set this aside for now and resume our way."

Cyrus went about returning the horses to the wagon. Aaron put the mysterious object into the back of the wagon. Once they had both taken seat in the wagon, Aaron started the horses again. Salem Town was only a few more miles away.

Although they were later than planned, Aaron decided to go a bit slower for the horses' sake. Thereupon, it took almost an hour to finish the drive in to the town of Salem. In the meantime, the sky had grown pinker and the daylight diminished.

Every year, they took a room at the Marble Wharf Inn, and so they planned to do so this year. They turned left from Bridge Street onto the main street, entering Salem Town proper; Aaron was delighted to see the somewhat-familiar buildings and homes. After almost half a mile, he spotted the inn and directed the horses towards it. He wanted the wagon near the entrance so that the horses would be in front of the inn stables.

"Ahh," Cyrus said with a deep inhale and broad smile, as the wagon finally halted in front of the stable barn. "Salem Town! There we are! Business, tea, women and rum!" He looked over to Aaron, who had already climbed down and was lashing the horses to the tethering post.

"What shall we do first, I wonder?" he asked impishly. He was mildly annoyed that Aaron seemed too busy tending to things to pay attention to his humor.

Aaron paused momentarily before replying, "Let us get our board at the inn, first," he said, finishing a knot.
"Besides, business is closed till the morn, tea ships through Boston, and, quite honestly, Anna would have me hanged with these witches should I even *consider* trifling with women."

"My dear friend, but of course I mean the women to be for me! The rum is for you," Cyrus winked, jumping down from the wagon.

The two walked up the short staircase that led to the inn's main entry door and went inside. A woman with wiry orange and gray hair was sitting behind the counting table working a needle through some fabric, apparently repairing a dress. She looked up, and then squinted to get a better view of the men entering. She sat forward.

"Greetings to you, gentlemen," she said with a thick Irish accent and a broad smile, her tone warm and welcoming.

"Good evening, madam Reilly," both said in unison.

After a moment, Madam Reilly's expression changed to one of recognition.

"Aaron Quincy! Cyrus! My dear boys! Has a year passed already?" she said. The delight in her voice was clear.

"Indeed it has. Have you any room this evening to lodge a couple of gentlemen on a business trip?" Aaron asked.

Madam Reilly placed her work on a table at her side and walked over to the men.

"I believe we do," she commented. After looking over her tenant register quickly, she said, "I have some rooms, all with two beds a piece. Do you wish to have the same room or separate?"

"Blind me!" Cyrus exclaimed and turned to Aaron, mocking a suspicious look at him. "I forgot to ask Anna – Do you snore?"

"Absolutely not," Aaron played along and feigned indignation; he turned to the Madam Reilly. "Four years married, and I have yet to hear a complaint from her."

"Is that so?" Madam Reilly replied, her lips pursed and an eyebrow raised.

"Anna tells the story somewhat different," Cyrus said, giving a wink to their hostess.

"Aaron, for four years have you brought your dear wife with you. Why is she not here today?" She asked pointedly. Her trilled r's seemed to linger, waiting for his explanation.

"She bears our first child soon, and was unable to make the trip," Aaron replied. He could not hide his grin.

"Ah, a new child. Such a blessing," Madam Reilly cooed with grandmotherly pleasure.

"Yes ma'am. We plan to conduct our business to morrow and return to Falmouth before Sunday," Aaron said.

"That is just wonderful. Christopher and I will pray for the safe delivery of your baby," Madam Reilly said, referring to her son. "So, how many rooms?"

"I think just one would be sufficient," Cyrus said, with Aaron nodding his agreement.

"Make your mark here," Madam Reilly turned the register to the men for them to sign in.

"I beg your pardon," Cyrus paused. "I have forgotten your preference. Shall we pay now?" Cyrus asked.

"No. You can wait until you check out before your bill is due. Here you go," she said, handing them a key. "You will room in number seven, 'round the back."

"Thank you, Madam Reilly," they both said.

"It is good to see you again," Aaron said, waving as he followed Cyrus out the door. "And I promise to share your sentiments with Anna upon our return."

"I want you gentlemen to have a nice evening. The tavern will remain open about three more hours. As usual, you will find Christopher tending in there. Good night," she said as they left.

They surveyed their room briefly as they set their effects. There were two beds as they had requested, which extended from the opposite wall to their left as they entered the room. The wall adjacent to the door had a single window, two clean candle mounts and a low bench, which itself sat next to the writing desk and chair. Along the right wall were another set of two candle mounts with long trails of wax that had frozen during their drip from the top of several long-used candles. Against the far wall sat a small potbellied stove for heat and a table for the chamber pots. The walls themselves were white plaster between the occasional square wooden posts.

"I am ready to have a beer and some food. Will you join me?" Cyrus asked, running his hand through his blond hair to get it out of his face.

"Help me stable the horses and we can go to the tavern," Aaron countered.

"Agreed," Cyrus said with enthusiasm. They drove the horses and wagon to the stables. "And the rum?"

Aaron took a deep breath, and then let it out slowly.

They removed the harnesses that fastened the horses to the wagon. "I do not know. I promised Anna I would keep clear in my head at least until the child is born. However," Aaron grunted as he nudged the younger horse, Perseus, into a stall, "this day has been long and I am tired. I would like to relax."

"I will not tell her if you indulge," Cyrus tempted his friend with raised eyebrows.

With the horses secured in their stalls and feeding, Aaron and Cyrus left the stables and walked around the inn and tavern, pausing near the threshold of the tavern.

"I have made up my mind," Aaron said finally. "My fatigue reminds me that I still have a few things to do for our meeting to-morrow. Besides the matter, I have the food that was brought with us."

"Then by all means, my friend, do retire for the evening," Cyrus said with his own sigh; for his part, he remained undeterred. "I find myself invigorated by end of the drive. I intend to go in here," he gestured the tavern.

"I shall finish organizing things," he took a step towards the boarding room, which shared a wall with the tavern door. "I expect to be asleep by that time you have returned. So, good night to you."

"Good night, my friend," Cyrus replied with a wave, and the two men went their ways for the evening.

CHAPTER III

Cyrus paused in the doorway to look over the drinking house. The room was large; he estimated it to be similar in size to Aaron's barn back in Falmouth. To his left, a desk and several benches lined the wall, which itself was painted with coarse images of various animals and plants. Along the walls were evenly spaced lamps; their flames casting small, flickering light and shadows on the wall hangings. Opposite where he stood was the fireplace full of a fire, in spite of the very warm August evening; it cast a good amount of light upon the whole room. To his right was a portcullis-gate-style bar, at which sat a few men hunched over steins of beer and cider, holding lazy conversation with each other or with the bar man. Approximately twelve men sat in loose groups at a few long tables, talking and drinking and making the familiar merry noise he had heard in many taverns. Cyrus stepped across the threshold and started towards the bar.

"Christopher Reilly," Cyrus called, letting his voice carry towards the man attending to the patrons.

Behind the bar, Christopher Reilly looked up from his conversation with a man, who also turned to see whom had interrupted his conversation. Recognition flashed on the face of the bartender.

"Cyrus!" Reilly said, pleased to reacquaint with a familiar face. "Mister Cyrus Bartle," he glanced sideways to the drinker and then back to Cyrus. "It is good to see you this day!"

"Good evening, gentlemen," Cyrus nodded in respect to the men drinking at the bar; only two responded, with muttered grumbles. He turned back to Reilly, and said with a formal tone, "Please, dear sir, tell me: what is there for food and drink in this establishment?"

"Is there anything else worth offering than beer or rum?" Reilly asked with a wry smile.

Cyrus began to reply when the drinker interrupted him.

"Where are you from?" the man demanded with a mild drunk slur in his speech. He was much older than Cyrus, and wore the face of a man who seen much but liked little in his life. He had gone several days without a shave, and had to squeeze his eyes to see Cyrus.

"What an interesting way to welcome a guest," Cyrus said, taking the man's rude manner with humor. He walked the last distance to the bar and leaned an elbow on it. "I am Cyrus Bartle of Falmouth, in the south of the Colony, near Rhode Island. And you, sir?" he asked the drinker in return.

"Pay no mind to Franklin, Cyrus," Christopher interjected with strained tolerance. "Did you say that you want something to eat?"

Cyrus took a seat next to the man. "Just some soup, please, and a dark ale."

Reilly turned to set up Cyrus' drink, and when he finished he left the bar and disappeared into another room. Cyrus looked around the tavern again, letting his eyes finish at his new neighbor. The man emptied his glass as he took another long swig. Cyrus considered this fellow's look; by his clothing, he had a general good standing, but had not attended to himself in at least a day.

"Do you do anything evil?" Franklin grumbled unevenly and without looking at Cyrus directly.

"I beg your pardon?" Cyrus blinked, taken unawares by this question.

"What I mean," Franklin said woozily, then turned to face Cyrus. "Can you create fire in the air?"

Cyrus chuckled lightly; perhaps this man simply enjoyed asking *non sequitur* questions. Reilly reappeared with a white bowl.

"I can *start* a fire, the same as any man, but it is nothing special, I think. I am a smith, so I work the forge regularly," Cyrus said. He threw Reilly a curious glance as the bar keep placed the bowl of soup beside Cyrus' beer stein on the bar.

"Now Franklin, we have talked about this. You must start a conversation *before* you become inebriated, not after," Reilly said with both a warning tone and an understanding face. "You know well also that the Constable will arrive within the hour to check for orderliness. I suggest you clear your head for the time being.

"He is a little shaken up after yesterday," Reilly said in answer to Cyrus' interested countenance.

"Indeed," Cyrus said. "Why? What happened yesterday?"

Franklin turned in his stool to face Cyrus directly.

"Now Franklin–" Reilly intoned before Franklin spoke; his voice was filled with stern warning this time.

"Three demons set to look like men!" Franklin declared, neglecting the warning. "Made to look like you or I do," he said, looking off between Reilly and Cyrus and clearly reliving the memory. "They have opened the gates of Hell!"

"Franklin!"

"Is that so?" Cyrus was intrigued. "News of your trials has reached our own village. In fact, His Excellency Governor Phips made a visit through Falmouth only a month ago, investigating our citizens for any possible witchery."

"Cyrus, please, do not get into that now," Christopher held his hand up to try to stop Cyrus from continuing. "Franklin claims to have actually seen the opening into Hell. He and his two companions did say this, while returning from a day of hunt."

"I tell you, I know what I saw!" Franklin said testily, jabbing the air in emphasis.

"I am sure you saw something. What I am not sure about is that what you saw has anything to do with those accus-ed. I do not wish for anyone to be accus-ed without fact."

Another man, sitting in the seat to the right of Cyrus, joined in the conversation.

"I too was one of the three hunting, with Franklin here, and another" the he said in hushed tones.

Reilly simply sighed, having lost all control of the conversation and now staring away into the distance. Cyrus took another spoon full of soup, and followed it with a deep drink from his stein as he listened to their story.

"You see," the man continued, "three men were seen on the road out of town as if going to Boston, when we came upon them. Suddenly, one made fire in the air at his mouth! There was no flint or steel, no lamps for other flame nearby. Well, we went after them to find out about this. They ran into the wood, and we gave chase, ending with those witches going back to Hell."

Franklin picked up the story. "In the bright light of day, I swear to you, I witnessed these men create a hole of fire in the air. It was black inside, bound ultramarine in color, as the sea, but bright as a fire. Hotter than your forges, I would stake on it, my boy." He looked back to the other drinker, then back to Cyrus. "The men walked into it and then were gone!" Franklin snapped his fingers in Cyrus' face to make his point.

"That will finish it for now, Charles, Franklin," Reilly finally said, his voice inarguable and resolute. Cyrus looked around; all men throughout the room had fallen silent and were watching this conversation intently. "This topic has gained too many listeners. This tavern is meant for relaxation, not starting more trouble.

"My friends, I implore you," he continued, his voice having tapered to a strong whisper. "Let us discuss other things?"

The men of the room slowly began to return to their own drinks and conversations and stories. The man called Charles slid back over to his stool, and took a long drink from his beer stein. Franklin requested a glass of brandy, and grumbled softly when Reilly gave him less than half a glass, but accepted the drink without further complaint.

Cyrus had finished his meal by now, and was full from the soup, bread and his beer. He swallowed the last of the dark brew he had, savoring the flavor as it flowed down his gullet. As he set the stein down, Reilly offered him another serving. Cyrus declined, and then paid for his meal. Both men exchanged their pleasures at reacquainting. Cyrus promised to return the next evening before they left town, and then Reilly walked down the bar to settle some dishes.

Cyrus stood up and turned to walk away from the bar. Feeling a bit playful, he paused briefly to whisper to Franklin, "I assure you, sirs, that if I or my companion lay eyes upon these…creatures…we will alert you at once."

Franklin made no reply, and Cyrus strode from the bar to the tavern exit, and left to return to his room.

Aaron lay stretched and relaxing on the bed in the boardroom, reading his bible. He had just read from the book of Exodus, chapter two, intrigued by the name which meant "stranger in a strange land." He pondered why the author of the Holy Book felt it was important to record the meanings of the names of children. His thoughts were interrupted by Cyrus returning to the room.

"Cyrus," Aaron said absently, trying to recapture his musings. "How was the tavern?"

"I did not intoxicate myself, if that is your main curiosity," Cyrus replied, sitting on his own bed.

"What did you eat?" Aaron asked, returning to his reading.

"The food of the body was bread and soup," Cyrus said, hinting with a mysterious tone.

"What other food would be in a tavern, after dusk?" Aaron was now piqued, and sat up properly.

"Only the gossip of two drunken men, and their stories of witch-men and fire that comes from air," Cyrus finished with a sinister tone, his eyes wide with mock malice. In his hands now sat the object they had found earlier that day, glinting in the candle light.

"Did you share our discovery with them?" Aaron asked, feeling a bit torn about the object. If it was made of precious metal and gems, he and Anna could certainly be helped by selling the object by pieces. On the other hand, such a thing must be valuable, and he did not want to feel as though he had stolen another man's treasure.

"No," Cyrus said, now viewing the fine silver-and-bejeweled item with intense interest. "I stopped at the wagon and brought it with me on my way back."

Both men fell quiet, but Aaron still felt unsettled.

"I wish to step outside for a moment," Aaron stood up

and stepped towards the door. He wanted to remove his mind from the distractions of the object, and he also sought the cool evening breeze.

Watching Aaron leave, Cyrus sat in study of the metal. He stood up, and started wandering absently around the room; as he ran his finger along the side near a long green jewel, he felt something odd. The jewel seemed loose, and there were strange contours that he could detect. He studied the green jewel closely, and noticed that there were words on the metal beside it.

"On," Cyrus read aloud without realizing. "Off."

He had stopped pacing to ponder their purpose. He was puzzled by the whole of the object. As it was, his curiosity had always overcome his sense of caution. He started to poke at the green jewel with a bit more force, when it suddenly moved. The object then began to make a loud humming sound, startling him and causing him to drop it. He yelped in surprise.

As it lay on the floor near Aaron's bed, it hummed in a peculiar way, but not loud or disturbing. Indeed, it reminded Cyrus of an agitated hive of honeybees. There was something almost soothing about it. However, the object was now shiny by its own lights, as many of the gems shone as though filled with their own flame. The prongs now spit lightning and fire to each other, creating glows unlike any fire Cyrus had seen. The floorboards did not seem affected by this fire.

"Aaron..." Cyrus said evenly and with growing concern. He leaned down to pick it up.

He wrapped his fingers gingerly around the handle of the object as it lay on the floor, and noted that it was warm, but not hot as he expected. He was forced to stand slowly, for the device seemed to be heavier as he lifted it. Moving the object reminded him of dragging an oar through water.

"Aaron!" Cyrus called again, this time louder and more urgency in his voice. Simultaneously amazed and afraid of this object, he noticed a glowing blue and yellow line of fire (but strangely without flames) that hung from the prongs of the strange object. The object then stopped humming, and released the glowing line. The glowing line was now about three feet long, Cyrus estimated.

He bent down to look closer, when the line suddenly split and opened into an egg-shaped hole. Cyrus instinctively jumped back a bit, losing his balance. The hole looked like a one that might be burned into a sheet of linen, except that instead of burn marks there were glow marks. Through the hole Cyrus saw darkness, splashed with gray and yellow lights behind unfamiliar dark shapes. In the deepness of the hole in front of him were lights of white and yellow and red, and lights that moved as though villagers with torches were running in the dark. He also heard sounds that were unlike any he had heard before.

It was then that Aaron had finally returned to the room and opened the door.

"Cyrus, I–" he began, but the door bounced off Cyrus' head and backside, sending him headfirst into the opening. Cyrus rolled and then bumped into a solid black form beyond the opening. He lay sprawled awkwardly, not moving.

Terror gripped Aaron when he saw the brilliant glow, and he watched his friend tumble forward through the hole.

"My God, Cyrus!" Aaron finally wheezed.

Cyrus, however, did not respond, but lay stunned and unawares beyond the hole that now existed in their boardroom.

"Cyrus!" Aaron cried again, trying to think of what to do. He hesitated to call for help, fully aware of the sensitivity Salem Town had regarding witchcraft. He knew Cyrus had no fancy for witchcraft, regardless of how heathen some of his ways may have been. He also was not willing to risk being put to the gallows on the eve of his child's birth.

The glowing circle that sat in front of him began to waver. In a moment of decision, Aaron made the sign of the cross and leapt through the hole, joining his best friend in whatever awaited them on the other side.

Even if The Old Deluder himself awaited them.

Wednesday, June 30, 2010

CHAPTER IV
The Research Laboratories
Edison, New Jersey

Doctor Troy Duncan sat quietly, taking a brief break from his work to stare at the large Renoir reproduction he had on his wall. It was his only true "view" from his office, which was deep inside a secure building in the middle of the research complex. He'd virtually been living in his office since the project went sour four days earlier.

He'd always tried to keep his office in good order, but the best he had been able to accomplish were nearly-neatly stacked piles of papers everywhere. Years of research (beginning with his graduate work) tended to pile up for a successful scientist. He felt proud that he had made a splash in his field of physics, developing several new advances in energy storage and production. Now he sat in windowless office, waiting, impatient but momentarily powerless, for some news to break on his pinnacle research experiment.

He continued to retreat into the Renoir, letting his eyes trace the lines, enjoying the contrasts in medium and bright colors. It was one of his favorite paintings, reminding him of places far from his office. Although he recently considered replacing it with a classic landscape, he always came back to enjoying this scene, and so it stayed.

Duncan glanced at the clock on his wall; it was almost a quarter to eleven at night. He expected his wife was annoyed, again, at his continued absence. Turning back to his computer, he resumed the grant request he had been working on. Between the research alone and the need to prepare grant extension requests, he had a lot on his plate; never mind his team's current predicament. They had made the most remarkable advance, not only in their field, but perhaps in all of human history. Still, when the funding is not there, the project cannot continue.

The difficulty Duncan was had with grant requests was giving away too much information. He could not just be candid about the fact that they had developed a method of time travel. Even respectable scientists, the few men and women who fully understood the consequences of tampering with time, could not easily be trusted with the responsibility of protecting it. Of course, that was assuming you could convince them of this new success in the first place.

Duncan's distracted mind became impatient again. Deciding he could not focus enough at the moment, he took in a deep breath, stood up and stretched quickly. He left the office and saw Darrell loitering a few doors down, reading a paper. Darrell looked up without word at the soft squeak of Duncan's door.

"So?" Duncan asked. He let his blunt tone suggest the obvious question.

Darrell eyes darted around, glancing behind himself. "Nothing yet, sir," he replied, shifting nervously.

Duncan had mixed feelings about inspiring such harsh reactions, but considering the stakes, he maintained his style. He knew his frustration was showing in his voice anyway. "Have we found out where they may have ended up?"

"Although they were targeting the mid-Twentieth, we are almost certain that is not where they went. There are no historical signs of them making it to the target zone. Plus, something was just not right when we saw through the portal."

"Keep working," Duncan replied curtly after a few moments.

The scientist frowned unconsciously. His team had targeted the year nineteen sixty-two, and had been expected to return within an hour. Four days later, things were going from urgency to emergency. He'd been holding off reporting their absences to the authorities; already, he'd started getting calls from their worried families.

"Yes!" came a voice from behind Darrell. Both Duncan and Darrell look down the hall, and then ran for the control room. Fervent tapping became noticeable as they turned the corner. Inside, Duncan saw Lewis, his second technician, staring intently at a computer screen.

"You have something?" Duncan demanded, rather than asked. He noted that he needed to work on that.

"Yep! Their signal reappeared," Lewis replied without taking his eyes off the screen. He worked the controls of the computer. "...But... they are not close," he said, and then turned to face Duncan. "It looks like they are in Massachusetts!"

"Massachusetts?" Duncan repeated, momentarily

stunned. Lewis pointed to his screen to show him the results. "What are they doing in Massachusetts?!" he demanded to no one in particular. He directed his next question to Lewis.

"Where?"

A few keystrokes followed by several moments' waiting had Lewis hummed with intrigue.

"Salem," Darrell read aloud, looking on from behind.

"Well, didn't you boys take a little trip?" Duncan muttered to himself. After a weeklong absence, it made a crooked bit of sense that they would show up in another state entirely. At this point, they could have turned up at the South Pole and he would be just as annoyed as relieved.

His cellphone started to ring. He glanced at his tense technicians as he reached into his pocket and pulled out the phone. He opened it in the middle of its third ring.

"Doctor Troy Duncan," he answered, trying to use his calm, professional tone.

"Duncan! It's me, Brent!" Brent blurted on the phone.

"Damn it, Brent!" Duncan burst out, no longer able to hide his frustration.

"Ok, don't worry, Duncan. We're all right," Brent continued with a hurried tone of reassurance.

"'All right'? You've been gone for four days!" Duncan shot back. He wanted to continue to scolding Brent, but stopped himself. "We need to get you back here, *now*. We have your position. *Do not move.* Darrell will come and get you tonight." He paused again to think if there was anything else he needed to say. Only one occurred to him.

"You'd better have a good, detailed explanation as to how the hell you ended up *not* in New Jersey!" He closed the phone, and walked out of the room.

Darrell looked at Lewis.

"How long does it take to drive to Salem?"

Brent closed the phone after Duncan hung up. He took a deep breath, and then turned and walked over to the woman from whom he had borrowed the phone. She smiled and took the phone from him. He thanked her, and turned to rejoin his two colleagues.

"How'd it go?" asked David, inhaling deeply on a cigarette.

"Dude, seriously?" Brent pointed at the cigarette. David simply shrugged, taking another drag. Brent rolled his eyes. "First, what does it say that she didn't bat an eye at these outfits?" Brent said, looking down at his clothes. He was still wearing the damp tunic and trousers of an old-time shipman, as were Andrew and David. "Also, Darrell is driving up here to pick us up."

"That'll be about a four-hour drive for him," Andrew determined after a moment of thought. "We aren't far from where my parents live." He said, thinking intently. He then shook his head. "Still, going there is not an option. It's way too late to go intruding on them."

"What time did you bring us back?" David asked, checking his useless watch. "What time is it, anyway?"

"It's probably eleven by now," Andrew guessed. "I set the Opener to ten-thirty."

David stood up, craning his neck to look up and down the streets. "Okay, maybe there's a bar nearby?"

"I'm not sure," Andrew replied with a shrug. "Even when I visited home, I didn't go to bars much at all. Getting drunk in public isn't my thing."

"Maybe we need to get you out a little more," David responded absently, taking a couple steps to see around the corner of the building. "Still, I want to find one."

"I'll go inside and ask the attendant," Brent volunteered.

"I should come too, since I know the area," Andrew said.

David put out his cigarette in the sand bucket, and the trio went inside to find their next destination to wait for Darrell's ride.

Thursday, July 1, 2010

CHAPTER V
Salem State University

The vibration of the cell phone in Jeremy Macer's pocket compelled him to hurry to his destination; he had no hands free to respond to its beckoning. It was probably his girlfriend Lisa, since most of his other friends were either in class or still asleep, or both.

Jeremy managed to get through the doors of the campus library, up the stairs to the third floor, and over to his usual study table. He had been rather careless gathering up his books after his first class this morning, so he was rather clumsy and loud when everything tumbled onto the table. This drew a few unfriendly glances from the other students who were already in the middle of their own work; Jeremy shrugged apologetically to them while reaching into his pocket for the phone. The display confirmed that it was indeed a text from Lisa, after all.

He read the message, deciding if he wanted to text or call her back. Making up his mind, he sent a text asking if she was close to a break yet. He sat down and began straightening up his stuff while he waited for her reply. A minute later, his phone buzzed again.

Yeah, my break is supposed to be in ten minutes, but I can go now. Will call you when I get to the break room, the message read.

Leaving his mess of books for the moment, he headed back to the stairwell to await her call outside. He opened the door just as his phone started playing his favorite ringtone.

"Hello?" he answered, making sure the door did not slam as it closed. With a clear sky and bright sun above, he looked for some shade while he talked.

"Hey!" Lisa's voice bubbled brightly. "I take it you are just now getting out of your class?"

"Yep. Actually, you buzzed me just as I arrived to the library," he said, finding a seat at the end of a long planter. "How's work going?"

"It's kinda slow. Not too many calls; I guess everyone is okay with their bills today. Which class was it you had first today…history?"

"No, that's later. I just left English," he corrected. Although he was sitting under a large tree, it still felt like the sun was beating down on him. He ignored the heavy warmth and continued, "We were given a big assignment, too. Check this: I have to come up with a fifteen-hundred-word essay by Monday."

"Wow. Do you have to pick your topic, or did your teacher assign you one?"

"No, I have to figure it out on my own," he said. "However, she said we should use a historical event and a personal perspective, and tell a story from it. I'm not terribly worried about it. Writing that will be no problem, it's just trying to decide which 'historical event' to write about. I'm thinking I'll decide between the War of 1812 and the colonial times here in Massachusetts."

"Shocker," she teased him. His fascination with local history was secret from no one. "Well, you'll come across an idea. You always do," she finished warmly.

"Yeah, probably. So, what time will you want me to pick you up for dinner tonight?" he asked, hoping to catch her off guard.

"Oh, we're going out tonight, are we?" she sounded surprised, just as he wanted.

"You bet. We haven't been on a good date in a few weeks, and I'd like to take the prettiest girl in Salem out for a good evening," he said, deepening his voice and trying to inject bravado and charm as he finished.

"A good evening, is that what you're planning?" Lisa played coy. "I guess that all depends on where you'll be taking me: Taco Bell or Pizza Hut?"

"That's not fair!" Jeremy feigned hurt, even putting a dramatic hand to his forehead, despite the fact that she could not see him. "I do mix it up once in a while. We went to Krystal a few weeks ago," he played along.

"Uh huh," Lisa muttered, pretending to be unimpressed.

"Actually," Jeremy said, switching tones, "I was thinking of an out-of-the-way Italian eatery just off Essex, near Summer Street. It's called Paolo's; I think you'll really enjoy the food there. I hear it's a great atmosphere, plenty of opportunity for me to get all romantic and mushy and stuff. What do you think?"

"Sounds good, Don Juan. I get off around four, then I have dance until six. After a little time for my girly prep stuff, I'll head over to your house, so I should be there by seven."

"I thought I was going to pick you up?" Jeremy asked, pretending to be stunned again.

"Being that this dinner will be in Essex, it's probably easier for both of us if we meet at your house, and then go from there together," she pointed out.

"Yeah, that does make sense," Jeremy conceded.

"Well, my break is almost over, so I'm going to let you get back to your stuff," Lisa said.

"Okay," he said. He grinned broadly. "I'll see you later."

"Yep, see you then. I love you!" She said cheerfully.

"Love you too," Jeremy replied, and then closed his phone after they both said bye.

"You LOST it?!" Duncan bellowed, struggling to make sense of how such an expensive piece of technology could be lost. He was already fully astonished by how this whole story was unfolding. Apparently, this team of intelligent minds had been befuddled by bad luck, unforeseeable challenges, and, most importantly, by stupid and careless mistakes. He stared angrily at the three men in the conference room with him.

"You have to understand: they were right on top of us, shooting at us!" Brent said first, moving both hands as if they were guns firing. "We were lucky to set it back to this time without getting riddled with buckshot. These guys were literally trying to kill us!"

"Ok, that part is understandable," Duncan began, taking a deep breath to recover his calm and refocusing on the problem at hand. "Let's start back from the beginning.

"You arrived, but realized that the date was way off after the portal closed," he said, looking around the table, "and, unnoticed in arriving, you were not able to get away from eyes to be able to get back here." Andrew, Brent and David all nodded tiredly at various points as Duncan recounted their experiences. "Somehow, you got yourselves pulled into service for a ship—"

"The *Voyage Maiden*," David offered, and then sat back quietly after a sharp glance from Duncan.

"—a ship that took you from here and took you to Salem. While on board you managed to trade for period clothes," Duncan gestured at the outfits the team was still wearing, "and so fit in better. Then, once docked in Salem, you slipped away unnoticed and made your way out of town so you could get back to the present."

"We agreed that we wanted to make sure that our return to the present didn't make any splashes today as much as in sixteen ninety-two," Andrew explained.

"I see," Duncan said. "Finally, on your way out of town, somehow you catch the attention of some locals who feel riled up enough to chase you with muskets firing. You race through the woods of Massachusetts, coming to a stop at some lake and return to the present, in full view of the locals you were trying to avoid disrupting to begin with. On top of all that, you manage to lose a piece of technology that not only cost hundreds of thousands of dollars to create, but can put a pretty deep kink into the history books if found and mishandled. Does that pretty much sum it up?"

Andrew, David and Brent exchanged glances, and then nodded their heads and muttered their agreement.

"So, what was it that got the hunters upset in the first place?" Duncan asked.

Andrew and Brent both turned to face David. He played with his fingers for a long moment, and then spoke up.

"I, uh," David began with a sheepish chuckle, and then cleared his throat to nervously say, "lit a cigarette, sir." He looked up to meet Duncan's eye.

Duncan grimaced, thinking about everything and how big a mess lay before him. He let out a slow breath, hoping the exhaled air would take with it some of his stress and frustration.

"We have the coordinates of where we opened the portal; we should be able to retrace our steps—" Brent began, but Duncan interrupted him.

"So we can spend hundreds of thousands of dollars looking for a prototype of a time-travel instrument that *already* cost us almost a million dollars to create, lost in the woods at a location we don't even have pinpointed, with a margin of error of nearly two and a half centuries of for it to be happened across?" Duncan shook his head. "No. There have been too many mistakes already. We need to find it quickly, but we also need to make sure that it hasn't been found. And we must proceed systematically, carefully.

"Andrew, I brought you on this team because of your historical expertise," Duncan began decisively. "I want you and Brent to do some historical research and see if there are any bizarre events, strange occurrences, or changed histories that might suggest time travel was involved."

"Wait—but if someone changed the past, how would we notice if any changes have taken place?" Andrew asked. "I've seen Star Trek; I know there are temporal effects to think about," he said, holding his fingers up to quote the word 'temporal'.

"That's difficult to say," Brent answered his friend, "there are lots of theories that have been published regarding temporal mechanics, but since time travel hadn't existed before we built the Time Opener, it's hard to say which theories are actually correct."

"Right," Duncan agreed, and then warned, "but I do not want you spending time thinking about writing a paper out of this. Your main focus is to look for inconsistencies. Andrew, you are going to look for anything out of the ordinary from what you knew before the trip; Brent, your job is to look for more obvious things like someone inventing the microchip before the American Revolution. You two should be able to mesh what you know quite effectively." Both men nodded at their new assignments while Brent yawned widely.

"As for you, David, I want you to do two things. I want you to retrace your entire journey in sixteen ninety-two and present a map for us to use. Since you are not sure where the second Time Opener was lost, we are going to develop a search plan based on your map to recover it."

"I can do that," David said, eager to get back in

Duncan's good graces.

"Look, I realize you boys are tired and ready to change into some modern clothes," Duncan said ready to bring the meeting to a conclusion. "I want all three of you back here within an hour to get started. I've got Darrell, Lewis and Adam assigned on rotating shifts, monitoring for any appearance of the Time Opener. Once you get back here, I don't want anyone to leave until we have some good leads."

"By the way; make sure to contact your loved ones so I will stop getting phone calls." He considered his young team; each man appeared somehow a bit older than they were when they left. "Okay, let's get started. Be back in an hour."

The three of them backed up in their chairs and stood. David stretched and looked at Duncan. "Duncan, what's the other thing you want me to do?"

Duncan stopped at the door to look at him.

"Quit smoking."

CHAPTER VI
Paolo's Italian Dining Restaurant

An Italian opera song played distantly in the dimly lit restaurant as Jeremy and Lisa were finishing their dinner. He had ordered some mixed ravioli while she was enjoying a chicken manicotti dish. Jeremy savored the last bite of his meal, and then gathered up the sauce with his garlic bread. He followed it with some water, and then looked up at his date.

"So, what do you think?" he asked, and popped the bread into his mouth as he indicated the restaurant.

She lifted her chin with pretended haughtiness. "Humph! Tolerable, I suppose." This drew an amused smile from Jeremy. She glanced at her plate and muttered, "I think I'll get that to-go."

"Want to get some dessert?" Jeremy picked up the small menu from the back of the table.

"No thanks. I had a *3 Musketeers* today," she deadpanned.

"Whoa, you're right. Let's not overdo it," Jeremy continued the game. "You're in a rather playful mood this evening," he observed.

"Yeah, I suppose I am," she said. The waiter returned with a carryout bag, and Lisa set about storing her food. "I think it was just that kind of day at work— the callers were not terribly troublesome. Besides, in this relationship," she paused, locking eyes with Jeremy, "at least one of us should be the funny one." She winked at him.

"Ah, yes, of course," Jeremy said, amused. "So, come on, share a banana split with me?"

"How about we go for a walk instead?" she countered.

"We could do that," he said, giving the dessert menu one last perusal. "I'm kind of in the mood for a tiramisu."

"Why not order that, and we can have it after our walk?" she said, folding closed her carryout box.

Jeremy took her advice, and after receiving the dessert and paying the tab and tip, they headed out. He opened the door for her, and after they got outside Lisa scooped up his hand and hugged his arm as they walked.

"There's a lot of history in this part of town," Jeremy commented.

"Yep, there sure is," she said, looking up and down the ancient road. She took a deep breath and detected the faintest hint of the nearby sea.

Jeremy checked his watch as they waited to cross the street. "So, it's almost nine o'clock. Where would you like to walk?"

"I'm not sure; I kinda feel like Collins Cove," she said, referring to the local public shoreline at the end of the small peninsula on which Salem lay. "But mostly I just want to walk a bit."

"We could do that. There's also the Commons," Jeremy offered. The light changed, allowing him to escort her across the street, where his car was parked.

"Nah," Lisa decided as they stepped onto the sidewalk. "Let's go to the Cove. I want to smell the sea air and feel the breeze," she said, smiling at the idea.

"All right, to the Cove then!" Jeremy smiled as well; he liked how the breeze swept her hair. The parking lot was just ahead; he chose a spot specifically so they could stroll a bit to and from the restaurant. It would be not quite a mile to drive to the Cove; they'd be there quite quickly. Jeremy intentionally slowed their pace.

"So what do you want to do this weekend?" Lisa asked. "Sunday's the Fourth, you know."

"Is it?" Jeremy raised his eyebrows, intrigued that he had lost track of the date. "What's today, the first?"

"Yep," she said.

"Cool," he nodded. "Oh, I don't know. Let's see, for tomorrow, maybe a movie?" he stopped them at the entrance to the parking lot; he had parked in the far right-hand corner of the now-empty lot, which had been filled with cars when they arrived earlier in the evening. He turned slightly to face her better.

"And then Sunday afternoon, we can drive down to Boston for some fireworks…" he leaned in and gave her a kiss.

"Keep this up and maybe you'll get some early fireworks," she said as they separated from their kiss, her voice sultry.

"So then for Saturday," he spoke abruptly, his ears feeling flushed and his heart bashful. "Well, I don't know. What do you think?"

Lisa opened her mouth to respond, but a flash of light snatched their attention before she uttered a word. Initially, Jeremy's first thought was that someone was lighting some sparklers at the end of the lot. Instead, in the corner next to his dark sedan, the light that had started as a flash had elongated to become a vertical blue-and-yellow glowing rod that sparked and fizzed softly, with long shocks of electricity pulsing across it randomly. Its flickering light reflected off the few vehicles that remained in the lot. Jeremy let go of Lisa's hand and started to tentatively walk towards it, entranced by the mystery of this sudden phenomenon. It was clearly not some ordinary firework.

"Jeremy!" Lisa hissed. Out of concern she reached out to try to restrain him; her hand grabbed only air.

"What is that?" Awe and curiosity had taken command of Jeremy's mind.

He made it only a few steps when the "rod" split apart, startling Jeremy and causing him to flinch backwards instinctively. The rod was now a nearly perfect oval hole, revealing a wooden room that was lowly lit, and a human figure crouched within. The individual appeared to be equally surprised by the blue-and-yellow mystery, for he appeared to fall back at the same time Jeremy had.

Curiosity again overtook his hesitating nerves, and Jeremy resumed forward, crouching down a bit to see better. The phenomenon was low to the ground and only a couple of feet tall. Something like a door moved behind the man, and Jeremy flinched again as the crouching person sprung through the portal. He heard Lisa's gasp as the figure stumbled into the parking lot and then collided head-first into the bumper of his car. The intruder instantly crumpled, and lay unconscious on the asphalt.

Back inside the glowing hole, another figure had appeared, and ducked down to peer out the rift. Jeremy stood and simply watched in disbelief.

"My God, Cyrus!" the second man exclaimed to the parking lot. Jeremy looked back to Lisa, who had a hand over her mouth. Lisa eyes darted back and forth between the spectacle and Jeremy: stunned frozen, she made no move and said no words.

"Cyrus!" the man hissed a second time.

Jeremy spun back to the rift and the other man; he wanted to call out in reply but curiously hesitated. Suddenly, the rift began to flicker and contort, as if the air was trying to heal itself by closing the unnatural hole. The second man had also noticed the rift's spasm; he made the sign of the cross, and then leapt headfirst through the blue-and-yellow loop. The peculiar phenomenon successfully closed itself; the air glowed but faded fast, and the parking lot fell dark again.

The man anxiously looked about as he scuttled nervously to tend to his friend. There was a moment of silence, as Jeremy waited for something else bizarre to happen, such as a leprechaun to arrive and offer him a pot of gold. When no leprechaun appeared, Jeremy took a deep breath, and then a step towards the men. His voice seemed to crack when he finally spoke up.

"Hey!" he said, perhaps a little too sharply.

The second man nearly jumped out of his skin; he whipped his head around to face Jeremy; his face was filled with terror.

"You stay back!" the blond man yelled, his fright suddenly transforming to a fierce self-preservation. He positioned himself between Jeremy and his prone friend.

"Whoa, easy, man," Jeremy held up his open palms, and stopped where he was.

"I will not be a prisoner of Satan!" the man exclaimed. He frantically looked between Jeremy, Lisa, and the nighttime surroundings.

"What?" Of all the first words Jeremy expected a stranger to say, this was certainly not on the list; not even in Salem. He was about to say as much when he took a closer look at the man's clothes, as well as that of his friend. He put it all together and realized that something even more remarkable was happening; his head seemed to clear immediately from the shock of last few minutes.

"I'm not going to hurt you," Jeremy began. Before he could continue, the visitor interrupted.

"What is it to be, then? Are you a witch?" he demanded with a hint of disgust. "A sorcerer?"

"I'm not any of those things, dude. Please try to calm down." Jeremy nodded toward the unconscious man. "How is your friend?"

The man paused, looked down at his friend, and then waited a few moments as his demeanor seemed to calm.

"His senses are gone from him," he began carefully. He was not ready to trust, yet. "Tell me truthfully, did you cast the spell to bring us to this evil place?"

"I told you, I'm not a witch. Can I—" Jeremy glanced back at Lisa, and noticed she had slowly moved towards him. "Can *we* come take a look at your friend?"

Eying them suspiciously for several tense moments, he agreed through clenched teeth. "Yes."

Jeremy walked cautiously towards the men, and gently crouched down to look at the unconscious man. He was watched closely as he pinched the man's wrist to check his pulse, and when he held a hand to his nose to check his breathing.

"He hit his head on the car—" Jeremy tied to explain, and then corrected himself. "He's hit his head. I think he's just out cold. I'm sure he'll be fine." He looked up at Lisa, who silently shrugged. He'd have to let her check him over later.

"Thank you," the man said, breathing a sigh of relief. He looked around, then at Jeremy. "Your clothing is strange," he said. "Things are not normal. What is this place? Where am I?"

"Hmm," Jeremy began, considering the situation. He chose his words cautiously. "Okay, let's just start with 'you're safe'. What's your name?"

"Aaron," he replied, "Aaron Quincy, sir."

"Aaron Quincy," Jeremy repeated. "Nice to meet you," he said, extending his hand, "My name is Jeremy Macer." Aaron tentatively took his proffered hand. He then nodded towards Lisa, who had joined them. "This is my girlfriend, Lisa."

"How do you do, ma'am," Aaron said. Lisa offered a meek "hello" and a friendly, if awkward, smile.

"Ok," Jeremy said, "we need to get your friend—"

"*Cyrus*," Aaron corrected him.

"Sorry; we need to get 'Cyrus' off the ground, and out from the open. However, we need to be very careful here. I can explain later, once we are safe," Jeremy continued, responding to the quizzical expression on both of their faces. "Lisa, can you open the doors while Aaron and I get Cyrus?" Lisa nodded moved quickly, doing as Jeremy requested.

"Aaron," Jeremy said, "You are going to see a lot of strange things until we get this straightened out. I can explain most of this stuff, but not right now. We need to get the two of you guys to safety, and we have to do that using my—" He paused to find an appropriate word. When none came to him, he shrugged and finished with "car."

Aaron did not ask any more questions as he and Jeremy lifted Cyrus off the ground. Jeremy struggled with the dead weight of a full grown man, and, with Lisa holding the door open, awkwardly spilled him in the back seat. As Jeremy worked to set Cyrus up and into place, Aaron stared at the dome light for a moment before he slowly reached for it. He caught himself, shook his head briefly, and then turned back to tend to his unconscious friend. Jeremy pulled the seatbelt out and went to buckle it into place when Aaron reached over and blocked his path.

"What are you doing, sir?" Aaron said with alarm. "Why restrain him?"

"Actually, Aaron, we all have to be restrained. It's the law here," Jeremy replied. Aaron paused, reluctantly allowing Jeremy finish buckling Cyrus' seatbelt. Jeremy indicated to Aaron to do the same.

Jeremy closed the door and stood, his back muscles offended by the work they just did. He noticed an older couple standing rather rigid across the street. They must have been watching for some time, for they wore concerned expressions on their street-lit faces. Jeremy hoped they had not watched the whole event, but since they did not interfere with things, he simply gave an exaggerated shrug and got into the driver's seat. Lisa more or less fell into the passenger seat; she did not seem to have noticed the old folks. Jeremy settled into place and looked into the rearview mirror; his eyes met with Aaron's, who was watching them closely, hesitant to buckle his own seatbelt. Jeremy then fastened himself in, and exchanged looks with Lisa as she did the same. He looked back into the mirror, and Aaron then began to secure himself as instructed. Jeremy closed his door.

Just then, the dome light extinguished itself.

"What game is this!?" Aaron exclaimed. "Cyrus!" Aaron started to frantically search for a way out of the vehicle.

"Aaron, relax!" Jeremy pleaded, turning the dome light back on. "It's just a light. It goes out automatic-ally."

Aaron settled down, but crammed himself into the corner of the seat. "I do not understand," he said, his eyes darting between the dome light and Jeremy's eyes in the mirror.

"The light turns off when doors are closed," Lisa explained gently. Jeremy was relieved that she had recovered from the weirdness and was now trying to help. She did not like surprises, and this was definitely a doozy.

Aaron's eyes lingered with Lisa's for a few moments, then finally reseated himself and joined his harness. Somehow, Lisa's entry into the conversation seemed to change the atmosphere. Aaron suddenly felt less fear and somewhat more at ease with this strange situation.

The car rumbled and shook then, as if a giant dog growling followed by a large cat purring from underneath Aaron, and the light extinguished again. Aaron felt himself become tense. Suddenly, the whole world burst into noise, throbbing and filled with sounds he could not identify, except for the voice of a man who seemed to be singing. He heard the words "won't you please, please help me" just before the noise vanished from his ears, replaced with a blessed silence.

"Sorry!" Jeremy said from the front, chuckling softly. "Forgot that we were listening to that!"

"What was that? Why does that man need help?" Aaron demanded.

"What man?" Jeremy asked. Realizing what he meant, he said, "Oh, that's just a song!"

"But I saw no one singing," Aaron replied.

"Trust me. There is a lot that you will not understand; you kind of have to be from around here for it to make sense." Aaron nodded his head after a few moments, still not fully comforted by this assurance from Jeremy.

"I'm going to take us to my house. We can sort all this out there, as well as try to wake Cyrus."

"Your house?" Lisa asked. "What about your – oh yeah, your parents are in New York for the holiday."

"Yep," Jeremy said. "Are you okay, Aaron?"

"I do not understand 'oh-keh', but I believe am prepared for what lies ahead," Aaron said. He turned his gaze uncertainly out the window. He saw many bright lights and lamps, and the buildings around him seemed foreign. Indeed, nothing was familiar to his eyes.

The car started to move backwards, and then stopped. "What is that?" Jeremy wondered in a whisper.

"What is what?" Lisa asked. Jeremy did not answer, but unbelted himself, and got out and walked in front of the car, standing awash in bright white light. Aaron stared in wonder; he had never seen such light that did not come from the sun. Even Cyrus' forges rarely glowed so bright.

Jeremy bent down to pick something up. Lisa and Aaron both craned their necks to see what he was up to. Jeremy returned to his seat and closed the door. In his hand Aaron saw the object that had started this whole experience, only now it seemed damaged.

"That thing is a tool of the Devil!" Aaron said with revulsion, shifting uncomfortably.

"What do you mean? You've seen this before?" Jeremy held up the metal item. He buckled in as he looked at Aaron.

"Aye, I have indeed. I found it in the woods just south

of Salem as Cyrus and I were arriving this afternoon," Aaron said. He braced himself as he felt the strange wagon move again. He marveled that there were no horses pulling it.

"There aren't any woods to the south of Salem" Lisa said to Jeremy. "At least not any major ones."

"I'm sure there used to be," Jeremy said absently, lost in thought. He pulled onto the road and began to drive home.

"What do you mean, 'there used to be'?" Aaron felt confused again. "What is going on? What is this place?"

"This place is Salem," Lisa tried to assure him.

"But not the Salem you are used to," Jeremy interjected quickly. He glanced up to look at Aaron in his rearview mirror. He asked the question he knew was cliché in the movies.

"Aaron, what year is it?"

"What...year –?" Aaron sighed and rubbed his temples. "Will nothing you say to me make any sense?"

"It might when you answer my question. I need to know what year it is for you," Jeremy insisted.

"The year of our Lord is sixteen hundred ninety two," Aaron impatiently recited, wondering where his answer would lead.

"Oh my," Lisa chirped, unconsciously bringing her hand to her mouth again. Jeremy let out a breath of air, a smile appearing briefly across his face.

"Aaron, try not to be too alarmed by what I am about to tell you. You say you've seen this device before," Jeremy said.

"I have."

"I think this device is what brought you here. That portal you two came through," Jeremy paused, marshaling his words, "brought you into the future."

Lewis Crenshaw sat at the computer in the darkened lab, watching a series of Charlie Chaplin video clips online and laughing at the comedy. He reached over and grabbed the package of Oreos, taking a few more out, and convincing himself that he was not going to have any more. He wanted to believe that fourteen of the tasty cookies was enough; he was pretty sure that in a few minutes, he would talk himself into believing that in reality, sixteen would be enough, and that would be it.

To his left, laughing alongside him, was Darrell, who had decided to stay late to keep Lewis company. Darrell had said he didn't mind, seeing as his roommates were always too loud anyway. Lewis and Darrell had become close friends since they started working for Duncan two years before. They had never had night shifts before, but since the Time Opener started working, they had to take turns sitting through the monotony of waiting for something to happen. Now they were sitting up, getting paid to watch old movies and wait for nothing to happen.

Then something happened.

A beeping sound prompted both guys to pull out their phones absentmindedly, still trying to enjoy Chaplin's classic slapstick. Once he realized that it wasn't a phone, but the computer, Lewis sat up straight and pulled up the tracking program.

"Darrell," Lewis said with urgency.

"What, do we have something?" Darrell asked, and he paused the video on his own laptop to take a closer look.

"I think we do," Lewis said, clicking and punching keys.

Darrell pulled his phone out again, and quickly dialed Duncan's home number. Lewis could hear a groggy voice on the phone answer "hello?"

"Duncan, we have a signal," Darrell spoke with a tone of excitement and urgency.

The voice cursed. "Ok, I'll be there in a half hour. Call the others; let's get the team together, ASAP."

"No problem," Darrell said.

"Hold on," Lewis said, concern in his words. He started typing and clicking in a flurry, and he felt his shoulders tensing. His monitor updated and changed, but nothing it told him had changed. Duncan would not be happy about this.

"We just lost the signal."

CHAPTER VII

Nothing seemed to make any sense to Aaron. His confusion deepened and was joined by irritation following Jeremy's proclamation about time.

"I do not understand," were the only words he could summon. He looked out the window and watched strange, powerful lights move past rapidly as Jeremy drove. Some were white and hung as lamps, without flame, others an ominous red and moving in the dark. Everything that had happened in the last several minutes raised both curiosity and fear in him. The two extremes collided inside him, and mixed with the shock of it all to leave him unsure where to begin to piece his reality back together. He looked over at Cyrus, and briefly envied his friend's condition. It was not his custom to accuse another man of witchcraft; until today, he did not believe that there was any truth to the matter. Nevertheless, he had seen the strange circle of fire, and had passed through it into another realm. Clearly, the world indeed held supernatural surprises.

"What is your meaning when you say 'the future?'?" Aaron asked after several seconds of uneasy silence. Another alarming thought came to his mind. "Did you summon me—us here? To," he finished with cautious acceptance, "the 'future'?"

"What? No!" Jeremy replied, his eyes reflected in the absurdly small mirror. He laughed as though the idea was the strangest thing to happen to him.

"Then what is all this? What is this wagon we are in? There are other such wagons out there, shining as metal and carrying red torches! What is all this?" he repeated, gesturing animatedly. Jeremy opened his mouth as if to answer, but now that Aaron had begun to ask the questions his mind was troubled by, he was inspired to continue.

"What has happened to Cyrus?" He became somewhat more demanding with each question. "Why have we come to this place? What is to happen now?!"

"Just calm down, now, Aaron," Jeremy said gently. "First things first; I think Cyrus hit his head when you both arrived. He is unconscious."

"Are you sure we shouldn't take him to the hospital?" Lisa wondered out loud.

"Do you mean to a physician?" Aaron asked.

"No," Jeremy answered to Lisa, hoping her first aid training should be sufficient.

"Why not?" Aaron demanded.

"Because you and Cyrus do not belong here," Jeremy explained. "You have no ID, no insurance, and too many questions would come up. Besides," he continued, "he doesn't seem to be in any danger. What time of day was it where you come from?" Jeremy asked, trying to change the subject.

"It was late, well past sunset. I believe it was around nine of the clock."

"Yeah, see, he was knocked out at first and maybe he is just sleeping now. We can check him once we get to my place. If worse comes to worst, we'll go to a hospital. Fair enough?"

Aaron considered his argument. He was beginning to feel like he could trust Jeremy. He knew he would feel more at ease if a doctor looked over his companion, but he did agree with Jeremy about one important fact: he and Cyrus did not belong here.

"What of my other questions?" Aaron said, moving on.

"Well, that's going to take more explanation," Jeremy began. He exchanged glances with Lisa, and then returned his view to the road. He always felt like she was the better socialite of the couple.

Lisa caught his meaningful glance, and spoke up.

"Aaron, tell me something about you and Cyrus," she said with an inviting tone, as if they had just met at the church luncheon.

Caught unprepared, Aaron asked, "I beg your pardon, ma'am?"

"You know," she said, "tell me a little about you guys. Where are you from, what do you do?"

He took a breath, and then released it slowly, starting to relax a bit. "We are from Falmouth, having traveled most of to-day by wagon to Salem."

"So you aren't from around here?" She asked.

"We are not," Aaron replied. "We have come to town to make some trades ahead of the season change. I am a tanner, and I bring furs and skins to sell in Salem. Cyrus," he nodded towards his prone friend, "is a journeyman smithy, and accompanies me as a friend would." Aaron smiled briefly with amusement; Lisa shared the smile. "Actually, I suspect he has his own motives for taking the trip that have more to do with Salem's unmarried than with keeping me company, but that is a matter between him and the Parson."

"Almost home," Jeremy announced. "We should be subtle taking Cyrus inside, but we probably won't have much of problem."

Lisa noticed Aaron's continued unsettled shifting as they traveled over bumps and turns. "To answer one of your questions, we call this a car."

"Ah, seems a natural name, for an unnatural carriage," Aaron responded. He gazed at the scores of lights surrounding the wheel-reigns of the 'car' at Jeremy's hands. Some lights were numbers in a semicircle, colored with blue and yellow. Looking to the area between Jeremy and Lisa, he saw more colored lights; some with pictures and strange symbols, that all made no sense to him. Most of those lights gave a soft green glow and the only thing he saw that he remotely recognized were the letters "AM", "FM", and "VOL". However, only the letters were familiar; their meaning was as mysterious to him as the rest of the car, let alone the whole evening.

The car halted in front of a house, and without warning, the carriage sounds and lights were extinguished.

The ceiling lamp light came on again when they opened the door, causing Aaron to start.

"I'll go unlock and open the door, and then we can carry him in," Jeremy said, removing his belt. Lisa also removed her harness, and both climbed out of the car. Aaron looked down, now able to see, and began to remove his and Cyrus' harnesses. He studied the door next to him, and then started to try to open the door. He was unsuccessful, as the handle seemed not to control anything, and the lever rotated but only changed the window. He began to feel trapped when Cyrus' door opened and Jeremy peered across at him.

"You can't open the door?" Jeremy asked, and then reached over to his own door to do something Aaron could not see; a soft click came from Aaron's door. "Try it now."

Aaron fumbled with the handle until he comprehend-ed the simultaneous clasp-and-turn required to get the door opened. Lisa helped pull the door open further, and Aaron stepped out, taking a deep breath and looking around at the future.

"There ya go," Lisa said. "Are you ok?"

"I believe so," Aaron said slowly. "I am just trying to get used to the world again."

The world was now peculiar; everything looked so strange and alien. It was night, yet he could see things as well as if it were early dusk. He saw many houses all around him, and in front of each were carriages (*cars*, he corrected himself) of a multitude of colors and shapes, and all bathed in the steadiest lamp light he had ever seen. The lamps were all along the street, which itself looked like no road Aaron had ever been on.

"I'm going to need some help here," Jeremy said,

breaking Aaron's thoughts. He joined Jeremy on the other side and together they pulled Cyrus' limp form from the car. They carried him into the house while Lisa held the door open for them.

The first room of Jeremy's home was unlike any Aaron had ever seen. It was bright, as if mid-day, apparently lit by the same unfamiliar, steady lamp flame as he had seen in the car and on the street. The floor was not dirt, but apparently of beautifully smooth fine wood. Further to his surprise, there was just so much *stuff*.

"What's wrong?" Jeremy asked with a strained voice, trying very hard not to drop Cyrus' lolling upper body.

"I beg your pardon?"

"Why'd you stop?" Jeremy asked through breathless gasps.

"Oh, do forgive me," Aaron marveled, having the luxury of holding his friend by the boots. "I have never been to a home so…decorated." Aaron continued into the room.

"Yes, my parents keep a nice place. Can we set him on the sofa over there?" Jeremy grunted quickly.

"Of course," Aaron uttered, and together they gently heaved Cyrus onto the sofa. Cyrus lay in a way that looked impossibly comfortable. Now that there was good strong light, Aaron could see a large red-and-blue bruise on Cyrus' forehead near his left temple. After a few moments, Cyrus let out a deep sigh, and somehow seemed to visibly relax.

Lisa leaned closer to inspect Cyrus. "It looks like he's

got REM." Aaron looked at Jeremy.

"It means that he's ok—er, rather that he will be just fine," Jeremy corrected himself.

"That does give me relief," Aaron said. "Still, I wonder if we should awaken him."

"Oh, I don't know if that's a good idea," Jeremy spread his arms to indicate everything around them. "I'm still not sure it would be wise to wake him only to shock him with all this."

"On the other hand," Lisa stood back up, "if he has a concussion, he'll need to be awakened anyway for precaution."

Jeremy furrowed his brow for a few moments, considering all the options available to him.

"Ok, how about this: Let's get all your questions out of the way. I'll answer what—," he paused midsentence; Aaron saw an unspoken argument live in a glance exchanged between Jeremy and Lisa. "—er, *we'll* answer what we can, and try to make you as comfortable as possible. Then we can wake him up, and let you help him adjust."

"Agreed," Aaron nodded.

"Excellent," Jeremy said, with a sudden excitement shining in the smile on his face. He extended his arm. "Have a seat. Ask away!"

"Ask away?" Aaron echoed. His new friends spoke so strangely, he at times had difficulty understanding them. "I suppose you mean me to…well, never mind that. My first question is: why do your candles not flicker?"

"Candles?" Jeremy cocked his head while Lisa glanced around, trying to locate what he saw.

"Oh, the lights!" she said softly after a beat.

"I'm not sure how to explain it in any way that makes sense," Jeremy began.

"Tis not magic, I hope," he smiled. "I have never seen a flame that does not smoke or flicker. There are no oil stains on the walls. Yet your light is as steady as sun light," Aaron stated, almost as a challenge. He was as curious as he was stymied in understanding.

Jeremy chuckled in spite of himself. "No, it's not magic. The candles are actually light bulbs."

Jeremy leaned over and picked up a lamp, tilting it for Aaron to see. "These replaced candles as indoor lighting a long time ago. They run off of electricity."

"Ah," Aaron said, only half as confused as he was before. "I have heard of 'electricity'. The philosophers in Mother England discuss such things. If my memory serves me well, it is suggested that lightning and thunder are made of this 'electricity'."

Jeremy nodded. "Well, no, not the thunder, but definitely the lightning. Anything else?"

Aaron hesitated momentarily, and then asked, "You say this is not Hell, but the future?"

"Right. Well, some might say—" A harsh, low *Jeremy!* from Lisa interrupted him.

"Never mind that. Yes, you are in Salem, Massachusetts; the future, not Hell."

"And who is our king in this age?" Aaron wanted to

know.

"King…" Lisa repeated; Jeremy detected a hint of mocking.

"Oh, that's going to be a touchy one," Jeremy grimaced. "Are you sure you really need to know the answer to that question?"

"Why should I not?"

"It can't be good to tell you too much about the future. We have to really be careful here."

"I must know; I am far too curious now. Please indulge me."

With a pause and glance towards Lisa, Jeremy said, "Well, we don't really belong to England anymore."

"What do you mean?"

"Ok, well, in about a hundred years from your time," Jeremy began, "the American colonies will revolt and fight for freedom."

"For freedom? But we are already free. It is why my family sailed to Massachusetts; for religious freedom," Aaron explained.

"Things will change, trust me."

"So we are in Salem, Massachusetts, but not in the British Empire?" Aaron tried to make sense of it.

"That's right. This is now the United States of America." Lisa said.

Aaron sat quietly for a few moments to consider this information, his eyebrows cramped with the continued surprises he encountered.

"It does not surprise me much to hear this, as I think it

over. Our own Colony seems to be perpetually changing allegiances. Why, it was only a few months ago that Reverend Mather's delegation returned to the Colony from England, having sought reinstatement of our royal charter. We had lost it upon becoming the Dominion of New England some years ago." He sighed with some impatience, and then stood as he continued.

"Instead, they returned announcing that King William was drawing a new charter that has combined Plymouth with Massachusetts Bay into a single Colony. It is not yet clear whether this was a good move; I suppose I should trust His Excellency." He paused briefly, and looked at Jeremy. "It would seem that in the future, we will have traded one king for another. Has it really made much of a difference?"

"I think so; but we don't have a king anymore. We have a president and a congress. We elect new presidents all the time. We have one of the greatest forms of government in the world," Jeremy finished with a swell of his patriotism.

"Perhaps that is an improvement; the ability to choose a new governor frequently has its appeal. Our governor is the recently appointed William Phips; he spoke at our town this last June while touring the colony since bringing the new charter. I shook his hand; however, I have suspicions of his competence to govern our Colony."

Lisa stood up. "Okay boys, I think that's enough of a history and civics lesson. It's getting late, and I need to get home. I have work in the morning, and you have classes first thing in the morning. I want to check his pupils when

Cyrus wakes up."

"Lisa is a lifeguard and likes to stay fresh on her first aid skills," Jeremy bragged.

"You, a woman, are in the militia?" Aaron asked Lisa, disbelieving.

"What?"

"A life guard is a soldier," Aaron said matter-of-factly.

"No, sorry, I mean that she watches over people as they swim, to keep them safe," Jeremy said though laughter. He excused himself and left the room, muttering that he would be right back.

Aaron leaned down next to his friend and peeled back an eyelid.

"Cyrus," he began. "Can you hear me?"

There was no response.

"Cyrus, wake up, my friend!"

Jeremy returned with something in his hand; it looked like a cup, but colored unlike any cup he had seen before.

"Any reaction?" Jeremy asked.

"He did not stir," Aaron replied.

"Cyrus, this is your last chance to wake up on your own!" Jeremy warned the sleeping figure. Cyrus did not move. Lisa noticed the cup in his hand.

"Jeremy, really?" she said, dropping her arms.

"What are you planning to do to him?" Aaron asked, grabbing Jeremy's arm that held the cup.

"Relax, it's just ice water," Jeremy said casually.

"Ok, you had your chance!" Jeremy said, and slowly poured the cup of water and ice onto Cyrus' face and chest.

Cyrus moved.

Gasping and hacking, he flailed as though he were drunk and falling.

"What the devil!" Cyrus sputtered as he awakened.

"Cyrus, calm down!" Aaron urged. He and Jeremy stepped back to be clear of Cyrus' arms and legs.

Cyrus wiped his face and looked at his attacker. He jumped up and started to go after Jeremy until Aaron grabbed his upper arm.

"Cyrus, get yourself calm!" he pleaded. "Everything is all right."

"This man has assailed me!" Cyrus was filled with fight and fury.

"He did what I asked him to! You were not yourself for some time, having hit your head as you fell!"

Cyrus stopped his attempts to reach for Jeremy. Cyrus finally took in his surroundings. After a few moments, Aaron let go of his tunic.

"Cyrus, let me introduce our new friends, Jeremy and Lisa," Aaron spoke in his formal voice.

"Nice to meet you," Jeremy said, extending his arm to shake hands. Lisa offered a soft "hi" and a wave of her hand.

Cyrus took the proffered hand. "It is a pleasure, sir." His words said pleasure, but his tone said otherwise.

"I'm sorry I had to douse you, Cyrus," Jeremy offered. "We needed to make sure you were ok."

Cyrus turned to Aaron and mouthed "ok?" Aaron shook his head subtly, and then spoke.

"Cyrus, Lisa needs to look at your eyes to make sure you do not have a sickness in the head," Aaron said.

Lisa directed Cyrus to a spot in the room where she could look at his eyes properly. The situation was made more challenging considering that he was a full head and a half taller than she. After a few moments of staring, she turned to the remaining two and announced "I think he'll be fine."

"Great!" Jeremy clapped his hands. "Listen, I'm going to walk Lisa out to her car. Aaron will explain everything to you in the meantime."

"Good night, ma'am," Aaron and Cyrus said together, both giving a slight bow.

"Good night, fellas," Lisa said with a smile, and stepped out with Jeremy, leaving Aaron and Cyrus in the room.

"Aaron, what is going on?" Cyrus asked, turning towards his friend.

Aaron rubbed his face with both hands.

"That is a question it seems I have been trying to answer for some time."

CHAPTER VIII

Jeremy pulled the door closed, and followed Lisa down the steps. She reached a hand behind her, subtly beckoning Jeremy to take it.

"Wow!" Jeremy blurted in a thrill. "Three hundred years! That's just awesome!"

"It is by far the weirdest thing I've ever experienced," Lisa said stiltedly. "And that includes the time my cat attacked your remote controlled airplane."

Jeremy laughed at the memory, recalling how the feline had actually caught the plane, and was subsequently flown. The surprised kitty dangled sideways by its two right paws about three feet in the air for about ten yards. It was as funny now to Jeremy as it was then, but at the time Lisa wasn't very amused. Jeremy had to endure an angry girlfriend and a disheveled cat that spring afternoon; *but it was worth it*, he mused.

"Weird, yes. The coolest thing ever? Definitely!" Jeremy waved his hands excitedly, emphasizing his point. "I mean, think about it: there's Back to the Future, and both Star Trek: The Voyage Home and First Contact," he said, ticking off each movie with a finger, "The Time Machine, Quantum Leap...The list goes on and on. But those were all just TV! This is *real*!" As the two walked past Jeremy's car, he made a mental note to grab the time device on his way back in.

"You're cute," Lisa smiled. Her expression turned serious, "What are you going to do?"

"I don't know. I really shouldn't have told him about the changes," Jeremy said. His previous elation quickly gave way to the need to be responsible about this situation. "I'm not sure. I'll make sure they are comfortable for tonight, and we will work out something tomorrow, a plan I guess, about how to get them home."

"And what about that thing?" Lisa asked, looking over towards Jeremy's car as she did. "You don't just find time travel…*whatevers*… lying in the woods. Especially back then."

Jeremy also turned and cast a glance back towards his car. "No, you don't," he said, thinking.

They stood quietly holding hands, facing one another. Lisa put her head on Jeremy's shoulder.

"You know," she started in a conspiring voice, "if I could use that thing, think of the boyfriends I could go back and warn myself about. Especially that Jeremy guy…"

"Har har har," Jeremy mocked, and hugged her, and she hugged him back.

"Maybe not," she said into his shoulder; Jeremy was certain he could hear her smiling.

They had been dating for over a year by now. An artist friend of Jeremy's, a girl named Claire, had once invited him to go to the Salem Arts Festival; he later discovered that she'd invited her friend, Lisa, as well. When the three had met up at the Festival, Jeremy's attention went quickly to how interesting he thought Lisa was. He remembered thinking that some of the exhibits at that event were kind of cool, but found most of the works were too eclectic for his own tastes; Jeremy did not really consider himself much of an art aficionado. He'd never tell his friend any of this, despite having known her since sophomore year in high school, because Claire seemed to really enjoy showing off her own work to him. Lisa, on the other hand, was a big fan of not only Claire's work, but many of the booths at the Festival. It wasn't the Art Festival that he had enjoyed that day; but listening to Lisa discuss the various art and exhibits. He had liked her immediately, and asked for her number before they'd even left the Festival grounds. He did his best to play down how crazy he was about her; nevertheless, or maybe because of it, it still took almost five months before they would become exclusive.

They separated from their hug, but still held hands facing each other. A thought occurred to him.

"Actually, I'm not sure you'd be able to use it. I think I ran over it with the car as I was backing out; it looked broken when I picked it up."

"Uh-oh," Lisa said, her eyebrows furrowing in the yellow glow of streetlight. After a moment of thought, she suggested, "Well, maybe you can try to find out who made it, see if they can fix it."

"I'm not even sure how to begin to do that," he said. "It's not like there's a Radio Shack for time travelling TV remotes."

"You know what I mean," she frowned.

"Yeah, but seriously, I thought about that. But what if whoever built it doesn't care much about preserving the time?" He felt it surreal to actually be saying these things. "Anyway, even if they are 'good guys', which may be likely, it will take too long to figure out who it is, return the device, blah blah and so on, in order to get these guys home. They really shouldn't be here if they are going back." There was a moment as he continued thinking it through. "This was so cool just a minute ago, but now I want to get them back as soon as possible. It's so weird that that's like that." He paused again, considering the scenarios, and finally coming to a decision. "No, I'd rather get them back to their own time as soon as possible, and then return this to its owners. Maybe I'll try to get Doctor Arvind to take a look at it, and see what he can do."

"Didn't you have him for chemistry?" she asked.

"Yeah, but you should have seen his lab," Jeremy answered, "There was electronic stuff and tools everywhere. I'm sure he'll be able to do something with it."

"Ok," Lisa said, and hugged him tightly to show her support for his decision. "Well, I gotta go."

"You know," Jeremy said, ignoring her remark and holding her tight, "now that I'm thinking about it, this may throw a monkey wrench into our weekend plans."

"Yeah, I know," she answered.

"We may have to host a couple of castaways for a few days. Can you settle for fireworks in this old town?" he asked.

"Well of course I would!" she frowned, a little peeved that he would say it that way. "I wouldn't care if we sat in a closet and lit sparklers all night," she said, before adding, "Of course, we'd need more champagne if that were the case. At any rate, as long as we're together, I'll be happy, and having fun."

"Aww," Jeremy hammed up the moment a bit. He leaned in and kissed his girlfriend. They hugged each other for a few minutes, not talking, just being in love.

Jeremy softened the couple's long embrace, and straightened up to his full height. "Well, I better get back inside, and get these guys set up for the night. I'll call you in the morning, after I'm finished at Salem State."

"Okay. Text me if you find anything out, but call me if anything happens. I do want to be there when they go home," she told him as she climbed into the driver's seat of her teal-colored car.

"I can definitely do that," he promised. She turned on the engine and turned down the stereo. He then leaned in and gave her another kiss. He felt the fullness of his feelings in his heart for her right then. "Drive safe. I love you."

"I really love you too," she said sweetly, gazing into his eyes from her seat. "Good night."

Jeremy stepped back as she pulled off, and then looked up at the sky. *Too bad you can't see the stars from here*, he thought. Between the time of their dinner date and now, the sky had gone from clear with dozens of twinkling stars to overcast, and the city and street lights created a dull gray glow in the sky. *It's not much of a view to offer visitors from the past*, Jeremy mused.

He walked over to his car, grabbed the time travel gadget and the tiramisu and Lisa's leftovers that had been forgotten in the evening's adventure, and walked back to the house.

Aaron stood near the door, and Cyrus remained seated on the couch. He had just told him of things that happened while Cyrus was unconscious; his friend had yet to fully react to the news. Because of the nature of the situation, Aaron felt that it would be most respectful to not say anything else until Cyrus spoke first.

This room had a strange but sweet and pleasant aroma to it; it reminded Aaron of the days of festival that the township had held at times when he was a boy. As he waited to allow Cyrus to decide his words, Aaron looked around at the things of this home. The couch that Cyrus now sat on was plain brown, and Aaron found it peculiar that he saw no wood at the arms or back of it; its design seemed both strange and bloated. There was a table at either end of the couch, on which were wooden disks and small paintings with intricate metal frames. There were two other large, plush chairs that did not have legs; instead, the lower halves were more akin to boxes that did not touch the floors. The rounded fullness of the upholstery matched the couch in its vanity.

"The things I see before me are strange, I agree, but to say we have come to the future? I do not believe it," Cyrus remarked defiantly, looking around the room and then at Aaron. He continued to try to dry himself and his clothing. In a brief moment of frustration, he exclaimed, "There is extraordinary light but I feel no heat! Where is the fire in this place?"

"Indeed, my friend, what I have told you, it is the truth," Aaron tried to reassure Cyrus. "It appears that the…thing we found is what took us from our home."

"Aaron," Cyrus began, and then apparently changed his mind on what he wanted to say in response. With a tone of suspicion, even concern, he asked, "Is it bewitched?"

Aaron was surprised by this question, when he considered that Cyrus had on many occasions dismissed not just witchcraft, but the notion of magic altogether.

For his own part, Aaron was skeptical but felt it prudent to be wary in such matters. "I do not know. When we first came here, I was certain we had been taken into the netherworld. However," Aaron said, looking at the items that Jeremy's house was cluttered with, "our new friends are far too friendly to be of such a place. And, they did not behave like it was an object of evil purpose."

He paused and looked at Cyrus thoughtfully.

"Quite contrarily, Jeremy seemed quite excited about it, as one might be excited to use a new hammer, or when they are to learn to ride a new horse."

"I am not sure I like him much," Cyrus frowned, and checked his clothing for dryness again.

"Oh, come come Cyrus," Aaron said dismissively with a smile and a wave of his hand, "you know quite well that you would have done the same thing, were our feet in their shoes and theirs in ours."

Cyrus simply grunted; Aaron expected this meant that Cyrus grudgingly accepted his argument as true.

Aaron continued to wander around the room, and came to the window. The shutters were, by some strange choice, on the inside of the window, and were unlike any shutters he had unclasped before. He separated the slats with his fingers and peered out the window. He saw the lights outside as he had seen them earlier, and in the road were Jeremy and Lisa in an embrace. He quickly returned his eyes to things inside, so as to lend them their privacy.

Just below the window was another surprise; a glass tank with a black lid that made a quiet, whispering hum along with the gentle sound of water pouring, and which was filled with water. Aaron knelt low to look into the tank more directly, and found several small fish in the water. Two fish were as orange as fire, one was black but otherwise identical to the orange ones, and in the back were two large fish with beautiful, elegant, blue-with-purple fins. There were plants in the water, but for some reason Aaron felt like they were not real. A tiny wooden chest (but not made of wood!) filled with tiny gold coins sat near the corner, its lid bounced as bubbles swelled and escaped from it. Most remarkable, however, was the pebble-and-sand bottom, wherein the pebbles were all as blue as the sky on a hot summer day. *Blue rocks, indeed!* he thought.

"They keep fish as their pets!" Aaron marveled out loud. *What a strange world we have entered into*, he thought. He looked over to his friend, saying, "Cyrus, come see this!"

"I am tired," Cyrus declared wearily from his seat across the room, rubbing his temple. "Also, my head hurts."

Aaron stood up and was about to respond when he noticed a stack of paper on a counter that extended from a wall. He stepped over to the paper, and saw that it looked like a gazette. There was a blood-red silhouette image of a figure sitting on a broom and wearing a hat, with a background of a map compass, and next to the words "The Salem News" which was printed in very large lettering. There were pictures that had been painted more perfectly than any painting Aaron had seen in his life, near which were more words: "In Mass., a politically correct casino debate." He did not know what 'casino' meant; in general, the whole expression did not make any sense. Something else caught his attention on the page.

"Cyrus, please come here," Aaron said, feeling unsteady and without his breath.

"What are you looking at there?"

"Please come here," Aaron repeated. Cyrus grunted as he stood, then walked over to stand next to Aaron. Aaron glanced at Cyrus, and then pointed his finger at the page. Cyrus read the words, looked at the all the painted images, then finally took in what Aaron's finger was directing him to read. His head still hurt, so he had to fight the impulse to look away altogether.

"I do not know what to say," Cyrus said, his mind swirling from the pain and the news. "You suppose it is this new date?" He gestured vaguely at everything around him.

"I think it is exactly that," Aaron said quietly. "If we have not lost all our senses, we now are in Salem, and it is July the first, in the year of our Lord, two thousand ten."

"Three hundred years, Aaron," Cyrus marveled with a whistle.

"Three centuries of years," Aaron repeated in shared amazement. Suddenly, a horrible reality struck him, stealing his heart and soul. He stumbled backward.

"By our Heavenly Father, Cyrus! Anna!" Aaron exclaimed, feeling faint. He took a step back as he was clumsy to find a place to sit; Cyrus reached out to steady him. Aaron found his balance again and looked at Cyrus.

"She is dead!"

CHAPTER IX

As Jeremy walked into the house, there was the familiar creak-squeal of the door turning on its hinges. It was not necessarily creepy, as in the horror movies; ordinarily, he would not even notice the sound. However, the night's bizarre events made Jeremy more aware of things, and he was amused that his mind briefly flashed on those spooky scenes in movies with creaky doors.

"Hey guys," he said as he turned to close the door. His creaky-door musings disappeared when he noticed Aaron sitting on the couch, head in hands. Jeremy looked over at Cyrus, who was standing next to his friend. Cyrus looked up at Jeremy briefly and uttered an indifferent "hello" in return.

"Is everything ok?" Jeremy asked, locking the door.

"It is not," came the muffled response from Aaron's hands; there was bitter anger in his voice.

"What's the matter?" Jeremy asked, feeling a little confused. He quickly considered anything that might have upset his guest this much, but came up with nothing.

"It is his wife," Cyrus said. "Also his family, and my family, and our friends. They are long since dead, are they not?"

"Well, yes," Jeremy answered. "It has been—"

"Three hundred years," Aaron cut him off, lifting his face from his hands and facing Jeremy with a piercing focus. Jeremy could see now that Aaron had not been crying or anything; his face, however, was long with sadness.

"Well, yes," Jeremy said again. "But—"

"Everything is gone!" Cyrus said testily. Jeremy wondered if the water had made him angrier.

"I know," Jeremy said. Seeing both about to respond, he quickly continued, "Ok, just relax. I know this is hard to deal with."

"Relax?" Aaron stood up, his face tightening in frustration. "How can you ask us to relax? This is not 'hard to deal with'! This is torture!"

"I know, but—" Jeremy interjected weakly.

"My wife is due to give birth to our baby," he continued. "Now I am here, and they are dead! Am I to be calm, knowing they died centuries ago?

"What have you done to us?" Cyrus demanded. Jeremy noticed for the first time that Cyrus was taller and had very muscled arms.

"Nothing!" Jeremy exclaimed defensively. He held up the device in his hand. "It was this!"

"And just what is that? Aaron found it after the horses raged this afternoon," Cyrus said.

"I don't know," Jeremy said, feeling beleaguered. "I've never seen it before. All I know is that there was a glow, and then it was a portal. You came through and banged your head on the car," he gestured towards Cyrus, and then towards Aaron as he finished, "then you followed, and the portal collapsed. That's all I know!"

"And that?" Aaron asked. "Are there more of those in this 'future'?"

"I'm not sure; I don't think so," Jeremy said, and held up the flash-light sized item, inspecting it closely for the first time.

It was about seven inches long, and about as heavy as a flashlight, and heavier to the bottom. Its casing looked like aluminum, and it was cracked on the upper left corner. The top of the thing was bulky and semi-forked, ending with two copper prongs. Just below the bulk was what looked like a three-line greenish-gray digital display, and below that was the ten-button keypad. To the right of the display lines were what looked to Jeremy like indicator lights. *It looks like someone gutted a cell phone make some kind of time machine*, he thought. On the side was the power button, and Jeremy noticed it was still in the "on" position. He toggled it back and forth between "on" and "off", hoping the thing would do something, but it did not.

"Ok, first things first. Clearly, this is for time travel. I don't know how it works, to be honest, but I think it's broken."

"Can it be repaired?" Cyrus asked with a hint of alarm in his voice.

"I don't know. I someone who might be able to fix it for us," Jeremy replied.

"May I see it?" Cyrus asked.

"Yeah, sure," Jeremy handed him the device. Aaron also

stood up to join the examination.

"The crack was not there before," Aaron offered. After a few moments, he pointed to the buttons and looked up at Jeremy. "Are these of gemstone?"

Jeremy leaned to see what Aaron pointed at. Amused, he replied, "No, those are just LEDs." Aaron looked at him, waiting for further explanation. "They light up when in use." Jeremy pointed at the lamp and ceiling lights to help make his point. Aaron nodded his understanding, and turned back to look it some more.

"It was not damaged like this when we found it. How did it come to be like this?" Cyrus asked.

"I must have run over it with my car as we were pulling out," Jeremy admitted, somewhat sheepishly.

"Car?" Cyrus remarked, and then rubbed his tired face with his free hand. "'Run over'? It is difficult just to have a conversation when you say so many peculiar things."

"It is a wagon, my friend," Aaron offered.

Cyrus sighed with irritation. "Yes, of course; two thousand ten."

"Yeah, hey, I was wondering how you found that out," Jeremy looked curiously at both of them.

"It was on your papers," Aaron pointed to the bar.

"Ah, gotcha," Jeremy realized that it should have been obvious to him. "That makes sense."

"What is to happen to us now? Is hope lost? Can this take us back to our own time?" Aaron asked, handing it back to Jeremy.

"I would imagine so, as soon as we fix it," Jeremy said,

and took the portable time machine back.

"I am a smith," Cyrus began, "but I confess that I do not believe I would be able to repair it."

"No, I wouldn't expect you to," Jeremy said. Cyrus looked as if he wasn't sure if he had been insulted. "Don't get me wrong; I'm not saying anything about your abilities. It's just that you guys have never seen technology like this, and so how could we expect you to know how to fix it?" He turned it over in his hands once more, and then set it down on the coffee table. He walked past Aaron and Cyrus, and into the kitchen.

"Are you guys thirsty or hungry or anything?"

"I am not hungry, but I could have a drink, after all this," Cyrus answered.

"Yes, the same goes for me as well," Aaron said.

Jeremy turned on the kitchen light, and smiled bemusedly when both of his guests flinched unconsciously.

"Relax fellas. Most things around here are safe. There will be surprises, but nothing that will hurt you."

"It is fascinating that you do not have to light your candles; I am not a believer in magic, but I must question if you are sorcerer," Cyrus commented, gazing at the ceiling light with interest, which was much brighter than the living room lights.

"Yeah, such is the magic of paying your power bill," Jeremy said, opening a cabinet. "Well, to be honest, my parents pay the bill; I just live here until I graduate."

"You are a student? The College of William and Mary is

quite a distance away," Aaron said, with surprise in his voice. He and Cyrus stood closer to the bar, watch-ing Jeremy prepare their drinks. Jeremy had pulled out a strange red jug of dark liquid and was pouring it into a glass cup. He was puzzled further when he saw it produce foam like a beer, which then slowly melted away, whispering a hiss as it did.

"I don't go to William and Mary. I'm just a sophomore at Salem State University." Jeremy paused to put the bottle back into what Aaron guessed was the pantry (it had a light inside, too, he noticed). He then took each of the other cups, set them in turn into a nook in the door of the pantry. To Aaron's surprise, it began to fill with clear liquid.

"It is remarkable, whatever it is," Aaron said in a soft voice.

"What is?" Jeremy asked, and then realized they were paying attention to the water in the cup

"You say you are a college student. I trust you are a gentleman, then?" Cyrus asked.

"What?" Jeremy stopped mid-motion. "I mean, I guess I am. I try to treat Lisa right; I think I do all right. Where does that question come from?" He handed the cups to his guests.

"No, that is not my meaning," Cyrus said, casting sidelong a glance at Aaron. "I mean, are you a man of wealth?"

"No," Jeremy chuckled. "Here; I thought you guys might prefer some water."

"Water?" Aaron said, but neither man made a move to

take the proffered drinks. "Are you sure it is good to drink?"

Jeremy did not understand. "What do you mean, why wouldn't it be?"

They took their cups slowly, and both looked at their water. Cyrus sniffed it, and, deciding there was no smell, shrugged at Aaron and took a big swig from it. He stopped himself when it did not taste as he expected.

"This water is...cold as the sea!" Cyrus exclaimed in awe. "How do you accomplish this?"

"I dunno," Jeremy amused by the unexpected reaction. "The refrigerator does it, that's all I know."

Aaron drank a long gulp of his own glass, and was surprised by the taste. "This is as clear and fresh as spring water! Please forgive us; we are not accustomed to drinking water that is not prepared, as it is insecure."

"Well, it isn't spring water," Jeremy said, taking a drink from his own cup of black foamy drink. "Just water, from the faucet. As far as I know, it's pretty clean and safe to drink."

"You say many unfamiliar words, Jeremy," Cyrus said with a grin, exhaling after drinking the entire serving, "but this is the best water I have ever drunk. It is as clear as glass, and as cold as winter. If this is the future, perhaps it may not be as bad as I first believed."

"Thank you, I think," Jeremy said, relieved at Cyrus' change of mood. "I'm glad you like it here."

"Yes, let us return to that conversation," Aaron said.

"Ok," Jeremy gulped his last bit of soda, and turned set

the cup in the sink. "Here's what I'm thinking: there's a professor over in the science building who I think I can take that to," he nodded his head at the time device. "I'm sure he will be able to help me fix it. He teaches physics, and I'm pretty sure he'll be in his office tomorrow morning. Once that's done, we simply take you back to the parking lot and send you back."

"I am satisfied to sleep until then," Cyrus said. "I still have a headache; it has been a long journey today."

"Yeah it has," Jeremy chuckled at the understatement. Aaron also began to laugh, and within moments, all three were laughing heartily.

After a minute, the laughter subsided and they tried to catch their breath. "Hold on a minute," Jeremy said, and headed down the hallway, towards the bathroom. He retrieved the bottle of Tylenol, and then after a moment's thought, also grabbed a couple of blankets and pillows from the hall closet. He returned to the living room, and tossed the bedding on the couch. With Aaron and Cyrus watching him, he walked back into the kitchen and refilled Cyrus' glass with water.

"Here," Jeremy opened the medicine bottle and held it towards Cyrus. Cyrus hesitantly extended his palm, and Jeremy shook the bottle until two tablets fell into Cyrus' hand.

"What is this?" Cyrus looked at Jeremy.

"It's medicine," Jeremy said, handing him his refilled water. "You swallow those with some water. It should make your headache go away."

Cyrus put the pills into his mouth and began to chew. His face scrunched up as the flavor offended his tongue, and quickly took the glass and drank until it was empty.

"That was…unpleasant," Cyrus grimaced. Jeremy laughed.

"I bet it was. You aren't supposed to chew them, just swallow them whole," Jeremy tried to hide his amusement.

"You could have said as much," Cyrus said with a frown.

"Yeah, sorry about that," Jeremy said. Stepping out from the kitchen, he walked back towards the hallway. "Ok, let me give you a quick tour," he began, walking down the short hallway. Cyrus looked at Aaron with raised his eyebrows and began to follow Jeremy.

"This is my dad's home office," Jeremy indicated the first door on the left. "To the right," Jeremy leaned halfway into the door way, "is the den."

Aaron and Cyrus paused to look into each room. Aaron lingered in the den door way while Cyrus continued after Jeremy, slowing himself long enough to look at the pictures of people that were behind glass set in frames of various carvings and designs.

"These are not paintings," Cyrus said. Aaron caught up with him, and Jeremy stepped back to where they were, and all three looked on at the several images that were on the wall.

"They are pictures," Jeremy said.

"Yes, I can see that," Cyrus sighed. "What I intended was that, aside from charcoal drawings, I have only ever seen paintings," he said, then amended, "*we*, have only ever seen, I must say."

"And never on paper," Aaron added, pointing back towards the kitchen. "These are fantastic; the images are so real!"

"Yeah, ok," Jeremy backed up. "Nowadays, when we say 'picture,' we mean photographs." They remained standing still, waiting, so he continued, "It's when we catch light on special paper using cameras." Both men just raised their eyebrows. Jeremy waved his hands. "It's not that important, never mind."

"Your image is up here," Aaron pointed. "And over here."

"Yeah, my mom loves to take family photos. She's got a ton of them on Facebook."

"They are so like life," Cyrus marveled, ignoring Jeremy's comment. He glanced back and forth between Jeremy's face and his photos. "Incredible."

"Ok," Jeremy said, turning back to the tour. "Here is the bathroom—er, rather, outhouse."

"We don't use outhouses," Aaron corrected.

"You don't?"

"The winters are far too cold," Cyrus said. "Are there no winters here?"

"Well, of course there are," Jeremy said. "So where do you, ya know…" he asked awkwardly, "relieve yourselves?"

"Chamber pots, of course," both responded.

"Oh, ok. Well, just think of that," Jeremy pointed to the

toilet, "as a chamber pot. Just push down on that silver handle there and it will flush it away when you are finished." Turning around, he pointed out his parents' and his own room.

"I'd show you into my room, but I think we've had enough scares for one evening," he said.

"Indeed," Cyrus echoed, and Aaron just nodded and yawned. They all headed back to the front room.

"So, I suggest you guys sleep on the couches in living room and the den. I brought out a blanket and a pillow for each of you. You are welcome to anything here."

"Thank you for your hospitality," Aaron said.

"No problem," Jeremy smiled. "Listen; don't worry about getting home to your wife. We'll figure this all out tomorrow. Need anything else, guys?"

"I do not believe so," Aaron said after checking with Cyrus.

"Great," Jeremy said. "Cyrus, sorry again about having to splash you with water earlier. I hope we're ok."

Cyrus looked down at himself, then back at Jeremy. "I am dry by now; I believe we can be friends," he said with a straight face, and then broke a wry grin. "I jest, of course. I am not angry any more. Good night, sir."

"Good night, guys," Jeremy said, and left for his room.

Aaron and Cyrus returned to the front room and began to sort out their bed linens. Cyrus volunteered to sleep on the couch in the den, and Aaron agreed to take the one in the living room.

"What are your thoughts, my friend?" Cyrus asked.

"When we left Falmouth this morning, I expected only to journey to Salem," Aaron answered. "Naturally, I did not expect any of this."

"It is unbelievable, is it not? Everything we knew— *everything* is different here." Cyrus walked over to the wall and flipped the light switch a few times. Both men marveled at its immediacy of going on and off.

"I keep thinking of Anna and the baby! It seems as though we are lost to each other right now."

"She shall be *fine*." Cyrus assured Aaron. "We'll be fine. I hope. We have plenty of time to try, as our visit to Salem was to be at least two days spent."

"Two days? Cyrus—three hundred years!" Aaron sighed, trying to maintain his grasp of their new reality and his own patience. "I am sorry, my friend. Perhaps I should have left that thing where I found it."

"It may not be as bad as we first believed. I find I am more curious and when I began. I would certainly like to explore this place…or time, rather."

"Well, you may do as you please, but I will not begin until tomorrow. I am going to get some sleep," Aaron sat down and began to take off his boots. "I pray that we wake up in our own beds in the inn, and that the reality has returned itself to its rightful place."

Cyrus half-smiled and headed to the den; his head still throbbed, yet not as much as before.

"Sleep well, Aaron."

"Good night, Cyrus."

CHAPTER X

Edison, New Jersey

Duncan rubbed his eyes, and yet again looked around his office, checking for anything that he could think of that might be helpful on the trip. He had already walked into the office four times already, making sure his tired focus didn't miss any ideas. He checked his watch, which reported the time as 10:32. He was not looking forward to having to drive to Salem throughout the night, but was also relieved to have a lead on the erstwhile Opener.

He left his office empty-handed again, and saw that Andrew had arrived, walking down the long hallway from the elevator.

"Good," he said, his tone curt. "You're here."

"Yeah, I just got here," Andrew stepped carefully over some equipment on the hall floor that had not been there earlier in the day.

Duncan sized up Andrew's fresh clothing and clean-shaven face.

"Did you bring a change clothes?"

"I did," he replied, joining Duncan to walk towards the control room. "It's in my car right now." They turned the corner and entered the room. "So, what's going on? All Darrell told me was that the signal for the other Time Opener was picked up, and then it disappeared."

"That's all we have so far," Duncan sighed, stopping to stand behind Lewis and Darrell at their terminals.

Andrew noted that David was sitting over at the corner computer, typing and printing out pages of documents. *I bet he's working on the maps that Duncan told him to make*, he thought.

"Where's Brent?" Andrew asked, noting his absence.

Duncan frowned. "We have not been able to get a hold of him yet. Darrell, have you tried again?"

"I did a couple of minutes ago. I also sent him a text message," Darrell replied without looking away from his screen.

"Ok, well, just keep trying," Duncan said, and turned to address David. "How are your maps going?"

"I just wanna make a few more adjustments," David said, brow furrowed in concentration as he moved the mouse carefully.

"Do you know where Brent lives?" Duncan asked Andrew on a moment of realization.

"Yeah," Andrew said. He and Brent had become friends quickly after he was hired; they had gone to Brent's place to watch the Mets play on his plasma TV the day before their trip to sixteen-ninety-two. "I can go check on him if you want. It's about twenty minutes from here."

"I don't know. I want to get things started soon, but I don't want to have to explain the plan over and over again." Duncan mulled his options for a few moments, and then made up his mind. "Ok, go get him, and get back quick. I want to get on the road before midnight."

"On the road?" Andrew had been wondering about the change of clothes.

"Yes," Duncan said as he picked up one of David's printouts and began looking it over. "We're going to Salem tonight."

"Alrighteythen. I'll be back," Andrew said as he walked out of the room with raised eyebrows. After a few steps, he began to jog down the remainder of the hallway to the elevator.

He reached his car a minute later and got on the road, heading toward Brent's apartment. He turned down his radio, which he'd kept on the local country station, so that he could call his girlfriend back; she was still asleep when he'd left rather abruptly less than an hour ago.

"Hey, it's me," he said into the phone when she picked up.

"Hey," came the sleepy voice on the speaker phone. "What's going on; where are you?"

"They needed me to go to Salem tonight," he said quickly.

"What?" she groaned with deep annoyance. "You just got back! What the hell kind of job is this?"

"One of our research equipment was..." he stalled momentarily, trying to think of a way to explain it. "...vandalized, and we need to get a replacement here as quickly as possible."

"Can't they just ship it overnight or something?" she asked. He knew she was not going to be happy with any explanation he might come up with. Andrew turned a corner as he thought out his response. He didn't like having to hide things from her.

"Well, this is a rather important piece of equipment, and if we don't go pick it up as soon as possible, there will be some major problems with the project," he replied; at least this was the truth. He saw the exit for Brent's apartment complex and took it.

"That sucks. Well, you better be getting paid overtime or something."

You have no idea, babe, he thought as he said, "I am, don't worry." He'd already decided that as soon as they got the Time Opener back, he would talk to Duncan about hazard pay.

"All right, well, just call me tomorrow when you get back, and we can have lunch or something," she said, finally resigning to the fact that she would be sleeping alone.

"I will," he said. "Have a good sleep, babe."

"Yeah," she said in an even, perturbed tone. "Good night." Just like that, the phone call ended.

He had just enough time to burn some energy by listening to some good old country music; "The Devil Went Down to Georgia" had just come on the radio. Andrew always got a kick out of mimicking the fiddle playing. After the song ended, Andrew climbed the steps and rang the bell; after a minute or so of no response, he banged on the door.

"Who is it?" yawned a sleepy voice on the other side of the door a few moments later.

"It's me, Andrew," he called back. He looked around to make sure no one else had been roused by his forceful knocking.

The door opened, revealing Brent standing with his robe half on, in basketball shorts. "Hey man, what's up?"

"Everyone is," Andrew said wryly. "Didn't you hear the phone ringing?"

"I thought that was a dream," Brent scratched his black hair, and turned to head back towards his room. Andrew took the unspoken invitation and went inside.

"Well, anyway, you gotta get dressed. Duncan wants us to drive to Salem," he said. "Tonight."

"What? Man!" Brent's scraggly face scrunched up. "I don't want to go to Salem! We just got back!" He disappeared into his room.

"I know," Andrew sighed. He dropped himself onto a beanbag chair in the living room. "I was asleep at Becky's when they called me."

"Uh-oh," came Brent's voice from the back of the apartment, "How pissed was she?"

"Not as much as when I told her I wasn't coming back tonight," Andrew said.

Brent walked back out a few moments later, with a black T-shirt that had the word "Metallica" and an indiscernible design splayed across it in gray. He had his shoes in one hand and was thumbing his phone with his other, staring blearily at the screen.

"'Bring a change of clothes'?" Brent read aloud. "How long do they expect we'll be there?" Andrew could only offer a shrug, although Brent did not notice as he finished getting dressed.

Brent paused when he looked at the long pack of firecrackers and three smoke balls that sat on the table near the door. After a few moments' consideration, he grabbed the noisemakers and the smoke balls, and stuffed them into the lower pockets of his cargo shorts. *At least I can still have some fun on the Fourth if we are there all weekend*, he thought, feeling resentful for the impromptu trip.

Once he'd gathered his spare laundry into a shopping bag, and grabbed his laptop ("I'm playing Lineage, I don't care what Duncan says!"), they headed out to Andrew's car.

It was about a quarter after eleven when they pulled in to the research facility. Each was carrying his stuff with him as they exited the elevator and trekked down the hall towards the control room. Along the way, David emerged from the restroom and joined them.

"Hey guys. Ready for a road trip?" David asked cheerfully.

"Hey," was Brent's only greeting and response; Andrew offered only a shrug. They all entered the control room.

Duncan was sitting at another computer, but stopped what he was doing as they came in and stood up.

"What took so long," he asked.

"I was sleeping," Brent replied with an edge.

Duncan frowned slightly; his expression shifted quickly to business as he said, "All right guys, we really don't have time to discuss things at the moment; we need to get going.

I'll give you a briefing in the car as soon as we get on the road. We'll take my Aspen, which is already loaded up with equipment we'll need." He pointed to the doorway. "It's out the back door at the lower parking deck."

The scientists and historian filed out of the room, Duncan turned to his technicians.

"You guys have things under control here?" he asked.

"Yep," both said in unison.

"Ok," Duncan said, standing in the doorway. "We'll call you when we arrive. Make sure you contact us if anything happens."

"All right," Brent said, once they were on the highway. He was still annoyed. "What's going on? Why are we going to Salem, tonight?"

"Well," Duncan began patiently from the driver's seat, "we need to go tonight because the signal appeared and then quickly disappeared. We have to find out anything we can about its brief reappearance, if we can at all. We are *all* going because we not only need as many eyes and minds focused on this as possible, but also because it was lost by the team."

"But I thought these things had a GPS in them?" Andrew asked.

"They do, but they still have to be powered on for the GPS to be useful," David answered.

"And by 'on' you mean…?" Andrew left his unfinished question hanging in the air.

"It only needs to be connected to the power source,"

Duncan interjected, "And that's what bothers me."

"You thinking that if the GPS is off, then it must not be connected to the battery, meaning someone has been tampering with it?" David guessed.

"Right," Duncan said. He leaned forward over the steering wheel and peered out into the darkness. "Oh, great, it's going to rain," he muttered to himself.

"Alright," Brent started thinking, "so, the GPS is not working, so the battery was removed."

"Or the Opener is somehow broken," Duncan countered.

"Then that's a good thing," Brent concluded, "since if it is broken, then no one is going to be able to use it to travel through time."

"Oh!" David blurted. "What if they used it to travel through time again, and that's why the signal disappeared?"

"Lewis determined that it was highly unlikely to have been that; the signal was too brief," Duncan replied. "Remember, if it came here, it came from the past, which means it had to be someone from sixteen ninety-two who brought it with them."

"Dang," David marveled with amusement. "Some dude from Witch Trials-era Salem comes through a time portal to the twenty-first century? That's gotta suck for him."

"Well, it sucks for us because we have to find this clown and get him back to his own time," Brent said, looking out the window.

Everyone sat in their own thoughts for a few minutes, when Duncan said, "Ok, guys, why don't you all get some sleep? We can hammer out the details in the morning.

We'll stop in a couple hours and change drivers so I can get some sleep too."

Everyone settled and began to drift into sleep; Duncan set the radio to soft classical music as the rain began to coat the windshield.

Duncan continued on to Hartford, but the heavy rain forced him to go slower; a short construction zone outside of Bridgeport in Connecticut didn't help either. They stopped in Hartford, and Andrew volunteered to drive the remainder of the way to Salem. After some bathroom breaks and Duncan refilled the gas tank, they got back on the road. It was almost six when the rain finally ended, and six forty-five when they started to see exit signs for the cities of Salem and Peabody. Duncan and David stirred and began to awaken.

"How are we doing?" Duncan asked through a gravel voice.

"Almost to Salem," Andrew answered, looking distantly to the pending sunrise of deep pinks and dark blues.

"I'm hungry," David said, hoping someone would endorse his suggestion.

"Me too," Andrew gave him the endorsement. "How about we stop and get some food?"

"Yeah," Duncan sat himself up in his bucket seat and started to play with the GPS, looking for some place to eat. "How about pancakes?"

With everyone's agreement, Duncan set the electronic navigator, and they headed to get breakfast.

Friday, July 2, 2010

CHAPTER XI

Aaron's eyes opened, the single bright sliver of the fresh sunlight made gentle through leaves beyond the window had found an opening in the curtain and landed at his brow. He lay on his back, face upward toward the white ceiling. He glanced around the room, letting his gaze linger on the wood of the shelves across the room, studying the craftsmanship that it showed. He realized after a few moments that there was no craftsmanship; the wood was dark and plain, with no engravings or any other distinguishing marks. The only thing he found interesting about the wood was that it appeared to be polished and smooth, almost like glass. There were colorful books on a couple of the shelves, along with small figures of various designs, some made of glass or wood or metal. It was the shapes of some of the trinkets that he recognized, such as a blue glass frog and a metal lizard. However, others were very strange, such as a diminutive green woman whose curious pose included holding one arm above her head, while holding a stone tablet close to her breast in the other arm.

He frowned at the unique predicament he was still in, and reflected on his far-away wife and their child. He and Anna had decided on the name John if the baby were a boy, and Marie if a girl. He resisted the tug of sorrow and loss that came with the memory of them and his current situation, remembering that Jeremy had promised to try to return them home to their own time.

The soft blue hue of the curtains reminded Aaron that the day was breaking, and he sat up and set his blanket to the side. He then noticed a giant, somewhat curved, black mirror across the room from him. *It is a most peculiar mirror,* he thought. *You cannot easily see yourself in the reflection.* He found it puzzling that the people from this time did not have better mirrors. *Perhaps they use this mirror for different purposes*, he decided. Beside the mirror was a stack of black boxes; some had small green and yellow lights. Aaron tried but failed to imagine the kind of flames that would burn so tiny yet remain steady.

Aaron looked around the room further; there were more pictures like the ones from the passageway between rooms. One of the pictures, a man and a woman smiling as though they were trying to be happy, appeared as though they were looking out of the wall at him; it was unsettlingly real to him and difficult to take his eyes away from. When he finally did look away, he saw a large, beige-and-black marbled vase in a corner, with five long stems of a sand-colored fern Aaron had never seen before.

On the table were two neatly stacked piles of pamphlets; one stack had several nearly-identical, yellow-bound books. The top one was titled "National Geographic", which was followed by the words "Water, Our Thirsty World". Aaron briefly was reminded of the glasses of water that Jeremy had given them the night before. Atop the second stack lay a dark blue Bible with pages of gold. He felt a wave of comfort seeing a Bible still existed in this future.

Between the stacks was a wooden board with paper on it, held fast to the board with a metal clasp. On the paper was a perfect drawing of dozens, perhaps hundreds, of tiny squares, some of which were black, and many of which were filled with manual letters, some of which had been several different letters written over. Scattered across the surface of the table were several long, dark items whose surfaces were cluttered and crowded with colors, gray or white circles, and each one had a number, symbol or word printed above it. A brief moment of mild unease swept through him as his eyes lingered on them for a few moments. In a way, they resembled the very thing that took him and Cyrus from their own world. At the thought, Aaron's eyes were led to the corner of the table to find the cursed tool that had taken him from his time and brought him to this strange New World. He snorted as the irony of the 'New' New World momentarily amused him.

The need to relieve himself captured his attention. Ordinarily he would have gone outside, but something in his spirit suggested that he not take that option this morn. He stood and went his way towards the—*what had Jeremy called it? A 'bathroom'?* As he passed the entrance to the other room in which Cyrus slept, he leaned in and saw his friend fast asleep. Cyrus lay on a red and yellow carpet near the couch, sprawled on the floor and facing away from the door; his blanket wound around him in a snug and seemingly uncomfortable fashion.

Aaron entered the 'bathroom' and walked over to the white bowl. He paused a moment, unsure if he would make a mistake and ruin the drinking water. The moment of consideration was brief, because he felt again the need to relieve himself, and so, deciding that there really is not much he could do to mess up, he did what he needed to. Once relieved, he quickly recalled that Jeremy's instruction was to push the silver handle. He tentatively put his hand to the cold, small handle, and jostled it lightly, but nothing happened. He pushed on it a bit more, when the handle gave up its resistance, and the bowl and water suddenly erupted into noise. Aaron jumped back in a start, shielding his face with his arms. When nothing attacked him, he slowly lowered his arms as he looked into the bowl, and saw a torrent of whirling water, slowly draining into the bottom of the bowl. Feeling somewhat embarrassed, he was amused in spite of himself, realizing that the bowl would cause him no more harm than would a bowl of water from his own well spigot. *Indeed, this place is quite filled with surprises,* he thought. Intrigued, he leaned closer and marveled as the bowl refilled with clear water, and all signs of his own urine were gone. Inspired to share this marvel, he rushed to where Cyrus lay sleeping.

"Cyrus!" Aaron exclaimed, prodding the prone figure in the shoulder. "You must awaken and see something!"

It took a few sharper nudges to finally rouse Cyrus from his slumber, until he rolled over and faced Aaron.

"What do you mean by this?" Cyrus asked blearily and

with mild annoyance.

"I want you to see something remarkable," Aaron said, his energy undiminished by Cyrus' grumpy demeanor.

"Must I see it now?" Cyrus said testily, pulling the covers over his shoulders. "I really want to sleep more."

"You sleep too late as it is," Aaron dismissed. He stood up, extending his hand. "Come with me."

"Oh, as you insist it," Cyrus took the proffered hand, and stood as well. He followed Aaron into the passageway and into the other room, which had blue walls and images of very yellow ducks near the ceiling. Aaron stood next to the large white chamber pot, and, resting his hand on the silver part, beamed back at Cyrus.

"Cast your eyes into the chamber pot and see what this does," Aaron said, and pushed on the handle. Again, it erupted with sound, from which Cyrus recoiled. As Aaron had, Cyrus quickly relaxed some as he too became curious when the water vanished, then refilled, as clear as before.

"Remarkable," Cyrus said, impressed by the demonstration.

"Yes," Aaron nodded. "You see, when I relieved myself, all of that happened," he indicated towards the bowl, and ran his hand in concentric circles, "and my waste was gone".

Cyrus looked about the room, and, upon seeing a beige shell on the counter near a small spigot, grabbed it and dropped it into the water.

"Cyrus!" Aaron hissed. "What if that is something important?"

"If it is important, they at least have two more," Cyrus said. He pointed at the handle. "Let me have a try at it."

Aaron leaned back, and Cyrus pushed on the handle. The now-familiar gush of water whirled in the bowl, and after a few moments, the shell had vanished.

"Amazing! Where do you think it has gone to?" Cyrus asked, gleeful at the new game.

"I do not know," Aaron said, his curiosity growing. "But I find that I am intrigued about our new world. I am going to go out side and see what can be seen." Aaron stepped past Cyrus, then paused at the door way and turned. "Do you wish to join me?"

"I will, after I have had a chance to relieve *my* self," Cyrus replied, closing the door.

Aaron made his way to the entry room, and pulled open the door. It was lighter outside than he first expected; the sun shone low in the clear blue sky, and there was the scent of dew still fresh on the ground. He considered it a moment and estimated that it was about half an hour after sun rise.

He stepped out onto the entrance of the house, and was vaguely surprised when he suddenly felt warmer, even in the shade. As his eyes adjusted to the bright morning, he looked around the street; it looked far different from the previous night. There were houses in both directions, and the street was not straight, but wended an irregular path between all the houses. There were vehicles in front of many of the houses; none were like the wagons and carriages Aaron knew so well, and there were no signs of horses. Instead, there seemed to be no two alike; some were big, some were small, they were all of varying colors and white, and some looked polished and clean, whereas others looked unkept and damaged.

Many of the houses had trees, but there were other poles that did not appear to be trees; they had several strands of black thread that joined poles together. Around many of the houses were strange fences, made of a gray metal but in a diagonal, cross-hatch pattern. In front of at least two houses, Aaron saw something very odd. Water was being shot rapidly across the grass; however, it was unlike any fountain he had heard of or seen before. In one yard, the water simply burst out of the ground and fell back to the earth several feet away in a lovely, misty semicircle. In the other lawn, the water was a stream that flew across the lawn in an arc. The stream itself swung around in a circle, and the rhythm of the water's hush changed when the direction that the stream flew changed. Aaron had never seen anything before like that in his life.

He could hear other sounds he had never heard before; mingled with sounds he was familiar with. It was a faraway sound, but he was unable to name any of the sounds he heard. Cyrus joined him on the porch as he was listening and looking around.

"Egad," Cyrus remarked absently, looking back into the house. "It is quite cool in the house."

"Would you see all this, which is to be the future?" Aaron said rhetorically.

"They live so close to each other," Cyrus said, his words carrying a subtle distaste.

"The land is so small. There is not enough land for even a single horse or even pig to graze, let alone a herd," Aaron pointed out.

"I have been told by visiting shipmen that London is a very crowded city. This is Salem, but three hundred years hence, and it is crowded like London. I do not think that I like if any town is destined to become like London," Cyrus said.

Aaron suddenly became aware of the rectangles of fabric fluttering in front of several homes.

"They fly a flag that is not British!" Aaron said, pointing to the several flags.

"Indeed," Cyrus squinted to see better, "but why would they refuse to fly the King's Colours? Does Salem no longer belong to England?"

"Jeremy told me that nearly a century from our day, several Colonies will revolt against the crown," Aaron recited.

"I am without words," Cyrus said after a few moments' consideration of this news. "There is truly nothing in this Salem that we can claim as familiar."

"It is a strange flag, as busy to the eye as their books and walls. What should all the stripes and stars mean? Do they truly believe themselves to be taken seriously as a nation?"

"Look at the flag yond," Cyrus indicated a house across the street and two houses down from them. "It is strange that they would fly different kinds in one place. What nation do you suppose 'redsox' would be?"

"No, it is not a national flag. Perhaps it is a family crest and flag," Aaron suggested. Cyrus considered this possibility, realized it seemed reasonable, and then frowned. "I do not like this 'future'."

As he said this, the door opened on the neighboring house, and a woman with deep red frizzed hair that was pulled behind her head, walked out into her yard.

"You were saying?" Aaron said, noticing Cyrus' interested gaze. Cyrus glanced back in return, one of his eyebrows lifted up. Aaron suspected that Cyrus was about to feel a lot better about this new New World.

Aside from not wanting to stand witness to Cyrus' attempts to misbehave, he was not accustomed to having a true day off from his labors. "Well, as we are not in Falmouth, nor a Salem in which I can conduct business, nor is it possible that we keep our appointment with Britson at this time, I am going to go back in and try to relax," Aaron decided.

"By all means," Cyrus said, his standard amorous smile spread across his face.

"You would never miss a chance, would you, my friend," Aaron asked lightly, walking back towards the door.

"Never," Cyrus grinned broadly, and walked down the steps, towards the fence that separated Jeremy's yard from the red-haired neighbor's.

CHAPTER XII

Somewhere in the background, Jeremy could hear an irritating, throbbing noise which he tried to ignore. He was having a conversation with a strange woman who wore a water barrel instead of clothes, but was having a difficult time understanding what she said. As the sound repeatedly faded and grew in his ears, she showed him a piece of paper, but he had difficulty reading what it said. However, he groggily realized that the noise was his radio alarm; the lady was part of a dream, and he had to adjust from dream to reality in order to wake up.

He opened his eyes, more tired than normal for some reason, and looked at the clock as he sat up. It was just after seven. His head lolled for a few moments as he lay still on his bed; he waited for the sleepy sting to leave his eyes before he could get up.

"Ugh," he grunted, forcing himself to stand. The details from the previous night flashed in his mind. Blinking tightly, the sting in his eyes faded and he felt almost fully alert. He walked to the door and headed down the hallway, pausing to glance into the den. He saw that one of the blankets he'd offered his guests was tossed about in front of the couch, but the couch was empty otherwise. Continuing to the living room, he saw Aaron sitting up, fully dressed, as though he had not slept at all.

"Good morning," Jeremy said through a yawn. "Did you even sleep?"

"Ah, Jeremy! Good morn to you," Aaron greeted him. "I did sleep, yes. Is this common for people now to awaken so late?"

Jeremy's brow furrowed as he sat heavily onto a stool. "What do you mean, 'so late'?"

"Are there no chores that need tending?" Aaron asked, furrowing his own brow and sitting back with his hands folded. Jeremy found Aaron's posture made him look a lot younger than he did last night. He had a youthful face, and sandy-brown hair, and looked strong but not muscular. He was probably in his mid-twenties.

"What, do you mean, like, milking the cow or something?"

"If you have a cow. However, your land could not support a cow," Aaron shrugged, matter-of-factly.

Jeremy chuckled at the image of a cow tied to the small tree in the back yard or wading in the pool. "No, no cows." He stood up and walked towards the front door. "Where's Cyrus?"

"He has gone out to your yard, and is talking to your neighbor," Aaron indicated towards the door. "We would have done some chores to pay for our lodging here last night, but—"

"No, no, don't worry about that," Jeremy dismissed Aaron's offer. Concern that Cyrus was talking to someone from the present began to grow in the pit of his stomach.

Opening the door, he had to pause a moment to let his eyes adjust to the brightness. Some days, waking up was just not a lot of fun.

"Really?" said a woman's impressed voice. Jeremy could now make out Mrs. Crandell standing next to the fence and Cyrus.

"Absolutely!" Cyrus replied, clearly in his element around a woman. He leaned casually and comfortably against the mesh fence, and oozed with a kind of charm that Jeremy had on occasion wished he had. "Although, I must confess to you that it was not my idea, actually," he grinned at Mrs. Crandell, who returned an amused smile with a touch of sheepishness. Jeremy stepped fully onto the porch, and Aaron joined him a moment later.

"He is as dangerous in your time as he is in ours," Aaron said.

"So it would seem," Jeremy agreed.

"Hi Jeremy!" Mrs. Crandell said, waving. Cyrus turned to see Jeremy when she had called his name. Jeremy waved back, and slowly descended the steps.

"Good morning, Mrs. Crandell," he said dutifully.

"Now how many times do I have to tell you," she said in mock annoyance, "Please, call me Elizabeth!" She was, after all, only about eleven years older than him. However, when his parents first moved to this neighbor-hood, she was already an adult and his babysitter for a short time; by now the habit was set.

"Good morrow, Jeremy," Cyrus said, clasping his shoulder as though they were good friends. "You did not

133

mention you had such a charming and beautiful neighbor!"

Jeremy felt himself blush, embarrassed to think that somehow Mrs. Crandell might find out about the small crush he had long had on her. Mrs. Crandell, however, simply smiled sheepishly.

"Yes, you're right. Sorry, Cyrus," Jeremy said, after a moment of pause, "I was preoccupied with other things."

"Indeed," Mrs. Crandell said, "How is Lisa doing? I thought I saw you two last night out here while I was locking up."

"Lisa is great, thanks for asking," he replied. "Yeah, we had a date last night.

"Oh, lovely," Mrs. Crandell smiled. "So, how do you know Cyrus? And who is your other guest?"

"Ah, yes, sorry," Jeremy stammered. "Aaron, this is Mrs.—er, this is Elizabeth. Elizabeth, this is Aaron."

"How do you do, ma'am," Aaron nodded his head in greeting. "It is a pleasure to meet you."

"Yeah, they are in town," Jeremy began, trying to put together a believable story. "Uh—"

"We have traveled here to visit Jeremy's college," Cyrus volunteered.

"Ah, that sounds interesting," Elizabeth said. "What will you be studying?"

"Right," Jeremy jumped in, "They are from—"

"Falmouth," Aaron finished. "We are considering a better study of our trades, and we have heard that—"

"Salem State University," Jeremy supplied.

"—Salem State University had the…uh," Aaron began

to lose his idea too. Elizabeth's brow creased slightly, trying to make sense of what she was being told.

"The new classes on what these guys do," Jeremy said. His improvisation was not great, but he suddenly felt clever, and said, "You know, a domestic-exchange- student type thing. You know what I mean?"

"Ah huh," Elizabeth said, her semi-suspicious glance passing among the three guys. "Well, that's interesting; unfortunately, I need to get going. I have to take care of a few things before I go in to work."

"Well, it has been a pleasure talking to you, Elizabeth," Cyrus said, taking up her hand and kissing it softly. Elizabeth blushed again, and withdrew her hand slowly.

"It's very nice to have met you boys," she said. "I hope you find what you are looking for at the University. See you all later!"

"Bye!" Jeremy said.

"Farewell," Aaron said.

The trio began to walk back towards the house, and made their way up the steps and inside.

"Alright, fellas," Jeremy began as they entered the living room. He walked into the kitchen and opened the pantry. "What do you want for breakfast?"

"May I have rye'n'injun?" Aaron asked.

"What?" Jeremy stopped rummaging through the pantry to pay attention to his guest's request.

"Do you not have it in this time?"

"I have no clue what you are talking about. What did you call it?" Jeremy asked, shaking his head; Aaron repeated himself.

"I've never heard of that. How about some Lucky Charms," Jeremy said, reaching back into the pantry. He got out three bowls, poured the cereal, and then went to the refrigerator to get the milk.

"I beg your pardon, but what is this you are making?" Cyrus asked.

"Lucky Charms? Just a cereal; it's one of my all-time favorites. You guys are going to love it," Jeremy ex-plained as he poured the milk. Aaron and Cyrus simply stood aside and watched, both with puzzled and uncer-tain expressions on their faces.

"Is that milk?" Cyrus asked, his face scrunched with mild repugnance.

"Of course," Jeremy said. "You do drink milk, don't you?"

"On occasion; we do not have much in our town. We certainly do not have it with breakfast, though," Aaron said.

"Ok, well," Jeremy said, putting spoons into the cereal and pushing the bowls in front of the two. "What do you normally have to drink?"

"At the smith, I have a cider and some bread," Cyrus said. "This is far too early in the morn."

"Right," Jeremy said, slightly stunned. He had no idea how to respond. "Well, try the cereal anyway. We don't have any cider."

Everyone took a bite of their food. Aaron thought that while it tasted strange, it was reasonably delectable, if overly sweet. Cyrus, on the other hand, had a frown on his face.

"What's wrong, don't you like it?" Jeremy asked.

"Not at all," Cyrus said with disgust. "Indeed, it is flavorful, but sweet to the point it is unpleasant. And I do not like the milk. It is far too cold."

"Cyrus," Aaron chided his friend, "he has been the most gracious host. The least we can do is accept and enjoy the food he offers us."

"I am trying," Cyrus said defensively. "Everything here is so different! I simply mean to answer his questions. I do not believe I am being ungrateful."

"Don't worry, Aaron, I'm not offended. It's really no problem to get you something else," Jeremy offered to Cyrus.

Cyrus considered it, and, after exchanging a quick glance with Aaron, said with a sigh, "No, what I have is fine. Perhaps I expect too often to get things to happen in my way."

They finished their cereal, and Jeremy offered them a second helping. Both declined it, and Jeremy went to the back and changed quickly. Upon returning to the living room, he said, "Okay, it's like I said last night. I'm going to see my professor. I hope that it won't be too long. If anything happens, I'll call you guys." He handed the house phone to Cyrus. Jeremy then began to dial on his cell phone.

"That phone is going to ring," Jeremy began. He pointed to the 'ON' button. "When that happens, you push this button and then say hello."

Jeremy pushed 'Send' on his phone, and the house phone began to ring.

The ring of the phone surprised Cyrus to the point of almost dropping the phone. He managed to hit 'ON', and then said, "Hello."

Jeremy chuckled, grabbed Cyrus' hand and guided it and the phone to his ear. "Say it again," Jeremy said, and held his cell phone to his own ear.

"Hello."

"Hey, can you hear me?" Jeremy spoke into his phone.

Cyrus yanked the phone from his hear, his face crumpled and unpleasant.

"What are you playing at?" Cyrus demanded.

"It's ok," Jeremy reassured him. "That's what it is supposed to do. It is so we can talk when I am away."

Cyrus put it back to his ear slowly, and said "Hello" again.

"Good, this should work." Jeremy hung up his phone, and then helped Cyrus turn off the house phone. He walked over to the coffee table and picked up the time device. "Now then, I really think it might be best if you two stayed inside. If you need fresh air, please go only in the back yard," he pointed towards the den.

"I feel like a child again," Aaron said.

"Come on, you guys are out of time! We have to take as many precautions as possible if we are going to get you back safely." Aaron conceded a nod; Cyrus simply shrugged.

"At any rate, I have books over there, and board games

in the wooden box," he indicated the box in the corner at the end of the couch. "Feel free to make yourselves at home; I'll be back as soon as possible."

"Right, then. We shall be all right until you return, father!" Cyrus said.

"Nice," Jeremy smiled and chuckled, and walked out the door.

Highland Avenue

Troy Duncan, Andrew, Brent and David walked across the parking lot of the pancake restaurant toward the Aspen.

"That was a good breakfast," David pulled out a cigarette and his lighter, then yawned and stretched. "Man, I'm still sleep—hey!" He reached out as Duncan snatched the cigarette out of his mouth.

"The lighter, too," Duncan looked steadily at him, his hand outstretched. The others watched the exchange silently; Brent looked on with a bit more amusement than David liked. Reluctantly, he slumped his shoulders and handed the silver flip-top lighter over to Duncan, who pocketed it and resumed his path towards the SUV. Andrew offered a "sorry, dude," and a shrug, and Brent patted his shoulder with a soft chuckle.

Duncan again took the front seat, and entered an address into the GPS. A night full of work back in the office in Edison yielded a best starting location to be Salem Common. Duncan had not told his team about this update yet, since he took the call from Lewis in the waiting area of

IHOP. Duncan, and then pulled into morning rush-hour traffic, following the directions provided by the GPS.

"Well, let's talk about a plan to recover the Opener," Duncan said to his rearview mirror.

"Finally!" Brent complained. "You kept shooshing us in there. I mean, I know we gotta keep this a secret, but still."

"'But still' nothing," Duncan said evenly. "'Secret' means secret. You signed the non-disclosure agreement; even casual conversation in public is prohibited."

Brent frowned and grunted softly. "Yeah, I know."

"So, what is our plan," Andrew said, trying to help defuse the mild tension.

"Alright," Duncan began, taking a deep breath. "Lewis suggested we begin in Salem Common."

"Oh yeah, I've been there before," Andrew remarked.

"Really?" Duncan asked. "Aren't you from around here?"

"Yeah, kinda," Andrew said. "I lived in Danvers for the last couple of years of high school. My parents actually still live there."

Duncan turned the corner, following the directions given by the dashboard computer. "Okay, so how familiar are you with this area?"

"I know it pretty well," Andrew said.

"Good," Duncan said, "That means you can be our guide up here. David, you have the Time Opener, yes?"

"Yeah, I got it right here," David said, holding it up.

"I've been thinking about it, and I wonder if we can modify it to be a detector of time rifts." The SUV's top leaned slightly to the left as Duncan turned right. There were a few moments of quiet as everyone considered this suggestion.

"How could we do that?" Andrew asked after a moment.

"You see, the way the Time Opener works is that when you select a time to travel to, the circuitry compares the target time and the current time, storing it automatically in the memory. It then generates the power discharge and electromagnetic frequencies needed to create the rift and connect it to the target time," Duncan explained.

"So what do you suggest? That we create a time rift and use it as some kind of compass?" Brent asked.

"We don't need to create a portal," Duncan continued, "but creating the conditions of a rift using the discharge, while reversing the power signal for the EM filament can turn it into the detector, and see if we can pick up any remaining waves in the area."

"It's a long shot, though, isn't it?" David asked, his face reflecting his focus on the problem. "I mean, we've never done any real research on the portals themselves. We don't know if they even leave any traces or residue of any kind once they close."

"It is a long shot, but we have to try everything to recover the other Time Opener," Duncan said determinedly. He steered the SUV to the right, and the GPS indicated that they had reached their destination. Everyone looked out the windows at the triangle-shaped park, which consisted of mostly grass and some crisscrossing sidewalks, a flag pole in the middle, a gazebo to one corner, and bordered with trees. On the opposite side was small building and what seemed to be a tennis court. Duncan found a parking space alongside the park and pulled the vehicle to a stop.

"Ok, does everyone have their cell phones?" Duncan asked, turning to face all three members of his team. They each responded yes. Looking at Brent, he said, "I have brought a tool box with pretty much anything you need to do anything to the Opener. How long do you think it will take to rewire it to use as a detector?"

"Actually, I can rewire so we can use it for both, I think," Brent offered.

"Are you sure?" Duncan asked.

"No, but I can try. It will probably take about half an hour, but I should be able to preserve its normal capabilities," Brent said.

"Good idea; we don't want to risk any further complications," Duncan said. "Please start working on that now. The tools are in the back," Duncan pushed a button to open the back hatch. Everyone followed Duncan's lead at this point and climbed out of the Aspen. He looked around the area for a few moments, and then turned to speak to the others as they gathered next to him.

"We need to see if anyone saw anything unusual last night." Duncan nodded his head towards the road that bordered the tennis court. "It doesn't look like any of those businesses would have been open late enough last night for anyone to know anything. Andrew, why don't you go start over there at—" he leaned forward and squinted to read the sign that was over two hundred yards away.

"—the 'Inn on Washington Square.' Head towards the Salem Witch Museum. David, I want you to start here," Duncan pointed across the street, "and work your way towards the Hawthorne Hotel over there. Be vague as best you can, but find out if anyone saw anything. We need any lead we can get. Make sure you answer your cell phones if I call."

Andrew and David headed off to carry out their assignments, and Duncan walked around the SUV towards where Brent was working.

"How does it look?" Duncan asked, knowing he'd only been at it for a couple minutes. As it was, Brent had just gotten the tools out and was working on removing the screws to open the Opener.

"I just started, Duncan," Brent said, his tone clear that it was obvious where he was in the process.

"Okay," Duncan said, deciding to back off a bit. "I'm going to tour the Common here and then make my way to the museum. Let me know when you've finished."

"No problem," Brent responded without looking up.

CHAPTER XIII

Jeremy walked across the lawn between the residence halls and the main sciences building on campus, the time device firmly clutched in his hand. He was hoping that Dr. Arvind would be in his office this morning; since it was summer, the professor might not come to campus. As he made his way, he tried to figure out how he was going to explain things to his former teacher. Since he'd probably sound nuts no matter how he described this, he decided that he would only explain when necessary.

He reached the science building and pulled open the blue-tinted doors which led into the atrium. Jeremy took the elevator to the third floor, and as he stepped off a few moments later, he saw that the door to Dr. Arvind's office appeared to be open.

Sweet! Jeremy thought, feeling relief that was then overrun by excitement.

The door was only half-open; he knocked on the door jamb.

"Just a second!" called Arvind from inside, amid the sound of papers rustling. After a few moments, Jeremy realized that his palms were sweaty. He had taken Arvind's physics class in the spring, and had gotten on well with the professor since, but this repair request made him feel unexpectedly nervous.

While he was pondering his tension, the door swung fully open, revealing the middle-aged, olive-skinned man wearing glasses with his full-yet-trimmed beard.

"Hi there!" Arvind said as delighted recognition spread across his Middle-Eastern features.

"Hi Doctor Arvind!" Jeremy responded.

"What brings you here, my boy?" Arvind asked pleasantly, if a little surprised.

"This," Jeremy said, going straight to the point and holding up the time device.

"Ah, what's this?" Arvind asked more to himself, tilting his head back to look at it through his glasses. Jeremy handed it over to the professor's care and put his hands in his pockets.

"It's broken," Arvind observed, playing his finger along the cracked casing.

"Yeah, I came across this yesterday, and I wanted to see if you could help me fix it," Jeremy explained.

"Jeremy, I am pretty busy. I'm not a repairman whom you can call upon at a moment's notice," Arvind reprimanded him lightly with a raised eyebrow.

"I know, Professor, but this is really important," Jeremy pleaded. "I'm really sorry to interrupt, but I wouldn't ask if I didn't need to have it fixed fast."

"Why, what's the rush? What is this?" Arvind gave him a wary glance after playing with the buttons briefly.

"Honestly, if I try to explain, you'll probably think I'm crazy," Jeremy said.

"Isn't that what they all say," Arvind said with a hint of wry humor.

"Yeah," Jeremy half-laughed. "Anyway, I think if we can get this fixed, it will be a lot easier to explain."

Arvind inhaled deeply as he considered Jeremy's request. He glanced back at his desk, then at Jeremy. Jeremy hoped his desperate expression was enough to sway his teacher to help.

"Let's go take a look at it," Arvind said, and a small frown flashed briefly across his lips as he exhaled. He pulled his door closed, and began walking down the hallway towards his research lab. Jeremy quickly fell into step behind the professor, and they entered the lab room.

The lab had plain white walls and a non-descript well-worn floor, with white-painted wooden cabinets jutting out from every wall and topped with a black counter top. One half of the room looked more office-like; there were stacks of papers on the counters, dozens of broad-spine books on shelves above the counters, three computers, a chair and a stool. The other half of the room looked more like a laboratory. Sitting on shelves sat equipment and labeled jars of various powders and fluids; beakers, flasks, and test tubes sat inverted on racks scattered across the counter spaces. In the middle of each half of the room were two countertop islands. Dr. Arvind set the device on the office-side island and headed over to a tool chest to gather a few tools. He brought his tools back to the center table and laid them out, pushing a few scientific journals aside to make some workspace. Picking up the device to inspect it more closely, he adjusted his glasses to sit on his nose more comfortably.

"Well," he began, "the casing is cracked, but the display and keypad look unaffected. Also," he continued while playing gently with one of the prongs, "this seems to have broken loose."

"Can you fix it?" Jeremy asked, a little more impetuous than he'd intended.

"No so fast. Let me open it up and see what damage may be inside," Arvind said with patience. "You are certain you don't want to tell me what this is before I begin?"

"Not yet," Jeremy said sheepishly.

Arvind grabbed a screwdriver and began to work on opening the casing. He finished removing the screws and carefully pried the two halves apart, making sure to keep the loose components in their proper positions. Jeremy leaned to see the innards of the gizmo, trying to see while keeping out of the professor's way.

"What made you decide to come to me to fix this?" Arvind asked casually while he set the bottom half on the table. He then set the top half, which had the display and keypad, face down on the table too, giving them both a clear view of several densely packed circuit boards. Jeremy counted at least four layers, with all kinds of electronic components jammed in between. At the top were a large silver-gray metal cylinder, and a huge grey plastic thing at the bottom that might be the battery, but seemed different.

"Well, mostly since you are a scientist, I figure you might know how to fix something like this," Jeremy finally answered as they both gazed at the disassembled device.

Arvind chuckled, as he gently prodded at it with the tip of the Philips screwdriver. He looked over at Jeremy briefly as he said, "I am a scientist, yes, but I am a chemist, not an engineer. You should know that I may be able to repair the damage, but I can't guarantee that I can return this thing to working order."

"I understand," Jeremy said.

Arvind poked at it for about another minute, and then grabbed another tool, one that Jeremy was not familiar with. Arvind brought it over and plugged it in.

"What's that?" Jeremy asked.

"A soldering iron," Arvind said. He gathered up some metal wire and continued to look at the electronics. "I can reconnect the prong, and the wire connecting these two boards," he pointed to the wire he was describing, "but after that we will need to test it to see if there are any other broken circuits."

Jeremy nodded soberly as Arvind began to make repairs. Jeremy decided that it would be best to just let Dr. Arvind concentrate on his work, and that he should just stand quietly and watch patiently, and not interrupt the scientist.

Cyrus shifted the colorful boxes that were in the wooden chest, crouched on his haunches as he read the titles on each box.

"I see no whirl-gigs or ninepins games," Cyrus finally remarked with a mild measure of dismay.

"Whirl-gigs, Cyrus?" Aaron remarked with playful disdain, glancing up to his friend while reading from the bible that had been on the table. "Perhaps our current predicament truly does make you feel like a child again."

Cyrus frowned briefly, and then pulled a couple of the boxes out of the chest. "No, I only point out that I do not see any games that we would know. Not even cup-and-ball. Here are some of their games," he said, setting a few more boxes on the first two.

"Scat-ter-gore-eyes?" Aaron's brow came together as he started to read from the red box at bottom. Cyrus pulled it from the bottom and showed the cover to Aaron. "Egad, it seems grisly, if the picture is to be believed. I hesitate to learn what is inside the box."

"Perhaps it is the brains of the loser of the game!" Cyrus suggested with a mad grin and wide eyes. He made to open the box, and once he lifted the lid, his shoulders slumped slightly. "How disappointing," he said with mock dismay, "it is only some kind of game of cards." Aaron smiled at Cyrus' dismayed humor as he closed the lid and set the box aside.

"Scrabble, Cranium, Clue, Risk," Aaron continued reading, noticing that each box was different in color, and the one titled "Clue" even had pictures of people on the side. Moving on, he said aloud, "Monopoly?"

"Yes," Cyrus said, and pulled it from the middle of the stack. "They do have a way of drawing images in this time," he said, pointing to the painted man in black who emerged from the middle 'o'. Submitting to his stimulated interest, Aaron set the bible onto the table and moved closer to the boxes. Cyrus lifted the box top and his eyes widened, followed by a slight smile and a look towards Aaron.

"What is it?" Aaron asked, and leaned further to peer over the box top.

"Could they be so wealthy?" Cyrus marveled, and moved the lid fully out of the way so Aaron could see as well. He grabbed the stack of papers with numbers on them, "Do you know what this is, Aaron?"

"It looks like a bill of shillings," Aaron said. In his own time, he most often traded according to the local barter system in use in the Massachusetts Bay Colony. There were times he might get paid in wampum or coins, and he had a couple pounds stowed in case of emergency, but only a couple times in the past year had he encountered paper bills as payment.

"Indeed," Cyrus said, and began to rifle through the bills, muttering their colors as he did. "Look at this," he said with notable excitement and a bit of admiration, "fifty, one hundred, *five hundred*. I cannot believe they have so much money that they keep some just for play."

Aaron looked on, but scrutinized them more than Cyrus did. "Perhaps they are merely game money, and have no worth. I do not think I would accept even five hundred for one of my pig's skins."

"Must you remove all fun from my musings?" Cyrus complained, as Aaron reached in the box and pulled out a metal figure.

"A flat iron," Aaron mused. "How odd; 'tis so small."

"Ah, a dog and a thimble," Cyrus said, picking up two more pieces, having set down his worthless prize. "And a shoe!"

"A most peculiar game, wherein property is traded using worthless paper money and coins shaped like things of random value," Aaron said. "This is not wealth; it is vanity."

Cyrus set down the coins and Aaron did as well with the flat iron, then picked up the thimble and shifted it in his fingers for a moment. His heart tugged again for Anna, and he hoped she was well with her parents. Before he let tears well in his eyes, he blinked a few times and took a deep breath, setting down the thimble and standing up.

"Are you all right?" Cyrus asked, looking up at his friend as he replaced the lid on the Monopoly game.

"Yes, my friend, thank you," Aaron said after clearing his throat. "Perhaps I should take some air."

"I shall come with you, then," Cyrus began returning all the game boxes to the chest, and closed the chest as he stood. They both made their way from the den to the front door, when Cyrus paused. "Wait Aaron," he said, "I believe he requested we should go into the back yard."

Aaron considered his point, and then pointed to the one in the den. "Then I think that is the door we seek."

As they made their way to the back door, the powerful glow of its large window made it difficult to see out, or even look at directly. Aaron turned the handle, and found that he had to push the door with some effort before it swung open. This prompted him to mutter "There we go."

"Dear me!" Cyrus exclaimed as the door opened wide. "A private pond!"

"'Tis as blue as the sky…" Stupefaction overcame Aaron as he was entranced by the clear water. A sudden noise followed by a steady hum gave him a bit of a start, but he was beginning to get used to the surprises that this new century presented.

"Are you boys just gonna stand there with the door wide open," came a musical voice from across the yard, "or are you gonna come outside and have a dip in the pool?" Elizabeth emerged from behind a bush with a shovel in her hand and a large, yellow hat on her head.

"Lady Elizabeth!" Cyrus smiled, not missing a beat. "It is a pleasure to see you again, and so soon!" He walked past Aaron and over towards the fence. Aaron cast a glance skyward as he closed the door behind him. He then went to join the other two, stepping around the odd white, low and long chairs as he did.

"We were just admiring the clarity of the pool" Cyrus said.

Elizabeth added a look of surprise to her pretty smile. "Your pools aren't clear?"

"It is as we said before, we are not from around here," Cyrus said, keeping his smile steady and trying to continue to charm.

"Where did you say you were from?"

"Falmouth, in the southern part of the Colo—"

"Cyrus!" Aaron shushed in uneasy alarm. The woman

seemed to sense the intrigue regardless.

"Were you going to say 'colony'?" Elizabeth's smile faded as she tried to follow of their story. "You boys really stay in character, don't you?"

"Character?" Cyrus repeated.

"Ah! She means for a play performance," Aaron said to Cyrus, realizing what she had meant.

"You guys aren't in any play, are you?" Elizabeth's tone suggested that they had been caught in their false story. Clearly, to continue the ruse would be to insult her. The men exchanged deciding glances.

"I do not wish to keep lying," Aaron said resignedly, "Let Jeremy have his concerns. We are, in fact, not visiting Jeremy's college."

"Then where are you from?" Elizabeth asked.

"That we are from Falmouth is quite true," Cyrus answered quickly. "However, we are not from *your* Falmouth."

"'My' Falmouth? I don't understand," She said with confusion. "I've never been down to Falmouth."

"What Cyrus means, my Lady, is that we come from a different time and year," Aaron explained.

Elizabeth's eyebrows nearly worked their way to her scalp. "Are you sure about this?" She asked, feeling like she was being put on.

"We do not understand it much ourselves," Cyrus said, gently putting his hand on hers where she was holding the fence. Her face filled with color at Cyrus' touch. "We arrived last evening and, with good fortune, will be able to return this day to our own home and time."

"Well," Elizabeth said, and then cleared her throat. "I suppose if you are visiting from out of town, you must take in our sights." She seemed to recover herself and was returning to her original color.

Aaron waited as he often did while Cyrus charmed women. After a few moments, he cleared his throat to move the conversation.

"Time travel is quite a story, guys," she smiled with skepticism.

"It is the truth. I would like to apologize for the ruse we attempted to deceive you with before," Cyrus spoke with a soft and deep voice, and looked steadily into her eyes.

She sighed and feigned royal haughtiness. "Very well, you are forgiven. As punishment for your misdeeds, you may relax in the pool." She then broke a full smile. "Seriously, though, don't worry about it. It isn't a big deal."

Cyrus returned her smile; Aaron had become weary of the coquetry and went to sit in one of the white seats.

"These seats are strange. I have never seen any material like it," Aaron said, tapping it with his knuckles. He looked up at Elizabeth. "This is not metal."

"I'm afraid not," she shrugged. "It's called plastic."

"Hmm," was Aaron's only response to her as he tried to settle comfortably into the chair, resigned to watching yet another of Cyrus' romantic conquest unfold.

CHAPTER XIV
Salem Commons

The sun was climbing into the sky and Duncan felt the heat of the sun's rays, but thanks to a light steady breeze he was not too hot. Duncan was glad for Brent's sake that the SUV was parked under the border trees, allowing him to modify the Opener in relative comfort. Andrew and David both were still going door to door and trying to find leads regarding the lost Opener. Duncan himself had no luck over at the museum, which would not be open for another hour and a half.

Everyone in the Common this morning was working on setting up decorations for the Fourth; unfortunately it was highly unlikely that any of these workers would have been strolling here last night. *What I really need is a bit of good luck to come my way,* Duncan thought wistfully. He had spent the last half hour mostly just waiting.

Duncan's cell phone began to vibrate and ring in his left pocket. He started to dig it out when Brent stood fully and casually tossed a tool onto the seat in the Aspen.

"I think it's ready," Brent declared as he turned to Duncan.

Duncan held up a finger as he nodded that he heard Brent, and opened his phone to say "Hello?"

"Hey, Duncan, it's me," said David's excited voice.

"What do you have?"

"I was talking to the desk manager over here at the Hawthorne and one of the guests overheard my question. She says that she saw something suspicious happen outside a restaurant down the street from here last night."

"What does that mean, 'something suspicious'?"

"Well, she said that there was a couple at the restaurant who left just before her and her husband, and then she saw them put a man into a car with another man. Apparently the two men were dressed in character, like in colonial times."

"That's gotta be them. Did she tell you the name of this restaurant?"

"Yeah, I got it. I'm headed your way—"

Duncan pulled the phone away from his ear when David's report was interrupted by another incoming call. It was the control room.

"David, get here quickly, I've got another call coming." He switched lines to the control room.

"Hello?" he said. His energy beginning to surge.

"Duncan, it's Adam. Just wanted to let you know that the tracking signal just came back up for the other Opener."

Relief flooded through him; if they acted quickly, they would not need to rely on the modified Opener as an untested detector.

"Where is it?"

"It looks like it's the campus of Salem State University. I'm still working on refining its location exactly."

"Try looking up the campus map from the university's website, see what you can find. Let me know if it moves or disappears again."

Duncan closed the call, a bit unceremoniously, but social protocol was not his priority at the moment.

As he tucked his phone back into his pocket, he noticed Brent also closing his cell phone.

"I overheard you talking to Adam, so I went ahead and called Andrew and told him to come back," Brent said.

"Excellent," Duncan's satisfaction was apparent. Moments later, David came jogging up, with Andrew appearing across the Common moments later. Everyone converged on the Aspen; Brent hastily tossed tools and shoved stuff aside to make room.

"Let's go. We need to hurry; we know where it is right now," Duncan informed them.

They had barely enough time to take their seats when Duncan threw the SUV into drive. The tires screeched briefly and the Aspen lurched forward, jostling its passengers. The hunt was on.

◊

"I think that does it," Arvind announced after nearly half an hour of work, setting down his soldering iron.

"Yeah?" Jeremy stood up from the stool he had been sitting.

"I believe so," Arvind was remounting the screws to close up the casing.

"Sweet," Jeremy marveled with a whisper. "Let's see if it works."

Arvind turned it on its side in his hands and, finding the power switch, pushed it on. The device began to vibrate and all the lights came on; it seemed to be booting up. Arvind watched it evenly, and then looked up at Jeremy only to see a grin spread across the young man's excited face.

"All right!" Jeremy cried out, and looked up at the professor.

"It seems to work. Now, before we do anything else, do you mind telling me what exactly this is and why it was such an emergency to repair it right now?" Arvind's serious eyes were intent on Jeremy.

"Ok, here's the thing," Jeremy began. "Last night, while my girlfriend and I were out on a date, a…portal or something … appeared. That's when these two guys came through it. I'm pretty sure this thing is for time travel."

Arvind stared at him for a few moments as he processed his story.

"Doctor Arvind?" Jeremy prodded gently after a few silent moments. He wasn't sure what to say next.

"I don't know what to say," Arvind finally responded, still stunned.

"They're from sixteen ninety-two, and I'm trying to help them get back to their own time," Jeremy explained.

"My goodness, young man," Arvind said. "This is a most remarkable situation to find yourself in. And what are your plans with this after you help your new friends?"

"Oh, I'll give it back to them, but not until I've gotten Aaron and Cyrus home," Jeremy promised.

"But why? Why not wait for whoever built this to come collect it, and let them return your friends to the past?"

Arvind peered at him with eyes that seemed to challenge Jeremy's reasoning and integrity.

"Well, think about it," Jeremy argued, "whoever made this left it in the past. Either they are careless, or it may have even been a trap! Who knows what else might be planning?"

"Jeremy," Arvind began, his tone suggesting a lecture was coming. "This is a *lot* of responsibility for anyone to be entrusted with. I am truly unsure what the right course is; part of me is obligated to confiscate this from you and wait for the owners to recover it, but part of me believes you can be trusted with seeing this situation through to its proper conclusion."

Jeremy' began to worry that Arvind would actually not let Jeremy have the time device back.

"Doctor Arvind," Jeremy said, and with a pleading touch to his words, "you have my word, I promise to not misuse that. I only want to get these guys home, and I will bring it back to you, today, to let you return it to its builders."

"I don't know, Jeremy," Arvind was still uneasy with the idea.

"Well, at the very least, can we try to figure out how to use it?" Jeremy requested, hoping an opportunity would present itself so that he could convince Arvind to let him have it back.

The professor considered it for a moment, and then turned study the front keypad features.

"Ok, it looks like you press this; let's see what format

this wants the date input," he said while pushing buttons. He had to try a few different number combinations before its discovering the right sequence.

"Ok, so, let me this to a couple minutes from now," Arvind explained, showing Jeremy how he had entered the target time information.

"Do you know anything about making the portal you described?" Arvind asked.

"Not really," Jeremy shook his head. "First, a line appeared," he drew in the air with his finger upward, "then it popped open and it was there."

"That's good," Arvind said, and then held the instrument at arm's length. "I believe I have figured out what to do. Please stand back."

Jeremy did as he was told, and Arvind carefully pressed another button on the other side, which caused the prongs to spit electric currents at each other, creating a glow between them. Arvind tensed as this happened, but proceeded to raise the device; it looked like it took some effort to do so. Jeremy watched as the same blue-and-yellow line emerged and remained in the place where the prongs had begun. It was as if the time machine was carving into the air. He stood in awe and excitement at the sight.

Arvind had lifted the device only about a half foot and when he turned it off. Almost at the same time, the line jumped apart to open the portal, bordered by the blue-and-yellow glow. The inside of the rift now looked completely empty, and Jeremy felt the urge to stick his hand through.

He began to reach when Arvind reached out his hand to stop him.

"Jeremy, don't do that," Arvind warned. He picked up a screwdriver and slowly poked at the air in the middle of the rift. Nothing seemed to happen, but a moment later, the rift began to pop in spots, as the hole in the space-time continuum tried to heal itself. Arvind looked at Jeremy and then shrugged, tossing the screwdriver through the portal. Within seconds, the rift border collapsed with a crack, leaving a faint, fading glow.

"Woo hoo!" Jeremy laughed at the thrill, unable to contain his excitement any further. "That was freaking awesome!" He whooped again.

Even Arvind was smiling. "Indeed, that was fantastic," he said with great wonder. "My boy, we are witnesses to a scientific marvel!"

All the fantasies he had of time travel, all the times he daydreamed, came flooding back to him. It was every sci-fi geek's dream come true, and he saw it firsthand.

Jeremy's internal thoughts must have played across his face, because Arvind's smile faded away as he watched him.

"Now you see why it is difficult to leave something like this to chance, a responsibility so big—"Arvind began saying before Jeremy cut him off.

"Yes, you're right Doctor Arvind," Jeremy said, regaining his composure. "I know I got excited about it, but this was totally the coolest thing I have ever seen. Still, I made a promise and I intend to keep it; both to you and to

Aaron and Cyrus."

"Jeremy, you are a bright young man," Arvind began, with approval in his eyes. He was about to say something else when the glow line reappeared over the work counter. Both teacher and student turned their attention to it and watched as the portal reopened, but this time the glow was muted and spread out differently. There was no longer a solid border and inside it was like looking through a bag of water. Jeremy and Arvind exchanged glances and then leaned to look around the singularity. They watched the screwdriver tip emerge from the floating portal, disappear, and then the whole tool fling across the counter before bouncing and falling to the floor. The portal closed again and faded away.

"Man, that just gets cooler and cooler every time I see it," Jeremy raved, but then quickly muted his expression.

Arvind regarded his former student for a few long moments, and then came to a decision.

"Your friends are from sixteen ninety-two?"

"Yes sir."

"That's the year of the witch trials. Did you take that into consideration?"

"Holy crap, that's right!" Jeremy had completely forgotten about that. "I can't *believe* I missed that! And I've lived in this town my whole life."

"You must be absolutely careful," Arvind punctuated the last two words to emphasize their importance, "When you send them back, do so in such a way that they won't be seen and accused of witchcraft. You know how they were back then."

"Absolutely, I will be careful," Jeremy said, making a mental note to see to that detail. A thought suddenly occurred to him.

"So you're going to let me take care of this?" Jeremy said, trying to hide a smile that showed his excitement.

Arvind handed the device to Jeremy. He tried to present the most stern face and voice he could muster. "I am allowing you to keep your promises, which can be the most important thing anyone can do."

CHAPTER XV

"What do you know about this university?" Duncan asked, checking the rearview mirror before glancing to Andrew in the front passenger seat. The urgency in his driving style leaving the Common was definitely different than it was arriving an hour earlier.

"I don't know," Andrew replied with a shrug. "Not much, really. I mean, it used to be just a community college, but they changed their name a few years ago."

A thought occurred to Duncan considered this as he followed the GPS. "Check the GPS route and see if it's taking us on the fastest path," Duncan instructed Andrew, who immediately followed his commands.

"It looks fine," Andrew said, looking into the distance as he mulled various routes between where they were and where they needed to be. "The only other ways there means taking neighborhood streets, which would only slow us down."

"Humph," Duncan grunted with mild impatience, and glanced back between the GPS' estimated time of arrival and the road. It said they would arrive in just about five minutes, but Duncan was already pushing the speed limit and driving more recklessly than he would ordinarily prefer. Quick glances to the rearview mirror told him that his abrupt change from passive to aggressive driver was eliciting mild alarm in his team of experienced time travelers. He realized that he felt a bit overcome with a madness to get to the campus now, reinforced by the hope to have the Time Opener back in his possession and to finally have this chapter of the time travel disaster behind him.

"Why would the Time Opener be at the university?" David asked out loud from the far back seat, bringing Duncan's attention back to earth. A few moments of silence followed David's question as everyone pondered the possible implications.

"That's a good question," Duncan remarked finally.

"Do you think a student found it?" Brent asked for his part. "Or maybe a teacher?"

"There's no way to tell until we find the person who has it," Andrew pointed out.

"Yeah, that's true," David conceded.

"It's still worth having an idea of what we should expect when we arrive," Duncan said. "David, when this woman told you about what she saw last night, what all did she tell you?"

"Let's see," David said, and drew in a deep breath as he corralled his memories from the exchange with the hotel guest. "She said that she and her husband were leaving some place called Paolo's and that she heard some yelling about a block away. She said when they got to where they were parked, they saw a couple of guys and a girl put an unconscious person into the back of a Chevy. She said she thought it might be a Chevy sedan or something like it," he recited. "'She seemed like such a sweet, pretty little girl when we saw them in the restaurant; I hope they aren't some in a gang or something'," David mimicked the woman's comment in a high-pitched feminine voice. This drew a few chuckles from Brent and Andrew. Duncan, however, was too focused to be amused.

"Alright," Brent said, as Duncan took a left onto a street called Mill Street. "So now we have an idea, that these people drive a Chevy."

"You said that she also said two of them were in period clothes?" Duncan asked from the rearview mirror.

"Yeah, one of them was out cold," David said, nodding.

"I'm guessing a student rather than a professor," Andrew declared, checking with Duncan, who refused to take his eyes off the road.

"Yep," Duncan swiftly wove between three vehicles that were closely clustered, but far enough apart to allow a Chrysler Aspen steered by a highly motivated driver to fit through. Traffic had picked up, and the streets were busier now, with the Fourth of July traffic adding to normal Friday morning commutes. Once they veered right and the road became Lafayette Street, traffic thinned and the two lanes became a wide one-lane avenue. His eyes darted quickly to the GPS; only about a minute or so left.

"Okay, so a student finds a couple of guys who just came from the past," Andrew began, trying to bring the details together that they had deduced so far, "but somehow one of them gets knocked out, so everyone loads him into the car and they just drive off to wherever."

"Don't forget, it was a guy and a girl," David pointed out, "they were out on a date."

"Big deal," Brent sneered. "A student, a couple, a dance troupe; it doesn't matter. You said it yourself: why would they have taken it to the school?"

David frowned at Brent's mocking. "Maybe they tried to turn it in to a professor or something?" he wondered.

"If you had a time travel device in your hands and just made new friends from the late seventeenth century, would you be quick to give it up?" Duncan posed with his eyebrows arched broadly.

"I wouldn't," Brent and David said simultaneously.

"Before I joined this project, I probably would have kept it," Andrew said soberly.

"My, my, dear Andrew," Brent said with pseudo-British accent and an amused smirk, "has the actual experience of time travel soured you on the idea of travelling through time?" David laughed; Andrew simply shrugged with a smile and shook his head.

"I don't know," he said. "I mean, who hasn't imagined riding in a DeLorean and going back to the Old West or something," Andrew said, making lightning-crash sound effects with his mouth. "The science is cool, but the actual travelling leaves a lot to be desired."

"There it is!" Duncan said, and began to look around more animatedly. "Everyone look for something, maybe somewhere to park. Andrew, whatever you can suggest," Duncan said.

"If you go down a couple more streets, the science building is to the south," Andrew said. Duncan pulled out his cell phone in the meantime. He dialed it up, and then held it out in front of him, having set it for speakerphone.

"Hello?" came the digitized sound of Adam's voice.

"Adam, it's Duncan. Any news?"

"Nothing has changed. The signal has not moved or disappeared, but I can see that you guys have reached the school."

"Okay, great," Duncan said. Andrew motioned for him to turn; Duncan took the SUV right onto College Drive. "We are getting ready to pull in somewhere; I'm going to keep you on speakerphone so we can get live updates." Duncan pulled into the parking lot to his left almost as soon as he had pulled onto College Drive.

"Where are we in relation to the other Opener?"

"Hold on, it'll take a moment to update through the satellites," Adam said.

"That's the science building over there," Andrew said, pointing to one of the buildings.

"Looks like you are almost directly south of it, by about a few hundred yards. You guys are really close," Adam said, a measure of awe and surprise carrying in his voice.

"Ok, here's what I want to do," Duncan said, working out a plan as he parked in one of the more secluded spots, further from the building than he liked because of its reduced visibility. "David, you stay with the SUV, but I'm leaving it running. Take the wheel, just in case we need it." David's head bobbed in the back seat as he received his directions. "Andrew, you are with me, we are going to the science building to check things out. Brent, I want you to follow us but keep some distance, and keep an eye on things around campus, just in case you spot something suspicious. I don't want to miss this chance to reclaim the Time Opener."

"You got it," Brent said, relishing the idea of action.

"Let's go," Duncan ordered.

Jeremy stepped out of Dr. Arvind's lab and paused momentarily to allow the professor to close up his laboratory door.

"Thanks again, Doctor Arvind," Jeremy said, studying the repaired time device's features. He felt like it was more familiar now, having seen it work for himself. He felt a strange sense of power.

"I think you should keep that thing secured when you are carrying it around. There is no telling who might ask questions about it," Arvind suggested. "Although, I'm sure it's highly unlikely that anyone would even think that that is used for...ahem... time travel," Arvind's voice dropped to a whisper at the words 'time travel'.

"Still, I gotta be careful," Jeremy agreed. As they began walking back to Arvind's office, he quickly took stock of his own outfit, which was a pair of cargo shorts and a t-shirt. The pockets of his shorts were pretty big, but the time travel instrument was too long to be concealed in them. "I think I'll just have to carry it to my car for now, but when I come back later, I'll be sure to hide it better," Jeremy promised.

"See that you do," Arvind said, looking at Jeremy seriously. The two reached Arvind's office and paused outside the door as Arvind searched for his key from the set.

"Okay, well, I guess I'll get back to my guests and try to get them home," Jeremy looked at his watch and at the time device.

"You do that, Jeremy," Arvind smiled. "Good luck, and remember, don't take any unnecessary risks. Open it up and send them back, and then bring it back to me."

"You got it," Jeremy smiled as he promised this. Using the time device to wave farewell to Arvind, Jeremy began to walk towards the elevator.

Suddenly, a blond guy in his mid-twenties turned the corner. He looked at Jeremy, and when his eyes found the time device in his hand, started to walk quickly toward Jeremy.

"Hey!" he said loudly.

Jeremy's blood ran cold, and he glanced back toward Arvind's office. Arvind popped his head out from his doorway.

"Hey, what's that you have there?" the blond man demanded as he continued walking briskly towards Jeremy. Jeremy froze for a mere moment, and then made his decision. He turned and broke into a full run in the other direction; there was a set of emergency stairs beyond Arvind's lab.

"Hey, wait a minute!" the blond man yelled.

"Jeremy!" Arvind cried out, reaching out his hand to try to stop him.

Jeremy dodged Arvind's attempt. He tore around the corner and dashed down the short hallway, slammed open the stairwell door, and began to take the steps three at a time. He passed the second floor landing and began to descend further when an idea hit him. He climbed the few steps quickly back to the second floor and ran to the door, yanking it open. He ran around the corner, ran to full speed down the lengthy corridor, hoping dearly that no one would emerge from one of the several doors as he passed them. He reached the elevators and pressed the button several times. The elevator finally responded, and the doors opened. Jeremy's heart was racing with exhilaration; he half-expected the blond stranger to be waiting for him in the elevator. When the doors' opening revealed an empty car, he rushed in and pushed the button for the first floor. The elevator doors closed and took him down.

The guy took off around the corner, but he had a commanding head start and Andrew was no track superstar. By the time he reached the corner of the hallway, the stairwell door clicked close at the opposite end of the short hallway. Feeling frustrated to have been so close to reclaiming their lost Time Opener, Andrew dug his cell out of his pocket and dialed Duncan. He walked quickly back to the professor who was standing silently at his office door.

"Duncan," answered the voice from his phone.

"Duncan, he's coming down the stairwell!" Andrew reported urgently. "He has the Time Opener in his hand. He saw me and took off, headed your way."

"Alright," Duncan said, "Get back down here quickly."

"Right. I'll be right down," Andrew said, and closed his phone.

"Okay, I need to know who that was," Andrew said forcefully. His voice cracked a bit with its rare use of full of authority.

"And just who exactly are you?" the professor said, looking suspicious and defiant. Andrew looked at the placard beside the office door and saw the professor was named Arvind.

"Sir, I believe he has something that belongs to us," Andrew softened his tone for respect. He did not expect this man to give him anything useful, so he did not want to push too terribly hard.

"I'm sorry, but until you give me credentials or badge or something, I cannot in good ethic tell you his name," Arvind shook his head stubbornly.

"Fine," Andrew said with annoyance, and turned and jogged back to the elevator. "We'll be back to talk to you later!" He called back to the professor. He heard the older man snort in derision as he turned the corner.

Duncan switched back to Adam after getting Andrew's report, and looked around the room for the stairwell. Seeing the gray door across atrium, Duncan headed towards it.

"Adam, Andrew says he made contact with the

individual," Duncan updated his technician. "I need to get off the line; I want you to call David's phone, and keep watching both signals."

"Yup," Adam said, and closed the call.

Duncan closed his cell phone, and started wonder how long it would take this person to rush down two flights of stairs. Just as he reached the door, he heard the elevator ding across the atrium. Duncan turned at the sound and saw a boy in his late teens or early twenties appear behind the parting doors, and then recognized the Opener in his right hand.

"Hey! Young man!" Duncan yelled sharply. The boy paused momentarily, and then suddenly broke into a pure run towards the doors. Duncan began running after him.

"Wait, stop!" Duncan ordered.

The kid glanced at him but easily reached the doors first, flinging himself through the double doors and out into the sunlight.

"Damn!" Duncan swore, and pulled open his phone again, dialing Brent's number.

Duncan followed outside and watched as the kid ran more west than south; evidently he parked in a different spot on campus. He frowned at the several pounds he'd put on since his college years; no way was he going to be able to catch a twenty-year-old kid who had a head start. Duncan hoped Brent would be able more successful.

"Hello?" Brent's voice answered.

"Brent! He's out racing across the courtyard," Duncan exclaimed breathlessly.

"Yep, I see him!" was all Duncan heard when the call ended.

He heard his name called out as Andrew emerged from the science hall. Duncan stopped and pointed towards their SUV.

"Go meet David; I'll call him! Hurry!" Duncan ordered. Andrew changed direction and ran towards the Aspen Duncan reached the street between the building and wherever the kid's car would be, punching up David's number as he did. This time he did not even wait for standard phone etiquette.

"David! Get over here, now! Andrew's on his way to you!" Duncan snapped the phone closed. He altered his path to keep Brent and the boy in view, but in such a way that David could also collect him quickly. Watching Brent's pursuit unfold, Duncan hoped his scientist could close the gap between himself and the kid before they lost track of him.

CHAPTER XVI

Jeremy saw the tall black man across the atrium, and something told him he was here with the blond man who had just chased him. When the man called out to him, he felt a chill like he'd just been caught with his hand in the cookie jar. He paused for a moment, and then realized that he was much closer to the atrium doors than the other man. He broke into a run for the door, threw them open, and pushed his legs as fast as they could go. He was not even sure he had ever run so fast before in his life, not even during that brief stint on his tenth grade track team.

He quickly reached College Drive and bound across it, having checked both ways as he approached it so that he could cross it without slowing down. When he looked left, he saw another figure wearing a black shirt and dark hair. Jeremy stole another glance backward after he was on the other side of the road and saw that this new fellow was also chasing him. Completely certain now that they wanted the time instrument he possessed, fear and an odd excitement fueled his speed and energy, and he continued to race towards his car. He knew if he let up even a little, the black-shirted guy would catch him.

He ran past the residential halls' tennis court and pulled out his keys with his left hand as he made it to his car. He was thankful he hadn't locked the door, and was able to plunge himself into the car and thrust the key into the ignition. The car seemed out of synch with his own energy as it started up with its characteristic quiet. He pulled the door closed, jerked the automatic shifter into reverse, and pulled backwards out of his parking spot. He inwardly thanked his friend Alan for living in the residence halls and letting him park in his spot occasionally.

He shifted to drive and pressed his foot to the floor; there was a thump at the rear of the car as it launched forward. Jeremy turned the corner and glanced back, and saw the black-shirted guy slowing to a stop; the thump apparently had been when the guy had pounded a fist on his trunk when Jeremy had backed out.

Jeremy sped through the short Rainbow Terrace Road which snaked through the University's residence complex. Reaching the end, he turned left and headed home. He had to get the guys and get them home, and there was no time left to make it happen.

The Chrysler pulled up and Duncan quickly climbed in to the middle seat. He was peeved because he desperately desired to be in the driver's seat, but he knew that any change in driver now would result in loss of time to catch the kid.

"Man, he missed him!" Andrew exclaimed breathlessly, staring out the windshield at Brent. David honked the horn; Brent heard it and jogged back to the SUV, hand clutching his side as he ran. David moved closer to meet Brent; Brent reached the SUV and climbed into the back seat, panting heavily as he did so.

"So," Duncan said in a dry tone, trying to catch his breath the same as Andrew and Brent. "We missed him."

"That dude can run!" Brent wheezed. "But I did get his license plate number."

"Do you have Adam on the phone?" Duncan asked David.

"Yes," David answered. Adam's voice rang from the phone, "Yeah, I'm here."

"See if you can look up the license plate number for someone in Massachusetts," Duncan said.

"Okay," Adam said. The sounds of keyboard typing came followed as several seconds passed while Adam was working.

"Okay, looks like I've got something here," Adam finally said. "What's the plate number?"

Brent quoted the number he had memorized, and another couple minutes of silence passed, broken only by occasional keyboard clicks and 'huhms' from Adam.

"Aha!" Adam hissed to himself. "I've got it here. This says it is registered to someone named Jeremy Macer, and for a blue, nineteen-ninety-eight Chevy Cavalier."

"That's the one!" Brent exclaimed.

"That's our man," Duncan declared. "Does it give his address?"

"Yeah, right here," Adam said, and began to read out the address. Andrew quickly grabbed the GPS and punched in the information as Adam gave it, and remounted it on the dash.

"Go, David," Duncan instructed. He was pleased with the growing information they had on the device, despite the setbacks. "We are headed there now and will check things out. Do you still see the other Time Opener?"

"Yep, still on my monitor," Adam answered, clicking away at his keyboard somewhere beyond the cell phone. "Based on this information, it looks like he is headed there now, if I had to guess."

"Keep tracking us and the other device, and let us know if anything changes. That's all I have for now," Duncan concluded, and closed the call with Adam.

David took a right turn, headed for their next destination.

Good news: Arvind fixed the time thing and it works. Bad news: the people came chasing me for it, and are after me now. How is your day going so far?

Jeremy hit "Send" on his cell phone, dispatching the text message to Lisa, and then wiped the sweat that seemed to suddenly accumulate on his face. The car was still warm in spite of the air conditioner, and he felt temporary wave of nausea after running so hard.

He felt briefly amused with his wording but quickly refocused on the situation at hand. He had to make a choice: take Aaron and Cyrus back to the parking lot where they first came to the present, and risk getting caught by the men chasing him, or simply send them back from his house, which according to them would be in the middle of the wilderness. His phone began ringing and interrupted his train of thought. He looked at the display before answering, saw Lisa's name, and then opened his phone.

"Hey," he tried to sound completely casual.

"What do you mean 'hey'?" She demanded, apparently perturbed by his unserious demeanor. "What do you mean 'chasing you'? The people who built that thing found you already?"

"Well, yeah," Jeremy stammered. He took a quick breath and began to fill her in about the events at the college.

"Why didn't you just give it to them?" Lisa pressed him in exasperation.

"Because, I told Aaron and Cyrus I would get them home. These people were way too aggressive," Jeremy defended. "I don't think they are worried about getting the guys back safe."

"Yeah, but Jeremy, you gotta realize it's not your job to take care of Aaron and Cyrus," Lisa replied.

"Look, after you left last night, I went back inside and they were all upset because apparently Aaron's wife is getting ready to have a baby. Aaron realized that she's dead in the present."

"Well, she kind of is, to be honest," Lisa said matter-of-factly.

Jeremy frowned at her Lisa's detached reaction to this highly irregular situation. "Well, at any rate, I told them I'd help get them back home, and that's what I plan to do," he pressed on stubbornly. "I'm on my way home now to get them and take them back to the parking lot where they came through. Do you want to come along?"

"I am working!" Lisa protested.

"Okay," Jeremy let his tone carry a strong hint of nonchalance, unsure what else to say next.

"Erg. Let me see what I can do. Maybe I can take a half-day or something," Lisa said with resignation. "I'll call you back in a few minutes if I can work something out."

"I'll be waiting," Jeremy said, and waited for her to hang up. She did so without saying a word. Jeremy frowned again, pulled up to a stoplight, and began to dial his home phone number. He put the phone on speaker and waited for it to pick up.

"Come on, guys," he muttered out loud, hoping that one of the guys would remember the lesson on how to answer the phone. After five rings, the answering machine beeped.

"Cyrus, Aaron?" Jeremy asked loudly into the phone, hoping they would figure it out and not get spooked. He repeated himself, adding an instruction to pick up the phone. After no response came, he hung up, wondering if something had happened.

He looked into the rearview mirror, then all around him, checking for signs of police. Satisfied that no cops seemed to around, and seeing the path home inside his head, he pressed down on the accelerator and worked his way through traffic. *This thing is quickly becoming a big mess*, Jeremy thought. *I hope it hasn't gotten bigger.*

About five minutes later, Jeremy was in his driveway and climbed out of the car. He rushed to the door, glancing around the neighborhood on his way up. There were no indications of the guys outside.

Tossing open the door, he quickly took in the living room and kitchen, and saw nothing out of place. The blankets he lent his guests the night before were neatly folded and sitting on the arm of the couch near the entrance to the hallway. Two glasses of water sat on the counter, sweating slightly; the kitchen light was still on. Jeremy mentally noted that he had forgotten to turn it off earlier.

Walking over to flip the switch to 'off', his eyes fixed on the phone he had called, and saw his parents' obsolete answering machine flashing the number two. Jeremy knew that one of the messages belonged to his voice, and the other had been left for his father a few days before. The phone itself sat quietly and unassuming, and Jeremy felt a mixture of annoyance and concern.

"Guys?" he called out. There came no answer, and Jeremy walked into the hallway towards the back. He glanced into the den, noticing that Cyrus had also cleaned up his sleep area, as everything was back as in its place. The bright morning sun created a strong glare in the back door and windows, and Jeremy walked past the entryway and down the hall. He called again for his guests, and again there was no response.

"Crap," Jeremy muttered irritably to himself. "I get the thing to work and now I have to try and find these two."

He passed the bathroom, wondering momentarily if Aaron or Cyrus had showered while he was out; both men had a strong body scent that Jeremy had been too otherwise occupied to comment on.

Jeremy picked up his pace and burst out the front door, standing with his hands on his hips as he scanned the yard and street. Everything was normal, with the expected addition of American flags on several front doors. A few yards had the familiar *chick-chick-chick* of sprinklers watering their lawns, and an older neighbor about five houses down was mowing his lawn.

A sense of helplessness washed through him as he realized that he had no idea where Aaron and Cyrus could be. Jeremy walked down the steps and out into the grass, trying to think of what he could do to find them. It seemed almost cliché to him that upon fixing the device, he would be chased and his charges would disappear on him. Jeremy frowned, and called out again.

"Cyrus! Aaron! Come on guys, where are you?" he bellowed.

"Jeremy?" Elizabeth's voice echoed from between the houses. Jeremy walked towards her voice, and the red-head came into full view.

"Mrs., ah, Elizabeth," Jeremy said, his voice betraying some of his mild panic.

"Jeremy, they're back here!" Elizabeth smiled pleasantly. "In your back yard!"

Jeremy felt a bit of embarrassment as he took the side gate to the back yard. How did he forget to check back there?

"Don't I feel a bit silly," Jeremy remarked, letting himself be amused at his foible. Elizabeth walked along her side of the fence as Jeremy followed the stone path. As he turned past the second large bush, he felt relief when he saw both Aaron and Cyrus. Aaron was sitting in a patio chair and looked quite relaxed; Cyrus was in the shallow end of the pool, floating with his arms out.

"Jeremy!" Cyrus called, a big smile splashed across his face. If Jeremy hadn't known better, he would have mistaken Cyrus for a regular guy from school. "Were you challenged in finding us?"

"Do you have news?" Aaron asked, his relaxed posture unchanged by Jeremy's appearance. Aaron was, to no surprise, still wearing the same period clothes he had been wearing since last night when they all first met. While Aaron could also pass for a regular guy, Jeremy found that he still seemed be out of time.

"Yeah," Jeremy said. He looked directly at Cyrus. "You probably should get out, and quickly. We gotta get going, ASAP."

"' A S A P'?" Aaron repeated him as he stood. Cyrus stood up in the shallow water and stared at everyone. Jeremy was about to answer Aaron when Elizabeth spoke up.

"What's the rush?" Elizabeth asked, keenly interested in the situation.

"I'm sorry, Mrs. Crandell," Jeremy said quickly and with the most respect he could summon. "But, I need to get these guys to an, um, appointment," he explained. Aaron stood up while Cyrus sloshed out of the pool.

"Oh," Elizabeth complained with a smile, then yelped,

"Oh my!" as she turned her head away from something. Jeremy looked over and saw that Cyrus had been swimming in pants that were lighter than his breeches, and that the water left little to the imagination.

"Yikes," Jeremy agreed, and turned his head away and shielding his eyes too. "Cyrus, can you get dressed quickly?"

"I shall," Cyrus' voice responded, with a mild chuckle. Aaron joined Jeremy and Elizabeth while Cyrus dressed.

"I apologize for my friend. He often forgets the line between vulgar and civility," Aaron offered to Elizabeth, who dismissed his apology with a wave of her hand.

"Don't worry about it," Mrs. Crandell said, her face still a little blushed. "Besides…," she said with an undertone and a raised eyebrow.

"Mrs. Crandell!" Jeremy gasped with feigned shock.

"Well, Jeremy," Elizabeth looked at him matter-of-factly, "you have to admit, with a body like that…I am still a woman." She winked at him and exhaled. She stole a quick glance at Cyrus.

Cyrus joined them, hair wet but now fully clothed. "I am prepared. Did you suggest we are to hurry?"

"Yes," Jeremy said, relieved now to be able to get moving again, as well as change the subject. "See you later, Elizabeth," he said awkwardly. Both and Aaron and Cyrus offered their farewells to her, and they followed Jeremy towards the back door of the house. Jeremy was already holding the back door open when they caught up with him.

They entered the den, and Jeremy absently noticed that

the windows on the door needed a very good cleaning, but set that thought aside as he marshaled his thoughts regarding the next few steps.

"I got the device repaired, and it works," Jeremy said quickly as they crossed the den and entered the living room. Both of his guests beamed at the good news.

"I am so very relieved, Jeremy," Aaron said. "When can we go home?"

"Right now," Jeremy said, and tried to look for anything that he might need to take with him. Since he never helped anyone travel through time, he quickly realized that he had no idea how to prepare for such an experience. He shrugged his shoulders. He stopped and pulled the time machine out of his pocket.

"Right when I was leaving the lab, these people showed up and tried to take this from me. I don't know how long it would take them to find me again, so we really need to get going fast. I want to get you guys home before they catch up again."

"What is your plan?" Cyrus asked.

"Well, we can do it right here if you like," Jeremy offered. Both Aaron and Cyrus both protested the idea.

"We are not familiar with this area, even in our own time," Aaron explained. "We would be lost for days before we found any settlement."

"Not to be inconsiderate, but so what? Aren't you guys used to hardship and adventure and exploration?"

"My wife is expecting to give birth any day now!" Aaron's impatience rose.

"I agree," Cyrus said. "We should go back where we were before."

"Ok," Jeremy relented after a few moments' consideration. "We'll go back to the restaurant. But obviously we have to make sure that you going back won't get you hung as witches. Those people were nuts back then!"

"I beg your pardon?" Cyrus said with a tone of warning.

"I'm sorry," Jeremy backtracked. "I meant only that those witch trials were no joke. You guys should know that better than anyone."

"We do," Aaron said. "However, you cannot deny that those witches present dangers that cannot be simply ignored!"

"I can deny it because all those people were innocent!" Jeremy said, and Aaron and Cyrus obediently followed him out of the house and towards his car.

"How can you say this for fact?" Cyrus demanded as they reached his car.

Jeremy got into his seat, but the other two did not immediately. Jeremy leaned his head back to see what the holdup was. Cyrus was looking at the door, then finally reached out and tugged on the handle, and the door popped open. Aaron then opened his door, and the two climbed in gently.

"Guys, I get it that things are still weird here, but can you get in a bit faster?" They each reached out and pulled their doors closed. Jeremy considered seat belts, but then decided not to waste any more time; he would just have to drive safely.

"I can say it because in a few months, everyone is going to be let go and the whole mess is going to end," Jeremy explained to them. "Even the people who were for it will admit it was a mistake."

He started the engine and backed out of the driveway. He started forward when a gray SUV turned the corner onto his street, coming his way. It could have been one of the neighbors, but he had a funny feeling that it was coming for him.

"Hang on tight, I think they're here," Jeremy said ominously. He threw the car into reverse, backed into another driveway, shifted again, and sped out. He quickly reached the end of the road and was turning left when he glanced in the rearview and saw that he was right. The gray SUV was racing to catch up with him. Jeremy floored the pedal and took the left turn.

CHAPTER XVII

"It looks like this guy is the guy," Adam's voice said from the phone, having called back to give this update. "The tracker's been stopped for almost ten minutes at address I gave you."

"Excellent," Duncan muttered satisfactorily. "Good work, Adam."

"We should be there in less than a minute," David said, switching the right turn signal as he prepared to turn the corner onto a street called Joyce Road. The GPS map indicated an upcoming left turn to arrive at their destination.

"So what are we going to do when we get this guy?" Brent asked. "I mean, what if I had managed to catch him; what then?"

"Well," Duncan began, leaning forward as if using sheer willpower to help get to their destination faster. He reflected that he should have taken the wheel after all. "Recovering the Opener is priority number one. But how to do so, while not hurting this young man—"

"There he is!"

David's exclamation cut into Duncan's words as they turned the last corner onto Wright Street, on which Jeremy was expected to live. Sure enough, the green-colored

Chevrolet belonging to Brent's license plate number was pulling out of a driveway and now faced them. After a pause, the car pulled into a driveway and then peeled back out, going away from them.

"He knows it's us!" Andrew exclaimed, giving voice to everyone's thoughts.

"Don't lose him!" Duncan said sharply, and David pressed the accelerator to the floor.

"Sweet," a mischievous grin spread across Brent's face as he wrapped his hand around the closest grab handle. "I've always wanted to be in a car chase!"

Jeremy glanced quickly right and then left without slowing down as he took the left turn onto Whitney Drive. Behind him, Aaron and Cyrus tried to keep their balance when Jeremy chuckled tensely and said, "Maybe you guys should buckle up after all, eh?"

"What was that?" Cyrus asked, looking to Aaron for possible explanation.

Aaron shrugged, and then remembered what Jeremy meant, and pulled his seatbelt as he had the night before. Cyrus watched him for a moment, and then did the same for himself.

Jeremy's cell started ringing; he flipped open the phone, saying, "Hello?"

"Okay, I was able to work it out to take the rest of the day off," Lisa said.

"Perfect, 'cause we're on our way to pick you up now," Jeremy said with urgency.

"You are?"

"Yep," Jeremy said, pulling up to Lynnfield to take a left, and watched the few cars on the road as he looked for his best chance to pull out. In the rearview mirror he saw the SUV turn onto Whitney and head towards him. Time was running out for this turn. "Meet me outside; I'll be there in a couple minutes."

Seeing an opportunity, Jeremy seized it and turned a quick hard left, cutting off an oncoming Toyota. He noted with mild disappointment that the tires didn't squeal as he had expected. Still, his reckless gamble had bought them a few extra moments, as more traffic was coming that should slow down his pursuers. Putting the phone back to his ear, he heard Lisa talking.

"Lisa, I'm sorry, but I gotta get off the phone; I'm driving."

"Alright, fine," Lisa said with an annoyed tone. "See you in a minute."

"K," Jeremy said, and closed the phone. Putting both hands on the wheel, he put his full focus on driving to pick her up.

"Crap, they're turning left," David uttered, mostly to himself.

"David," Duncan said with a warning tone, "I hope you are up to this."

"I do too, sir," David said. He went heavy on the brake at the stop sign, causing the vehicle to lurch with the suddenly deceleration. He waited for the best spacing of cars to take his turn.

"It's moving northeast along Lynnfield Street," Adam reported.

"Maybe we should have switched seats after all," Duncan grunted as he watched openings pass that he would have tried to slice through.

"I got this," David said with a hint of indignation, and pulled the SUV out onto Lynnfield, inspiring some offended drivers to honk their horns.

"Your fault for being in the way," David muttered with mild aggravation.

Coming up was the left turn onto First Avenue that Jeremy hoped would buy even more time for him and his party to make their way. *Hopefully these guys aren't from around here and don't know Salem well*, Jeremy hoped. As he pulled closer to the intersection in the left turn lane, he glanced back, but was not sure where the SUV was; there was a white car and a large red truck immediately behind him blocking his view.

"You guys okay back there?" he checked, waiting for the oncoming cars to give him an opening.

"I am well but Aaron has a weak stomach for hard travel," Cyrus quipped, winking at Aaron.

"I have no such trouble, you know this well," Aaron protested. "I am quite well, Jeremy."

"Good," Jeremy said, "Hang on!" He floored it again, tearing into the left turn.

There were no cars on the road front of him, so Jeremy

cautiously met and exceeded the speed limit. He desperately hoped no cops were lurking along this road. He got halfway down the road when he noticed in the rearview mirror what might have been the SUV turning onto First Avenue behind him, about a quarter of a mile back. Looking ahead, he saw his desired target, and turned right onto Centennial Drive.

Up ahead on his right, he saw Lisa's building; after moving past a large bush, he saw Lisa standing at the entrance. Jeremy took the right turn onto her parking lot and, while slowing down, was still rushing through the parking lot faster than he normally would have done. He braked hard, stopping abruptly in front of her.

"Hurry!" he said, gesturing her over vehemently. She skittered to the car, and then climbed in. She had barely gotten the door closed when Jeremy set the car in motion again and swerved out of the parking lot, taking a left instead of a right on a sudden whim.

"Jeremy!" Lisa cried out, trying to regain her balance in the seat. She clutched the seatbelt, and then reseated herself as Jeremy tore onto the road, and clicked the buckle into place. "Slow down!"

"Sorry," Jeremy said, slowing instead of stopping at a stop sign. "We've gotta stay ahead of those guys."

He pointed out the window at the gray Aspen they passed as both vehicles turned the same corner, but in opposing directions. Lisa turned around in her seat and watched the SUV disappear behind the trees. Aaron and Cyrus both turned also to see what she what she was looking at.

"Hello, Lisa," Aaron said as they turned forward again.

"Hi Aaron," Lisa said sweetly, momentarily forgetting her annoyance with her boyfriend. "And…Cyrus, right?" she tried to remember as she smiled at him.

"Indeed," Cyrus bowed his head cordially. "I'm delighted you could join us."

She turned in her seat, a frown returning to her face. She gave a glare at Jeremy as he pulled to the stoplight at the Lynnfield intersection and said, "What's with the reckless driving?"

Jeremy met her eyes, and then quickly checked his rearview mirror and then the light. "They caught up with us at my house just as we were pulling out."

"Why didn't you just send them home from there?"

"Because," Jeremy explained, hissing a "yes!" when the light turned green, "They're not from here in the past; they'd be completely lost. I can't do that to them. We need to get them back at the restaurant."

"Well, do you really need to drive so dangerously?" she asked through clenched teeth, clutching the armrest on the door to keep herself from falling over as Jeremy wove between cars.

"This isn't that dangerous," Jeremy defended while speeding over the limit by almost ten miles per hour. "Let's just call it my own rush-hour driving."

Everyone in the SUV did a double take when they saw Jeremy's car pulling up next to them at the stop, then speeding away to their rear.

"Dang it, man!" Brent exclaimed.

"Well, at least he's making it interesting," Andrew quipped.

"I don't like it," Duncan said, as David pulled into the first driveway and began to turn. Adam's voice chimed in on the pursuit from the phone.

"Hey, guys, stay on that road," he said. "It connects back with Lynnfield Street; you might be able to get ahead of him if you get around it fast enough," he suggested.

David checked with Duncan, who nodded.

"Do it."

David peeled back out and was soon pushing the speedometer past forty.

"That should be fine," Duncan said smoothly. "Be careful around that corner, but in the meantime let's not get pulled over and risk losing track of the device again."

"What is this guy up to?" David asked.

"My best hope is that he wants to return whoever came from the past back to where they came from before we get there," Duncan answered.

"How do we know this guy didn't just find it in the dirt or something?" Andrew posed out loud. "I mean, can we be sure he even knows what it is?"

"You were up there with that professor," Brent pointed out. "Did he seem like they had no idea what the Time Opener does?"

"I didn't talk to him much," Andrew said while in thought. "I pretty much told him we'd be back, and then took off to catch up with you all."

"*I'll be back*," quoted David the clichéd monotone, causing him to chuckle at himself. Andrew also smiled in brief amusement.

"Nobody finds anything like that 'in the dirt' around here; not with this level of urban development. Besides, I'm sure he is fully aware of what that thing can do," Duncan said, bringing the focus back to the task at hand.

Up ahead about a quarter of a mile was the red light at Lynnfield Street. As they approached the light, Jeremy's car passed in front of them. Immediately after he crossed through the intersection, the light turned green for them, and David used the momentum to take the corner with nearly full speed, garnering muted shrieks from the strained tires. Duncan chose to say nothing, as it might affect his driver's dedication to catching up with the car.

◊

"Holy smokes!" Jeremy cried out as he sped through the yellow, then saw the SUV appear immediately in his rearview mirror. "These people are relentless!"

"You should have just given it to them," Lisa argued. She felt very uneasy that Jeremy insisted on racing through the streets and trying to avoid these people instead. "At least we wouldn't be risking our lives, tearing through the streets of Salem like—like—"

"Stampeding cattle," Cyrus volunteered from the back seat. Lisa gave him a double-take, briefly thrown for a loop by the uncommon metaphor.

"Okay, right, like stampeding cattle," Lisa finished

saying to Jeremy. She noticed that Cyrus pleased that she used his proffered phrase.

"Please let's not get into that again right now," Jeremy said. "Besides, we're already 'stampeding', as you put it." He glanced up in his rearview, and consulted his mental map for upcoming turns in the road.

"Well, I don't think I'll be able to trick them again; and they *are* just behind us. Hopefully we will be able to pull this off before they can interfere." He paused a moment to consider the scenarios. He then spoke out of the side of his mouth to address the rear-seat passengers. "When we get to the restaurant parking lot, we'll light up the time thing and get you home before they can stop us."

"That's your plan?" Lisa exclaimed. "'Get there first, hope for the best'?" She was quickly becoming impatient with Jeremy's handling of this situation.

"Yup," Jeremy said firmly.

"What do you know of our pursuers, Jeremy?" Aaron asked, hoping his curiosity might also take his new friends' attention off their disagreement.

Jeremy hastily told them about his experience in Arvind's office, how the blonde guy had tried to tackle him and his inspired decision to change from stairwell to elevator (the accolades he expected for disappointingly never came; he'd thought it had been a pretty clever idea, if he said so himself).

Jeremy then told them about being chased by two other people, one of whom almost caught him at his car, as well as his surprise and thrill at the fact that he'd outrun them all.

"And you are certain they wish to do us harm?" Aaron wondered; he certainly wouldn't want Jeremy to get in to trouble on their account, especially over a misunderstanding.

"I have no idea what they want to or might do. For all we know, they may want to do experiments on you or something, since you are from the past. We already know they were in your time for some reason," Jeremy said.

"I do admit, Jeremy," Cyrus spoke up, "that I appreciate your efforts to try to keep your word. Furthermore," he leaned over to look out the window, "while your wagons and carriages are beyond the imagination, you seem to have maneuvered yours quite effectively to evade and elude our enemies. I thank you for these this."

Jeremy smiled, and cast a glance at Lisa. She rolled her eyes; however, he was sure they to rolled much further than ever before.

Everyone in the Aspen had fallen into a silence since they had gotten behind Jeremy's car. They had been following the Chevrolet for a few miles, and were now on Boston Street when Adam spoke up over the phone from the control room.

"You know what, guys," he started, "I think they are going back to where whoever arrived last night."

"What makes you say that?" David posed.

"The road you are on is going that way, for one," Adam answered back. David shrugged his shoulders and his eyes, realizing how obvious his answer had been.

"You don't recognize having driven this way?" Brent asked.

"My sense of direction is a bit screwy," David said. "That's why I love the GPS in my car. I never have to think about how to get where I am going; I'd probably get lost in my apartment complex without it." This made Andrew laugh out loud.

"Do you have an address?" he asked Adam. "Maybe we can put it into the GPS and see if we can get there faster."

There was silence as Adam could be heard typing; after a moment, he read out an address. "That's my best guess."

"It'll do," Duncan said. "We just need to be close to them."

"Uh oh," David said. "This doesn't look good."

"What?"

"That light is green," David noted, and then added with dismay as it changed. "Now it's yellow. They're going to make the turn, and we're gonna be stuck at a red light!"

Duncan cursed as David's prediction came true. The light turned red, but Jeremy's car sped through the yellow as it turned red. David slammed on the brakes just in time for the Aspen to lurch to a halt just past the crosswalk lines. Even though he'd sped up too, had he continued behind Jeremy into the intersection, he would have caused a wreck with at least three cars. Once again, they were helplessly stuck at a stoplight, and the Time Opener and its current owners were getting farther away.

CHAPTER XVIII

"Come on come on come on," Jeremy repeated through clenched teeth while clutching the steering circle. Aaron looked on and saw that he was staring intently at a black-and-yellow object that hung from the end of a metal pole and had two black voids and a steady green circle at the bottom. Aaron did not physically flinch, but felt his breath catch a bit when the green circle disappeared and a void became yellow. Perhaps it was the steady deluge of unfamiliar curiosities that was having an effect on him; Aaron never thought of himself as one who was weak in his constitution until this experience.

He felt the car go faster while Jeremy continued his steady chant. Lisa perhaps felt more tense as well, with her arm outstretched and bracing herself for what Aaron expected would be a turn. In a high-pitch voice, she said, "We aren't going to make it!"

"Yes we will," Jeremy said, his teeth still tightly closed, and Aaron felt the car quicken again. The yellow circle vanished and a red circle came into being just as the yellow box disappeared out of Aaron's view. Jeremy whooped in joy as Aaron was abruptly pulled to the side of the car as it turned the corner, causing him to collide with the door. His shoulder and head smarted after having struck the door;

Aaron cursed internally and felt mildly annoyed with himself for not being ready.

"Yes!" Jeremy hissed in exhilaration, looking back in the mirror to check his pursuers as he sped along on this new street. "They couldn't make the turn!" His shoulders dropped slightly as he exhaled in relief.

Regaining his own balance, Aaron sat back up and looked out the window again, but while buildings and carriages still seemed foreign, something about this road seemed more familiar to him. He couldn't quite place it, but it was nice to feel a sense of familiarity. There were vibrant signs of red and blue that featured the words "July 4th" on nearly all of the buildings they were passing. Aaron also noticed an extraordinary number of the striped flags he had seen earlier while at Jeremy's house now adorning these buildings as his new friends drove the strange, unfamiliar streets of Salem.

Aaron felt a hopeful joy to be able to get home, with promise of his wife no longer being dead for centuries, but alive and well at her parent's farm in Falmouth. He decided that as soon as he crossed the threshold of his and Cyrus' room at the inn, he would send notice to Britson to meet an hour earlier than agreed. Aaron was anxious to see his wife, to feel her in his arms, to know she was safe.

"Aaron," Cyrus summoned him from his thoughts in a whisper. Aaron turned to look at him. "Do you see the gait with which this carriage takes us? No horse can go this fast," Cyrus whispered.

"Indeed," Aaron nodded.

"And there is no wind in our hair, yet it is cool to the skin," Cyrus continued, prompting Aaron to look at the skin on his own hand.

Shifting his position to sit up more erect, something caught his eye in the distance, above the wall of buildings and trees (which were moving by so fast they were a blur to his eyes). He spoke up to address Jeremy and Lisa, who were in the middle of a muted but heated discussion.

"Did I just see an 'M' rising beyond, above the trees?" Aaron asked. Cyrus leaned over to see what Aaron referred to. However, neither Jeremy nor Lisa seemed to have been aware that he had spoken. He suddenly felt weary of this new century, with its strange quirks and myriad of 'cars' which traveled at unseemly speeds on roads with yellow lines and white lines and the red-white-and-blue-striped flags that decorated the buildings and the dizzying assault of colors seemed to be on everything. He was ready to go home.

"Only a few more minutes and we'll be there," Jeremy announced, as if he had been listening to Aaron's thoughts. Lisa turned in her seat to face Aaron and Cyrus.

"I hope you don't think I'm a terrible person," Lisa said, "I just disagree that these people want to hurt you."

Aaron thought he saw the side of Jeremy's face crumple with annoyance. For her part, Lisa seemed a bit less angry now that they had put some real distance between themselves and those who sought them.

"I do not think such of you," Cyrus answered, then turned to look at Aaron, who tried to show a friendly face as he shook his head in agreement with Cyrus' words. Absently, Cyrus then ran his hand through his blonde hair, which was still wet.

"Why is your hair all wet? Did you take a shower or something?" Lisa asked, noticing Cyrus' features for the first time.

"He went swimming," Jeremy said, pulling the car to a brief stop before speeding up again.

"Ah, I see," Lisa said.

"Gadsbodikins!" Cyrus cried out, his eyes wide with understanding.

"What?" Jeremy asked as Lisa said, "What's the matter?"

"What is it?" Aaron asked. There was a moment of tense silence as Cyrus stared at his feet, his countenance one of someone attempting to gather his thoughts.

"There was an incident here," Cyrus began slowly. "Well, in our Salem, a day ago. Last evening," Cyrus paused again, and then said, "Yes, it was last evening that I was at the pub. So it was when some patrons in the pub told me of three 'demons' who raided Salem Village. It has just now come to my mind that these fellows who chase us now would have been those witches."

"It makes sense," Jeremy said, and picked up the time device as he reached another stop. "They go back, leave this, whether by accident or on purpose, then you find it and come here."

Lisa repositioned herself as everyone considered Jeremy's theory, taking out of Jeremy's hand the device that Aaron hoped would successfully return him to his own Salem.

"So how will this work?" She asked as she toyed with it, turning it over in her hand much as Jeremy and he himself had done.

"Ah, yes, okay, so," Jeremy said, suddenly animated, "We're almost there, so here's the plan." Aaron and Cyrus both sat up to give better attentiveness to him. "We need to turn it on," he pointed to the side where the green button was, "but don't push anything else yet."

Lisa put her finger to the side of the instrument, and it began to hum loudly; its adornments lighted up to glow once again. She jumped a bit and gave a high pitched, but soft, yelp of surprise, and looked to Jeremy.

"Don't worry, it's supposed to do that," he answered her unasked question. He turned left into the parking lot they had first met Aaron and Cyrus, pulling into a space near the lot entrance. Jeremy and Lisa quickly removed their restraining harnesses, and Aaron and Cyrus then copied them; Aaron needed to point to the red part of the harness that Cyrus needed to push to be able to free himself. All four clambered out of the car and closed the doors.

"Let me see that," Jeremy requested of Lisa, who handed him the warm, humming metal item. He looked at it intently, and then began to push buttons on the keypad, following the sequence that Doctor Arvind had figured out only an hour before. Hitting the hash key, the both the first red light and the green light next to the display began to glow steadily. Nervously, he looked around at his girlfriend and their two unwitting time-traveling friends. He walked over to the side of the parking lot, near the cement curb, and readied himself.

"Okay, here we go!" Jeremy said, trying to sound confident but feeling the burn of excited anxiety as he pressed and held the star key. With a crackle and some flames, the prongs burst to life and began to cut into the space-time continuum.

The light was not terribly long, as measured by the day-to-day motorist, but to Duncan and his crew, it seemed to stay red far too long. During their wait, Andrew had finished entering the target address into the GPS. The light changed, and now they were on Essex Street, and speeding to each of the stop signs and stoplights that lay along their way.

There was a growing tension in the SUV as David maneuvered the streets of Salem, occasionally cutting off drivers as he tried to make time on his pursuit.

Duncan wanted to warn David of traffic safety in light of the situation, but also felt that David was acquitting himself quite effectively with his driving skills. He decided to let him drive without nagging.

"I'm fed up with this. It's time to get this situation under control," Duncan said; Andrew turned his head to face Duncan and Brent leaned forward. "Andrew, Brent, I don't care what you do," he said determinedly, "tackle them, knock them down, restrain them, I don't care. We can deal with straightening things out after we have the Opener safely in our possession."

Brent smiled broadly; he evidently wanted to finish the job that he started at Salem State University. Andrew, on the other hand, wore an expression of concern and uncertainty.

"Doctor Duncan," Andrew began, "What if they are just trying to return a traveler back to 1692?"

"We can do that," Duncan responded quickly, already having planned his reply. "But first, we need to know what this person has learned since being in our time, and make sure this traveler understands the gravity of what he or she knows about our time. We cannot risk contaminating the past!"

The GPS reported that their destination would arrive in half a mile. Brent searched around as they crossed a street labeled Summer Street on one side of the intersection, and North Street on the other side. Something caught his eye as David pressed on towards the address given. Duncan was fervently looking forward and to his right; Andrew was doing the same.

Brent saw a sign on the storefront to his right. "Sao Paulo's!" He exclaimed. Everyone turned to see what he just saw, but Brent was one step ahead of them. It was just as he turned to his left that Brent noticed four people, two of whom were in period clothing, standing across the street in the back corner a parking lot. A familiar bright yellow-blue glow burst into view a millisecond before the Aspen's forward progress took it out of view.

"That's them!" Brent exclaimed, and tore off the seatbelt, barely waiting for David to realize that he needed to stop, and Brent crouched next to the door. "Stop the car!"

David hit the brakes, and a car that was behind had to swerve to not hit the SUV, pulling around on the spare asphalt to the right of the SUV. The driver leaned out his window, cursing at David.

"Shut up!" Brent yelled as he leaped out of the side of the Aspen and tore across the street. Duncan and Andrew had unbuckled themselves and now followed Brent's zealous lead, having to cautiously duck around another oncoming vehicle.

It was perhaps one of the strangest, if not the strangest, sensation Jeremy had ever experienced. The time machine hummed loudly as it vibrated; Jeremy felt its high warmth as he held it tightly clutched with both hands. He did not expect resistance as he pulled it from chin height to the ground, creating a beautifully soft glow of blue and yellow light. There was the sound of static and other energy noises that he had heard in when they tested it in Arvind's lab. He was reminded of a light saber for a moment, and a part of him desired to swing the handheld time machine around as if he were an expert Jedi swordsman. He ignored the urge, and released the star key; the prongs ceased creating energy, and he stood from his squatted position.

"Jeremy, I thank you, for everything," Aaron said, and offered his hand. The portal popped open with a ripping bang, startling everyone, and there now hung a darkened hole inside of a border of soft blue and the sound of nighttime crickets in the middle of the day.

Jeremy was about to speak when they heard a screeching of tires out of view from on the street. Jeremy felt a rush of adrenaline as Lisa turned back to face him.

"Jeremy," she said urgently, "They're here! If you're going to do this, get done fast!"

He extended his arm around Aaron, and indicated towards the portal, forceful urgency in his voice too. "Just walk through. That should be it; I set it so you'll arrive an hour after you left."

"*Hey!*" yelled a man who appeared at full sprint from around the parked cars. It was the guy who had chased Jeremy at the university.

Aaron and Cyrus took this cue to step through the portal; two more men whom Jeremy recognized from the school chase earlier appeared, running full tilt towards the group.

"Go!" Jeremy yelled, and started running towards the Brent. Brent was ready for Jeremy, however, and deftly sidestepped him, and kept running for the portal. Lisa leaned back as he ran past her, a focused fury on his face as he reached out. Jeremy stopped and turned to see Aaron halfway through the portal when the black-shirted man let out a guttural sound and clotheslined Cyrus. Aaron, however, also had his hand on Cyrus sleeve as he had stepped through and gave a firm yank at the exact same time, and Cyrus was pulled through the portal. Brent, having a firm grip Cyrus, was pulled through as well. His momentum carried him crashing into both men and all three tumbled into the black hole.

"Cyrus! Aaron!" Jeremy yelled, and started for the portal.

"Brent!" yelled both Duncan and Andrew, who had come to a stop when Brent disappeared into the hole. Duncan started to race for the portal again, with Jeremy nearby as it started to close itself. There was a screech of tires again, this time as the SUV swerved into view in the parking lot, blocking any exit.

"No!" Andrew yelled, extending his arm out as if to be able to reach Brent from across twenty feet and three hundred years. With the same ripping sound as when it opened, the portal finished closing, and Duncan, Jeremy, and Andrew all came to halt. David, for his part, had gotten out of the vehicle and was now caught up with them. For a few moments, everyone gazed dumbfounded at the spot where the portal had just been. Brent was now trapped in the past.

Duncan looked at Jeremy, then Lisa, then at Andrew and David, and finally back to the spot where Brent disappeared. He sized up the situation, thought for a moment, then ordered Andrew and David to action.

"Hold them," he demanded, and walked over towards Jeremy. David grabbed Lisa by the elbows from behind, and uttered an "I'm sorry" as he did. Lisa struggled, and he tightened his grip; he felt bad for having to be rough with a girl.

"Let go of me," she demanded as she wriggled.

"Let go of her!" Jeremy yelled as Andrew grabbed him

in a choke hold and with an arm awkwardly held behind his back. The pain in his elbow convinced him to stop struggling for a moment.

"We will let you go once we get this situation back under control!" Duncan said forcefully; the power of his anger with Jeremy and the disappearance of Brent would no longer remain restrained. He reached Jeremy and furiously snatched the Time Opener from Jeremy's white-knuckled grasp.

"Not bad. You figured out how to set it properly," he said after a few moments, inspecting the formerly damaged device. "It appears Brent is now in...August 22, 1692."

"Why do you need to hold us hostage?" Lisa cried out, her elbows and shoulders aching from David's grip holding them behind her.

"We're not holding you hostage, young lady," Duncan chided. "But you just performed time travel with a tool that you have no business using." He pressed a sequence of buttons on the time device as he reset it for a couple minutes after the first target time of midnight. "You won't be arrested, but we will need to ask you some questions before this will be over."

Jeremy felt as indignant; this guy reminded him of his Aunt Regina, whom he often felt was unnecessarily antagonistic with everyone. "Why don't you just ask us now, and be done with it?"

"Because, Mister Macer," Duncan turned to face Jeremy, every ounce of impatience balanced itself inside him against every other ounce of self-restraint and his focus on the task at hand, "I have to go back and get Brent. He fell through the rift, and now he's stuck in the past with your buddies." Duncan held up the active time machine, "And he doesn't have this to come back." Letting his glare linger as he bent down, Duncan began to open another rift, which opened with its crack-rip sound and blue-yellow glow.

"Hopefully he'll be expecting this and come through momentarily," Andrew said

"Brent?" Duncan beckoned his student, talking into the black hole.

After a few moments of silence, Duncan looked back at the other four, and then addressed his assistants. "Hold them until I come back. There may be something wrong."

He started to step through the rift; Jeremy felt Andrew relax ever so slightly, and he took advantage of that lapse to spin through his grip and stun Andrew with a back-kick to the shin. Andrew cried out in pain and collapsed. Seeing this, Lisa made to elbow David in the gut, but missed; however, the unexpected attempt to assault him managed to free her left arm. She called on her self-defense training and outstretched her right arm, pulling David closer to her; she then clasped his hand as it gripped her right elbow, peeled his fingers off, and elbowed him with her right elbow. This time, the shot landed, and David doubled over with an "oof".

Jeremy smiled momentarily at his girlfriend's moves, and then turned to go through the portal after Duncan.

"Jeremy, what are you doing?" she exclaimed, running

to catch him.

"I gotta make sure!" he answered, jumping through the hole. "You stay here!"

"Like Hell!" Lisa said indignantly. No way was she going to let him go through without her, let alone tell her what to do. Grunting with annoyance at her boyfriend's carelessness, and glancing down to see both captors still on the ground in pain, she said, "Somebody's gotta keep an eye on you!"

She ran and leapt through as the portal began to close again.

Passing through the portal brought an odd sensation; she felt a temperature shift somewhat like passing through the doors at the supermarket, and she felt a subtle tingle in her spine. She could not see anything after she passed through the portal; she had that temporary blindness that happens when walking into a darkened room from the bright sun outside. Still moving with momentum from running, Lisa collided with someone in the pitch dark and they tumbled in a mess of arms and legs. She smelled Jeremy's scent, but she also detected an unfamiliar scent of someone with mild aftershave and strong deodorant. Though she could make out shapes amid the grunts as the three bodies struggled in dirt, she was suddenly thrust into full darkness when the portal closed behind her.

"WITCH!" someone yelled in a shrill voice, and with an echo that she would have associated with movies set in the Old West. Whoever yelled it apparently then ran into a building, judging by the footfalls Lisa heard.

"Jeremy?" she said, her eyes fighting the adjustment to abrupt darkness.

"Shut up!" Duncan hissed, hoping that the alert did not refer to him. However, his hopes were in vain, as about five or six men then spilled out of a wooden door, a couple of them holding torches, and started walking towards them.

"Them, I seen them! Those evil witches have returned!" one cried out, his silhouette pointing excitedly towards them.

"Damn it," Duncan cursed. All three stood slowly as the men walked closer, slowing with caution and one raising a musket.

"You will not move, lest I fire a bullet into your brains," one man warned loudly. "You are hereby seized into custody, and you shall be indicted and tried tomorrow by the His Majesty's Court of Oyer and Terminer, for your evil conduct as witches in our sight. May God have mercy on your souls, for none you will find here."

Wednesday, August 20, 1692

CHAPTER XIX

As soon as he had heard the man appear from behind the cars, Aaron felt the urgency to enter the blue-and-yellow glow that encircled the path to his own day. This time, the frightening spectacle offered him a haven of safety, and not the evil netherworld he took it for the night before.

As he set foot on dirt that was from his own year, sixteen hundred and ninety-two, he felt the entirety of his body come alive momentarily, as if ice had passed through him. It was followed by the shivers one felt crawling along his backbone. While not a powerful sensation, but it was neither dreadful nor comfortable. Turning to look back, he saw the man running fast as a horse, having already passed Jeremy. Behind everyone were a Negro man and another man, both of whom were also running. Aaron reached out and clutched Cyrus' waistcoat, and gave a firm tug; Cyrus had set his feet for the battle, so Aaron knew his effort would need to be strong.

He heard the man in the black short-sleeve shirt grunt loudly as he collided, arm outstretched, with Cyrus. The power of his running carried all three through the passageway between eras, and they fell into one another and onto the ground. The ring of fire and light snapped closed with a muffled crack as they rolled. Aaron pushed to get both Cyrus and the intruder off his person, as he quickly realized the need to reacquaint with his now-darkened world.

"Cyrus!" Aaron said urgently, finally loosing himself from the other two men and leaping to his feet. "Cyrus, we must move quickly!"

"Aaron!" Cyrus said, also separating himself from his assailant.

"What is the matter with you two?" Brent demanded sharply, his voice carrying through the alley. He rolled onto his haunches, as best as Aaron could make out.

"Be quiet!" Aaron hushed him. Cyrus was on his feet now, and looking around.

"I cannot see well, Aaron," he said, a touch of concern in his voice. "Where is our room?"

There was a sound of a door being opened not far from where they stood. Aaron felt his heart beat loudly in his chest. "This way," he hissed urgently, and clutched Cyrus' sleeve.

"Hey!" Brent exclaimed, standing up and looking back at the opening door, out of which sounds of men talking and boisterous laughter emerged. He reached out and grabbed Cyrus' coat by the shoulder. "Wait a minute!"

"Fool!" Cyrus hissed, letting go of Aaron's arm and clutching the boy with both hands. "If we are caught out here," he hissed, "it will be the end for all of us! Now be quiet!"

Aaron quickly ducked back towards the corner around which lay the safety of their room, and Cyrus followed, his eyesight already beginning to adjust to the night.

Brent paused for a moment, considering the situation, and then followed Cyrus after he saw a man finally stepping out of the door and into alley.

"Enter here," Aaron directed, holding open the door into their room. Brent allowed Cyrus, still crouched down, to enter the room first, then quietly shuffled in himself. Aaron swiftly entered the room, and closed the door behind him, taking care to close the last few inches with great gentleness.

Aaron walked over to his cot and sat on it. Cyrus stood from his hunched position and also took a seat on the end of his bed. Brent watched them, then looked around the inn room, and sighed.

"Well, at least this is better than that stupid ship's cargo hold," he remarked.

"I beg your pardon?" Aaron asked as paused from rubbing his face with exhaustion.

"I was forced to live on a ship for a week last time I was here," Brent said.

"So, it *was* you," Cyrus said; Jeremy had been correct. "You and your curs-ed friends were here yesterday?"

"'Curse ed'? Really?" Brent sneered. "Yes, we were here, but it's not like—"

Brent had stopped, having turned his head and listening intently. "Wait a minute," he said, holding a finger in the air.

"What is the matter?" asked by Aaron and Cyrus. Brent stood and opened the door a crack to hear better.

"Do not open the door!" Aaron exclaimed, his voice still not much above a whisper. He jumped from his seat and rushed to the door.

"Stop it; I think that's the Time Opener!" Brent protested, and pulled hard against Aaron's attempt to push the door closed.

"WITCH!"

Brent felt his stomach lurch and his blood run cold; he let the door go, as if the handle had become too hot to touch. After a moment, he realized that it must have been Duncan. He reached out again to open the door. Aaron blocked him, and this time Cyrus had also gotten up to help.

"We gotta help him!" Brent exclaimed.

Cyrus slapped him flat across the face. Brent was momentarily stunned by this move, and he hardly had time to react before Cyrus pressed him against the wall. "You cursed fool! Your voice will beckon them to investigate us!"

With his face stinging, and considering Cyrus' build and height advantage, Brent decided not to let his temper cause more trouble. Aaron waited a few moments before he slowly and cautiously opened the door again, just enough to listen to the events outside.

By now, there was the sound of several pairs of shoes shuffling in the dirt of the street, and a man exclaimed, *"Them, I seen them! Those evil witches have returned!"* Aaron could see shadows cast by torchlight play along the alley, dancing faintly in the darkness of the late summer evening.

"*Damn it*," they heard Duncan curse.

"*You will not move, lest I fire a bullet into your brains*," someone warned loudly. "*You are hereby seized into custody, and you shall be indicted and tried tomorrow by the His Majesty's Court of Oyer and Terminer, for your evil conduct as witches in our sight. May God have mercy on your souls, for none you will find here*."

"We gotta do something!" Brent insisted in a whisper. "Let go of me!"

Cyrus looked at him, and then he and Aaron exchanged glances.

"We would be implicated along with them. It would be best to let the events play as God would have it," Aaron whispered. "Perhaps we can discover a way to help them tomorrow."

Cyrus considered this a moment, then shifted his stance, reaching to open the door.

"I have an idea," Cyrus said. "Let me pass, but remain here," he said. He then glared at Brent. "Do nothing to interfere!"

"What is your idea?" Aaron asked.

"There is no time," Cyrus said. "Please trust me, my dear friend." Aaron nodded curtly, and Cyrus stepped out through the door.

He walked around the corner, and the full view of the arrest was present before him. In a circle were six men, including his tavern-keeper friend Christopher Reilly, as well as the men who told him of the story of the three witches, Franklin and Charles. Christopher held a bayonetted musket, Franklin held a pistol in a tremulous right hand, and Charles a folding gully blade. Two other men in this hastily-assembled squad held torches, while one other man, whom Cyrus had seen in the bar earlier now also held a pistol. At the center of the group were Jeremy, Lisa, and the Negro man who had chased them in the future. After a moment, Christopher looked up and noticed Cyrus.

"Cyrus," Christopher said without humor. "We have seized these who apparently would practice witchcraft among us! I hope that we have not disturbed you."

"Nonsense, my friend," Cyrus smiled, and slowly strolled closer to the group, taking care to not get too close. Lisa had a hand on Jeremy's arm, and her expression was of pure dread. Jeremy stood with his mouth agape; he almost began to speak twice after Cyrus appeared, but stopped before uttering a sound each time. The third man, whom Cyrus assumed was somehow the master to Brent, stood with an elegant dignity. All three held their hands raised in the air. The threesome looked at him, but no one said a word; Cyrus was thankful that they did not. "I did hear some sounds of commotion, and thought to come see for myself what the matter was."

"The matter is that these three have been seen and witnessed practicing sorcery of remarkable power," Franklin grunted.

"Ah, witches you say?" Cyrus broke into a delighted smile. "We have had but one case in Falmouth, although over eleven years ago. I dare say to you that this," he extended a hand to indicate the three people with their hands in the air, "is not what I imagined."

"Those who would practice the magic of the devil always make themselves known in ways men would not expect," said the man with the pistol, who spoke slowly as he considered the captives. "What business brings you a day's travel from the home?"

"My friend and associate," Cyrus pointed back to his cabin with his thumb, "one Aaron Quincy, is here on business to sell hides he has tanned. It is an annual trip. I have come as his travelling companion."

"I see," he replied. "And where is Mr. Quincy now?"

"Ah," Cyrus said, trying to gather an idea to answer. One came to him, and he said, "Well, as it turns out, I permitted him to drive most of the way here, and he has all but passed out, asleep. He is one who would not wake were a herd of horses to stampede his bed!" Cyrus made himself laugh, which drew only a couple of mild smiles from them. The man was not amused, but he seemed satisfied with his reply and turned back towards the prisoners.

"We have sent for the Sheriff," one of the torch-bearers remarked with glee; he was a man of no more than nineteen. "I think that he should arrive within these several minutes, to take custody of our prisoners."

"Prisoners!" Jeremy blurted. Duncan quickly turned to him.

"Quiet, Jeremy!" Duncan said sharply.

Several of the captors began to laugh. The unnamed

man with the pistol spoke, saying, "You would be ordered by a Negro?"

"So what if I did?" Jeremy turned and stood to his full five-foot-ten-inch height, his hands dropping to his waist.

Suddenly, Jeremy's vision was filled with lights, and he was confused, his head solid with pain. Christopher had stepped forward and struck him with the butt of his musket; Jeremy fell to his knees, doubled over. Lisa gasped his name and bent down to tend to her boyfriend, and Duncan also reached one hand down as he carefully turned to check on him. Cyrus had to restrain himself from also going to assist, or let down his false smile.

"Realize your station, boy!" Christopher said. "You will show respect for Reverend Mather."

"Reverend Mather!" Cyrus said with recognition, and bowed respectfully towards the minister. "You honor us with your presence this evening!" Mather simply nodded his head in return, but kept his gaze on the three.

"Indeed. I had decided to delay my return to Boston," he began, his throaty baritone resonating in the street, "since I wished to be sure that Salem saw calm after the executions that did take place on Tuesday. However," he sighed, "it would appear that my continued presence is needed."

"What is to be done with this unholy group?" Cyrus asked with his feigned smile, hoping to keep conversation continuing so as to avoid another confrontation. In the distance, he could hear a wagon and the beating of hooves of the horses pulling it. Jeremy looked at him, and Lisa also watched him, both wearing faces of confusion; he hoped they did not feel betrayed.

Mather answered, saying, "The sheriff or constable will arrive and secure the prisoners. This town must be rid of such blatant evil doings, and not continue to be tormented as it has. Immediately I will request an emergency meeting with the several magistrates and court officials. This matter shall be dealt with speedily."

As he finished speaking, an oxcart pulled by horses came round the corner at the Main street, driven by a man in a black dressing coat and white frock, accompanied by a second man, who apparently had been sent to summon the constable. The cart drew to a stop, and the constable dismounted and strode to stand next to Christopher.

"Mister Flint here has said to me that you have arrested new found witches?" the man said.

"Joseph," Christopher said, dropping the muzzle of his musket as he turned to address the man, "We do surrender these individuals to your custody. Would you escort them to the jail for the night?"

"What are the charges?" Joseph asked, his small mustache twitching in the torchlight.

"Let us begin with that most simple of charges, disturbing of the peace," Mather said pointedly, "for it is well after dusk, and in the view of the public, these people have agitated us from our drinks and recreation." After the briefest of pauses, he continued, "I intend to hold audience with the magistrates in order to organize and identify the remaining charges, and present them to the accus-ed by morn."

The constable came prepared, as he was swift in going over to his cart, pulling out black mass of metal chains and irons that rattled and clanged as he walked back to the captives. By now Jeremy had recovered to be able to stand, and while the constable prepared the irons, Franklin spoke.

"What is your name?" he demanded.

"My name is Jeremy," said Jeremy with a thick voice.

"Your surname, boy?" Franklin growled, a very clear impatience in his voice.

"Macer, *sir*," he said back. Franklin paused, looking back to Christopher and the other arresting party members.

"I do not recognize such a name," he glanced back to Mather, hiccoughing as he spoke. Constable Joseph finished laying out his irons in front of his prisoners.

"There is no such surname in the Colony," Mather said with suspicion. Joseph paused before beginning to bind them to allow this exchange to finish without incident. "Do you lie to me, boy?"

"No sir," Jeremy said. The constable took the heavy moment of silence to clasp the irons onto Jeremy's wrist.

"Ouch!" he jerked backward; however, Joseph was experienced and much stronger, and Jeremy only succeeded in scraping his wrists up in his action. He glared at the jailer, who smiled at Jeremy's winces as he finished closing the irons. Cyrus quietly watched while his mind worked to take in as much of the details as it could. Having heard the stories of the trials over the past several months, he could not help but also be curious to watch this affair proceed in person.

"Woman," Christopher said. Lisa looked toward him, her eyes red and full of dread. "Tell us your name, and your relation to Mister Macer."

"Um," she said, biting her lip as she glanced at him and Duncan. Jeremy and Duncan both nodded for her to go ahead. "My name is Lisa Carson," she said softly, with tears in her voice.

"And your relationship to Mister Macer?"

"My boyfriend, sir," she finally said. She jumped when Constable Joseph grabbed her hand to apply the iron. Her face crumpled in pain as he put them on, but she bit her lip to avoid crying out from the pain when he applied the shackle bolt. His hands were coarse, black and cold, in spite of the warmth of the evening air. She looked up and bit her lip more as he clamped her ankles as he had Jeremy's. Jeremy hoped her jeans would help mute the discomfort, even a little bit.

The men exchanged glances, and then Christopher shared their lack of understanding by asking, "'Boyfriend'?"

"Sir, if I may say," Duncan spoke up, bowing his head in a manner he hoped would be seen as respectful, "they are betrothed."

"You will mind your manners, slave," Charles, who had been silent this whole time, said to Duncan. As he was standing closest to him, Charles held out his blade and waggled it towards Duncan, who looked at it with great wary.

"Charles, now do mind your own manners," Christopher

said. He turned his head toward Duncan and said, "Your clothing is strange, to be sure, but you also have a good hygiene. You neither look nor speak like a slave. Perhaps you are a house servant who has run away from his Master?"

"No sir," Duncan said carefully, and in a low tone. He had tried to be ready for this moment. Inside, he wanted to reach out and wrestle the men around him, to exact revenge for wrongs that he had for so many years felt he had abolished from his heart and soul, wrongs that were done to people of his race simply because of their color. However, he also knew that to misstep would likely bring about his death swiftly, and perhaps those of Jeremy and Lisa. He could not risk anyone's life over his own pride. Thinking quickly, he told them a story.

"I am recently come from Port Royal by way of New Amsterdam, arriving just two months ago. I was trained to be a gentleman by a man named Shawn Lassiter, who bade me to become free and find my own wealth upon his death last summer. Sir." He said, never looking up.

Jeremy and Lisa both stood slack-jawed, temporarily forgetting the pains of their shackles. They did not know he had read a lot about sixteen-ninety-two the moment his team had returned. It also helped that he was a major pirate buff and had seen nearly every pirate movie (good and bad) that he had ever been able to lay his hands on.

Christopher glanced between Mather and Franklin and Charles, both of whom simply shrugged. Mather, however, tilted his head back and squinted an eye.

"And your name?"

"I am called Duncan, sir," Duncan said, keeping his head bowed. Joseph began clamping the irons around Duncan's arms, and then his legs.

"There, you see, Charles?" Christopher said, smiling. "He does have manners."

"Perhaps," Charles spat, disgruntled thoughts reveal-ed on his face. "Although I doubt his being learn-ed. His Master surely did a poor job of educating him, or perhaps was an idiot himself. He has taught him to call New York New Amsterdam."

Duncan frowned at his mistake. He detested the way they were talking about him in front of him. He had not felt this kind of humiliation since his undergraduate days, when he was stopped with some friends by police while traveling through Georgia on his way to Spring Break in Florida. Nevertheless, he made himself try to appear as though he knew and accepted the life of a slave in the seventeenth-century New World.

Joseph stood and announced that they were fully shackled, and directed them to go to the back of the oxcart, slowly. Jeremy, Lisa, and Duncan shuffled in the heavy metal irons and chains; their clanging jingles a somber sound in the silence, one accompanied only by the sound of their shoes as they kicked the uneven dirt.

As they reached the back, Joseph ordered them onto the cart platform, and they complied quickly. Mather, watching this unfold along with the rest, abruptly turned and began to address the posse.

"Mister Flint," he called out. Flint stood from his perch on the oxcart driving seat. "I request you to, with haste, go alert and gather the magistrates of this town, and inform them that I should join them at Magister Corwin's house for an urgent matter before the hour is up." Flint nodded and jumped down, and ran off to carry out his duty. At this point, the cart had begun to move. Cyrus made eye contact with the three fugitives from the future; he hoped they could be spared the fates of those accused before them.

Mather turned to the rest.

"As you are all witnesses to this evening's events, you must accompany me to this meeting to give testimony on your parts," he said with authority. "The sooner that it can be arranged for the indictment of Mister Macer, Miss Carson, and the freedman Duncan, it will be all the sooner that we can dispatch them back to Hell and let God do with them as He will." Everyone turned to walk back to the tavern to settle their drinks.

"What about me, Parson?" Cyrus asked.

Mather paused and turned to face him. "You did not witness the evil event, so you have no testimony on that. You were here for the arrest, so you may come along and give testimony or you may go back to your bed. In truth, it is of little consequence what you choose to do tonight. Good night, Mister Cyrus." Curtly, he turned and continued to follow the rest.

Cyrus thought on that for a few moments, watching them walk. He then realized that there truly was little else he could do, so he turned and walked back to his and

Aaron's room. Things would have to be arranged immediately in the gravest of secret in order to save his friends.

CHAPTER XX

Brent and Aaron stood in quiet tension as they listened to the events that were transpiring outside. They had difficulty hearing everything, since things were taking place around the corner. Neither spoke, although when they heard Duncan speak, Brent had to smile at his boss's clever response. He uttered a low and impressed "Nicely done!" which prompted Aaron to glare up at him before turning his ear back to the cracked wooden opening.

They could hear their friends' jangling couple with the sounds of clambering onto some kind of wooden platform (*that must be the wagon*, Brent thought). The noise of the receding horse and wagon then drowned out any further conversation that was taking place. All Brent or Aaron could discern was the voice of Reverend Mather, resonating unintelligibly among the jingling, squeaks, and thuds of the horse-and-wagon. The sounds faded, and Mather's instructions became clearer; he was directing various men to tasks. Finally, they heard Cyrus' hearty voice, followed by Mather's indifferent reply.

"That should conclude the activity of the evening," Aaron stated, standing from his crouched position, and stepping back from the door. Brent watched him for a moment.

"So what now?" he demanded. Cyrus entered the room just then, and closed the door with more care and attention than usual. "Do we just let them take everyone to jail?"

"What did you see?" Aaron asked, ignoring Brent's question.

"Well, Jeremy and Lisa have arrived," he turned to face Brent, "Along with a Negro man. I presume this man is your acquaintance?"

"Yeah, he is my 'acquaintance'," Brent mocked, holding up two pairs of fingers in the air to quote Cyrus. Cyrus' expression twisted as he flinched marginally at this gesture. Brent also noted Cyrus' reference to Duncan as a Negro, and while he did not detect any hint of racism in his tone, Brent did not like it.

"Actually, he's my boss," Brent explained with a bit of crankiness, but directed his remarks more towards Aaron than Cyrus. "His name is Doctor Troy Duncan, and he's the one who came up with the idea for the Time Opener. He's probably smarter than all of us combined."

"I – the 'time opener'?" Cyrus repeated slowly, shaking his head.

"Ah!" Aaron said with the raised eyebrows of sudden enlightenment, holding up a forefinger. "That which we were curs-ed to find!"

"I see," Cyrus said, giving Brent an angry glare.

"What?" Brent said defensively.

"What is done," Aaron interceded, standing up and straightening his shirt, "is done. We are now in a situation of exceeding danger."

"You mean these witch trials?" Brent scoffed, pointing a thumb behind him. "Please, we can just break them out in the middle of the night!"

"We can do no such thing," Aaron shook his head seriously, incredulous at the idea. "We would likely be shot by the sentry man upon any assault and escape, as would they."

"So, what then? Do you plan to just let them sit and rot there until they get burned at the stake?" Brent was becoming impatient.

"Burned at the stake?" Aaron frowned with disgust. "How barbarous! No one will be burned as a witch; at least, no one has that I have heard."

"They do practice such things in Europe; France and Sweden I believe," Cyrus pointed out, leaning back against the writing desk and folding his arms. Noting the curiosity his friend had, he explained.

"Remember the last spring, during the planting season, when the Dutch ship," he snapped his fingers a couple of times as he tried to remember, "—*Callantsoong*, set port? The old ship man told drunken stories to several of us about 'twice having the misfortune of witnessing human beings aflame'." He looked towards the ceiling as he recited the remark. "He said the first time was in back in seventy-six in Sweden, and then again three years later in Paris."

"Guys, I really don't care about how the crazy people here kill witches," Brent said impatiently. "I just want to get the Time Opener—" he paused midsentence as his expression went blank.

"What is it?" Aaron asked.

"Did you see the Opener in Duncan's hand?" Brent asked Cyrus in a slow, careful cadence. *Oh man, if we lose it again…*, he thought soberly. A long moment passed as he waited for the answer; Cyrus, however, only shook his head.

"I believe not," Cyrus answered with a subtle shrug, looking alternatively between Brent and Aaron.

"You did not see it on the floor?" Aaron offered. He shifted his stance to straighten his posture in light of the new problem.

"No, I did not," Cyrus said, looking innocently back and forth between the other two.

Abruptly, all three men moved towards the door handle at the same time. Cyrus, being the closest, grasped it first. Brent frowned and rolled his eyes as Cyrus chided him, saying, "I will seek it. You must be more patient."

Cyrus stepped out of the room and disappeared around the corner. He returned a moment later, needing to excuse himself to pass between both Brent and Aaron who were crowding the doorjamb. He picked up the grease lamp, lit it with one of the wall candles, and then made his way back out the door while they looked on.

He turned the corner and walked out to the spot where the arrest had happened. He searched in the dirt and grass, which seemed an unnatural color in the lamplight. The dancing flame cast tottering shadows behind the rocks and blades of grass. Cyrus paused for a moment and tried to remember the direction they had returned. As he turned to face the inn, he saw something light and gray lying against the wall, behind some tufts tall grass and a bush, just under the lower edge of the wooden wall of the inn.

"Ah!" Cyrus uttered to himself, glad to have found it. He walked over to it and knelt down. Reaching to pick it up, he set his fingers around it. He paused momentarily, reflecting on his last experience with it, a day (*an hour?*) ago. Gently but swiftly, and watching for spies as he did, he picked it up and set it in the pocket of his knee pant. Just then, the door to the tavern burst open, giving him a start and thrusting his heart into his gullet.

Christopher, Reverend Mather, and the men called Franklin and Charles walked briskly towards the main street. Christopher saw Cyrus and called out to him.

"Cyrus! Are you coming along?" he asked. The other three men paused and turned, not expecting this interruption.

"No thank you, Christopher," Cyrus said loudly, standing up again. "I have nothing to offer."

Reverend Mather cast a skeptical stare at him. "What brings you back out into the night, using up your lamp grease?"

"Reverend," Cyrus said, thinking quickly, "I admit that at least one of the criminals appears familiar to me, but I do not know why. I came out here for a moment to jog my memory." He shrugged and shook his head. "Perhaps I simply saw him somewhere previously."

"Perhaps," Mather repeated. "So you *are* going to accompany us to give testimony?"

"Respectfully, sir," Cyrus said, "I fear I must follow your advice from earlier, as I do not believe I would be able to provide any useful evidence."

Mather regarded him silently for a few moments; Cyrus stomach felt tight as he hoped to avoid raising the suspicion of the minister.

"Indeed," he said finally. "Very well; I will check on your memory in the morn. You may return to your business."

"Yes, thank you. Good night!" Cyrus said with a smile. After Christopher had finally turned to follow the other three who had already resumed their gait, Cyrus went back to the boarding room. Turning the corner, he could hear Aaron and Brent having a tense, whispered exchange.

"—will only make matters worse!" Aaron hissed, with one hand wrapped around the frame of the door. His other hand clutched the black shirt across the chest of their uninvited visitor.

"I have it," Cyrus announced, pushing open the door. Brent looked up and glared at Cyrus, his eyes filled with a sense of betrayal.

"You did that on purpose!" he accused, pointing with his left hand towards the wall beyond which Cyrus had just been.

"Of course I did!" Cyrus spat back. "Now we have a possible excuse to have an interest in any trials, and so can explain our attendance!" Cyrus was now tired of this boy's rudeness. He strode strongly forward and grabbed Brent by the shirt, pushing him back.

"It is time you settled yourself," he said forcefully, pushing him across the room to the bed. Brent stumbled backwards, finally tumbling over the side of the low, wood-frame bed and rolling over onto the floor behind it. He quickly tried to regain his bearings, and Cyrus stepped a bit closer to him. Aaron stepped toward his friend and reached to set a hand on his elbow.

"Cyrus," he said gently, "please be calm."

Cyrus inhaled deep to register Aaron's plea without letting it show on his face. "What is your name?" he demanded.

Brent stood up, trying to smooth his clothing and brush off some dust that now covered patches of his clothes and skin. He looked angrily at Cyrus, and then at Aaron. He face was warm with embarrassment at being so easily manhandled, in spite of the fact that he'd been spending a decent amount of time in the weight room.

"My name is Brent," Brent answered. "Brent Robertson."

Cyrus took another deep breath and remembered his father and his gentleman's training. "It is a pleasure to meet you, Brent Robertson." His words were cordial but terse. "I am Cyrus Bartle, of Falmouth." He glanced back to Aaron, who then spoke up.

"I am Aaron Quincy, late also of Falmouth," Aaron said, walking across the room and extending his hand. He was relieved that Cyrus had not yielded to a fight Brent. "Welcome to Salem!" he said with an awkward pleasantry and smile. Brent reached a tentative hand out and accepted the handshake.

"Yes, welcome indeed. Welcome, in fact, to sixteen hundred ninety-two," Cyrus said evenly, now extending his own hand; their handshake reached across the bed. Cyrus made his grip strong, and then tugged Brent towards him, so that they were close in eye contact.

"I warn you now, however," he said in a low voice. "If you cannot settle yourself to be more calm and respectful, I will strike you with a hand that will make you sleep until your own time arrives by nature's course."

"Fair enough," Brent said back, also through clenched teeth. The defiance in his heart was defeated by the pain in his hand. Cyrus broke the grip and leaned back; Brent lost his balance from his awkward posture and fell forward, again onto the bed.

"I have a thought," Aaron interceded in a quick and diplomatic manner, hoping to diffuse the tension. "Let us now rest, so that on the morrow we can begin to decide how to save our friends from the gallows."

Several seconds of fierce glares lasted before they took his advice, and the three men began settling down for the night.

In the Home of Jonathan Corwin

Cotton Mather stood in a small sitting room within the home of the honorable Jonathan Corwin, late a magistrate and presiding official for the special Court of Oyer and Terminer, established and entrusted to act on behalf of the

Sovereign Lord and Lady William and Mary, here in Salem. This unexpected and rushed meeting led to several of the attending gentlemen to appear less formally prepared than was ordinary; two of them had not even worn their wigs.

Elizabeth Corwin, the magistrate's wife, moved quietly and quickly through the room, providing a brandy for each man present. In attendance were William Stoughton, who also prosecuted the cases, Bartholomew Gedney, Samuel Sewall, and their host, Jonathan Corwin, all of whom had taken to sitting in couches and chairs. Additionally, assistant judges Peter Sergeant and John Richards stood behind the main magistrate panel, while John Hathorne, who interrogated the accused, and Wait Still Winthrop, who represented Governor Phips' Council, stood attentively to the side.

Sitting across from this esteemed council of judgment stood David Flint, who saw the three individuals appear, Franklin Peters and Charles Martin, the men who gave chase to the previous mysterious individuals just the afternoon before today and were part of this arresting party, and finally Christopher Reilly, who also helped during the arrest. For his own place, Reverend Mather stood at the entrance of the sitting room, addressing both groups of men.

"Reverend," Stoughton addressed him first, a nasally deep voice carrying a hint of impatience through the room, "I do allow you a good deal of latitude in the participation of the affairs of this town, but it is late and I am very tired.

I ask you to explain yourself and why you have summoned us to a matter that might have otherwise been held on the morrow?"

"Indeed, your honor," Mather quickly said, bowing his head briefly in respect. "I thank you for gathering at such a late hour," Cotton began. "As you may already know, an event has happened which is serious of nature that, if left to develop as things have in the past, shall likely create panic in this town, and perhaps eventually in the whole of the Colony." He pause a moment to allow this warning to settle in their minds.

"Continue," Corwin said, extending a hand in invitation after a few moments before bringing his hands back together into a contemplative position.

"We were having drinks and good company in Mister Reilly's establishment this evening when the good Mister Flint did go outside to leave, and witnessed the appearance of three people to this town: a young man, a young woman, and a Negro. I will leave him to describe what he saw to you, but I believe there is evidence that this event is the most outright and defiant performance of witchcraft this Colony has ever seen. Misters Martin and Peters have their own tale to tell, and were also joined with us in arresting the accus-ed."

Glances were exchanged, and several magistrates changed their positions to provide better attention to the speakers. Mather saw a range of countenances on their faces that included all from disbelief to shock to intense curiosity.

"By all means, then, Mister Flint, please tell us what you saw," Stoughton said, his impatience now replaced by intrigue.

"Thank you, sire," Flint said with a soft, raspy voice. He held his hat in front of him, both hands nervously clutching its brim. Mather willed him to have more strength of voice, but this internal effort was to be for naught. The man told his story as he would.

"I was at the door at the Marble Wharf Tavern, taking leave to go home, and I heard a sound that was to my ears like the sound of waves landing on the sea shore, sire," he said. It was quite clear that he was intimidated to be addressing so many important men.

"I stepped outside to see what I would see, and that is where I saw a circle of fire which did stand in the air with no support. That is also where I saw the accus-ed," he glanced nervously quickly to Mather, then back to the magistrates. "They came through and began to fight and grapple. I yelled to alert those who could hear me and went in to summon those who would come. When we returned outside, the fire-circle was gone but the devils remained."

"I see," Stoughton uttered with astonishment. He glanced over to the host Corwin, and then at Gedney, and finally Sewall. "Did no one else witness this fire-circle?"

"No sir," the four witnesses said together.

"This would be spectral evidence, then," Bartholomew Gedney commented. The middle-aged magistrate squinted his eyes briefly, and then wiped his gaunt face with his handkerchief. "We will need to verify with the girls whether they have had any fits," he said to Stoughton. Stoughton nodded in agreement. His remark sat uneasy with Cotton, who had on many occasions questioned the value and legal validity of such evidence.

"Sirs," Charles Martin spoke up. "If I may, sirs?"

"Yes, by all means," Corwin responded. "I believe you also witnessed something which is bizarre and fantastic as Mister Flint?" He continued his steady countenance.

"Yes, sir," he said. He was not terribly nervous, speaking quickly with more excitement than Flint. "I wish to tell you that we saw just yesterday a group of men who also were associated with a circle of fire. However, what we witnessed, sir," he explained, indicating himself and Franklin who quietly sipped his brandy, "these men created the fire-circle and then vanished from our eyes into it."

"This is all very damning for the accus-ed," Corwin pointed out. "You say you have them under arrest now?"

"Yes, magister Corwin," Mather said. "The Constable did arrive and collect them; they are surely to be in their stalls by now."

"And you are of the opinion that we must hasten the trial process in this particular case?" Corwin probed.

"Yes, your Honor," Mather responded. "Considering the anxiety and fears the community is having in regards to the executions Tuesday just past, to allow this current situation to sit and to allow these powerful individuals to live would raise these fears and could devastate all of Salem."

"We are not a panel who would condemn people without just cause, and on the whim of men who have been drinking for the better part of the day," Stoughton reprimanded, his features tense with offence.

"Of course not, sir. My apologies," Mather offered, again offering a subtle bow of his head. "I only mean that to not act quickly on this particular matter could require more aggressive means in the coming days and weeks. Perhaps these witches will empower those who have already been arrested and condemned, and so endanger the people of this town. Regardless, the citizens must know that we are willing to take whatever measures necessary to protect them from any and all evil."

"I agree," Gedney said. "We should move with great speed in this case." He looked to Stoughton and to Corwin.

"As do I," Sewall volunteered. Stoughton sat quietly, his eyes meeting each official in turn and awaiting their position.

"We can issue the warrants to validate their arrest tonight," Stoughton began after brief consideration.

"Very well," Corwin took over. "We should assemble a jury to meet tomorrow in the afternoon. Around ten of the clock in the morning we shall hold court to hear testimony, and they will be try-ed after supper. If they are guilty, we may be able to have a conviction by the fall of night."

"That would allow an execution by mid-day Saturday," Gedney calculated. "Let us not have this linger beyond Sunday, thus creating distress in church. Perhaps you could deliver a few words to help comfort the congregation, Reverend Mather?"

Cotton bowed respectfully, saying, "It would be an

honor, Magister Gedney."

"Yes, that would likely be the best course," Corwin said. "Provided, naturally, that the accus-ed are in fact guilty of all charges," his voice even with responsible warning. He turned to address John Hathorne. "Will you interrogate them during a mid-day session to morrow?"

"I can," John responded, nodding slowly.

"Please raise also the good doctor William Griggs, and require him to perform an examination of the bodies of the accus-ed before we meet with them," Stoughton ordered. "I will, in the mean time, prepare my own examination for the case."

"I will check for any reports of fits among the children of the town," Gedney offered.

"Very well," Corwin said. "Let us adjourn this meeting and set about our tasks, so that we may remove this unexpected blight swiftly."

"Thank you, Magistrates," Mather said, satisfied with the successful meeting.

CHAPTER XXI

Man! These are heavy, Jeremy complained inwardly as he sat against the rail of the oxcart. He guessed that the chains on his wrists were somewhere between fifteen and twenty pounds. Although he had never worn handcuffs, he expected that these were orders of magnitude more uncomfortable than the modern version. The shackles bit into his lower arms, irritating the raw skin he'd earned a few minutes earlier. He absently massaged his kneecap, having cracked it on a rock when he'd run blindly into Duncan while jumping through the time portal. Combined with his mild headache and sore shoulder where the butt of the gun had landed, Jeremy decided his first time travel experience was rather unpleasant.

It was surprisingly dark, with the only light coming from the constable's lantern; it was as though there was a power outage in Salem. In the open spaces a person could make out shapes and some features, but when underneath the cover of large trees, you might as well close your eyes altogether. Jeremy looked up to find the moon, which was low and largely obscured by clouds. Although he knew that this was supposed to be August, the sky was more reminiscent of a spooky Halloween night.

The ride in this wagon was bumpy; the last time Jeremy

was in the back of a wagon was when he and Lisa went on a hayride last Thanksgiving. However, this ride was much less comfortable, and was far less trivial.

Lisa sat to his right, and he could just make out Duncan, sitting cross-legged across from them. Jeremy exchanged glances with Duncan, who must have been able to tell he was about to say something, because the older man put his finger to his lips to indicate to Jeremy not to talk. He obeyed this time, and then looked over to Lisa, to see how she was doing. She had sniffled softly a couple times so far, and seemed to be avoiding looking at him. She even righted herself quickly after she fell into Jeremy's right side when the wagon turned a corner. Even now, in the dimness of night, he could see a few glinting trails where tears had trod her cheeks. He immediately felt guilty, like he should have done more to protect her.

He looked up and tried to get a feel for where they were. He had a reasonably good sense of direction, and decided this might be a good distraction for the moment. To his left was the road off which they had just turned, which he assumed was Essex Street. Even in the darkness, he could easily count at least six well-separated houses and a smattering of trees. Above those trees was the moon, which occasionally peeked out from its hiding place behind black clouds with blue-grey edges. Two of the houses had yellow-lit windows, and Jeremy saw some movement in the form of shadows that crossed the windows.

Directly in front of him and behind Duncan's back were the shadowy silhouettes of trees and at least three more dark, wooden buildings. To his right, beyond Lisa and the driver and the horses, silhouetted against a dark gray-black sky as a background, tree lines met about a half-mile in the distance. Jeremy guessed that would be where the street opened onto the North River. Halfway to the river was a single light, a dancing flame that cast a weak yellow light on the wall of a building from which it hung. He could also hear a couple of dogs barking somewhere in the distance.

He became aware of an odor, or rather, a mixture of odors. It was the tart scents of wood burning; he detected the telltale aromas of maple and white pine, but he wasn't sure what the other wood was. However, there was also a very distinct stench that offended to his nose. It was not a pleasant smell, and it was faint and inconsistent; at first it reminded him of that stink when someone steps in dog poo and then tracks it inside. However, he realized that it was closer to human sewage than dog waste. The scent itself and the thoughts it conjured made him crinkle his nose, and he subtly raised his forefinger to his upper lip to help block the stink. Thankfully, faint as it was, it subsided after they had passed the three houses.

The building with the single light grew closer. By now, some clouds had parted enough for the moon, which was three quarters full, to cast its own light on their surroundings. The building was long, receding from the street; Jeremy thought it was at least twice as long as his parent's house. It was made of what looked like, in the moonlight, gray wood, but the roof appeared to be made of bunches of straw rather than wood. There were only a couple of white windows, one on each end near the corners of the building. The windows themselves were the characteristic grid style, but after a moment Jeremy realized that the white of the window *was* the window and not a curtain behind it; there was no glass. The entrance to the building was a simple door on the short side of the building, facing the street. A man holding a musket and sitting on what appeared to be a large, bark-stripped wood log stood as the oxcart pulled to a stop. The man repositioned his musket to his other shoulder and walked over to meet the carriage.

"Do you have any news?" Constable Joseph Herrick asked with authority as he dismounted the front of the cart.

"Nothing has stirred, Joe," the orange-haired man said with a thick Irish accent. He began to tend to the horses.

"Come here and help me with the prisoners," Herrick commanded; the man gave one of the horses an affectionate slap as he made his way back to join Herrick.

"Come down from off of there, now," Herrick demanded, and all three shackled captives began to scoot towards the edge and climb down. Jeremy's ankle chains landed loud and heavy, as did Duncan's and then Lisa's.

Herrick gripped Duncan by the left arm and gave him a shove, pushing him towards the building. "James, take the girl and settle her into a stall," he directed his associate. "Be wary as you go, Mister Smith, for as you heard reported, these accused are perhaps the most powerful of all the witches we have yet encountered."

James Smith nodded curtly and walked over, taking Lisa

by the chains and yanking her to come with him. Jeremy became incensed at this treatment of his girlfriend, and he stepped forward, grabbing the man's wrists.

"Take it easy, man!" Jeremy protested, feeling more aggressive than ever. He was not a fighting type of guy, but he felt ready to plow this jerk into the ground. Suddenly, he again experienced disorientation and sharp pain, and released Smith's arms. This time, Herrick had back-handed him across the cheek.

"Jeremy!" Lisa exclaimed, struggling against her chains and captor, who held fast to the chains. Jeremy did not fall this time, but merely stumbled about for a few moments before regaining his full senses. Herrick glared angrily at him.

"You shall get lashes for that action, boy!" he warned.

"Jeremy," Duncan's baritone said softly and carefully. Jeremy looked up to him, tasting some blood in his cheek. "Now is not the time for chivalry."

"Indeed," Herrick said with a mild amusement. He took Duncan's left arm in his own right hand and then clutched a handful of hair of Jeremy, and began to pull them both along. "I promise you, *Jeremy*," he sneered as Jeremy painfully tried to keep up with his scalp, "I will not endure your brassy behavior. I may have to shoot you to make sure you do not attempt to escape before your trial." The casual tone in Herrick's voice unnerved Jeremy to the core. He suddenly felt a lot less defiant than he had up until now.

As he was being pulled to the jail, he stole painful glimpses of Lisa's silhouette walking awkwardly over the uneven ground, arms out in front of her like some kind of zombie or marionette. Smith walked to the other end of the building with purpose, gun in one hand and Lisa's chains behind him in his other hand. That was the last he saw of her before the wall obstructed his view.

They reached the door of the building, and Herrick released Jeremy's hair and Duncan's arm. He opened the door, and a strong stench struck Jeremy's nose, reeking of urine and feces, hay, sweat, and body odors. It was like a dumpster had been parked in a gym locker room where no one flushed the toilets.

"Oh, dang, man!" Jeremy muttered as he gagged, burying his nose and mouth into the inside of his elbow. He looked at Duncan, whose face was also hidden in his own elbow. Herrick looked at them and smiled.

"I see." He gave a firm shove to both of their shoulders. Duncan and Jeremy both staggered into the jail, simultaneously trying to obey and resist. "Let us stall you both, shall we? I should like to return to my wife, who was kind enough not to be offended when I had to leave to arrest you."

He grabbed Jeremy's chains, pulled him further into the dark room. Jeremy felt some apprehension, since he couldn't see a thing beyond ten feet.

"Here, boy," he said, flinging Jeremy and causing him to stumble and slam into a stall's back wooden wall. He fell to the dirt ground, and now his forearms were to be sore. He was already tired and was feeling all his pains, and slowly rolled himself over into a slumped, sitting position, leaning against the wall.

Duncan watched Herrick throw Jeremy into the wall; he struggled desperately to keep his composure. Jeremy was irreverent, but Duncan detested the harsh abuse the boy had already endured. Duncan felt an urge to lead an escape, but he quickly decided that to try would probably bring about all their deaths before midnight. Hopefully after Herrick left he would be able to talk to Jeremy, and try to get them both on the same page. He expected that this girl Lisa must also be terrified over in the other part of the jail, and there was no telling how she would fare under whatever torture or punishment these Puritans would levy. He prayed that she behaved better than Jeremy.

Herrick took Duncan's shackles and led him across the room to another stall, slinging him in a fashion similar to how he had thrown Jeremy. However, Duncan was ready for it and simply caught himself with his hands on the wall. He turned slowly, and Herrick considered him.

"You are an educated Negro," Herrick said, almost impressed and with an eyebrow raised. "It is a pity that you will probably die for your crimes. A good manservant who is educated is perhaps impossible to acquire." Duncan seethed, and was glad the darkness hid his seething expression.

Herrick walked slowly towards the door, and then stopped to look back, and idea coming to him. "Perhaps I could arrange with the Court to purchase you from the town, once you have been convicted. Of course," he smiled genially, "we would have to make sure you never practice evil sorcery again." Duncan felt repulsed both by his suggestion and by what he meant when he said "make sure".

Before he left, he spoke once more. "See that you do not cause any more disturbances to night. There will be penalty for any who break this curfew." The door closed and the room fell dark.

Duncan carefully took small steps over to where Jeremy sat, hoping his eyes would adjust to the blackness. He could hear snoring and coughing, shackles rattling as bodies shifted in the darkness; they were clearly not alone. He knelt down in front of the young man, and spoke in a hushed voice.

"Are you ok?"

Jeremy groaned. "I'm fine, I just hurt everywhere."

"You have to be more careful here," Duncan chided him. "You can't go around seventeenth-century Salem acting like a teenager from the twenty-first century!"

"I wasn't acting like a teenager!" Jeremy defended himself. "I was trying to protect Lisa from these jerks."

"Well, these 'jerks' currently have all the cards," Duncan pointed out.

"Let's just get out of here! I didn't hear him lock the door." Jeremy said. "You have the time thing, don't you?"

"No, I don't," Duncan said worriedly. "I dropped it when you ran into me."

"Are you serious?" Jeremy complained. "Do you think they found it?"

"There's no way to know right now," Duncan said.

"Tell me about those men you helped come here."

"You mean Aaron and Cyrus?" Jeremy asked. "They came to us by accident after they found *your* time machine lying around some woods somewhere," he said with mild derision. "While we were on a date, no less!" Jeremy gestured between himself and where he figured Lisa would be; however, in the dark, Duncan would not see his movements.

"Ok, fine," Duncan said diplomatically. "What do they know about the future? Tell me everything."

Jeremy took a few minutes and tried to relay to Duncan everything he remembered from the last day. Duncan listened quietly.

"So they rode in a car," Duncan said, more to himself than Jeremy. "Anything else?"

"Not really," Jeremy said. "I know you're probably trying to figure out if they're going to mess up history or time or something, but they really did not do much while they were in the future. You don't have anything to worry about."

Duncan hoped Jeremy was right. "Do you think they will be friendly to Brent? I never saw him when I stepped through."

"I don't see why not," Jeremy said. "Although, I could see him and Cyrus having trouble getting along after that tackle."

"Yes, well, I'm sure I'll have something to say to Brent about that after all this is settled, and we are safely back home," Duncan remarked.

"So now what," Jeremy asked, sitting up more. "Do we just sit here in the dark and wait?"

"I suppose so. There's not much we can do right now in the dark," Duncan said. It really was absolute darkness. "I say we get through tomorrow, and give ourselves time to come up with a plan."

"Fine," Jeremy said, and tenderly leaned back against the wall. "I'll try to get some sleep and not puke in the meantime."

"You really need to settle down," Duncan advised gently. "Stop trying to be the hero; it's like they say, 'When in Rome…',," he quoted the clichéd phrase.

"Yeah, yeah, yeah," Jeremy said. "Do as the Romans do." *Although I'd love to do go Gladiator on these people*, he thought as he drifted to sleep.

Lisa stumbled and nearly lost her footing when her foot caught a large root as they passed under a low hanging tree. The constable was pulling so hard on her wrists that she had to lace her fingers together just to keep from feeling like her hands were about to get pulled off at the wrists. She was angry that Jeremy kept getting hit by these people. She loved him for trying to stand up for her, but she also was annoyed that he kept doing it and getting himself hurt as a result.

"Where are you taking me?" Her voice betrayed her concern.

"Ye are to be jailed with the rest of thy kind," he said with disgust. She could smell the rum he had been drinking.

She looked back and saw Constable Herrick's dark figure pulling Jeremy by the head and pushing the man named Duncan. She turned her attention back to keeping up with her jailer when other three figures disappeared behind the building.

Beyond her side of the building, she saw an open field with a couple of trees, bordered by scraggly black tree silhouettes. They seemed ominous, set against a dark gray cloudy sky with deep black smears where the clouds parted and revealed the true darkness of night. She could see her own moonlit shadow as she emerged from the tree's shadow.

The jailer dropped her chains so he could open the door. Her nose was immediately assaulted by the most horrible stench she had ever experienced as it opened.

"What's that smell?" she asked, turning her head away from the door. She moved her hands to cover her face but Mister Smith snatched her chains so that she could not do so. The jailer started to chuckle.

"That, my lady," he said with glee, "is the smell of thy new home! At least it is until ye are hanged."

"What?!"

"Oh, yes, my dear," he burred through his thick accent. "Ye ought to know that witchcraft is forbidden in the Colony. Ye will pay for thy crimes," he said, pulling her in to the black hole that was the doorway.

Feeling powerless, she followed him. He took her about fifty feet into the room, where it was so dark she could barely make out Mister Smith's back.

"Ye will find that ye are in good company, I think, here. There be more than a dozen of ye foul criminal witches here. Just be sure that ye do not make any attempt to cause any problems, lest we be given cause to punish ye," he warned. They reached the spot he was taking her to. He guided her into the stall and finally let go of the chains. She was not prepared for it, so as they swung down heavily they pulled her arms as well. They struck her in the legs just above the knees; luckily, her jeans softened the blow, if just a little.

"So what do I do now?" she asked softly and fearfully.

"Sit quietly, go to sleep, pray," he suggested dismissively as his voice moved in the dark. "I do not care." She could almost see Mister Smith as he walked back to the open door. She began to sit down after he walked out and closed the door. She was blind in the darkness, had no idea what was going on, and did not have any way to talk to anyone she knew. She had never felt so abandoned and alone.

The floor was dirty (*or was it actually just dirt?*) and the stall was surprisingly cool, considering how warm it was outside. She could hear other sounds within the jail, mostly breathing or an occasional clinking of chains as other prisoners shifted. Somewhere to the far right some-one was snoring.

"Pardon me," whispered a feminine voice directly across from her; Lisa's heart lurched, and she gave a small squeak.

"Who's there?" she asked, fear shaking her voice.

"I am the widow Elizabeth Proctor," the woman said mournfully.

"Oh my God," Lisa breathed. "You mean *the* Proctor, as in Proctor Street?"

"I beg your pardon?" the woman sounded confused.

"Never mind," Lisa said, realizing that this was not the time for that sort of thing. "I'm sorry."

"Oh," Elizabeth said. "Please, if I may ask, what is your name?"

"Lisa," she replied. She extended her hand, but then felt silly when she realized that Miss Proctor would not be able to see it in this utter dark. She quietly lowered her hand. "It's nice to meet you."

"My dear," Proctor ignored her greeting. She seemed awkward, even in the darkness. "I came to ask you, why have you been arrested?"

Lisa looked down at the chains and shackles she could not see but definitely felt. "I don't know, exactly. I followed my boyfriend here and then some nut called us witches, and the next thing I know, there's a bunch of these guys standing around us, pointing guns at us and stuff." She was crying by the end of her explanation.

"I see," Elizabeth said after a few moments. Lisa could hear her scooting closer. "So you have been accused of being a witch?"

"Yeah," Lisa said, a little indignant now. "What's that all about? I mean, I know that was 'the thing' back in this time, but can they really just go around saying people are witches?"

Elizabeth sighed a sigh that was heavier than any that Lisa had ever heard.

"They can, my dear, and they have, and they will," Elizabeth said sadly.

"But they can't get away with it, right? I mean, I'm not a witch!" Lisa said defensively.

"I am certain that you are truthful and good," Elizabeth said, "but that will not matter. In happier, more thoughtful times, you would not be guilty. No woman in this jail has truly practiced witchcraft or anything evil of the sort. Yet we are prisoners and we await the judgment of the Court to dispatch a ruling on our lives."

"So what happens now?" Lisa asked.

"Have you been examined yet?" the woman asked.

"No," Lisa shuddered at the idea of being 'examined'; she'd been to several of Jeremy's museum field trips.

"My dear child," Elizabeth sighed sadly again, "you have a great deal of trouble ahead of you."

Lisa pulled her knees into her chest, and began to cry quietly.

Thursday, August 21, 1692

CHAPTER XXII

"Child!" Elizabeth Proctor's voice rasped. "Awaken!"

Lisa slowly roused, and quickly remembered the situation when she felt the weight of the shackles on her wrists and ankles, and then began to cry again. She was as uncomfortable as she had ever been, she didn't know quite where she was other than some kind of jail in the past, and she felt scared.

Miss Proctor scooted over to her across the dirt on her hands and knees. The only light came through a window that lay over ten feet away, beyond one of the stall walls. It wasn't made of sunbeams; actually, it was muted, but just strong enough to keep much of the very long room in low light. Still, she was able to see Miss Proctor now; she was probably in her forties, but her face seemed older than that. Her face was haggard and dirty, but there was a simple prettiness to her features. Her clothes seemed to be years old; she wore a long white dress that now was covered with varying splotches of black and brown dirt, and yellow dust. It had grey-dusted black sleeves which had small tears in it and threads of different thicknesses that were long and jagged stuck out from the holes. The front of the blouse reminded Lisa of an apron; it was as if this woman was a period re-enactor who had taken her role as serious as any

Shakespearean actor ever had.

"Oh, my dear," she scooped Lisa into her arms. Lisa just wanted to go home and back to her own bed, and to take three or four showers in the meantime.

"Thank you," Lisa sniffed after a minute, her tears subsiding. "Sorry to cry like that for no reason."

"Do not be sorry," Miss Proctor let her go, but still held her shoulders. "We each have shed the tears of sadness for this sorry place."

Lisa looked around. The room was half of the building in both directions, and to her right, going away from the door, was a long row of stalls, about twenty, as if this were a stable for horses. There were other women in the receding light, legs that emerged from long dresses of varying shades of black, white, and brown, extending from the stalls; Lisa suspected they were still asleep. There were shackles on the feet, and only about half had shoes. For a moment Lisa thought she saw a smaller pair of feet among the group, but it was too dark that far back to be sure. She quickly dismissed such a horrible thought.

She looked at the stalls themselves, and at the ceiling. The ceiling was actually a network of wood that held up a roof that looked somewhat like the hay roofs that Lisa associated with primitive huts in prehistoric times. The unfinished, jagged-surfaced wood beams were going in all directions, and the room had a subtle chill that reminded Lisa of being inside the stupid Old Salem Jail museum that Jeremy would drag her to on a few Halloweens. However, this was real and Lisa had never been here before, and that alone made her feel uneasy. In fact, even though there were other people here, Lisa was sure she had never felt so isolated.

Feeling embarrassed for crying for no reason, she looked down and began to pick off the hay fragments that had collected on her shirt in her sleep. "So you said your name is Miss Proctor?" Lisa asked, trying to change the subject while sniffing away the last of her tears.

"Yes, but please, you may call me Elizabeth," Miss Proctor said softly and invitingly. Her eyes were warm and friendly, and that made Lisa feel just a little bit better.

"So what are you in here for?" Lisa asked her, looking around for a moment and then giving up on finding something to wipe her nose with; she just used her sleeve.

"My husband and I were arrested in four months ago when our former maidservant and her conspirator friends accused us of evil deeds," she explained.

"Those children need to be arrested and put in chains, and then given a series of lashes until they each cannot remain on their feet, if you ask me!" a boisterous voice spoke up from a few stalls down and across the way.

"They will be dealt with by God in His own way and in His own time, Wilmot," Elizabeth said sideways, turning her head towards the voice but not enough to face her.

The woman called Wilmot emerged from her stall and jingled her way over to the two women, also on her hands and knees. She was much older than Elizabeth, and her skin seemed loose on her body. Lisa made a guess that she was in her seventies and had been in jail as long as Elizabeth.

She looked as though she were formerly plump, but had lost a lot of weight in an unhealthy short time. Her clothes, a uniform grey with dark smudges, also were tattered much like Elizabeth Proctor's. Lisa briefly noticed that the fabric quality of both women's dresses was much rougher and the threads were not always the same size; all the period actors in Salem that Lisa had ever seen had crisp, nice looking clothes. This world was beginning to feel more and more real to her.

"You are far too forgiving, Goody Proctor," Wilmot told her darkly, "especially in light of the fact that they are the purpose and reason behind John being hanged yesterday."

Proctor gasped, looked upward, and then turned her head sharply away from Lisa and Wilmot, jingling her shackles while hiding her face in her lower dress. Wilmot looked at Lisa with her pale blue eyes, and her contemptuous expression softened to one of sympathy. "Oh, my friend," she reached a hand to Elizabeth's shoulder. "I am sorry. I…" she trailed off.

The door suddenly creaked to open, and all three women turned towards the sound, and they saw a man in a beige Puritan outfit and with a black buckled hat, and wearing one of those waist-length capes. He stepped through, and Lisa felt a chill in her stomach and her spine when he made eye contact with her.

Both of the other women skittered briskly and meekly back to their stalls as the man entered.

"You are to come with me," he said formally. As he approached her, another man who was middle-aged and wearing a large, curly white wig, a grey vest and pants that stopped at his knees, also entered the door. He followed by three women dressed in traditional Puritan dresses.

"What's going on?" Lisa asked nervously. She started to feel scared again, this time wondering if she was going to get beheaded or something. She stood slowly just as the jailer reached her, not wanting to feel the hurt of getting yanked by her chains. He grabbed her by one of the links anyway and started walking back to the open foyer area near the door; Lisa quickly stepped forward to keep some slack at her wrists.

The other people who had entered had taken various places around the foyer, and in the light, Lisa could see far more than she expected. There were several sets of shackles hanging from the wall, and various whips and several straps also set in their place on the walls. The daylight that lit the foyer area came through a window that did not have glass; instead, the panes looked more like the white plastic that milk cartons were made of. Over in the opposite corner from the stall hallway she had come from was a single post that stood away from the ceiling, and there were splotches of brown on the dirt and hay around it. Her eyes filled with tears again, and she prayed inside that they would not torture her.

"Woman," the wig-wearing man spoke, "I am William Griggs, a doctor in this town and village. I have in attendance with me my assistants who will aid me as I examine you for the Devil's mark." While he spoke, the constable began to remove her shackles. She felt a moment of relief from the shackles, but then started to dwell about his Devil's mark comment. Fear of what that might mean made her begin to breathe quick and shallow breaths.

"Disrobe," the constable ordered, standing back. Lisa looked at him, then at the doctor, and finally at the three women in turn.

"You want me to take off my clothes?" she asked him, unbelieving the request. She looked back to the two women in front of her, hoping that they might protest, or offer an alternative. However, their faces were stoic; not even the women seemed to sympathize with her hesitation. She feigned courage. "Um, I don't think so."

"You will or I will," he warned. After a moment he started to step towards her, and she backed away and began to unbutton the top of her shirt. He stepped back into his spot and she paused. She stopped with her shirt buttons and then bent over to remove her shoes and socks first. After that, she slowly rose, and stopped when she saw the leering constable watch her.

"Turn around!" she squeaked pleadingly, sounding more pathetic to her ears than she had hoped to. She felt powerless as it was, and definitely did not want to expose herself to this cruel man. She tried to convince herself that at least the other man was a doctor. Still, the constable did not move and just smiled.

"I am required to be a witness, you see," he said gleefully. Lisa felt creeped out, and kept waiting for this nightmare to end with her waking up.

No such ending took place. After she took off her jeans

(all the women chirped a gasp when they could see her panties), she began to remove her shirt, which was a pullover. She hated being made to do this; even in high school gym she preferred to wait until everyone else had changed, busying herself with her locker until nearly all the girls had gone. She was almost tardy to gym class every day throughout the four years of school because of her private nature.

She had gotten down to her underwear, and leaving her bra on also, desperately praying inside that they would not force her to completely go nude.

"Oh dear," the doctor uttered to himself. By now he was standing directly behind her, and God only knew what his remark meant. She felt sickened by all this attention to her body, and by the fact that there was nothing she could do about it. She then felt rough, moist fingertips jab at her left shoulder, where she had a birthmark. She fought the urge to pull away.

"It's just a birthmark," Lisa said feebly, looking to the ceiling, fighting not to let herself break down again into tears. She was being forced to give up her privacy to these horrible people; she desperately did not want to give them the satisfaction of her losing control of her emotions.

"We shall see," Griggs said simply. Suddenly, two of the other women walked over to her and took her hands, separating her fingers and carefully looking at her skin as if looking for clues to sunken treasure. They began to twist and contort her fingers and hands, prodding her every square inch of skin. She could feel the third woman's hands working over her back; the very sensation of these strangers touching her made her skin crawl. She wanted to smack all of their hands away and run and hide.

After a few moments, he jabbed at her lower back, where Lisa knew she had a sequence of three or four small moles (or so Jeremy had once told her at the beach). "Elizabeth, please hand me a pin," he said, not to Miss Proctor, but apparently to the third woman Lisa could feel but could not see. A few moments later, she felt a strange series of pokes at her lower back. They were not sharp, so it did not hurt as much as it was uncomfortable. Feeling that she was supposed to not react to the pokes, she stood silently as the two women continued to pinch and twist her skin on her arms and worked towards her armpits.

Finally, without warning, the women removed her bra and inspected her breasts, then replaced it and pulled her panties down. After a few more moments of having to endure the pinching and poking, tears began to stream down her face. Lisa suddenly felt more violated and humiliated than ever before in her life. Finally, at long last, the women stood, and returned to their places, shaking their heads without a word at the doctor as they did so. They did not even have the courtesy to bother to pull her bottoms back up.

"You may redress yourself," the doctor intoned absently, as if treating a patient this way was a common thing to him. Lisa could not hold back her emotions any longer and finally broke out into full tears, and they dripped from her face as she awkwardly bent down and began to reposition her clothing to cover herself, then quickly and angrily pulled on her jeans and shirt. She stood up and buried her face in her hands as she cried silently.

"Do you cry for your guilt?" The doctor asked her.

Lisa looked up, her face a deep pink and her eyes red and puffy. "Guilt? For what?" she asked with confusion. *Doesn't he realize how horribly he just treated me?* She wondered, the pang of embarrassment flashing in her heart for a moment as she reflected on the experience.

"My child, if you confess now, you can prevent yourself more pain, and begin your repentance for your dealings with Satan," Griggs said in a fatherly manner.

Feeling as if she was being blamed for something she didn't do, and afraid to give the wrong answer, she exclaimed, "I don't even know what you are talking about!" She looked at the other three women, hoping they might give her a clue to know what the right answer was, and then at the constable, who simply stared at her without expression. She looked back to the doctor. Strangely, the woman behind him whom he called Elizabeth wore an expression almost as if she was enjoying watching Lisa's examination. Lisa wanted to go over and scratch the weird, subtle sneer off the girl's face.

"As you wish it," Griggs sighed, reclaiming her attention. "Very well. Constable, you may return the prisoner into custody and to her stall, so we can proceed with the examination of the men."

The constable worked without a word, squatting down to return Lisa's wrists and ankles into shackles, and then again took her roughly by the chains and placed her in her stall. She did not try to fight or keep up with him, but simply was led there; she was so numb from the experience that the pain in her wrists barely registered to her. He paused as he looked at her after she sat back down in her place.

"'Tis a pity you have allied yourself with the Devil," he commented, looking down at her with both interest and disgust. "You are a beautiful woman."

With another moment's lingering gaze that made her feel gross, he turned on a heel and walked towards the door without looking back (which Lisa was thankful for), where the last woman was exiting. Lisa turned to see Elizabeth Proctor and Wilmot across the walkway. They apparently had been able to hear the entire ordeal, as both of the women also had eyes red with tears.

At least she was no longer alone.

Jeremy stood next to Duncan, and both men were unshackled and reduced to their boxer shorts. For Jeremy, it was awkward and weird, standing next to a man in his underwear. It did not help that there were girls around. He was self-conscious of his physique, mostly because he was lanky and did not have a lot of muscle on his frame.

Duncan, for the most part, was not terribly uncomfortable being half-naked around other people, but he did hope this examination would be over quickly. He had joined the Army reserves shortly after he got his first post-doc appointment, and was familiar with the concept of group exams. He had to undergo a series of them when he was first enlisted, and at least twice more during his single three-year stint.

"I have been informed of your rebellious nature, young man," the doctor spoke slowly, as if considering whether what he had been told was actually true. "I believe that you will find that any sort of such behavior in this examination will result in a very painful punishment. Do you understand me, son?"

"Yes," Jeremy said with resentful humility, after wrangling for a few moments with his defiant desires to not answer the man.

"Good," Griggs said with a hint of satisfaction. "Let us begin. We shall examine Macer first, and then the slave."

There was a deep sting in Duncan's spirit that quickly became a passionate fire of fury. He tamed it equally quickly, but he was compelled to speak.

"Sir," he said, keeping his head low, "May I speak?"

"What do you want to say, Negro?" Doctor Griggs displayed his fullest haughtiness in that question.

"Sir, I informed our captors that I am a freed man," Duncan said carefully. "I am not a slave." He almost choked on that last word. In all the years of developing the Time Opener and being fascinated with time travel, he had never considered the possibility that he would be confronted with having to say that phrase. He missed two-thousand ten, where at the very least nearly everyone treated him as an equal, or even a respected scholar.

"Man, you have been caught in the company of those in

the possible practice of witchcraft, and may very well be guilty of doing dark magic yourself," Griggs almost laughed at the audacity of Duncan's expectation. "I think you and I both understand that your days as a freedman have ended."

Duncan tried to maintain a stoic in the face of this man's treatment of him. There was no malice in his voice; it was simply a fact of the situation; Duncan was a black man who had been given his freedom, and wasted the chance by doing something forbidden. Duncan did not sense racism from this man; at least, not like the racism he had experienced in his youth. This was as degrading, however, as if he were a second-class citizen. Duncan realized that no matter what he might do or say going forward, no man in this era would ever look at him with any level of respect. He now understood a lot better the stories his grandparents had told him about life before the sixties.

Duncan raised his head, and tried to feel his dignity, as injured as it might have been at that moment. He could see Jeremy looking at him out of the corner of his eyes. He hoped Jeremy would have the sense enough to go through this examination without any kind of altercation.

Jeremy's gaze upon Duncan lingered for a few moments, as he mulled his dislike for the doctor and his rude remarks. He had never known discrimination personally, nor anyone who was racist; it infuriated him that Duncan would be treated like this. However, he sensed that Duncan would be offended if Jeremy said anything about it, and he restrained his fury as best he could and waited for the examination to begin.

The women suddenly moved towards him and Duncan, and each took one of their hands and began to play with his fingers, but not in a playful way. Jeremy found it a strange mix of feelings to both enjoy human contact but also to not want them to touch him. He thought immediately of his girlfriend, and felt a little guilty that he enjoyed the touch of another girl, even though he did not like the fact that they were touching him while he was so exposed. Each girl closely examined a hand of each of the two prisoners, then pinched and prodded their arm, up to their shoulder, and then switched arms. Behind him, he imagined that the doctor was staring at his back, looking for this Devil's mark he had mentioned as they had disrobed. Jeremy was not sure what that mark might be, but he knew they wouldn't find anything; after all, he'd even been an altar boy for a while as a kid. There was no way he did anything that would get that kind of mark.

The girl who was examining his arms reached his other shoulder, and then began to poke at his face, moving his hair and ears around while not making any eye contact. He did not like her being this close to him, for several reasons, including the fact that she was not his girlfriend and that he did not know her. On top of that, she smelled like old body odor, and he was sure that it was her breath that smelled bad too when she exhaled through slightly parted lips.

Both girls finished simultaneously, and both backed up and spun themselves to face away from him and Duncan when Griggs appeared in front of them, and began to examine Jeremy's lower half.

"Hey!" he snapped when the doctor began to remove his boxers. As promised, the sting of a lash suddenly burned on his exposed back, and he glanced back through welled eyes at the constable, who was smiling happily while holding the short whip. By the time he returned his attention to the doctor, the physician had already finished much of his work and was examining Jeremy's feet.

After several more moments and Duncan quietly experiencing his own round of humiliation, Doctor Griggs stood up and looked at the constable.

"I have finished my examination," he said formally. "You may have them reclothe, and returned to their stalls."

Jeremy did not wait to be told directly, and bent down to pull his shorts back up. The bending motion sent a stream of fire across his back, from his right shoulder to his lower left side; apparently, the lashing broke his skin. When he began to put his shirt back on, he tried to let it tenderly lay over his frame, but unfortunately, this sting wasn't going away. Duncan waited a few moments, and then also began to dress. The doctor and his assistants disappeared out the door, and Smith began to reclose their shackles.

"You okay?" Duncan asked him quietly as the constable worked.

"Probably," Jeremy said, trying to find a position that did not bring pain to his back. He arched his back a small bit backwards, squinting an eye. "I think that one's gonna hurt for a while."

CHAPTER XXIII
9 A.M.

Brent sat on the bed, reading through the only book he could find: the Bible. He had not slept much that night, given the adventures of the evening as well as his own internal clock, which was still timed to Eastern Daylight Time in the year two thousand ten. Now, he was having a bout of cabin fever, having been relegated to sit on his haunches Aaron and Cyrus' room.

They had forced him to destroy his clothes before allowing him to sleep, for fear of his presence being discovered to be "otherworldly", as Aaron had put it. *You could have at least let me keep my shirt*, he pouted: *that was my favorite one!* Still, he also knew they were right, and had grumpily complied, watching his futuristic clothes burn in the iron pot-bellied stove. His shoes put on the best show, melting and hissing before being engulfed by a blue-green flame. However, he drew the line at his underwear; he wasn't about to go another week in period loincloths, nor was he willing to go commando. He won that argument, and now wore a dark brown, three-piece outfit loaned to him by Aaron; he felt like a pilgrim. All the anachronistic things that had been in his shorts pockets now sat in a sack on the desk.

He was randomly flipping through the Bible, looking for

a chapter to read. At least reading the Good Book felt familiar; even though he only attended Mass from time to time, the formality of the King James Version gave the same comfort as his family church back home. He liked the stories in the middle of the Old Testament, particularly those of David and Solomon. However, it was difficult to settle on anything specific; his mind kept wandering out the door to the unknown dungeon which held his boss and two other time travelers. After about fifteen minutes of flipping randomly and reading sentences one or two at a time, he closed the book with a slam, and then felt a tinge of guilt at being so rough with God's book.

The door opened and Brent looked up; Aaron appeared, some sweat on his brow beneath his brown, pulled-back hair.

"Are you ready to do your part?" he asked, glancing around the room and finally settled his eyes with Brent's.

"What took you so long?" Brent hissed impatiently, standing up from the bed and checking his wrist for the watch that was no longer there. "It's been, like, almost three hours!"

"Business deals require finesse of conversation and skilled bargaining," Aaron said casually, closing the door and walking over to Brent and checking out his clothes for anything out of place. "Skills I suspect that you may not have or understand fully. Nevertheless, it has in fact only been two hours," he said as he tugged at the frock that hung from Brent's neck. He stepped back and to look him over once more.

"The news as we know so far is that there is to be a first hearing today at the tenth hour this morn. We have only a short time to work; I am told the court wishes to accelerate the process." Aaron let his concern weigh his tone. He took a deep breath, held it for a moment, and then let it out. "As I asked, are you prepared?"

"Yeah," Brent sighed, letting his concern for Duncan focus his mind on the plan they had agreed upon. He nodded to Aaron, who nodded back and disappeared out the door. Brent bent a bit low, and snuck out the same door, turning to the right.

When Cyrus had awakened him earlier that morning, they told him of a plan that Aaron had just come up with. After their meeting with some merchant named Walter Britson, Aaron and Cyrus were to go to the tavern for drinks and breakfast. Brent's job was to pretend to arrive from Falmouth with urgent news of Anna's beginning stages of labor; Aaron would be free to "leave", thus making it possible for them to develop a plan from behind the scenes. It would also easily explain Brent's sudden appearance in town.

Ducking low, he passed several doors and windows (Brent snorted at the thought of considering them real windows), making his way along the back side of the building that was both inn and tavern. Checking out the lay of the land from the corner when he reached it, he saw the barn about a hundred yards off. There were several trees that were widely spaced out between where he was and the barn, raising concern that he would be easily spotted. There was some cover before he became exposed, though; at least two wagons were parked near where he was hiding. The one closest to the wall looked like it had been sitting unused for dozens of years, with wooden barrels of various sizes and levels of decay littering it on top and underneath.

Looking around, he ducked behind the wagons, and checked to see the activity on the street. There were about a dozen people dressed as Puritans walking around on the street, each going about their daily business. Finally, he got impatient with his own trepidation and decided to make a walk for it. *Hide in plain sight*, he remembered hearing somewhere.

He stepped out, walking as assuredly as he could make himself feel, and strode with confidence towards the barn. He was surprised when no one had even looked his way by the time he reached the barn doors.

Brent passed out of the sunlight and into the darkened, warm barn. It smelled like hay, dust, and animal feces. Brent's nose crinkled subconsciously as he set about looking for Aaron's stall. His eyes adjusted quickly, and he managed to find the horses, stored in the eighth stall on the right, just as Aaron had told him.

Perseus was easy to identify of the two horses, having one white leg and three chocolate brown legs. Just as Cyrus had promised, the horse was already saddled. Brent had to insist on that point; for some reason it was beyond the guys' ability to grasp that he had no idea how to saddle a horse. He'd be lucky to make his way from the barn to the road without losing control.

It was tough at first because Perseus refused to obey Brent. However, after some insistent clicking and cooing and petting from him, the horse finally agreed to move. Brent quietly pulled him to the rear barn entrance.

He peeked out the door, and saw a fenced-off lot that did not have anything but grass and trees in it. He looked up at the sun, and estimated that he was facing north. To his right were three wooden buildings, about four hundred yards away. He looked among the trees that littered the land between him, the fenced lot, and the three buildings, and decided on a path.

Ushering the horse out the door, he mounted the horse (*Sweet!* he thought, pleased to succeed at climbing into the saddle), and tried to guide the horse in the right direction. Again, the horse did not respond. Brent tried to shake the reigns, which did not work, and then he tried bouncing on the saddle, and then finally he shook himself and the reigns, feeling foolish and hoping that no one would see him convulsing like that on the back of the horse. Not only would he probably be arrested for having fits, and the plan ruined, but it also would just be flat out embarrassing.

He stopped. "Come on, Perseus," he said to the horse, patting its neck, "I need you to trust me. Aaron needs you to trust me."

He tried again, and this time the horse responded. Realizing he had nudged the horses' ribs as he clicked, he found the horse began to obey. After a few minutes of experimenting, the horse had managed to walk a zigzag along the intended path. Now came the difficult part.

Brent emerged from behind the buildings, onto a wide street made of dry dirt that had very recently been mud.

"Heyah!" Brent said self-consciously, spurning the horse to move. Unfortunately, Perseus only began to walk a bit faster. There were a couple of people on the street, and a horseman in the distance; luckily, no one still seemed to pay attention to him. He kicked Perseus' ribs again, and clicked more insistently. Perseus responded with a faster walk, and eventually a trot after a few more nudges.

Finally, Brent got his message across, as the horse began to run at a fast pace. He felt the wind in his hair as he bounced violently enough to almost lose his seat on the saddle. His lack of control was fun, making him laugh out loud at his first-ever ride on a horse. Realizing that he a job to do, he tried to regain his composure and began to guide the horse around the bend of the street. The horse complied by veering to the right, and Brent could see the front of the inn.

He pulled the reigns back and told the horse to whoa when they were in front of the tavern; Perseus was still unused to this rider, slowed at his own pace to an eventual stop. Brent grabbed the horn of the saddle and eased himself down. He led Perseus over to a horse post, and tied the reigns down next to another, solid grey pony.

Brent felt giddy from his first horseback ride, but stayed with his path. His adventure with Perseus was enough to leave him looking naturally tired and sweaty; he finished the part by racing into the front room of the Inn.

"I'm looking for Aaron," he gasped to the woman who

he was told would be called Madam Reilly. "Aaron Quincy!"

"Calm down, young man!" the lady stood and walked briskly over to him, squinting. "What is your rush?"

"I bring news of his wife, in Falmouth," Brent said quickly, trying to remember his lines. "Is he here?"

"He has rented a room, and I have not seen him today," Madam Reilly answered him, her demeanor becoming immediately maternal.

"Can you guess where I might find him?" Brent asked.

"You might try the tavern," Madam Reilly said quickly, walking from behind the counter. "Out the door, around the corner."

Brent, knowing this already and trying to play the role right, had already started back for the door. He stumbled out the door, having misjudged the uneven edge of the floor.

He raced around to the gray-brown wooden door, and yanked it open, and ran inside a few steps.

As if on cue, Aaron and Cyrus both stopped their conversation and turned from their tankards at the bar, along with about fifteen other men of varying levels of diminishing sanitary conditions.

"Aaron!" Brent yelled, a little more energetically than he preferred. He had never been an actor.

"Brent!" Aaron and Cyrus both smiled as they said his name. The men of the bar sat silently and watched; Madam Reilly stepped wordlessly into the tavern.

"What brings you to Salem, my cousin?" Aaron said, his

voice carrying a bit of ham-acting too.

"It is Anna, your wife!" Brent gasped his pre-chosen words. "She has begun the labor of giving birth, and demands your presence, the deal be damned!"

"Anna?" Aaron chirped oddly, but he made the faces convincingly. Cyrus, as per his part, watched as he let them exchange their lines. Aaron began digging in his belt to pay for his drink, and faced the bartender. "I must leave at once!"

"I will prepare our things," Cyrus volunteered. He made to turn to the bartender as well.

"No, my friend," Aaron said, grabbing Cyrus by the elbow. "I will make this ride alone, and be with my wife this evening."

"It is not safe, Aaron!" Cyrus protested, quite believably.

"I will be fine, Cyrus," Aaron said, and started to walk to the door. "We have made our deal. You said you were curious about the trial today; please, stay and enjoy yourself." He reached over to Brent and put a hand on his shoulder. "Indeed, Brent, I insist that you stay and keep Cyrus both in company and out of trouble!"

"Really?" Brent asked excitedly, forgetting for a moment that this was all an act. Aaron frowned so slightly but recovered that no one seemed to catch it.

"Let us at least help see you off," Cyrus insisted. Aaron nodded after a dramatic pause, and then smiled to the tavern of men.

"I am to be a father today!" he bellowed joyously,

shooting both fists high above his head.

Fifteen arms raised steins of beer into the air, saluting the news of the new birth. "*Huzzah!*" the men bellowed back, not in unison. Madam Reilly put a hand on his shoulder as he turned for the door; Aaron turned and she gave him a quick, strong hug.

"Congratulations, my boy," she smiled proudly at him. Aaron smiled back, nodding his appreciation. He stepped again to the threshold and took his leave of the Reilly's.

Aaron, Cyrus and Brent quickly left the tavern, and made their way back to their room.

"Well done!" Aaron congratulated Brent. "You performed most admirably!"

Brent felt good to have been able to pull off his performance; it seemed like the first successful thing he'd done in weeks. Even Cyrus smiled at him and patted him on the shoulder without a word.

However, he tried to put his pleasure at success aside, for now they needed to work out a plan to rescue Duncan and the couple who, only hours before, they themselves had tried to capture.

After trying to find the best way to sit or stand without feeling the searing sensation on his back from the lash he'd received, Jeremy found that lying on his side helped the pain subside to a manageable level. Duncan had inspected the laceration and told him that it was basically a broken welt, with a few streams of blood droplets at points. Had they been in their own time, with some Tylenol and strategically-placed Band-Aids, Jeremy imagined that he would probably not even feel an injury like this. However, he realized that he would just have to figure out a way to block out the pain.

This jail is nothing *like the museum*, Jeremy mused as he lay in his stall.

When they were told the night before that they were being sent to jail, Jeremy had visualized the stone walls and iron bars that enclosed tiny, black-backed cells in the re-created Witch Dungeon museum which existed in the twenty-first century. However, now he was inside the real thing, and it looked far different. There were some short stone walls that divided several of the cells towards the darkened end of the long row of stalls in which he now sat, but the walls above them as well as the dividing walls closer to Jeremy were built of rough wood planks. The dividing walls themselves were not much more than about five feet high; apparently, people did not spend much time standing while in here.

The wood was course and unfinished, as though the builders had chopped the planks and beams from the original trees in a hurry, and put them on the wall without much concern for woodcraft or beauty. The floor was dirt, rough and uneven, with straws of hay littering about. The dirt near the middle of the alleyway that ran between the two rows of stalls was compacted and clear of most hay, but towards the wooden cells the dirt was looser and there were even occasional tufts of grass, struggling to survive in the limited light of the jail.

As he drifted in and out of sleep, Jeremy glanced over towards Duncan from time to time, who lay on the dirt floor on his back, with his hands laced behind his head. Jeremy found himself impressed with the older scientist's way of maintaining his composure here, considering all the bigotry he was being confronted with.

Things had been quiet for a couple of hours; occasionally Jeremy heard whispered murmuring from a couple voices in the darker regions of the jail's hallway. However, he was sore and feeling very hungry, and so was not terribly interested in finding out who owned the voices.

He heard the jail door open, and he opened his eyes. He could hear the footsteps as someone walked towards him, and he turned, ignoring the discomforts his movements provoked.

"Get up!" Constable Herrick ordered. "You have a first hearing which begins in a half hour!"

Jeremy stood slowly, during which Duncan had stood and, with what Jeremy sensed was defiant dignity, walked over to join him.

"I trust you have begun to learn that there are consequences to your disrespect," Herrick said evenly to Jeremy. Jeremy could not help but notice the long, bell-ended barrel of a musket that sat in Herrick's right hand.

"Yes sir, I think I do," Jeremy said after a moment, feeling more humble than he wanted to, but not resisting it. His hunger and injuries seemed to take any bite out of his resentment towards the constable's punishments.

"Follow me, then," Herrick ordered, and turned to leave

the room. After a wordless glance at Duncan, who looked at him with sympathy, Jeremy followed Herrick. As he walked towards the door, he passed one of the first cells of the jail, and realized that it contained the mess of waste that was responsible for the stench that filled the jail's air. Apparently, the prisoners were not allowed to go outside to relieve themselves. Jeremy shuddered at the prospect, considering that he was likely going to have to use that stall very soon. Toilet paper probably hadn't been invented yet.

They stepped outside behind Herrick, who closed the door and led them towards the wagon that carried them to the jail the night before. As he and Duncan passed the horses and reached the back, Jeremy looked over to the last place he had seen Lisa, hoping she was ok. His heart jumped and he felt relieved when he saw her walking towards them, her head low as she maneuvered the rocky, uneven grass. The other constable led her by her chains, and he too was carrying a musket. Jeremy kept watching them as he climbed onto the cart, feeling anger that his girlfriend was being treated like a common criminal, regardless of what year it was. Still, he made himself sit quietly as she reached the back of the cart.

When she tried to reach up to begin climbing on, he leaned over to help her; her appreciative blue eyes quickly turned furious when she looked up at him. He saw that the dirt and dust on her face had been shaped by many tears, and her eyes were swollen and red. *She must have been so scared and alone last night*, Jeremy sympathized. *At least I sort of had Duncan, even though we didn't talk at all.* He offered his hand to help her up.

She glared at him in a way that somehow made his gesture to help seem feeble and insulting. He and Duncan had had a rough night and morning, which meant she probably had a pretty rough time too, but he didn't figure there would be any reason she would be angry at *him*. He sat back against the side of the cart and looked at Duncan. Jeremy offered a small shrug, to which Duncan merely replied with a raised eyebrow.

Lisa paused before sitting down next to Jeremy, as if that was the last place she wanted to have to sit. Once she had settled and the constables had mounted the wagon, the three were jerked backwards without ceremony due to the horses' rough start. Regaining his balance, Jeremy leaned towards Lisa.

"Hey," he said in a low voice, hoping to break the ice that suddenly and unexpectedly appeared between them.

"Don't talk to me right now," she said in a voice that betrayed both anger and hurt.

"What?" Jeremy asked, turning to her. She sounded like he had done something to her. After a few moments without response, he pressed on. "What happened?"

"Seriously, just shut up right now," she whispered, looking away from Jeremy and out towards the distance.

"Come on," he said, "It can't be that bad."

He apparently said the wrong thing, for she turned to him and there was a glint of something in her eye that he had never seen before.

"'Not that bad'?" she growled through clenched teeth.

"What are you mad at me for? So you had to sleep on the floor," he said, suddenly annoyed that she was taking this out on him.

"That's what you think is wrong? Did you get 'examined'?" she was getting angrier by the moment.

"Yeah," he said. "It wasn't that bad. He just looked at us and poked at our skin for a few minutes. No big deal!" Jeremy shrugged again, showing her how stupidly clueless he was to her pains.

"No big deal!" she said loudly, and could not help but laugh maniacally.

"Be silent back there!" Constable Smith yelled back over the noise of the cart and horses.

"Seriously," Jeremy said back, now mad at her for putting the blame on him. "Besides, you'd have been just fine if you hadn't followed us through!"

For a moment, Lisa was so incensed that she suddenly felt far away from herself. Without thinking about it, she reached back her right hand and punched Jeremy full on his left cheek. He apparently never saw it coming, for he spun and rolled over to the front of the cart, lying sprawled on his back. She came back to herself quickly after hitting him, and felt suddenly terrible for having done so. She wanted to both comfort him and hit him again, but ultimately took a deep breath and sat where she was, looking out towards the distant trees, tears welling in her eyes again. As she was turning, she noticed Smith laughing at Jeremy's new punishment.

Jeremy reached up to his face where Lisa had hit him,

and found a small cut from her shackles as well as the throbbing tender areas under his eye from the punch.

"Seriously?" he groaned, bouncing limply with the cart as it hit bumps in the road.

Duncan looked down at him sympathetically.

"It's really not your day, is it?"

"This is what I'm saying," Jeremy said pitifully, covering his face with both hands.

CHAPTER XXIV
Salem Town Meeting House

Cyrus and Brent took their seats in the last row of the small Town Meeting House. Brent had also been in town the day of the most recent hanging only two days before, but he, Andrew and David had not disembarked from the ship until the middle of the afternoon. They had heard the townsfolk gossiping over the matter as they were making their way across the village. Although they'd tried to look as casual as possible, the three time travelers had basically speed-walked across town before to avoid any suspicion. Now, Brent was sitting here on the dusty wooden bench in the very room where so many people had been condemned as witches. He felt very self-conscious and a little paranoid that somehow the twenty or so people who were currently milling about the room would figure out that he did not belong.

"You must calm down," Cyrus said in a low voice to his ear, making him jump. "At least stop your leg from its fidgeting movements."

Brent looked down and realized his right knee had been bouncing very rapidly; he made his leg slow down and do so less obviously, but he did not stop it. He expected to be agitated throughout the trial.

Brent looked up and took in the room and its occupants.

The room was small as it was; Brent would have expected a larger building with more decorations. He and Cyrus had entered behind where they now sat, at the very middle of the long side of the building. Along the short length of the building, on either side of the room, were wooden staircases leading up to lofted balconies, both of which overlooked the central area of the room. There were about ten or so people up on the balconies, all dressed in very Puritanical clothes; they seemed more formal than the clothes Aaron had loaned him. After a few moments, he realized that only men were on the right balcony, and only a few women had attended, and they were up in the left balcony.

His thoughts were broken when a man brushed against his left shoulder, struggling to drag a little girl who couldn't have been much older than ten or eleven. The child was alternating between going fully limp and flailing her arms and legs wildly, but she was not uttering a sound. Brent frowned watching this odd behavior, and followed the man with his eyes as he took a seat on the right, two benches ahead of Brent and Cyrus. The girl kept sliding to the floor, and flailing, then going limp, continuing on without interruption. Brent felt like she could use a good swat on the hindquarters using a good-sized twig from one of the trees outside, and marveled that the father simply let her act out.

Another man brushed up against Brent, and this time he responded by scooting in further. Looking up, the older man who had bumped him gave him a quick apology, and then stepped forward to sit right in front of him. A young woman, who in Brent's era could probably be a senior in high school, followed the old man and sat across the aisle on the neighboring bench as indicated by the man. She kept her head down when she addressed him, but stole a quick glance back at Brent. She had a pretty complexion, but very plain; her white bonnet hid her dark hair, which Brent guessed was probably wavy but not tightly curly. She offered him a sidelong smile, and her one visible green eye making contact with Brent's own. Brent was intrigued by the girl, and suddenly felt compelled to wave 'hi' to her when a voice bellowed from behind him.

"This audience shall now take your seats," said the round-faced man behind him, wearing a black robe and some kind of a white neck ruffle, which was like a long rectangular scarf tied like a tie. He gave the assembled citizens a few moments to collect themselves and sit down. The room fell quiet, except for the little writhing girl.

Two more black-robed men, both wearing dusty grey wigs, entered the room and strode swiftly towards the front of the meeting chamber. There were three chairs that sat behind the wooden table they would be seated at, and the table itself was placed on a sort of stage that was three steps above the rough wood floor. The two men reached their seats, and the announcing man followed them up. The man in the center, whom Brent thought looked like a mean Mister Rogers, cleared his voice before speaking loudly.

"We assemble this day, the twenty-first day of August, in the year of our Lord, sixteen hundred and ninety-two, to examine the charges that have been brought against three individuals who have been witnessed performing serious and terrible acts of witchcraft in this precinct." He paused and surveyed the audience. His eyes darted quickly down to the flailing child, and then he looked over to the man who first called the chamber to order.

"The honorable John Hathorne and Jonathan Corwin will now hear the complaints of those who wish to be heard by the court." As he said this, the older judges took their seats and began to organize the papers that lay in front of them. The announcing man remained standing.

"Thank you, Mister Sewell," The magistrate named Corwin said, and the two exchanged nods.

If this had been his own church, Brent would have leaned over to Cyrus to ask what was going on. However, the cramped space and nearly forty people made it virtually impossible to speak without being heard by everyone here. He decided to just watch the proceedings and see what happened.

"Your honor," the man with the rotten child stood and spoke, removing his wide-brim had to do so; he too wore a wig, but his was dark brown and wavy. "I wish to speak first, if it pleases you."

"It does, Reverend Parris," Judge Hathorne said evenly. "What is your business?"

"My daughter Betty Parris, whom you well know, has come into another bout of fits just this morning," Parris said to the court. He pointed down to her as she lay in one of her limp periods, and as if on cue, she began to flail about, but now she started to grunt as if she were some kind of rabid dog. Brent was stunned that her father was putting up with her antics in public, and even more astonished that he was taking her to court for it.

"Do you believe she has become afflicted with illness or malady?" the second judge, Corwin, asked.

"I do not, sir," Parris answered. He turned back and extended a hand towards the doctor. "Doctor Griggs was by this morning prior to his physical examinations of the accus-ed to inform me of the news, and confirm-ed that her fits were not of the body, but of the spirit."

"What be his diagnosis?" Corwin asked Griggs, his hands steepled together attentively.

"Magistrate, it is his belief that she again has become bewitch-ed by some unknown practicer of evil spells," Parris responded, very much convinced in what he was saying. The judges looked to Doctor Griggs for confirmation, who deliberately nodded twice. Brent had to remind himself that he was not watching a movie; this was really happening.

"Then we shall again verify if this is so," Hathorne said, interjecting with his nasally tone. "Bring in the accus-ed, and we will now determine if effluvia will identify one or all as the guilty soul."

Brent didn't know what effluvia was, but it led some whispers to start flying in the room, as several men and women leaned to mention what they had already seen in the short testimony. Brent took this chance.

"What?" he whispered in confusion to Cyrus.

"Effluvia," Cyrus answered him in whisper. "It is a touch test. If she is made well by their touch…" he said, and simply shook his head in place of the rest of the sentence.

That's messed up, Brent thought. He turned and saw Duncan, Lisa and Jeremy led in one by one, all blindfolded and wearing long, black, shackles that rattled noisily. Duncan looked the same, Lisa looked disheveled and upset but none the worse for wear, but Jeremy looked like he had been through a couple rounds of kickboxing since Brent had chased him the day before. They were led by the constable, who wore a gray outfit with minimal neck accoutrement, and walked down the center aisle, passing Brent, then Doctor Griggs, and finally leading them around the girl and to the left side of the room.

"Constable," Hathorne intoned, "Will you now see the first accus-ed to touch the young Betty Parris on her left arm?"

Constable Herrick took Duncan by the arm, and guided him by his left arm to reach down and touch the girl on the arm. The limp child did not move for a moment, her head hanging so that she was facing the audience, and then she suddenly burst into another fit of grunting, flailing, and whipping her head about. The magistrates exchanged looks that Brent registered as surprise, and then signaled Herrick to do the second touch test. Duncan was awkwardly guided to step backward, and Jeremy was grabbed. Brent looked back to the child on the floor, and for a moment thought she had locked glances with the doctor's assistant.

Jeremy was guided down, and just before she was touched, she rolled on the floor onto her belly, then back again, as if her fits were getting worse.

"No! No! No!" the girl wailed and cried out as she flailed, and when the blindfolded Jeremy touched her forearm, the girl screeched as if in great pain.

What the— Brent was overcome with astonishment at this charade. He glanced at Cyrus, who caught his look and stared at him with a hard glance warning him to not make a sound. *This is unbelievable!* Brent thought angrily, turning back to the bogus touch test. *It's totally ridiculous!*

Lisa was next. Brent now gave the exchange the keenest attention he may have ever watched anything unfold. Lisa kneeled down as her wrist was guided by the constable, and the child again began to cry out in pain, and Brent was distracted a brief moment when he thought he saw out of the corner of his eye a subtle nod from the nurse to the child. Suddenly suspicious, he looked to Cyrus, whose eyes were also on the nurse.

"No! Nooo!" Betty Parris flailed and cried, emptying her lungs with the effort. Suddenly, Lisa's hand made contact with the child's wrist, and the child screeched again. This time, though, the screech broke into tearful giggles, as if she was giddy to have her pain lifted.

"Thank God!" Reverend Parris exclaimed, and he bent down to scoop up his daughter. She clenched him by the shoulders as he lifted her off the ground; the senior Parris gave a disgusted look towards Lisa, who could not see anything but was crying beneath her blindfold.

"Lisa?" Jeremy called out loud blindly.

"What's going on?" she said tearfully. The constable blocked her attempt to remove her blindfold. "Why are you picking on me?" she pleaded out towards those she could not see.

Brent watched in silent shock as the crowd burst into whispered gossip. He could not believe this farce. He was astonished by the whole performance, and by the fact that everyone seemed to buy it.

"Constable, please remove the blinding of the accused," Hathorne instructed.

As the constable complied, Reverend Parris sat back down, his daughter wrapped around his torso as if scared to let go. She simply looked to the floor, breathing heavily from her exertions, and the nurse seemed to have a look pleased, even though Brent could only see her profile from behind.

"I am concerned whether it is wise for us to remain," Cyrus whispered to him as the court began to settle down. "You are perhaps too agitated."

"I'll be fine," Brent grunted defiantly. As the court settled down, however, Brent let himself agree that Cyrus was correct; he was in danger of making a scene. He needed to be careful, knowing already that although they were a violation of modern human reasoning, these infamous trials were something he was out of his league to confront on his own.

Magistrate Corwin spoke as he read from his parchment paper. "We will now begin the examination of the accus-ed, so nam-ed as the following: Lisa Carson, Jeremy Macer, and the former slave and now freedman Duncan."

The three accused individuals stood still for a moment as their names were called out and entered into record by Sewell.

After an exchange of glances between Magistrate Hathorne and Reverend Parris, the judge began his examination.

"Betty Parris," the magistrate's voice softened a bit as he addressed the child. She turned in her father's lap and faced the judge. "Do you know who hath hurt you?"

The little girl nodded, and pointed to Lisa. Lisa gasped and covered her mouth with one hand, taking an unconscious step back and bumping into the wood paneling of the left lower pews. She started shaking her head without words.

"Lisa Carson," Hathorne turned to face her, and most gravely asked her, "What do you say, are you guilty?"

"What? No!" she said, looking horrified. Brent saw Jeremy watch the exchange, and could tell that he was preparing to fight for his girlfriend. Brent hoped Jeremy would stay calm. He then remembered he needed to hope he himself would stay calm, too.

"This woman hath come and pinched me since I was awakened this morn," Betty whined, her outstretched arm pointed an index finger at Lisa. The tone in the girl's voice even made Brent wonder about the truth, despite the fact he knew that there was no possible way her testimony was true.

"I've never even seen that girl before! I wouldn't ever hurt anyone!" Lisa cried out, looking pleadingly to the magistrates and then the audience. The magistrates made no face, but simply returned to their papers, while Sewell diligently wrote down minutes of the proceedings.

"You see this girl accuse you. She was afflicted but until you laid your hand on her," Hathorne leaned towards her from his seat. "Before God, tell us now, what have you done to this child?"

Lisa shook her head incredulously. "Nothing!" she said defensively, then looked at Jeremy, who leaned towards her nearly imperceptibly. She then looked back towards Hathorne. "Why won't you believe me?"

"How can you say you know nothing, when you see this tormented, who accuses you," Hathorne demanded without mercy, "Would you have me accuse my self?"

Lisa suddenly turned and buried her head into Jeremy's shoulder, sobbing hard.

"Is this really necessary?" Jeremy asked the judge as he wrapped his shackled arms around her. "Your honor, we have never seen this kid before!"

"No, Jeremy," Lisa sniffed as she pulled back from him. "I don't want you trying to protect me. They'll just keep hurting you." She wiped her tears away and turned to the magistrate, gently stepping out of Jeremy's arms.

"Your honor," Lisa began, and then after a short sniffle, said, "All I can tell you, sir, is that I have never seen her before, and that I have not done anything that would hurt her. You can believe me or don't, but that's the truth."

The magistrates both raised their eyebrows and exchanged surprised glances with each other. Lisa suspected they'd never been talked to like that before.

"How far have you complied with Satan whereby he takes this advantage against you?" Hathorne continued, his tone softer yet carrying a more suspicious tenor.

Lisa gave a resigned chuckle as she wiped some remaining tears. "Satan? Really?"

After a few moments of steady stares by the judges, she sighed heavily and said with a hint of irritability, "No, I have never done anything for Satan."

"How do you explain her fits, then?" Corwin asked.

"I don't know," Lisa said with slumped shoulders, and then putting her hands in the back pockets of her jeans. Jeremy stepped back to let her have their full attention, and Duncan put his hands in his own pockets. "Has it occurred to you that she might be faking it?"

"You dare claim my child to be an agent of sin?" Reverend Parris shouted at her as he stood abruptly, pushing the bench back a few inches; Betty remained clung to her father's side.

The magistrates swiftly faced Parris with expressions of extreme disdain, but before they could speak, the doctor's assistant suddenly screamed and stood. Her hands were flat against her hips; for a flash, Brent thought she was getting ready to draw a gun.

"Elizabeth?" Griggs stood and reached an arm to her with concern.

"Please don't touch me, Doctor!" Elizabeth pleaded.

"Young Elizabeth Hubbard? What is it, girl? What is the matter?" Corwin demanded. Brent sensed that Corwin did not appreciate his courtroom getting out of control like this.

"My arms!" She cried out, and flapped her elbows to convince them that her hands were somehow stuck to her sides. "I cannot move my hands! And I feel pain in my wrists!" She wailed briefly.

"Who or what is doing this to you?" Griggs asked with great concern. The rest of the audience hovered above their seats, trying to follow this chaos.

After a few moments, she looked up at the three shackled people, and cried out, "Him! It's the Negro man!"

Everyone looked to Duncan, his face frozen in disbelief, and he quickly pulled his chained hands out of his pants pockets. As soon as he did, Elizabeth Hubbard yelped as she pulled her hands from her hips. A number of voices in the audience gasped and began murmuring about this new evidence. Brent fought as hard as ever to remain calm at this whole circus. It was becoming nearly impossible: everything was a frame and setup; there was no real justice happening here.

"For a moment, he appeared to me, holding the Devil's book!" Hubbard said, pointing her hand towards Duncan. Brent had only seen the perplexed expression on Duncan's face a few times before, when with really bad results during initial testing of the Opener. Suddenly, frustration and protectiveness took over his brain. Without realizing it, Brent stood up.

"You lying b—"he began to yell, but was knocked to

the ground, suddenly wrestling with large, strong hands. He tried to regain his grasp of what just happened.

"Please forgive us, your honors," Cyrus' voice quickly pleaded. Brent realized that it was Cyrus who had tackled him. His fury grew towards Cyrus as he continued wrestling him. "I believe my friend has now suffered a fit!"

"What?!" Brent grunted, offended to a level he never knew he could reach. He fought harder to free himself.

"Constable, remove these men from this house!" Hathorne ordered.

"Please, sir," Cyrus said, still struggling with Brent while sitting upon his chest. "If I may, let his tormentor touch him so that he be free of torment, and we would then leave peaceably!"

"Get off me!" Brent demanded, swinging wildly at Cyrus. Cyrus had been holding his wrists, but now he had to find a way to tell Brent something in front of thirty witnesses.

Hathorne waved his hand in gesture to Herrick to lead the prisoners to the scuffling men. The whole room watched this in utter silence, except for the shuffling of feet and jingling of chains.

"Tell us who afflicts you, man!" Corwin called out.

"I'm not—oof!" Brent was again interrupted midsentence, this time by a bounce on his solar plexus by Cyrus.

"You must share who torments you, Brent!" Cyrus said loudly and with dramatic flair. He continued to wrestle Brent, who was quickly becoming tired.

"Have the boy touch him first, Joseph!" Hathorne ordered with curiosity. Herrick complied, roughly grabbing Jeremy's wrist by the shackle and yanked him down.

Thinking quickly, Cyrus twisted Brent around and then wrapped his arms around the younger man's neck, making it possible to nestle his mouth near Brent's ear.

"*Accuse him now, or we die,*" Cyrus whispered harshly and very quickly.

Feeling pure hatred at Cyrus, Brent did not see but felt Jeremy's hand touch his upper arm. He struggled against Cyrus, but then let himself obey. Brent fell completely limp, earning a gasp from everyone in the room. Cyrus relaxed his hold on him.

I'm so sorry, Duncan, he thought impotently as he looked up into their astonished faces. Even Duncan was taken aback by this unexpected turn of events. Brent felt horrible, and he knew that there was nothing he could do to undo it.

"We have heard enough. Take the accus-ed back to the jail while we prepare the indictment hearing," Magistrate Jonathan Corwin ordered. "This court will meet again at two hours of the clock this day after noon, for the trial of Lisa Carson, Jeremy Macer, and the Negro Duncan. You will be tried for the high crimes of practicing witchcraft in the presence of this court and God."

CHAPTER XXV

Cyrus remained atop Brent while the magistrates regained order in the meeting house, which took some time because of the difficulty of being heard above all the shouting. Brent fumed from his prone position on the floor, but did not try to wrestle or move Cyrus. *At least he is finally cooperating*, Cyrus mused.

As soon as Magistrate Corwin broke court, Doctor Griggs turned to tend to Brent.

"My boy," Griggs said with concern in an odd, throaty nasal voice, "Are you all right?"

Cyrus got up slowly and allowed Brent to move. The room was almost too noisy to hear the doctor speak, and the movements of the prisoners and court officials leaving briskly were distracting as well. Brent stirred a bit, and slowly began to get up on his elbows.

"Yes, I think so," Brent said with resentment, maintaining his unfriendly glare at Cyrus. Cyrus inhaled deeply and looked around, hoping he could get Brent out quickly before the doctor asked too many of the wrong questions. A few townsmen had encircled Brent; some out of concern, some out of curiosity. Behind the doctor, Cyrus could see the maidservant Elizabeth Hubbard speaking with the Parrises, and glancing occasionally back towards Brent.

He was sure that he had seen eyes of conspiracy and cunning in the maidservant's visage. He turned his attention back to Brent, whose skin was being investigated by Doctor Griggs in the area where Jeremy had touched him.

"My friend," Cyrus forced a smile and grasped the hand of Brent, "Come, let us retire from this excitement and find some rest for you."

Brent did not grasp Cyrus' hand back for a few moments as he sat on his haunches, but after a tight squeeze by Cyrus, he returned the grasp and stood up with Cyrus' help.

"Gads bodikins, my man," Griggs exclaimed, standing to continue his examination. "Let me make sure you are healthy."

"Stop!" Brent said with annoyance, then remembered himself quickly, and added a more respectful "Sir, please. I promise I'm fine."

Griggs froze for a moment, looking suspiciously at Brent. Brent felt it awkward that this man was so closely studying his face, and after a moment, he asked, "Is there something I can help you with, sir?"

"You are a strange boy," Griggs remarked. "You speak rather oddly."

Cyrus heard this, and put a strong hand on Brent's shoulder. Still grasping Brent by the right hand, he began to guide him to the meeting house doorway.

"We really must retire, good Doctor," Cyrus said, smiling with charm and natural good nature. It seemed to work, as the doctor seemed to start forgetting about his suspicions and returned a smile to Cyrus. "Please understand. We thank you for tending him so well!"

"It is my pleasure," Griggs said absently, now sounding a bit confused. Quickly, Cyrus made for the door, and he and Brent walked through. The August sun was nowhere near a cloud, and so it was as warm on Cyrus' face as he had felt in several days. After they had walked several dozen yards, Brent started to wriggle in Cyrus' grasp.

"You will not make another scene," Cyrus said firmly with his hushed tone.

"Well let go of me!" Brent hissed, still wriggling.

"In due course, naturally," Cyrus said tersely, casually tossing smiles to Salem passers-by. After a few hundred more yards, when they had reached an area of the road that was much more sparsely populated, Cyrus let go of him completely and began to walk even more briskly.

His mind was working quickly, thinking about the events that had just occurred in the meeting house and how they impacted the plan Cyrus and Aaron had begun to put together that morning.

Brent had to jog every few steps just to keep up with Cyrus' tall stride. He was seething and wanted to confront him about what had just happened, but he was frustrated that Cyrus kept walking without pause.

"So where are we going?" Brent's voice was filled with anger as he hopped over a pile of horse manure in the road. They turned a corner onto the street where the Marble Wharf Inn and Tavern sat.

"Back to our room," Cyrus said simply.

"You don't even want to talk about what just happened?" Brent asked with amazement.

"No," Cyrus said, keeping his answer brief and disinterested. He was again tired of Brent's manner, and was now in the mood to aggravate him more.

Brent wanted to stop and knock the guy down, but he had enough difficulty just keeping up with the man's tall stride. *This is infuriating*, Brent thought angrily. After a couple minutes of walking, during which Cyrus continued waving his greeting to every person they passed by on the road, they arrived at the front of the Inn. The horse was still tied to the wooden post; Brent briefly wondered if it was okay that it had been left for the past couple of hours like that.

They walked along the side of the building, past the entrance to the tavern, and around the back to where the room was. As Cyrus opened the door, Brent made up his mind and steeled himself. As soon as the door was open and Cyrus had stepped in partially, he turned to allow Brent passage through. Brent reached back and focused every ounce of his anger and hatred into his balled up fist, and landed a right hook on Cyrus' jaw.

Cyrus was not prepared for it, and went tumbling into the room, rolling to a stop at the foot of the bed, his vision spinning dizzily. He blinked several times to and tried to shake his head back to normal. Brent stepped in and closed the door.

"Damn your impetuous nature!" Cyrus spat loudly,

slowly getting up. Brent continued walking towards him. Having traded fists in taverns on many previous occasions while inebriated, Cyrus was more than capable to launch his fist back to Brent's charging form. His knuckles met Brent's face as he stood to his full height, and sent the boy reeling backwards into the door.

Cyrus did not follow with a charge, choosing instead to stand unsteadily as his head finished clearing. His left cheek and teeth tingled and felt dense and numb. Cyrus looked over at Brent, who had slumped somewhat against the door, but did not fall to the ground.

Brent's whole head vibrated, as if he had been lying on a massager too long. He tried to remember what had just happened, but he knew he was angry. Quickly, he began to remember Cyrus' manipulation, and he let out a yell and charged the man. He went in for a mid-section tackle, but Cyrus was ready for it, and grabbed Brent over the back as Brent wrapped himself around Cyrus' midsection. The two men flew onto the bed and tumbled onto the floor, now a mess of arms and legs. After a minute or so of wrestling, Brent grabbed the wooden leg of the bed and pulled himself out of Cyrus' grasp. Cyrus held fast to one of Brent's legs, and Brent kicked out with his free leg, landing on Cyrus' shoulder with his heel. Cyrus let out a grunt of pain and released Brent's foot. Brent scrambled to the other side of the room, stumbling as he tried to catch his breath and his balance. Cyrus stood with one hand clutching his sore shoulder, panting heavily as he did so.

"What the hell is the matter with you?" Brent hollered

angrily.

"Me?" Cyrus yelled back, matching Brent's anger. "You struck first!"

"You made me betray Duncan and them!" Brent accused him, pointing a wobbly forefinger at Cyrus.

"Yes, of course I did!" Cyrus declared, annoyed that Brent did not understand his motive.

"So this is how you people do things here?" Brent demanded with bewilderment. "Betrayal at a moment's notice? 'Save your skin'? 'Every man for himself'?" he ranted madly.

"That 'betrayal' actually helped them and protected us!" Cyrus retorted. "You let yourself become uncontrolled, and in doing so you nearly put us on trial!"

"She was lying!" Brent said, his exasperation growing. "You expected to just let her lie like that?"

"Yes!" Cyrus said with eyes wide and eyebrows high. "You must come to understand a fact of this time," Cyrus began, lowered his voice to a conversational level, "The people of this precinct are uneasy of mind and anxious about witchcraft. This court is appointed by His Majesty's Royal Governor to hear cases of suspected witchcraft; every act that you do, every word that you say, and every man or woman you offend will raise in their minds the specter of you being a witch."

"And you don't believe in witches," Brent asked sarcastically, putting his hands on his hips.

"It does not matter what I believe," Cyrus shot back. "What matters is what the magistrates believe! Every thing you witnessed is evidence against them."

"But there was no evidence!" Brent protested. "Just a spoiled-rotten kid who pretended to be hurt by their 'ghosts'!" He finger-quoted the word, again drawing a puzzled look from Cyrus.

"That *was* the evidence," Cyrus replied. "It is called 'spectral evidence', and this court permits it against the accus-ed in the trial."

"So then how did you making me accuse them help?" Brent asked, raising his eyebrows with skepticism.

"Most anyone who accuses another person will be found innocent," Cyrus explained calmly. "Further to the point, now the court will have reason to convict all three as one instead of separately. This will help with our plan; at least they will be in the same place at the same time."

Brent considered Cyrus' points, working out how this development fit in with their rescue plans.

Cyrus walked out from behind the bed and over to the writing table, beginning to tend to his clothes. Brent watched him quietly for a few moments; his anger at Cyrus was subsiding as the realities of witch trials settled in his mind.

"So now what," Brent asked.

Cyrus retied his cravat, which was simply a long white towel that was like a floppy, oversized bowtie. "Now," he said, "I will return to the town and attempt to learn more about what is to come. You will stay here and wait for Aaron to return from Boston, and plan further in the meantime."

Brent bristled at being told to stay in the room. "You don't trust me?" he challenged Cyrus.

"No, I do not," Cyrus said simply. "I will tell them that you are tired from your ordeal, and that you have remained in the room to rest. Do not leave." he looked seriously at Brent, who rolled his eyes in resigned agreement.

"Fine," Brent huffed, holding up his hands in defeat. "I'll stay here and see what ideas I can think up."

Cyrus began to open the door, but then paused. "You have a strong arm," he complimented, rubbing his cheek briefly. "Yet you are impatient and emotional. Let us see if you are also clever as you claim. I shall see you later," he said, and disappeared out the door.

As soon as Brent had fallen limp and quiet, Jeremy stood dumbfounded. The entire room suddenly burst into outrage and calls for their immediate execution. At least in Jeremy's mind, the magistrates were able to successfully conclude this first part of the trial with dignified control. Unfortunately, the mob was quick to rejoin their fury after the judges began to leave the room. They now were converging on the accused as the Constable Herrick led them out.

The constable was joined by Constable Jonathan Smith as they emerged from the meeting house, assisting him in securing the now dangerous path back to the oxcart. Jeremy, Duncan, and Lisa huddled close to each other as they walked fast towards the wagon; ironically, the jail now would become a haven of safety for them.

The three chained prisoners clambered onto the oxcart, each one helping the others to get on board and to their spots. At least a dozen protestors continued to surround them while yelling and grabbing at them, until the constables called on their horses to start the ride back to the jail. As the cart lurched and sped away from the curious meeting house that sat in the middle of the street. People continued spilling out of the single entrance of the house, and even a few were jogging furiously after the cart, yelling and shouting in a wild chaos of sound.

"What the heck was that?" Jeremy said to Duncan with exasperation as he shifted from sitting on a knee to his bottom.

Duncan looked at Jeremy, and then at Lisa, whose expression asked the same question. He considered his protégé briefly, and then shrugged his shoulders.

"I don't know," Duncan said, frowning at his inability to see the logic behind Brent's accusation. "I really did not see that coming at all." He thought about it further. "Whatever it is, however, I'm sure he has a good reason for it."

"Ha," Jeremy laughed singly and without humor. He looked at Lisa.

"Are you ok?" Jeremy said, glancing up to check to make sure that he was not being so loud that he got the attention of the constables.

"Yeah, I'm fine," she said with a tone of acceptance. She still sniffled a little bit from time to time, but her tears were otherwise all but gone. Jeremy sensed that she had finally accepted the reality of this situation. "This whole thing is so stupid, but I'm not going to let it upset me anymore."

Jeremy regarded her for a moment, and exchanged glances with Duncan, who shrugged lightly with his shoulders and eyebrows, mouthing the word *women*. Jeremy agreed; even after being with the same girl for over a year, and the previous one for three years, he didn't know what to do. He looked back at Lisa.

"How's your face?" she asked, reaching up to touch him where she had punched him earlier; Jeremy flinched, almost imperceptibly.

"I'm not going to hit you," she said, almost as if it was silly of him to think so. Her hands stopped short of him, restrained by the shackles.

"I know," Jeremy said quickly, trying to inject some toughness into his voice. He leaned forward let her touch his bruise, and for a brief moment they connected.

"I am sorry that I did hit you," Lisa said, sweetness and remorse in her tone carrying the weight of her apology.

"It's all right," Jeremy said, smiling lightly. "I'm sure I had it coming."

"You think so, eh?" Lisa returned the smile.

"Well," Jeremy said, turning to include Duncan in the surprisingly casual conversation. "I'm not sure what it was I said that got under your skin enough to do that," he said bemusedly, "but if it made *you* hit me, it can only mean that I must have made a big error somewhere."

"What on Earth possessed you come through in the first

place?" Duncan asked Lisa abruptly. "I mean, I can guess his reasons, but yours aren't so obvious."

"I was concerned for him," Lisa said matter-of-factly, looking at her boyfriend as she answered. "He was walking through some time portal thing to God-knows-where, and I didn't want him to be alone."

Jeremy felt appreciation for her concern for him. He picked up a straw of hay. "Yeah," he sighed, twiddling the hay with both hands as he glanced up to Duncan. "I probably should have thought twice before jumping in after you."

"What makes you say that?" Duncan asked casually. He extended a hand towards Jeremy's bedraggled appearance. "That is, of course, aside from your collection of bumps and bruises."

Jeremy hung his head low for a few moments as he summoned up the courage to admit his faults.

"I wasn't sure what you guys were up to," he began, clearing his throat. "With the time thing just left carelessly in the woods, and people popping in from the seventeenth century, and you guys chasing me, I wondered if you wouldn't care to try to help Aaron and Cyrus." Jeremy looked at Duncan, who did not allow his expression to change. Duncan wanted to give Jeremy the full chance to say all he felt he had to say. After a few beats, Jeremy continued.

"So, I jumped through to make sure you didn't try anything," Jeremy said sheepishly, realizing how silly the idea sounded, now that he was sitting shackled in a wooden

311

oxcart and being pulled to jail as an accused witch in Salem, sixteen ninety-two. "Anyway, when I jumped, that wasn't all I was thinking about."

Both Lisa and Duncan watched him intently, each waiting to hear what else he'd been thinking.

"I jumped through because I wanted to travel through time," Jeremy finally admitted, feeling ridiculous in front of both his girlfriend and a man he had known for less than a day. "You know," he laughed at himself, "I promised Doctor Arvind that I would be responsible with the time machine," he explained, randomly picking up hay straw bits and tossing them aside. "I let him down." Jeremy felt like a complete jerk. He turned to Lisa. "I let you down. And now we're in this mess. I'm sorry." Jeremy turned back and stared at the top of a house as they turned the corner onto the street where the jail lay, avoiding the eyes of both Duncan and Lisa.

Everyone sat in silence for a few moments. Lisa felt a mixture of understanding and forgiveness, and a bit of anger at Jeremy's recklessness. She had on many occasions fussed at him for doing things without considering the consequences. However, Duncan spoke up, breaking her from her thoughts.

"Jeremy," Duncan began gently, now as a father would with a son, "It's all right. Everything you have said and done is completely understandable. *We* were careless; both in the past and in the future. I probably should not have stepped through either." Jeremy looked up in surprise, and Lisa did too.

"Hey, don't forget," Duncan smiled, "I invented that thing, and it was because I wanted to travel through time, too." He let his remark sit for a few moments. Then, Duncan extended a hand, which Jeremy slowly accepted.

Jeremy appreciated Duncan's effort to make him feel better. He turned back to Lisa. "So we're okay now?"

"Yeah, I guess so," Lisa said coyly, hamming up her words with a smile.

He'd resolved that he had indeed broken his word to Doctor Arvind, that Lisa's issues here were the result of his decisions; he must work better at keeping his word properly. He also wanted to figure out a way out of this; there was no way he was going to let a bunch of paranoid villagers hurt Lisa any more. They had to find a way to escape.

"Then let's figure a way out of this," Jeremy said resolutely.

"Yes, let's do," Duncan said, sitting up straight as the cart pulled to a stop in front of the jail.

"Hey guys," Lisa said quickly, knowing they had only a few moments before being separated again. "Just for the record," she began, scooting to the edge of the cart first, "I *don't* want to travel through time again. Except to get home."

She hopped off the cart, her chains jingling as they hit the crusty mud-dirt, and waited for Constable Smith to escort her back to her side of the jail.

CHAPTER XXVI
Around 1:45 P.M.

Lisa sat on the dirt floor surrounded by about fifteen other women, most of whom had told her of their own imprisonment due to accusations of witchcraft. She couldn't help but notice that a majority of the women were past middle age. The stark, sad exception was that one of the prisoners who sat around her was a four-year old little girl named Dorcas Good. The small girl was listening quietly and nestled against a seventy-year-old woman who called herself Martha Corey. Lisa felt horrified and even angry that a small child had been imprisoned and now sat in her own set of shackles and chains.

Dorcas herself had said little around Lisa, and seemed very shy, but the women of this impromptu support group had told Lisa of the child's plight. Dorcas' mother was a woman named Sarah Good, and was one of the first people accused of being witches earlier in the year, back in February. Lisa's heart broke further for Dorcas as she learned more about Sarah Good, who had been accused while pregnant, and had given birth in jail (Wilmot showed Lisa the cell where Sarah had given birth to her doomed baby, Mercy Good. Mercy died within weeks of her birth). Sarah's husband, William, had testified against her at her trial, saying he believed that she either was or would soon be a witch. Dorcas had been arrested herself in late March, over a month after her mother; worse still, she had been forced to testify against her mother at her trial. The women said Dorcas had a wild streak, occasionally running up and down the long hallway of stalls and cells, and even biting the Constable a couple of times on the hand. Since Sarah's hanging a month ago, Dorcas' behavior had become odder. She had less frequent wild fits, but when she had them, she was far more inconsolable than ever. Her father visited her once every week or so, but only briefly at that. Lisa would have loved to meet William, her so-called father; she wanted to string him up by his testicles for treating his child so uncaringly.

Lisa had almost broken into tears while the women shared each of their own personal stories of how they became accused and imprisoned as witches.

Lisa asked them at one point about why they did not try to escape. A few told her that they did not want to risk being killed by the constable's musket as they escaped, but most of the women simply shook their heads in honest confusion. "We may be guilty by the words of children and men," one sweet old lady called Ann Foster told her, "But God has put us in here. Who are we but to decide our own innocence and flee lawlessly?" Several ladies nodded in agreement with Ann. Lisa struggled to see her point of view, but simply could not; she realized that debating it would get her nowhere, and let the conversation drift elsewhere.

Nearly every woman in this circle strongly agreed that

there was not a real witchcraft in either Salem Town or in Salem Village, but that the problem was in fact the girls who had accused them. Lisa told them of her own experience a few hours before, to which Wilmot reiterated her feelings that the accusers needed some time in the stocks outside.

Lisa was about to ask a question to Elizabeth Proctor when the jail door opened up, revealing the Constable. Lisa felt surprise and pity as the women suddenly scattered along the straw-and-dirt floor back to their darkened cells at his appearance.

As Constable Smith came over to her, Lisa heard a skittish woman further down the row of cells beckon him. Without word, Smith walked past Lisa and went to talk to the woman, who had stayed in her cell while the others had been gathered a few minutes before. After a few moments, as Lisa watched them interact soundlessly, she suddenly felt a cold chill in her stomach when both turned to look at Lisa; she must be the topic of their conversation. The woman was probably in her fifties, as best as Lisa could estimate, and she had shoulder-length grey hair, except for one longer lock that was solid brown and was several feet long.

Lisa wondered what they could be talking about when Smith turned back to the woman, nodded quickly and then began to walk back to her.

"It is time now fer you to return fer your trial, witch," Constable Smith said, grabbing Lisa roughly by the elbow just as she had gotten to her feet. His attitude seemed to have changed; this morning he had been lustful and harsh but now he was disgusted and impatient. As they exited the jail and stepped into the August midday sun, Lisa could not help but suspect that the old woman in the back was responsible for Constable Smith's new level of disdain for her.

2 P.M.
Salem Meeting House

Jeremy surveyed the room, having just been led into place between Duncan and Lisa by both constables. The small meeting house, serving as a courthouse today, seemed to be twice as full since the morning's examination. There were people standing outside the building, unable to get in due to the overcrowding. Through the single entry door, Jeremy could see mid-afternoon sunlight bouncing off the white collars and cravats as the genteel and common men milled outside, presumably gossiping about the trial that was going to start soon. Up in the balcony, Jeremy could see Cyrus, but neither Brent nor Aaron. Jeremy wondered about their absence, as well as Cyrus' own actions earlier.

Duncan and Jeremy exchanged a brief glance. "Remember Jeremy, keep your cool."

"I will," Jeremy sighed as he turned back to face forward. His stomach growled and popped for the first time in several hours. He felt like he could eat anything given to him, but he no longer felt the strong pull of his hunger. He knew that the other two felt similar, having discussed their hunger pangs in the cart ride back to the courthouse.

"Come to order!" bellowed the man who was called Stephen Sewell, the court clerk. The murmur died down rather quickly, and the sound of wood against wood barked throughout the room as men took their seats, including the overhead balcony above Jeremy's head.

Sewell stepped aside so that several men could enter the room, all of them apparently magistrates. Jeremy recognized only two of them from the morning session; Sewell called out their names as they reached the raised wooden stage and took their places behind their table.

"Lieutenant Governor William Stoughton, chief and presiding magistrate," Sewell bellowed, now unnecessarily, into the room. "Honorable Jonathan Corwin," he continued in turn, "Honorable Doctor Bartholomew Gedney, Honorable Jonathan Hathorne, Honorable Samuel Sewell, Honorable Peter Sargent, and Honorable John Richards."

The only sounds in the room after his voice went silent were that of robes and footfalls of the court officials taking their seats. Sewell the Clerk walked up the middle of the room and took his place opposite from the prisoners, as he had stood previously. The magistrates set about reviewing the papers prepared for them at their seats.

After several silent moments, the Chief Magistrate Stoughton spoke.

"Is His Majesty's Governors Council appointee present?" Stoughton spoke with a deep, nasally voice that reminded Jeremy of a bad Bob Hope impression.

"The man is here," Sewell the Clerk responded. "I

present Mister Wait Still Winthrop." At that, a man entered the room and walked towards the front, taking a seat on the only clear bench in the whole room, directly in front of the panel of judges. He bowed slightly before taking a seat and opening a book he had with him.

"Also representing the Crown and the good town of Salem is Mister George Herrick," Sewell the Clerk said. A tall man, perhaps in his mid-thirties and very handsome with well-groomed black hair and a very crisp appearance, strode with great dignity into the room, bowed upon reaching the front, and took a seat near Winthrop. Jeremy suddenly realized that seated on his own side of the short aisle were several men from the group who had arrested his trio the night before.

"Let us now begin this session of the Court of Oyer and Terminer," Stoughton said. "Please proceed as you will, Mister Sewell."

"Hear Hear, sir," Sewell the Clerk responded officially, and then addressed the congregation. "Oyea, Oyea, this Court is now in order and will hear any concerns that men may have. I invite the good man Nicholas Noyes to lead us in prayer."

A man in the second row of the center benches stood and began to pray in a fashion not unlike, to Jeremy's mind, those semi-rambling prayers he'd heard on television or radio or occasionally at church. When the man finished, the entire room concluded with a unison "Ah-men," and he sat.

Two justices exchanged glances, and Magister Corwin

spoke.

"In deference to the chaos and concern with regard to events that did transpire during the examination of the accus-ed," Corwin spoke clearly, "These who stand accus-ed were not present when the evidence was presented to the Grand Jury assembled at that time. This Jury has concluded a verdict on the indictment of these individuals, and will now read the indictment for the Court to hear," he finished. A man seated in the lower benches under the balcony and behind Sewell the Clerk rose, and accepted a parchment handed to him by Sewell.

"The Juror for our Sovereign Lord and Lady the King and Queen presents that Lisa Carson of unknown place…" the man read unevenly, apparently having difficulty reading the paper.

"…and Jeremy Macer of unknown place, and the former slave Duncan of Port Royal. The aforesaid Woman, Man, and Negro, sometime in this August last 1692 aforesaid and diverse other days and times as well before as after. Certain detestable arts called witchcrafts and sorceries, wickedly, maliciously and feloniously hath used, practiced and exercised at and in the Towne of Salem, in the County of Essex."

Jeremy sighed as he listened, choosing to be bored rather than get riled up. The man drew a breath before continuing, still sounding like a first-grader trying to read, "Aforesaid upon and against one Betty Parris of Andover, a child, and one Elizabeth Hubbard, a single Woman, by which wicked arts whence the said Betty Parris, on the day and year aforesaid, and diverse other days and Times as well before as after, was and is tortured, afflicted, tormented, consumed, pinched, and wasted against the peace of Sovereign Lord and Lady the King and Queen, their Crown, and dignity and the laws in that case made and provided."

Jeremy looked around the room, then at his girlfriend and finally Duncan as the man finished. He turned back, raised his right hand, and the jingling of the chains drew the attention of the entire court. Corwin raised an eyebrow and exchanged a glance with Stoughton.

"You wish to make a statement?" Stoughton asked unhappily.

"Well," Jeremy said, hearing Lisa's hushed *Jeremy, please don't* behind him. "It's more of a question."

"Proceed," Stoughton intoned.

"I have no idea what that guy just said," Jeremy said plainly, shaking his head and spreading his hands wide in a broad shrug. "What?" he said to make his point clearer.

"I warn you now, boy," Hathorne interceded, "That this honorable court and its members will not tolerate outbursts or childish irreverence. I have been told of your indiscretion towards members of this town, and you will be removed if you prove to behave in such a manner during this trial."

Jeremy became annoyed quickly. He took a breath and chose his words carefully, however. "Your honor," he said slowly, trying to sound as respectful as possible. "I didn't mean to offend you. I only mean that we are on trial, and I have no idea what he just said about us, and what we are accused of," Jeremy said, indicating towards the jury man.

"To put it plainly," Magistrate Gedney said, "you three have each presented yourselves to young Betty Parris and to Elizabeth Hubbard, as well as to the man called Brent, as spectral spirits. This can only be performed and happen if you practice the detestable evil of witchcraft. You will be tried on that evidence, and on other evidence that the court will now hear." At that, Gedney turned his attention back to the court and made it quite clear that the members of the court would not hear any other requests from the accused.

Jeremy felt fury at this treatment, and was astonished at how far it was from the kind of court proceedings he'd seen on TV. Still, he simply took a couple of deep breaths, and shrugged his shoulders to loosen his tightened muscles.

"With the accus-ed so indicted on these charges," Corwin said, "We now permit those with further evidence to present such for the consideration of our minds."

At this point, the slender man named George Herrick stood and took to the area in front of the Judge's cloth-covered table and the benches, so all could see him.

"If your worshipful honors will permit, I wish to present Elizabeth Hubbard for her testimony to be entered and recorded," he spoke in a friendly tone, although he was sincere in his words and demeanor. The full court nodded their approval, at which the girl who had accused Duncan rose from her seat on the center benches where she had sat earlier.

She spoke clearly, with nervous glances towards

Jeremy, Duncan and Lisa, as if she expected them to perform more pretend acts of witchcraft.

"I visited with the good Doctor Griggs up to Reverend Parris' house on the morn of this day, only to see Betty Parris who laid speechless and in a sad condition. I saw there the apparitions of all three of those who now are in irons, in a most dreadful manner, which did affright me most grievously." Hubbard began to crack in her voice. "And immediately the slave Duncan did set upon me most dreadfully and tortured me, and he was almost ready to choke me to death and urged me vehemently to write in his book. He did most grievously afflict and torment me during the time of his examination also," she explained, conjuring tears as she testified.

Jeremy checked Duncan, and continued to be amazed by his stoicism.

The panel of judges listened intently to the girl; Sewell the Clerk writing fast to record her statements, while some magistrates took occasional notes and the rest simply sat and paid attention. Duncan fought the anger her false accusations, and he was further upset as he could not think of any other explanation than that she knew she was lying. Duncan lifted his chin unconsciously as he listened to her continue.

"During the time of her examination," Hubbard continued, "I saw the woman Lisa most grievously afflict and torment Betty Parris by twisting and almost choking her to death. And I verily believe in my heart that the Negro Duncan and the woman Lisa each to be most dreadful witches, and that she and he hath very quickly afflicted and tormented me and the child Betty Parris." Duncan raised his hand this time, and though his sounds drew glances from the court, none responded to his raised hand but instead turned to face again Elizabeth Hubbard. Duncan was unsure if they ignored him because of Jeremy's remarks or because he was, in their eyes, a former slave. He tried to convince himself that it was to do with Jeremy's sarcasm, but deep inside he felt pretty sure it was the other reason.

"Do you make these statements and give this testimony as the true oath of your experience?" Magistrate Gedney asked her.

"I do, Magistrate," Elizabeth said, giving a subtle curtsey as she did. "May God strike me with His wrath and fury should I speak falsely." She bowed her head in conclusion; the magistrates spent a minute or so each taking notes on the things she had said. Every word out of her mouth now seemed to spark a nasty flame in Duncan's stomach. He tried at first not to, but found himself quickly despising the young woman.

"Very good, thank you," George Herrick said to her and the court, and she sat down. "I wish now to present for the court the eyewitness accounts, as given by those who actively did see and watch the accus-ed perform hideous magic."

Magistrate Stoughton simply waved for the prosecutor to carry on.

"Will the man Mister David Flint please rise to give

your testimony," George Herrick requested evenly. A middle-aged man with unkempt, shoulder-length dirty blond hair, dull brown clothing, and perpetually squinting eyes, stood at the mention of his name.

"You have given testimony in private to the members of this court, related to the misdeeds of the accus-ed," George Herrick stated; Flint began nodding even before Herrick had finished. "Will you, in the sight of God and this court room, please do tell us the things you have seen of these people?"

"Yes, I will," Flint said. For the next minute or so, he repeated much of the same story, about having stepped outside and of the tavern, and seeing Duncan, Jeremy and Lisa appearing out of nothingness, and that he had summoned others to arrest them.

"So these people did not appear to you and molest you in any way?" Herrick suggested.

"No sir," Flint responded.

"Nor did they try to afflict your or seek to have you sign the book of the Devil?" Herrick further pressed, his demeanor reflecting that he knew the answer.

"No, sir, I have not been visited by their apparitions," Flint said.

"Then please share with us that which makes you believe that the actions of the accus-ed were magic and the result of witchcraft?" Herrick challenged him.

"It was the manner in which they appeared," Flint rasped, his tone mystified and eerie. "I did see a circle whose height was that of a tall man, and that circle was made of a strange fire. I have never before seen flame that behaved as that did." Flint mimed his fingers in a circle as he described what he saw. "It was yellow and blue," he continued, "and as it burned in the air without wood or grease, I witnessed them come into our world from it and then fight."

"On your oath do you swear this testimony to be the truth?" Magistrate Corwin asked, watching the man closely.

"Indeed I do, Honorable Corwin," Flint nodded in punctuation.

"The guy can barely see," Jeremy whispered sideways so that Duncan would hear; Duncan quietly grunted an amused agreement. His words drew the suspicious attention of a couple of judges, but Jeremy straightened up quickly and felt that he had successfully played it off when they turned back to take their notes of Flint's account.

After a few more minutes of note-taking, Flint sat back down, and George Herrick spoke again.

"I now call upon the good men and citizens Misters Franklin Peters, Charles Martin, and Jefferson Smith, who also have seen similar acts of magic."

The men stood, and Herrick asked them to recount their experience. Franklin, who had appeared disheveled and not very hygienic the night before, now stood clean-shaven and sober, and wore well-kept clothing. He spoke for the three men.

"Gentlemen of the Court, I would say that we," he indicated his two colleagues, "that is, me, Jefferson and

Charles, was on a hunting party just returning that afternoon on August the nineteenth when we encountered three men on the main road to Boston." He paused for effect, and then continued. "They was without horse or wagon, and their dressing was strange; I give you my word that I have never before seen them here in Salem."

Sewell the Clerk continued writing without pause. Once he and a couple of judges had finished making notes, they looked up to him for further testimony.

"We asked if we could help them any, they said they was just passing through. They did not want our help," he said. Then he faced Duncan, Jeremy and Lisa and said with deep disgust, "I bet they got their help when they sold their souls to Satan!"

Several hushed comments made their way amongst the many spectators at this accusation. Duncan could not help but notice several satisfied smiles from the court members and Prosecutor Herrick.

"Please tell us what you witnessed, sir," Herrick prodded with satisfaction.

"At this point, we wished them good day, and as we passed by, one pulled out a white cigar and a sort of silver broach, and created fire in his hand!" Again, murmurs of intrigue wound through the courtroom, prompting several magistrates to look at their prisoners with disgust.

"David!" Duncan cursed under his breath. "I'm going to kill that kid when we get back."

"Well," Franklin continued, "Jefferson was first to pull his musket on them, but they did then run when we demanded they identify themselves properly."

"The men you met," Hathorne interrupted, "Are any of those three men here now?"

"Your honor, I tell you that they are not here, but I know these three have conspired with them," Franklin accused, then looked around the room as he finished, saying, "for as we gave chase, upon reaching a large pond, we did see the man create fire and lightning with his hand, and he did certainly create the very circle which the respectable David Flint has described to you. The men walked through it, over water, and then disappeared to our eyes and were gone from this world!"

CHAPTER XXVII

The implications of this startling testimony drew a collective gasp from the audience. Duncan watched all the people react; his jaw set as his mouth tightened. He chastised himself inwardly for not anticipating this piece of evidence as various shouts for their immediate execution rose above the din. His mind raced for a solution; as the leader of the first expedition, he felt the desire to take responsibility for his team's actions, especially since it aggravated an already-paranoid period in history.

Jeremy and Lisa both turned to face him, both confused and a bit angry.

"You didn't say anything about that!" Jeremy hissed through gritted teeth; luckily, he'd kept his voice just low enough to be unheard over the continuing furor.

"Shh! Not now!" Duncan hissed in return. He looked at both of his fellow prisoners, still trying to think of how to get them out of this mess. Regardless of how brash Jeremy and Lisa had been in following him, Duncan still was responsible for this whole issue. He had to do something to protect them, even if it meant his life.

He was about to call out, but then raised his hands again instead, hoping to be given the chance to speak this time. To his surprise, Constable Smith saw his hand and indicated as much to the magistrates; several wig-wearing heads turned to face him, exchanging glances in the process.

"The accus-ed Negro man Duncan wishes to speak," Hathorne announced loudly after a few moments. The room fell silent with abnormal abruptness at this news, and Hathorne continued, "Do you wish to contest this testimony?"

"No, Your Honor, Sir," Duncan said evenly, although almost forgetting the requisite 'sir' at the end, "I wish to corroborate it."

The collection of seventeenth-century American Britons in the room seemed unable to handle any more surprises, as they again broke out into discussion. Even the magistrate panel did not seem to expect this and were conferring on what to do next. Jeremy and Lisa turned to face him again; this time Jeremy stepped in front of Duncan.

"What are you doing?!" the younger man exclaimed, his eyes wide with confusion.

"You're just going to have to trust me," Duncan said, trying not to move his lips much. As he said it, the two constables and the man called Nicholas Noyes had been summoned to the Magistrate's table. A moment later, they began to walk through the room, apparently warning every man to be silent. The din faded slowly, until Corwin rejoined his fingertips in a steepled fashion and spoke loudly.

"This Court, as a representative of our Sovereign Lord and Lady the King and Queen, demands good conduct of the people of this town in which we hold this trial," he spoke very clearly and with great authority. He looked at every person in the room, both on the lower level and the balconies. "The facts and truths of the acts of the accus-ed perhaps are certain to unsettle you and take you unawares, but if the gentlemen of this room cannot behave in a dignified manner during the trial, the meeting house shall indeed be cleared. We will have justice, in the name of God and our Sovereign, and we shall achieve it with dignity. Is this warning clear to the congregation?"

Collectively, dozens of voices echoed their affirmation in the small hall. Stoughton turned to Duncan and spoke for the panel.

"Beware, Negro man," Chief Magistrate Stoughton said, lighting the fire in Duncan's heart that he had to work to suppress, "your testimony will not likely save you from the gallows. Perhaps your soul, but that is for God; this court is only interested in your actions among men."

Duncan began to feel hatred against the judge, and had to fight it. He did not like the idea of hating anyone, and he knew that this man simply lived in a different era, and could not grasp Duncan's equality. At best, however, Duncan was only able to reduce his feelings to loathing. He nodded his understanding as sweat beaded on his brow.

Gathered his thoughts over a few more tense moments, he spoke, making eye contact with both the man who had seen his team's time travel and with the magistrates.

"I am the leader of the men of whom you speak," Duncan said to Franklin. The crowd inhaled audibly, but did not make further sound after a fierce look from Corwin. Franklin drew himself up with a deep breath, as if Duncan's affirmation only made the man angrier. Duncan continued. "I directed them to come here, and I came here after they left. It was not our intention to interfere or harm anyone, and I am truly sorry to have upset you, your party, or the good people of Salem."

Duncan felt a little better after saying that. He looked back at the magistrates, waiting for their response.

"Yet you have afflicted individuals since that time," George Herrick stepped towards him, seemingly out of nowhere.

"No." Duncan replied defensively. "We came here by accident, and we simply want to leave. End of story!"

George Herrick eyed Duncan warily, and then walked back to his spot across the room, sneering along the way.

"We shall see if that is indeed the end of the 'story'," Herrick said. "I now invite the good Doctor William Griggs to give a report of the details of his physical examinations performed this very morning!" Franklin and his friends finally took their seats uncertainly as Griggs rose, parchment in hand.

"Doctor Griggs," Magistrate Gedney spoke this time, saying, "you have dam-ning evidence that was found on the bodies and persons you examined to-day?"

"I do, sir," Griggs replied professionally. He glanced up to Sewell the Clerk to make sure he was ready to record the testimony, and seeing he was ready, Griggs began to read.

"On this very morn by order of their Majesties' Justices,

I went to the prison in Salem to search Jeremy Macer and the Negro slave Duncan, and likewise Lisa Carson." He looked up for a moment, then looked back at his parchment and continued reading. "John Smith, the constable, was in presence, as was my maidservant Elizabeth Hubbard and assistants. All was concerned with me in the search where upon the said Carson, her lower back we found a teat about a quarter of an inch long or better. So, it was that I took a pin from said Hubbard and did run it through the said teat, but there was neither water, blood, nor corruption, nor any other matter. I saith that the said Carson was not in the least sense-able in what we had done, for after I told the said Carson and she knew nothing about said pin."

Duncan and Jeremy looked over at Lisa, who had a hand covering her mouth and a few tears welling in her eyes. She caught their glances and waved her hands dismissively, clearly not wanting them to make a fuss. Jeremy looked up at Duncan, who simply shook his head. Jeremy's face scrunched with annoyance, and he looked back at the doctor. The doctor read further.

"Having searched the bodies of Jeremy Macer and the slave Duncan in the jail, I saith that we do not find anything to farther suspect them by their bodies." Griggs let his words linger as the judges wrote on their own parchments.

"Do you have any more facts of your examination to report?" Magistrate Gedney pressed, his voice implying that he was waiting for more information.

"Yes, I do," Griggs replied. "While examining the said Lisa Carson, we did see that she wears strange clothing as her garments that covered the lower rump of her body. This garment, your Honorable, was most full of colors, being red and white and blue, and spangled with stars, and it shone as though it were silk. This woman has in her mind indecency and she wishes to destroy our Holy ways," Griggs finished with conviction.

Duncan looked at Jeremy, whose eyebrows were almost as high on his head as they could have gone before they furrowed again, but Duncan was glad that the boy had enough courtesy and sense not to look back at her during this awful production.

With Griggs' testimony completed, the court moved on to their next 'witness', which turned out to be Cotton Mather himself. Mather had been sitting beside Griggs, and stood as George Herrick called his name.

"Reverend Mather," Stoughton spoke this time, "the members of this court have become aware of your objection to the testimony gathered this morning during the preliminary examination. Do you have any further evidence to provide for or against these witnesses?"

"Governor," Mather spoke lightly and respectfully, "As I did not personally witness the appearance of any of the accus-ed, I have little direct evidence against any one save for their peculiar dress. I only wish to repeat my concern for the legitimacy of the testimony gathering during the examination."

Stoughton frowned and responded testily. "This Court has accepted the testimony as given and as truth; I warn you, even in your well-received status, do not test our patience in the matter. We invite you to give evidence or be seated."

"Very well, sir," Mather said with grace and dignity. "I then call upon one Mister Cyrus Bartle, late of Falmouth to the south."

Duncan looked up at Cyrus as he stood in his place on the opposing balcony, then back at Jeremy and Lisa; all three shared the same curious confusion. They each returned their attention to Cyrus, whose blank expression betrayed nothing he planned to say in this public forum.

"Mister Bartle," Mather said, craning his head up. "Good day, sir."

"Good day to you, Reverend," Cyrus responded with measured words. "How may I serve you and their Majesty's Court?"

"You spoke to me last night, saying that one of the accus-ed was familiar to your eyes," Mather said.

"I did," Cyrus nodded.

"Tell me now," Mather instructed him, "Do you still suspect familiarity with one of the prisoners?"

"I do not, Reverend," Cyrus said respectfully, smiling and shaking his head.

Cotton Mather frowned almost imperceptibly; however, everyone was watching Cyrus, so it was not noticed.

"Are you most certain of this?" Mather pressed on.

"I am," Cyrus replied. "It was dark when I did see him, but in the daylight I have come to know that I have never before seen the man."

"Which man, I pray you will tell us?" Mather asked.

"'Tis the younger man we speak of, and who is now in shackles and chains, sir," Cyrus said, pointing directly at Jeremy. Duncan saw the young man's shoulders relax somewhat, as though he was relieved after Cyrus' apparent betrayal from earlier.

"And yet your friend became afflicted by this very man," Mather scoffed.

"Please forgive me, Reverend," Cyrus said, his voice echoing in the hall, "but did you not only minutes ago declare uncertainty about how valid his affliction was?"

Several eyebrows raised, but before more than a few whispers began to grow, one of the magistrates spoke.

"Reverend," Bartholomew Gedney said to Cotton Mather's suddenly red face, "I do not believe that you have provided any testimony or evidence for our consideration."

Mather looked back and forth between the magistrates and Cyrus. Duncan wondered if Reverend Mather was about to accuse Cyrus of being party to them. Instead, Mather inhaled deeply, regathered his composure, and nodded in deference to the judges.

"Forgive me, Your Honor," Mather said. "I shall now return to my seat, as I have nothing to offer at this time." Meekly, Mather took his seat again, but looked up at Cyrus with repugnance. Apparently, Cotton Mather did not like being embarrassed, especially in court.

"We do not have any further evidence to present for your Honors to review," George Herrick announced after a few moments of quiet judicial note-taking. Just as he finished, Constable Jonathan Smith stepped forward and spoke into the prosecutor's ear. The man straightened up in surprise, and Smith stepped out of the room as Herrick addressed the panel.

"Do excuse me," Herrick requested. "I have been informed that there is a woman who wishes to give testimony."

"This Court has not been informed of any such person," Corwin pointed out with annoyance. Duncan suspected that he did not protest the surprise for any reason other than proper protocol; surely, he would welcome any further evidence that would doom the accused. The rest of the several judges were flipping through their documents and trying to figure out what was going on. After several long moments, Constable Smith re-entered the room through its singular door, followed by a woman that had short grey hair, except for a very long lock of brown, natty hair. Duncan noticed Lisa's expression, which suggested she knew this lady; in fact, she'd gone pale at the appearance of this woman. Duncan formed a guess about what was about to happen, and decided to intervene.

"Your Honors!" Duncan blurted, stepping forward unconsciously before Constable Joseph Herrick placed a bell-ended gun barrel in his chest. Duncan remembered himself and stepped backward. His outburst seemed to stop everyone, including the woman.

"You test the patience of this Court!" Stoughton pointed at him.

"But sir!" Duncan protested. "I want to confess!"

"What?" Jeremy and Lisa both said.

The magistrates exchanged words as they considered this. Finally, they turned and Stoughton said, "Very well, say what you mean."

"I am responsible!" Duncan announced to the entire room. "I am the man who has made these rings of fire, and I sent the men." Jeremy and Lisa both stood with their jaws slack and their mouths open in shock. "I am the man who brought these two here."

"NO!" Jeremy said, jumping in front of him, and Lisa taking a step in the same direction. Duncan put his arm out to block Jeremy's face. Many of the magistrates and the prosecutor had an expression of satisfaction at his confession.

"I kidnapped them and forced them to do my bidding!" Duncan declared.

"What the hell are you doing!" Jeremy cried out.

"Duncan," Lisa cried, "They'll kill you for that!"

Duncan frowned, trying to contain his genuine, twenty-first century reaction, which would have been to talk freely about the Time Opener. He had no such luxury here, and he had to act fast to keep them from letting it slip too.

"I have done my deeds," Duncan said. "You are innocent; there is nothing to do now for me."

"But –" Jeremy began. He could not finish because Duncan pushed him such that he spilled onto the floor, landing on his rear.

"I must follow the Prime Directive," Duncan said tersely through clenched teeth, hoping that Jeremy would understand his Star Trek reference. Jeremy got it, but his reaction was, as expected, not as Duncan wanted.

"Prime Directive?!" Jeremy shouted angrily from the floor. "Duncan! We're in sixteen-ninety two! There IS no 'Prime Directive'!"

"Young man!" Duncan said in his most authoritative voice, making Jeremy's expression change quickly from defiant to surprise. "There was ALWAYS a Prime Directive! Even from the day I first made…the 'Fire Circle'," Duncan caught himself just in time. "You need to get that! It is time for you to be quiet!"

Both Jeremy and Duncan were panting when George Herrick interrupted their altercation.

"If it pleases you, Honorable Stoughton," Herrick said, "we have another confession, which will destroy the claim of innocence of the accus-ed by the Negro man!"

"It pleases," Stoughton said grumpily. "Get it over with, and do be quick about it. I have had my fill of this trial!"

Herrick obliged and sped the woman to the front.

"Woman, give your name to the assembled," Herrick demanded haughtily.

"I am the widow Dorcas Hoar," the older woman said. Duncan noted her clothing was tattered all over, dirty, stained, and she clearly had not bathed in weeks, perhaps months. George Herrick spoke next.

"The good Constable Smith and I wish to showeth that it hath pleased the Lord, we hope in mercy to the soul of Dorcas Hoar of Beverly, to open her heart out of distress of conscience," he said with a car-salesman smile. There were once again hushed mutterings, which quickly died out as

Herrick prodded her to speak more.

"I professeth," she said with a husky but shaking voice, "to confess myself guilty of the heinous crime of witchcraft, for which I am condemned." She looked around the room, then back at the judges. "I will confess how and when I was taken in the snare of the Devil, and that I signed his book with the forefinger of my right hand."

"Did you take these actions alone?" Magistrate Hathorne asked.

"No, I did not," Dorcas Hoar said. "Also I give account of some other persons that I hath known to be guilty of the same crime, namely, the woman stands now accus-ed."

"Oh, My, God!" Lisa said pointedly, and her mouth fell open, and then she looked at Jeremy and Duncan, her eyebrows raised in disbelief. She looked ready to go toe-to-toe with this Dorcas Hoar. Constable Joseph Herrick stepped closer to her in warning; she closed her mouth but still appeared ready to strangle the woman.

"What do you seek for your confession?" Hathorne asked her.

"Being in great distress of conscience," Dorcas said slowly, seeming to want to garner sympathy in the panel, "I crave a little longer time of life to realize and perfect my repentance for the salvation of my soul."

"What is your petition, George?" Corwin asked the prosecutor. George Herrick conferred briefly with the constables, and then answered.

"We humbly petition in her behalf," he said, "that there may be granted to her one month's time or more, to prepare for death and eternity. Except by her relapse, or afflicting others, she shall give grounds to hasten her execution. And this we conceive if the Lord sanctifies it may tend to save a soul, and to give opportunity for her making some discovery, and be providential to the encouraging of others to confess and give glory to God!"

The magistrates spoke quietly amongst themselves, this time with disagreement in their whisperings. After a few minutes of discussion, all turned to face forward.

"We agree to your petition, approving as according to your request," Hathorne ordered. "We accept her testimony as further evidence against Lisa Carson."

Dorcas Hoar broke down into tears and fell to her knees, thanking God and the magistrates repeatedly. Duncan looked on as the pitiful woman was given her freedom, and contemplated the price she paid in her spirit to accuse a perfect stranger of being a witch.

After the confession/accusation of Dorcas Hoar, the magistrates of the Court of Oyer and Terminer declared that all the evidence had been presented. They adjourned the court for the day, ordering a reconvene as early as eight of the clock in the morning. Until then, Duncan, Jeremy and Lisa endured a quiet, awkward ride back to the jail, to stay the night in a putrid cell, to continue to be increasingly hungry, and to face the prospect of conviction with a sentence to be hanged at the gallows.

CHAPTER XXVIII
Dusk

Jeremy had to fight his gag reflex as he used the waste stall to relieve himself. The whole jail smelled like an open sewer all the time, but to be standing inches from many ages of human waste, with the dozens of flies swarming it, was perhaps the most disgusting experience of his life. He had tried to hold his breath, and then hid his nose in his shirt, but all he succeeded in doing was to make himself dizzy.

Jeremy finished and stepped quickly out of the cell, retching as he did so, unable to hold it back anymore. However, it had been nearly a day since he had had anything to eat or drink, so his only result was a dry heave, which hurt. Once he returned to his own small cell, he allowed himself to breathe normally. The air still reeked, but at his stall it was mildly easier to ignore.

"Ohh," he moaned. "What time is it?" Jeremy asked as he pulled out his cell phone and looked at the time.

"My watch says seven-seventeen," Duncan said dryly, looking at his wrist. "A.M."

Jeremy chuckled at his report; they had returned to the jail about an hour ago, so it was still late afternoon here. His own phone read seven-eighteen A.M.

"I think we're eleven hours off," he scrunched his face

in thought as he tried to work it out. "No, ten hours—"

"What time did you set it?" Duncan asked after a moment, bothered that he could not recall the time setting on the Opener.

"Nine o'clock, I think," Jeremy said absently, "I was under some pressure at the time," he arched his eyebrows with friendly irony at distinguished-looking scientist. Duncan snorted a half-laugh dismissively.

"I put us at eleven hours ahead, give or take about ten minutes," Duncan said. "I'm hungry."

"Yeah, me too," Jeremy said. He folded his phone and set it in his lap as a question came to him. "Duncan, can I ask you something?"

"Shoot," Duncan said, looking up from his bored slouch.

"I think I already know the answer to this," Jeremy began. "But how come we haven't told them the truth?"

"I don't know about you, but I've been completely honest with them," Duncan replied with pretend snootiness, amused with himself briefly. "But to be serious, the answer is the same as the one I gave them back in the court room."

"The good old Prime Directive," Jeremy cited with some beleaguered dismay. "I mean, I feel like we should try anything we can to get out of this, including the fact that we are time travelers."

"We can't tell them that," Duncan said. "First, it introduces a very dangerous unknown element into what is already an unstable society. If we tell them we're from the future, who knows how that would affect the outcome of the Salem Witch Trials."

Jeremy reflected on his own numerous visits to the many tourist attractions in Salem through the years, and realized that things in this time were already bad; why arm these people with a new weapon to use against defenseless citizens? *If there was already pretty much no way to prove you were innocent of witchcraft, forget about defending against time travel!* Jeremy thought.

"Second," Duncan continued, "There's no convincing these folks of anything they don't want to believe. And finally," he said, opening his palms wide and shrugging his shoulders for effect, "we have no proof."

"You mean aside from our clothes and this," Jeremy said, holding up his phone. Duncan frowned at him. Jeremy laughed at the response he inspired in the scientist. "I'm kidding, of course!" He opened his phone again; the screen glowed bright in the dimming light of the stall. The battery still had half charge.

"Man, I wish I could call her," Jeremy said with mild frustration and longing to hold Lisa. She'd said in the oxcart that the women over on her side had been really nice to her, but Jeremy couldn't imagine that being as comforting as being next to someone you've known for years.

"Won't work," Duncan remarked. "No towers."

"I know, "Jeremy said defensively. An idea hit him, and he began to poke at the keys.

"Texting won't work either," Duncan said, resting his head against the wooden post. "Still no towers."

Jeremy felt warmth in his face as he realized his gaffe. "Doesn't matter anyway," he said as he gave up trying; he instead settled on gazing at the picture of Lisa, who had been wearing a giant silly smile and a Patriots hat while they were at a Red Sox game back in April. "She keeps hers in her purse, which is in my car, and that is about a quarter of a mile and three hundred years away."

"Put away that thing, boy!" hissed an old voice from the darker regions of the hall, startling Jeremy from staring at his picture of Lisa on his phone background.

Jeremy quickly closed his phone, moving to stand and see who had just addressed him; Duncan raised his head as well, and exchanged raised eyebrows with Jeremy.

A man shuffled into better lighting, and Jeremy saw that his clothing was dirty and torn in several places; his waistcoat was grey but his trousers were dark brown. He had a white beard, shocks of white hair around his head and smooth skin on the top; his skin was wrinkled and loose and covered with dark liver spots. Jeremy was concerned he had just been busted for having his cell phone out during the seventeenth century, and this guy was going to accuse him just like the woman had against Lisa earlier.

"I beg your pardon?" Jeremy asked, quickly shoving the phone into his back pocket.

"Do you want to get into further trouble?" the old man asked testily; Jeremy got the impression that the possibility of incriminating himself made the man very annoyed.

"Why," Jeremy decided to be bold and test the waters. "Are you going to turn me in?"

"Turn you in what?" the old man asked, and then waved his long arms dismissively. "Does not matter. I have no intention of telling others of your secrets."

"Then why –"Jeremy began to ask, but was cut off by the old man.

"Because that constable and his magistrates will use anything against you as proof that you practice witchcraft!"

"They've already made up their minds," Jeremy shrugged. "Besides, we still have our defense."

"Defense? How do you mean?"

"They made their case, and we get our turn," Jeremy said nonchalantly, then began to feel uncertain. "Right?" He exchanged looks between the old man and Duncan.

"Did you speak when they asked you questions during the trial?" asked the old man.

"Yes," Jeremy answered, wondering where he was going with this.

"You thus defended yourself, lad," the old man said, and nodded to punctuate his point. Jeremy considered his words for a moment, and then frowned in aggravation.

"Of course," Jeremy said with resignation. He glanced over to Duncan, who just shrugged and rolled his eyes at the fact that something else didn't go their way.

"Okay then," Duncan spoke up. "What about food? We haven't had anything to eat since we arrived," Duncan said, taking in the haggard old man's appearance as he posed his question.

The old man laughed heartily. "Do you have money?"

Duncan and Jeremy looked at each other quizzically,

and then Duncan replied, "None that anyone here would take."

"Well," the old man said after his laughter ended in a harsh wheeze. "I beg your pardon for my trifling of your misfortunes," he said genuinely. "Yet if you have no money, you cannot buy food."

"Wait a second," Duncan said with surprise, "you're telling me that if we want to eat while we are in jail, we have to *pay* them for it?"

"Indeed, my slave friend," the old man said. Duncan reacted almost unconsciously to the man's reference, but Jeremy picked up on it and stepped in between the two. Duncan regained himself and took a deep breath, looking away for a moment and walking back towards his stall.

"Please," Jeremy said pointedly, "don't call him that. He's not a slave." The old man eyed him, and then Duncan, and then shrugged to himself and walked back a few steps.

"Very well," the old man said casually as he shuffled back into the darkened recesses of the jail hall. He spoke over his shoulder as he faded, "Do remember, though, lad, to let not your light glow again."

Cyrus strode across the lane, two bags in hand and a handful of coins in his other. The jail was within sight; and the sun had disappeared from sight beyond the trees, leaving behind a deep blue sky with pink clouds. He went over his planned points, and he hoped that it would be sufficient to convince the constable on duty.

"Holla there!" cried out the guard; it was Constable

Herrick. Cyrus breathed a sigh of relief; Constable Smith would likely have been less agreeable to Cyrus' goals. "Who are you, and what is your business?"

"Salutation!" Cyrus tried to sound formal, but quickly gave up on it. He spread his arms wide in a gesture that showed his lack of armaments. "I am Cyrus Bartle of Falmouth."

"Yes, I know of you," Constable Herrick studied him briefly, and then noticed the sacks hanging from Cyrus' left hand. "And your business this evening, sir?" Herrick requested in a relaxed tone.

"I bring meals for the newest prisoners," Cyrus declared neutrally. Herrick looked suspicious.

"Why do you bring food to those who have and would afflict your friends?" he asked.

"As an act of forgiveness, sir," Cyrus said. "They have performed evil against us, and they shall pay the penalty by the law and by the court. Still, I wish to forgive them in person." He waited for Herrick's decision. After a few moments without response, Cyrus rubbed a few coins noisily against each other, and nonchalantly dropped three coins on the hard dirt. Herrick looked down at the fallen minted money; there was a penny, a sixpence and a shilling. Herrick took another look into Cyrus' eyes in the twilight, and then spoke.

"If a man shall ask me of your business—" Herrick asked with a hinted request.

Cyrus tried to hide a grimace as he reluctantly let one of the tuppence in his fingers slide out of his grasp and land on the ground. Herrick stepped aside and rested the wood of his musket rest on the ground. As Cyrus opened the door to the jail, he glanced back and saw Herrick crouched down, collecting the bribe.

Cyrus had noted how pleasantly fragrant Jeremy's house was when he had been in the future. Upon his return to his own present, he had become more aware of the odor that existed in Salem. As he stepped into jail, the foul stench struck him; perhaps it was more noticeable after having been in the future. Cyrus dismissed the thoughts as he looked down the two parallel corridors of cells, looking for his friend.

"Cyrus?" Jeremy's voice called from the corridor to his right. Cyrus strode quickly over to Jeremy, who was standing at his cell; Duncan had stood also, watching Cyrus from his own stall, but did not make any moves to join the other two.

"Jeremy," Cyrus said in a hushed voice. "I trust you are well, as you can be?" He glanced over at Duncan too, noting his scrutinizing eyes.

"Yeah, we're fine," Jeremy said. "There's not much to do here except sit and wait for things to happen."

"Indeed," Cyrus said. He held out one of the bags in his left hand. Jeremy took the bag, looking curiously at Cyrus and then over at Duncan. Duncan finally let his own curiosity draw him over to Cyrus and Jeremy.

"What's this?" Jeremy asked as he opened the coarse-fiber sack. He realized what was in it, and an excited smile burst on his face.

"Food!" Jeremy said, looking at Duncan. He opened the bag and knelt down to get to its contents better.

Duncan looked at Cyrus, who returned the glance with uncertain, awkward silence. He bent down and joined Jeremy as his chains jingled in the course of his digging through the bag.

"Whoa! Lobster!" Jeremy exclaimed, keeping in mind to try not to be loud. "This is awesome! But why would you spend so much just to feed us?"

Cyrus gave him a perplexed look. "This meal did not cost me more than threepence," he said. "Had I bought you pork, I would not have been able to buy anything. It was necessary to spend a half-day of wages alone to gain permission to bring this to you."

"Thank you," Jeremy said hungrily. He reached into the sack and felt around. He also found potatoes in the bag; however, Jeremy was surprised as he realized the lobster was lukewarm and the potato was cool. He looked up at Cyrus with puzzlement.

"They're cold," Jeremy said, hoping not to sound ungrateful. He broke the potato open and took a bite as he waited for Cyrus' reply. Duncan had already done the same, and even tore his lobster in half. It did look cooked thoroughly.

"I regret the delay," Cyrus said, squatting to their level. "After the trial, I spent time with several towns-men to learn the likely verdict. Then, Brent and I had conversations regarding our plans to save you," he explained.

"How is he doing?" Duncan asked, still leery of the man who brought them sustenance.

"He has his, ah," Cyrus began, searching for the right word, "passions." Duncan snorted in amusement; he appreciated Cyrus' attempt to be diplomatic, and found that he now felt less distrust towards him. Cyrus continued. "Yet he is well. He is drawing pictures and writing things on some parchment. He tells me to tell you that he promises to save you."

"And you?" Duncan asked. Jeremy chewed some of his lobster tail and watched as the two men worked their way through an awkward conversation. Cyrus stood.

"I am here to help you," he declared, almost with an offended tone. Duncan regarded him for a moment, then looked at the food, and then at Jeremy. Jeremy raised his eyebrows, curious to see what Duncan did next. Duncan stood up.

"I thank you," Duncan said at last, extending a clean, shackled hand. Cyrus accepted the proffered hand. "For the food and for the effort. We were simply confused by this what happened this morning."

"Yes, of course," Cyrus replied. "Unfortunately, that could not be helped. Had I left things to chance, it is very much likely that I and Brent would be in here with you."

Duncan nodded in understanding and agreement. Jeremy stood to rejoin the conversation.

"So what now?" Jeremy asked, taking a bite.

"Yes, tell me what Brent has cooked up," Duncan said. Cyrus gave a puzzled look, and then Duncan clarified his meaning, saying, "The plan. What is his plan?"

"Ah," Cyrus said. "Actually, the idea was formed by Aaron. We devised a deceit, wherein Brent came and posed as a compatriot of ours from Falmouth, bringing news that Anne had begun her labor. Aaron, thus free to move about in secrecy, went to Boston to retrieve some supplies we need in order to save you. He should be returned as we speak; Brent has gone to meet him on the road to Boston."

"So how are you going to save us?" Jeremy asked, now eating his food as though it were popcorn as he paid close attention to Cyrus.

"It would be unwise to explain the details here. The walls have ears," Cyrus warned. "However, I am also to tell you, Duncan, that Brent has with him some explosives," he said, his voice tapering with interest.

"Explosives?" Duncan knitted his eyebrows.

"Let me think for a moment," Cyrus looked upward in thought. "He called them, what was it," he mulled out loud, and then finally said, "Firecrackers!"

Jeremy's face lit up with intrigued excitement at the news; Duncan laughed. *Only Brent would have smuggled fireworks into the past,* he thought.

"Well, all right then," Duncan said. Suddenly, a thought struck him, and his laughter gave way to focus. "Hang on a second!" he said with some urgency. He thought for a moment as his hands patted at his pants, looking for the lighter he had confiscated from David just the day before. He found it and pulled it out of his pocket. Jeremy looked on with curious confusion, not seeing what Duncan was looking for.

"Give this to him," Duncan said, placing the metal lighter into Cyrus' hand. "Don't let anyone see you with this. I don't need to tell you the danger otherwise," he said with a wry seriousness.

"Indeed I do," Cyrus stuffed it into his boot. "Well, I must get along, as I must deliver food to Lady Lisa."

Jeremy sighed in relief, appreciative of the lengths that Cyrus was going to in order to take care of them. "I'm glad you're going over there. Can you tell her I'm sorry we can't be together through this?

"I will try," Cyrus said. "Be warned, my friend, that entrance to see her will be watched far more closely. I cannot appear to be familiar with any of you."

"Last question, then," Duncan said. "When are you going to get us out of here?"

"Ah, yes, the very decisive question indeed," Cyrus said with a sigh. "We cannot remove you safely from the jail; the journey through the main part of town would be fatal for us all." Jeremy and Duncan leaned close; this would probably be their only chance to discuss the plot. Cyrus continued in whispers.

"The only way to safely remove you from danger and to protect our own lives is if we do so at the gallows. Hangings are performed outside of town, and in such a place that we can claim you from the gallows and leave Salem in one fell swoop, as it were."

"So," Jeremy said slowly, "you need us—"

"To guarantee your guilt," Cyrus finished. "It is most

important that all three of you are sentenced to die by the same hand on the same day and time." Cyrus looked at both imprisoned men, ensuring that his instructions were clear. After only a few moments of silence, the jail door opened; Jeremy jumped with a start when Herrick leaned in. Cyrus cleared his throat.

"Very well, then," he said crisply, raising his voice a bit so as to be heard by the Constable. "While you refuse to repent, I repeat my offer that your sins against my companion are forgiven. May God have mercy upon your souls." Cyrus turned to leave, reaching the door when Jeremy became curious about something.

"Excuse me," he said; Constable Herrick and Cyrus both looked at him. "What time is it?"

Cyrus looked at Herrick, who answered, "It is near seven of the clock." Cyrus barely made it out the door when Herrick closed it. Jeremy looked at Duncan, barely able to make him out at this point in the dim twilight.

"What is it?" Duncan asked.

"It's not that important, but I just realized it's dark outside," Jeremy remarked, baffled. "It's the middle of August here; why would it be dark so early?"

Both he and Duncan stood in silence; Jeremy believed he saw Duncan shrug. After a few moments, Jeremy snapped his fingers as both men realized the answer simultaneously and said in unison, "Daylight Savings Time!"

"Hasn't been invented yet," Duncan sighed with a wry laugh.

CHAPTER XXIX

The door opened, and Lisa sat up instinctively, feeling ready for whatever abuses the Constable might bring her. Instead, she saw the face and figure of Cyrus, and she felt an unexpected rush of emotion. It was nice to see a familiar face finally, even if she had only known him about a day. She noticed he was holding a bag in his hand while he exchanged a few quiet words with the Constable; Lisa could tell even in the darkness that it was actually Constable Herrick. She felt like Herrick was far more trustworthy and professional than Smith. Cyrus closed the door and made his way to her; hopefully Cyrus brought good news.

"Lisa," he whispered. She became overwhelmed with her emotions, this time stepping forward to give him a hug. Actually, what she really needed was to receive a hug. However, Cyrus recoiled at her advance.

"What is it?" she asked, suddenly embarrassed by her lack of control.

"We must be very cautious," Cyrus whispered. "I know you are upset by all that has happened here."

Lisa laughed cynically, wiping her eye to clear her vision even though it was dark. "Upset? That's an understatement!" She looked at the dark dirt floor, wondering what to say next. Then, she just said the first thing that came to her mind.

"It's just that this whole trial, it doesn't make any sense!" She blurted. "All those people believing in witches—I mean, when Jeremy and I would go to the old Witch Museum and stuff, all those were just mannequins, you know? But here, I just can't believe it! *And that old woman!*" her tone turned to a growl as she ranted. "I could just rip her eyes out for that! And those girls!" Lisa's eyes were furious slits by now. "How could they just lie like that? How come everyone just *believes* them? It's crazy!" She finished, breathing heavily from the outburst of emotion.

"Yes, of course," Cyrus said carefully after a moment, considering her. He then continued, "As it goes, I do have a meaning for being here." He handed her the bag. Although it was getting dark to the point that she had to rely on her senses other than sight, she looked at him curiously.

"What is this?" she asked.

"Lobster and a boiled potato," Cyrus said. Lisa smiled, remembering that she felt famished.

"Aww," she cooed, "that's so sweet of you! Thank you!" She accepted the bag with more of a snatch than she intended, but she sensed that he did not mind. She reached her hand into the dark of the bag and felt around; her fingers brushed against what she could only guess was the face of the lobster. "Oh my goodness!" she said with a mixture of surprise and ickiness. She made herself overcome the gross factor in light of the fact that she was really hungry and that this was her only option. "Beggars can't be choosers," she remarked under her breath.

"I beg your pardon?" Cyrus said.

"Oh, nothing," Lisa said dismissively, taking a bite out of the potato, noting that it was still warm in its center. She was pretty sure that she had never enjoyed a potato so much in her life.

"I see," Cyrus said. He glanced back to the door, then back at Lisa.

"Lisa, there is a couple other things, and there is very little time to say them," he whispered urgently. Lisa stopped chewing so she could hear him better.

"Go ahead," she prompted.

Cyrus repeated the news he had shared with Jeremy and Duncan regarding the plan to be saved at the gallows. After a few moments, he paused and asked her if she understood.

"So you're telling me I have to let them say I'm guilty of being a witch?" Lisa uttered with her mouth full, the defiance she felt crept into her tone.

"It is of utmost import," Cyrus replied. "There would be no other way to help should any of you be separated from the rest."

Lisa swallowed the potato remnants in her mouth, gulping louder than she meant. If she'd been in the mood, and perhaps safe in the twenty-first century, she might have laughed at the ominous gulp. She mulled the plans he'd presented, and finally settled on her reaction.

"Alright," she sighed, "that's fine. Let's do it." *Better to face this risk with my head held high, just like Dad always*

says, she thought. *"Fear is no reason not to do a thing."*

"Wonderful," Cyrus said with relief. "I must be on my way. I have a message from Jeremy: he says he wishes he could be with you amidst all this."

Lisa smiled, wishing Jeremy was there so she could bury her head into his shoulder. As frustrating as he could be at times, there was no doubt in her mind how much she loved him.

"Thank you, Cyrus," Lisa said sweetly. "Good night."

"Good night, madam," Cyrus said formally, bowing slightly as he did. He began to walk back to the door when Herrick opened it. Cyrus was pleased that he had been generous with the time he had permitted the visit. He took the opened door, nodded his unspoken appreciated at the officer, and made his way back to the Marble Wharf Inn.

"Lobster! Now we're talking!" Brent exclaimed when Cyrus arrived with some more lobster from Christopher's tavern. Aaron, who had just returned from Boston, took his serving off the wooden plate and tore the cooked red sea animal in half at its tail.

Cyrus took his piece and began to tear into it. He looked up at Brent as he chewed. "You join the others in your excitement for this food," he remarked. "Are they so rare in your time?"

Brent chewed thoughtfully for a few moments, then swallowed and said, "I dunno, actually. Lobster is just usually so expensive; I guess we all really appreciate you spending so much on us."

Aaron and Cyrus both chuckled in amusement. Brent watched them, feeling like the butt of an inside joke.

"What's so funny?" Brent asked defensively.

"We do not mock you, friend," Aaron said with half-chewed lobster in his cheek. He turned to Cyrus and asked, "How much did you spend on this royal meal, Cyrus?"

"A sixpence and a farthing for the lot," Cyrus said proudly. He smiled good-naturedly at Brent, who relaxed himself at the answer, even if it meant nothing to him. He shrugged.

"I don't get it," he said. "Is that a lot? Did you get a good deal or something?"

"There are two things that any man can find lying around to eat in Plymouth Col—" Aaron corrected himself, saying, "rather, in the Colony of Massachusetts: corn and lobster. One cannot wade into the sea more than a few feet without the need to step over a lobster," he said. His tone shifted to one of fatigue as he glanced at Cyrus. "There are times when Anna and I cannot but afford only this, and perhaps some bread."

"Well, you may have tons of it here," Brent said, "But for us it is fine dining. And, it's delicious, let me tell you. All it needs is some garlic butter." Brent kissed his fingertips in the classic French chef pantomime.

"Have you finished your own ideas for the plot?" Cyrus asked after a few moments of odd silence that followed Brent's mime.

"I think so," Brent said. "After looking at the things Aaron got while in Boston, I think we need to go back and get a few more things."

Aaron sat up with curiosity, and with some disappointment that his choices were not sufficient. "How do you mean?"

"Well," Brent said, taking a deep breath. "The cloaks I think will be a great idea, flowing in the wind as we ride the horses," he began, intrigued by the mental image, "But we still have the problem of disguises."

"Why not take my advice of dressing as the Indians?" Cyrus asked.

"Well, two reasons," Brent said. He held out two fingers, ticking them off as he hit his points. "First, it might set off a war or something with the Indians, and we can't let our actions affect the original timeline."

"Time line?" Aaron asked, and took a drink from his wooden cup which contained cider.

"The natural flow of the events of history," Brent answered. He continued with his second point. "Second, it's been done. All the movies and stuff do the Indian thing. I want to do something that really rattles them; you know, makes 'em hesitate to follow us!" He finished with a dose of passion, ignoring their somewhat puzzled expressions.

"What else do we need from Boston?" Cyrus asked.

"Well, we've got the replacement horses and wagon, so that the people won't possibly recognize them as yours, parked outside of town near the hill," Brent said. He wiped his hands on his lower pants, since there were no napkins. This drew a grimace of dismay from Aaron, but Brent carried on with grabbing the parchment on which he had drawn up some plans and figures. "Also," he said, "if we can get our hands on some wire and iron rods, we can magnetize them on the ride back from Boston."

The two men indigenous to the seventeenth century leaned over and gazed at Brent's drawings and calculations.

"What's this writing here?" Cyrus asked curiously.

"Just the calculations to see what I'd need to make this work right," Brent replied. Aaron and Cyrus exchanged glances and then looked back at the page. He stood up and stretched.

"Yes, it would be a wise idea to get some rest," Aaron said, standing as well, tossing his empty lobster shell into the bag that Cyrus had brought. "We will need to leave before the light of dawn if we are to be unseen," he told Brent.

"What can I do while here?" Cyrus asked, feeling a little useless.

"I'm not sure," Brent shrugged. "I guess just keeping an eye on the guys, making sure that things go according to plan, and no surprises."

Cyrus considered that for a few moments, when he remembered Duncan's message. He crouched and reached into his boot to retrieve the lighter, and then stood to hand it to Brent.

"David's lighter!" Brent said with excitement. "That's awesome!" When he looked up at his hosts, he explained. "This will make things a *lot* easier," he said. He flipped the silver top, and thumbed the notched wheel, which ignited the gas and made the flame. Both Aaron and Cyrus flinched, and then leaned in to look at the fire closely. Brent could not help but be amused as he watched them study it. After a moment, he flipped it closed and extinguished the flame. Both men looked at him with stunned amazement.

"Impressive," Aaron commented. "I say, the men of your time have become remarkably clever."

"Maybe," Brent said dismissively. "But you want to know what makes this ironic?" Aaron and Cyrus waited for him to answer his own question. After a few moments, he obliged.

"This stupid lighter may make the difference between success and failure," Brent said, "and it is the very reason we're in this mess to begin with!"

Friday, August 22 1692

CHAPTER XXX
An Hour Before Sunrise

Aaron and Brent had to walk for the first hour; they needed to go beyond the town boundary, crossing a wooden bridge that then became the road to Boston, and then a mile past that. The horses were camped about a hundred yards from the road; on the night before, Brent had been able to take a horse (with mild improvement over his first horse riding experience) out to meet Aaron and smuggle him back into town. This time they used the cover of darkness to begin their trip to Boston, with Brent yawning frequently and Aaron taking decisive strides in the lead.

"I expect we should arrive in Boston perhaps within two hours," Aaron said as they climbed onto the wagon seat, taking the reins in his experienced hands. "Once there, let us take no more than another two hours; we must try to return by midday to have the best time to prepare for tomorrow."

Brent nodded through a thick yawn at Aaron's words, wrapping his arms around himself to ward off the coolness of the summer morning. He did his best to doze as Aaron guided the horses on their way, and only had limited success. By the time the sun had broken between the trees, casting long, interrupted shadows to their right, Brent had given up on sleep and his mind had sharpened enough to keep going over different disguise ideas. Along the way, they discussed different aspects of their plan, trying to put together an order of events to anticipate. Every so often, Aaron would break into tangents about the highway to Boston and life in the seventeenth century, and about his excitement about finishing this adventure so that he could return home and begin the adventure of being a father.

They reached the outskirts of Boston, crossing a few long bridges in the course, and began to make their way into town. Brent could not help but marvel at the reality of Boston being made of wood and dirt. They reached the center of town, which was full of activity, and Brent could smell the sea of the famous Boston Harbor, which made Brent briefly flash on the well-known Boston Tea Party. *That's not going to happen for, what, another eighty years?* he thought.

They stopped at a smith shop and came out several minutes later with lengths of wire, as well as four lengths of heavy iron bars. Combined with the three they had salvaged from the decaying wagon behind the Marble Wharf, which gave Brent seven potential iron magnets, once he built the generator.

They moved on to tour various supply shops of Boston, searching for ideas for their disguise, and purchased a few more minor supplies and materials, including lengths of rope. It had already been two hours of randomly wandering around the merchant district, and Aaron was becoming adamant about getting back to Salem in order to keep their schedule. Brent, too, was getting dejected as they walked along Main Street, when something caught his eye.

"Hold on," Brent said, and leaned backward to look past a large white horse that stood tied to a post in front of him. Across the street, a woman had walked out of a shop carrying a stack of linens. The woman was well dressed, but not in Puritan clothing; she was wearing a long, large dress shaped like an upside-down wine flute—wide at the hips and narrowing towards the feet. The dress had no collar, but was a broad neckline that exposed her shoulders; the sleeves were poufy and bulky, and her hair was done in fancy blonde curls, from her shoulders and arching over her head. However, none of this mattered to Brent, who was paying attention to the dark blue linens that sat in the middle of the stack she carried.

"Wait a minute," Brent said to himself, walking across the street, pausing a moment to let a horseman trot by on a black horse with brown splotches. Aaron had to jog a moment to catch up with him, completely at a loss to know what Brent was up to. The two men stopped in front of the shoppe, and Brent read aloud the wood-burnt sign that was nailed to the door post.

"Draper's Shop, Wool and Linen," he muttered. He looked at Aaron quizzically, and then walked in.

It was a fabric store. The man who ran the shop bragged to Aaron and Brent that he was one of the only two wool dyers in the town, and that he could do any color and any linen, which was something his competitor could not claim. Along the smooth golden-brown wooden walls were several swatches of linen of various weave patterns and colors, apparently to show off the merchant's skills. However, an idea was developing in Brent's mind.

"I've got it," Brent said, a grin spreading across his face, growing bigger as he mulled the fantastic nature of his thoughts. It was so wild and crazy that Brent was convinced it was the right idea.

"How much to buy some of your blue dye?" Brent asked the hairy merchant. The man looked at Brent as if he asked him how many fingers he was born with, but then quoted a price, and Aaron almost lost his composure with Brent at the cost.

"Relax," Brent assured him, "I'll find a way to pay you back, I promise. Please trust me, this is a great idea."

Reluctantly, Aaron paid the man for about a quart of dark blue paste in a ceramic jug. Brent was beaming with pride at his idea, and excitement about putting it in action. As soon as they reached the wagon, Brent and Aaron made sure to wrap the jug in protective fabrics for the journey back to Salem.

"Now all we need are some candles and we can go!" Brent declared.

"What is in your mind?" Aaron asked him suspiciously.

"I promise to tell you on the ride back," Brent said. "Trust me; this will be worth every cent!"

10 A.M.
Salem Meeting House

After a night's rest, the men who packed the court to

367

witness the verdict in the trial of Jeremy, Duncan, and Lisa seemed to have an energetic excitement about them. They went quiet almost immediately upon oyeas called by Stephen Sewell, the Clerk of the Court of Oyer and Terminer. He called the meeting house officially to order, saw to the seating of the Magistrates, and then took his own place beside them to once again make his record of the hearing.

Looking around the room, Jeremy spotted Cyrus again sitting in the opposite balcony, along with the other accusers, seated as they were during the afternoon trial. A few of them would occasionally cast a disgusted glance in his direction, which was then followed by a smug smile which irritated Jeremy. He tried to make eye contact and frown at their looks, but they had looked elsewhere and so did not see his reactions.

Again, the session was opened with a prayer, only this time Cotton Mather was invited to lead. He spoke of the importance of repentance for few minutes, quoting scripture along the way, as skillfully as any preacher Jeremy had heard. He had to remind himself at moments that despite the man's presence and oratory, he was still wrong about Jeremy and his friends.

"I pray thee God to see that the three prisoners, whose fates shall be decided this day, would by Your grace humble themselves before You and the worshipful Magistrates," he intoned soulfully, "that we may witness thy glory as they would confess their guilt, and repent of their evil doings by that old Deluder, Satan."

Jeremy had bowed his head during the prayer, and used the brief privacy to roll his eyes. He sighed a deep breath as Mather concluded and the congregation responded with its amen; he cast a quick glance at his girlfriend and then at his jail mate. They'd barely had an opportunity to discuss their brief visits from Cyrus during their oxcart ride to the court this morning.

"How can we make sure they sentence us to death?" Lisa had whispered, constantly checking to make sure the driver did not hear her over the noise of the horse and wagon.

"Easy," Jeremy had said, having given it thought before they were collected for the drive. "When in doubt, deny, deny, deny! Everything is backward here; everyone who was found guilty in these trials pleaded innocent." He paused to check the driver, and continued in a strong whisper. "If you want to be set free, it'll be like that lady yesterday. Admit you're guilty and then accuse someone else, and you're off the hook!"

And so now they stood beside the seven magistrates, each wearing their black robe, white cravat, and wig, and prepared to admit guilt. Magistrate Stoughton spoke first.

"This court hath heard the testimonies of the several good men of this town against the accus-ed," Magistrate Stoughton sounded almost bored to Jeremy. "The evidence of their wicked acts and tormenting of the diverse individuals, and of their creation and use of their fire-circle, has been presented to the Court and the Jury. We now confront the accus-ed and hear their plea of innocence or guilt, God have mercy."

This apparently was a pre-arranged signal for Hathorne to speak, for he began with a serious and stern glare at them.

"Lisa Carson," he said. Lisa's chains jingled as she brushed her hair out of her eyes.

"Yes, sir?" she answered. Jeremy saw steady calm on her face.

"The several charges against you are that you hath wickedly and feloniously used, practiced, and exercised at and within the Township of Salem, in the County of Essex, certain detestable arts called witchcrafts and sorceries," Hathorne said evenly, almost in a hypnotic monotone. "The case has been made against you that you tortured, afflicted, and tormented upon and against one Betty Parris, a child. Further, upon examination of your physical body it was found that you bear the Witch's teat, given only to persons who have conspired with the Devil, all against the peace of our sovereign Lord and Lady, the King and Queen, and against the form of the statute in that case made. Tell me now; are you guilty of these actions? How do you plead this day?" He locked eyes with Lisa, who stared back at him with a steady, unfazed expression. Hathorne opened his mouth to speak further when Lisa finally answered.

"Whatever," she said with a sigh, waving her shackled hand dismissively at them. "I didn't do it," she followed up with a measure of impatience in her words.

"You deny the evidence against you?" Hathorne demanded, now angry at her impertinence.

"What evidence?" Lisa argued back, just as peeved as the magistrate. "A kid throwing a tantrum on the floor, a few freckles on my back and some sicko "doctor" (she finger quoted) and his twisted staff poking at my privates, then telling everyone what color my panties are? Ha!"

"You will show respect to the court and its witnesses, woman," Magistrate Gedney warned her, his voice loud and his words quick enough to make her feel like he was yelling. She quickly turned to see where Constable Smith was; he was about two feet away from her. She frowned at him and turned back to the panel of judges.

"Fine, whatever," she huffed. "I'm sorry. But I'm still innocent," she staccatoed the last few words. Hathorne stared at her for a few more moments, and then faced the jurors.

"Foreman, please recognize that in spite of the facts presented, the accus-ed aforesaid Lisa Carson has denied her actions, and hath pleaded not guilty."

Jeremy heard Lisa huff another sigh, and mutter another "whatever" just quiet enough that he did not think anyone else heard it; he restrained a proud smile.

"Jeremy Macer," Hathorne said, snatching Jeremy's attention. Hathorne continued as he had with Lisa. "The several charges against you are that you hath wickedly and feloniously used, practiced, and exercised at and within the aforesaid Township of Salem, the aforesaid witchcrafts and sorceries. In this very court room," he tapped indignantly at the cloth-covered table with his forefinger in punctuation, "you have tortured, afflicted, and tormented upon and against one Brent Robertson, a man from the town Falmouth. Further, you have walked through a circle of fire which was not fire, and came to this town against the peace of our sovereign Lord and Lady, the King and Queen, and against the form of the statute in that case made. Tell me now, how do you plead this day?"

Jeremy paused for a briefest moment, momentarily hoping in a prayer to God that he had made the right call on the oxcart ride. He took a deep breath to compose himself, and said with as much respect as he could muster, "I plead not guilty, sir."

Hathorne frowned, apparently not expecting them to deny such obvious and damning evidence against them. He raised his eyebrows.

"You saith you did not perform the acts I have read?" Hathorne asked. "Did you afflict the good man Brent Robertson?"

"No sir, I did not," Jeremy responded honestly, standing a little taller and holding his chin high in his confidence.

"Did you enter this town by way of a circle of fire as witnessed by Mister David Flint?" Hathorne pressed, gesturing towards Flint.

"Oh yeah, that I did," Jeremy said, allowing a bit of playfulness to color his tone.

"Yet you deny having performed witchcraft," Magistrate Corwin interjected. "How can you use magic yet be innocent of performing magic?"

"I dunno," Jeremy shrugged his shoulders obnoxiously. "I just am. Innocent, that is. I'm no witch."

Hathorne directed the jury foreman to record Jeremy's plea of innocence. Jeremy suddenly felt self-conscious in such a quiet the room, considering how many people were in the small meeting house.

Hathorne turned to Duncan. Jeremy looked at Duncan; although the older gentleman had not offered any hints to his internal thoughts during the oxcart ride, Jeremy suspected that the consistent references to Duncan's skin color was wearing on even his most dignified and sophisticated sensibilities.

"Freed man, Duncan," Hathorne addressed him. "The aforesaid charges against you are the same as those spoken against the aforesaid Jeremy Macer and Lisa Carson; that is to say, the aforesaid witchcrafts and sorceries performed feloniously in this God-fearing town." Hathorne suddenly dropped his public-speaking tone for a softer tone. "In this very court room did you torment, torture, and afflict upon and against one Elizabeth Hubbard, a single woman and maidservant in the house of the good Doctor William Griggs. Further, you claim to be leader of the men who have walked through the aforesaid circle of fire, which was not fire," Hathorne's voice was gradually rising in volume and agitation, "and came to this town. You further claimed to be responsible for the terrors and visions that have been unleashed to the several persons of this town." He paused for a few moments, letting the accusations settle. He dropped his voice again, this time adding a knowing smile to it. "Tell me now, how do you plead this day?"

Duncan had his eyes closed throughout Hathorne's

rambling, as if meditating. Hathorne looked on patiently at first, then rose an inch out of his chair as if to see closer, and was about to signal for the Constable to prod him when Duncan finally did open his eyes a few moments later.

"Your honor," Duncan said slowly. "You are a superstitious old fool." Almost a hundred gasps followed that remark. Constable Smith raised the butt of his gun and was about to strike Duncan in the neck when Hathorne signaled him to hold. Hathorne smiled as though Duncan had fallen prey to his trap.

"Am I?"

Duncan glanced at Smith, who had lowered his gun but remained close to Duncan as warning. He looked back at the magistrate.

"Yes, you are, as are the rest of you," Duncan replied calmly, drawing more gasps. "That is all I wanted to say. I am *not guilty.*" His voice was almost a growl.

Magistrate Corwin stood abruptly, glaring furiously at the whispering congregation, which fell silent as quickly as they had started.

"Indeed," Hathorne said slyly. "Tell me, did you murder your master?"

"What?" Duncan reacted almost without thinking. Jeremy and Lisa both took a step towards him, and Duncan waved them back, his chains jingling.

"You are perhaps a man who has seen, say, forty years?" Hathorne asked with suspicious eyes.

"Forty-three," Duncan answered, mirroring Hathorne's tone and expression.

"And you are in remarkable health," Hathorne pointed out.

"Thank you. I try to take care of myself."

"Yes, of course," Hathorne chuckled. "The only negro slaves who earn long lives are those who serve their masters as house servants and valets. Your master would then be a man of good wealth and standing. Yet," Hathorne paused for a moment, "upon his death he freed you and bequeathed you his wealth. I cannot help but be curious; where is your wealth?"

"I don't understand," Duncan replied. He cursed inwardly for having been unprepared to have his cover story dissected. He tried to come up with something.

"If your master died of natural causes and gave you what was his, where is it?" Hathorne persisted.

"I," Duncan began, searching for an answer, "left the majority of it in Port Royal. I am simply on holiday."

"You lie!" Hathorne spat angrily. "Those who met you as you entered through your circle of fire say you were told to 'find your own wealth'. Now you claim you possess it, yet you left it in the Caribbean. I argue that you either murdered your master, or perhaps you never had one, and you are guilty of piracy," Hathorne concluded. He softened his composure, and then leaned back in his chair casually. "No, you are no pirate. Yet perhaps neither have you been a slave."

More gasps; Jeremy had to stifle an inappropriate smile of amusement at the crowd's predictability.

Duncan was at a loss for a response; however, he made

sure to maintain his poker face and eye contact with Hathorne.

"No reply? Fascinating," Hathorne taunted. "Lieutenant Governor Stoughton, do you have remarks you wish to make for the court to hear and consider on this matter?"

Magistrate Stoughton leaned forward. "On what date were you freed by your master's death?"

Duncan's mind raced. While he was prepared to take the risk of getting sentenced to the gallows, he had no idea what punishment would come for this set of charges. Now it was a matter of luck; either he would guess a good date or a bad date.

"June fifteenth."

He looked upon Duncan meaningfully. "I received notice on the twentieth of June, the year of our Lord Sixteen Ninety-Two, which did tell me of an earthquake which sunk parts of Port Royal on the sad date of June seventh of this very year. This accident of Nature, which would be the work of God, saw the deaths of many thousands of English subjects," Stoughton reported soberly. "This notice further told of plunders by the few who did survive."

"That doesn't mean *I* had anything to do with that," Duncan defended himself. "I was there for the quake, yes," Duncan lied. "But I helped my master with rescue efforts."

Hathorne laughed heartily. "You may continue with your deception, Negro Slave," he said through fading guffaws, "but you will surely be punished for it."

Duncan sighed and his shoulders sagged. He could not

win; no matter how prepared he thought he could be, there was no way he would have guessed to read up on the history of Port Royal. At least, not for the purpose of an alibi.

Hathorne regained his regal composure, and turned to address the jury. "Foreman, please recognize that in spite of the facts presented, the accus-ed aforesaid Negro Duncan has denied his actions, and denied the Will of God, and hath pleaded not guilty."

This apparently ended this session of court; the foreman nodded as he stood to leave the room, followed by seven other men. During their absence, the Magistrates broke court, but did not leave. The room erupted into fervent conversation, wherein there were dozens of smaller debates about the drama they were witnessing. Jeremy turned to Duncan, and Lisa leaned in as well.

"Don't let it get to you," Jeremy whispered. "We *did* want them to find us guilty."

"I am angry because," Duncan replied quietly, looking Jeremy in the eye, "I am not used to lying, and I am not used to being made a fool out of."

Lisa reached a hand out and patted his arm at the elbow, hoping to show him some support. He did not refuse her comfort.

"Man, I guess we all are getting tested here, in our own ways. I wish I knew what to say that would help," Jeremy offered.

"Thank you," Duncan said. "But it's not necessary. I just hope I haven't derailed the plan."

Jeremy was about to respond when the door opened, and the jury began to return. The onlookers in the room heard and saw this, and swiftly took their seats. Jeremy could now see why the Magistrates did not bother to leave their chairs. Corwin reconvened the hearing.

"Captain Thomas Fisk, senior, Foreman," Corwin said to the foreman, who stood with a parchment in his left hand. "Have you reached a verdict?"

"We have, your worshipfulness," he responded. After a beat, he read his verdict.

"Lisa Carson, of unknown town, indicted and arraigned for the crimes of failing to wear clothing fit for a chaste and holy lifestyle, and of the felony by witchcraft committed in evidences being called and sworn in open court," Captain Fisk read unevenly, even though Jeremy guessed he had just written it while outside. "The Jury finds Lisa Carson of unknown town guilty of the felony by Witchcraft, committed on the body of Betty Parris, also on her very own body."

Lisa slowly sat down on the floor, sliding along the white plaster wall behind her. Jeremy wanted to embrace her and remind her that they would be rescued in the morning, but he guessed also that being found guilty of anything, especially this, must strike a deep chord in any person. He was about to find out for himself.

The foreman read on, moving on to Jeremy's verdict. He found it interesting to listen to them spout nonsense, and he realized that he was intrigued as he waited to hear his name; he would have to reflect on that later. Jeremy made himself pay attention again. "The Jury finds Jeremy Macer, of unknown town, guilty of the felony by Witchcraft, committed on the body of Brent Robertson, and in the sight of David Flint."

It didn't feel much different, but Jeremy was not Lisa. She was not a weak-willed person, but she did not like things that did not make sense; it was one of his unspoken favorite traits of hers. And if this trial could be described by any one word, 'nonsense' would certainly be it.

The foreman moved on to Duncan, and when he announced the guilty verdict, Duncan barely changed expressions except for the right corner of his mouth, which twitched. Jeremy was impressed at his stoicism.

"What sentence does the Jury recommend for these guilty witches?" Hathorne asked.

"The sentence of death is passed on Lisa Carson, Jeremy Macer, and Negro Freed Man Duncan," Captain Fisk said. The three leading magistrates, Corwin, Stoughton, and Hathorne, picked up dark iron bell-shaped items and slammed them on the table simultaneously; these apparently were their gavels. The course was set; hopefully the plan would work, and in time.

Now Jeremy felt a bit woozy.

CHAPTER XXXI

Upon their stealthy return from Boston, Brent had set about making the several trips, inconspicuously, necessary to bring the supplies in to the room. The task had been largely easy to accomplish; even at midday, the town was either consumed with the trial or busy working in their shops. A few back paths between properties were sufficient to hide Brent's multiple treks. Meanwhile, Aaron had gone to scout Gallows Hill, as it was called here.

Over the past three or four hours, the humble boarding room had transformed from two beds and some candles to nearly full of various half-finished projects. Along one wall were two open sacks filled with black powder, which sat next to the keg barrel with the rest of the powder. Next to the keg was Aaron's hunting bow, together with a few modified arrows. On the bed lay a pile of black cloaks and several coils of rope. On the floor, just under the bed, were several iron bars which were now powerful magnets, thanks to Brent having converted the wheel axles of the wagon into a generator prior to their journey back from Boston. To Brent's right, beside the writing desk at which he sat, was a small sack of flour and the pint of blue dye paste he'd convinced Aaron to buy.

Brent and Aaron were now leaning over a few

parchment pages, working out the plan for the next morning and studying the layout of the wooded area where the hangings would take place. Aaron had been able to identify a few paths to get in and out of the area, as well as the hanging tree itself. Aaron shook his head in sad dismay as he mentioned the four cut ropes that still hung from the long branch of the tree. Both men swore an oath to make sure they were successful in seeing that their friends did not join the list of the victims of Salem's Witch Trials.

Brent was sketching one of his several ideas to present to Aaron; they wanted to have the right plan in place by the time Cyrus finished his politicking and socializing. Although he still sort of resented Cyrus' decision to go and make friends while they developed the plan, he understood that it was critical that the townsmen not suspect Aaron or Cyrus of having in part in the rescue.

"What is this?" Aaron asked as he opened Brent's black Velcro wallet. Brent tried to. The first thing he noticed was a white piece of strange, hard paper that had a picture of Brent on it. He showed it to Brent, who finished what he was sketching before he glanced up.

"Ah, that's my driver's license," Brent said quickly.

"It is peculiar, but this does not look very much like you," Aaron said, shifting the photo in the light.

"Yeah, well that was taken about five years ago; I had different hair ideas then, and now I have contacts," Brent said, going back to his work.

Aaron read the information on the license, noting that Brent's date of birth showed the year nineteen hundred eighty four. Aaron moved on to look in other parts of the black wallet.

Aaron poked at the strange looking papers that sat in it. "Is this your money?"

"What?" Brent said through his distraction. He looked up. "Yes, ah, looks like eight bucks." He returned his attention to his work.

"Even in your splendid future time do you put kings on your money," Aaron remarked with amusement. "Perhaps things do not change much as I would think."

"Actually, the guy on the ones is the first President," Brent said absently. A moment of pride captured him briefly. "He earned his place on that bill; before he was President, he was something like the commander of all the American forces during the Revolution."

"Hmph, 'Washington'," Aaron grunted with mild interest. He pulled out another bill and examined it from several angles. "Even your money is full of color. I presume this 'Lincoln' was also another president?"

"Yep," Brent said, dragging his futuristic pen down the page to divide one sketch from another. "Freed all the slaves."

Aaron dropped his arms in shock, staring at Brent. After a few moments, Brent realized Aaron was gazing at him.

"What?" Brent asked impatiently. He wanted to get this plan done.

"'Freed all the slaves'?" Aaron asked with a mixture of perplexity and amazement. "What reply can I say to such a thing? It is unthinkable!"

Brent looked at him oddly. "I haven't even seen another black person since I've been here," he said with furrowed brow. "And there was only one guy on the boat when we were made to join the crew. Why does that matter to you?"

"Because I have a slave," Aaron said slowly. "In truth, I share him with my father, to tend our farms. Why would you free them?"

"Because," Brent said, bothered that the idea of slavery was not naturally offensive to Aaron. He set down his pen and leaned back in a stretch. "I don't know. The war was dragging on and I guess Lincoln thought that would change things a bit." He scooted his makeshift chair back and rubbed his face. "Besides, it was the right thing to do. No one should be a slave; it doesn't make any sense."

"This war, was it the revolution?" Aaron asked, suddenly deeply curious about the things to come.

"No, this was the Civil War," Brent said. He thought about it for a moment, then said, "About a hundred and fifty years from now, actually."

"Unbelievable," Aaron said softly, marveling that this land would be separated from the Royal Throne and then suffer civil war, only to become the peculiar world he had visited not two days before.

"Yeah, it is. Listen," Aaron said as something occurred to him. "I really shouldn't be telling you this stuff anyway, so you should probably forget everything I told you. Plus, we should probably get back to work; I want to get this right, and we still have a lot to do."

Glad that Brent was finally ready to discuss his plans,

Aaron put the wallet down and moved closer so that he could see Brent's newest round of suggestions.

There was a strong, clear knock at the door. George Corwin, son of Magistrate Jonathan Corwin and son-in-law to Magistrate Bartholomew Gedney, was now expected to perform his duty as High Sherriff of Essex County. As he strode towards the door from his desk, he checked that his vest and petticoat sat well on his shoulders.

The courier who stood at his doorstep was no more than eleven years old, entrusted with delivering an important letter to Sherriff Corwin. Corwin accepted the delivery and excused the lad, allowing him to leave and report that his task had been carried out successfully. He broke the wax seal of the Magistrate and began to read the enclosed message:

Whereas Lisa Carson of unknown place Jeremy Macer of unknown place and the Negro Duncan fmr of Port Royal, in their Maj'ts Province of the Massachusetts Bay in New England Att A Court of Oyer & Terminer held by Adjournment for Our Soveraign Lord & Lady King William & Queen Mary for the County of Essex at Salem in the s'd County on the 21st day of August were Severaly arraigned on Several Indictments for the horrible Crime of Witchcraft by them practised & Committed On Severall persons and pleading not guilty did for their Tryall put themselves on God & Their Countrey, whereupon they were Each of them found & brought in Guilty by the Jury that passed On them according to their respective Indictments and Sentence of

death, did then pass upon them as the Law directs Execution whereof yet remains to be done:

Those are Therefore in their Maj'ties name William & Mary now King & Queen over England: to will & Comand you that upon Saturday next being the 22nd day of this Instant August between the houres of Eight & eleven in the forenoon the same day you Jeremy Macer & Duncan, Negro, Lisa Carson From their Maj'ties Gaol in Salem afores'd to the place of Execution & there Cause them & Every of them to be hanged by the Neck untill they be dead and of the doings herein make return to the Clerke of the said Court & this precept and hereof you are not to fail at your perill and this Shall be your Sufficient Warrant Given under my hand & seale at Boston the 22'nd day of August in the fourth year of the Reign of our Soveraigne Lord & Lady Wm & Mary King and Queen:

*Wm Stoughton
Annoq Dom. 1692 –

Sherriff Corwin folded the Death Warrant closed, flipping the letter over and again in his fingers absently as he considered the actions he needed to take to carry out the orders. It was unpleasant business on any day, but it was especially unsettling, in light of the fact that he had to do this for a second time in the same week. Dedicated to upholding the law, he knew that this had to be completed before noon the next day; it was in the best interest of the town. He placed the letter in his pocket and made his decision. He called out to his wife, who was in the adjacent room repairing clothing.

"Lydia, I am summoned and must go meet with the Constables," he said, striding towards the door. "Town business."

Lydia responded agreeably from the other room, wishing him to bid good tidings to them while Corwin grabbed his hat from the wall nail, setting it upon his head. He walked out the door; there was much planning to do in the next few hours before the fall of night.

"Man, I'm not sure I have ever been this bored in my life," Jeremy complained.

"Good!" Duncan remarked with sarcasm.

"What?" Jeremy asked.

"At least you have stopped complaining about the stench," Duncan said with amusement and a little fatigue.

Jeremy was immediately reminded of the gut-wrenching odor that hung around his nose in this putrid jail. "Man," he moaned. "I'd forgotten about that; thanks a lot!" Duncan chuckled at him.

"Seriously, though," Jeremy said, sitting up. "Can I ask you a question?"

"I suppose," Duncan said, facing him.

"How bad does it bother you, you know, when they say… you know," Jeremy looked for the right words to say.

"That I'm a slave?"

"Well, yeah that too," Jeremy said, relieved that Duncan

did not seem uncomfortable discussing such a sensitive topic. "And when they call you 'Negro'. I mean, don't you just want to reach out and smack them around for it?"

"Jeremy," Duncan said after a few moments' thoughts, "first you have to understand that not every black man or woman feels like society owes them something for a tragedy that ended over a century and a half ago. In fact, it's probably a majority these days."

"I know," Jeremy said, trying not to sound presumptive.

"Now, if you're asking whether there are still bitter feelings, then yes, many people still remember life before the Sixties," he said, giving a pause to collect his next thoughts. "As for me, yes, the things these people say, and the way they look at me and treat me, is rather demeaning, and it does upset me. The trick, however, is to put things in context."

"What do you mean?" Jeremy asked.

"Look around you," Duncan said. "This is the seventeenth century! Slavery has been a universal constant for thousands of years, at the very least. It will continue to be so for another hundred-fifty years. Of course a part of me wants to react, but it wouldn't help; *these people simply don't know any better.*"

Jeremy nodded as he thought about what Duncan had said. The conversation ended there, and he began to look around, thinking about how Brent, Aaron and Cyrus would get them out of this. All the things were in place that he had been told; specifically, *get yourself condemned,* he amused himself in thought. An idea struck him.

"Hey, how come we just don't decide that once we are safe in the future, come back to this place and use the Time Opener to get us out of the jail now?" Jeremy asked.

"Because," Duncan said, mulling the question, "Let's say we did that. How would we get ourselves safe to begin with?" For a moment he felt like his brainstorming sessions.

Jeremy thought for a moment, and then answered, "I don't get it. Wouldn't we be safer by not going through the gallows thing tomorrow?"

"Yes, on its own that makes sense," Duncan said, but then pointed out, "But don't forget: if the rescue tomorrow fails, we would never make it back to be able to come rescue us from the jail, right now."

Jeremy tried to make sense of Duncan's time logic. It seemed so strange to try to make sense of paradoxes; somehow they had seemed so easy when Doc Brown explained it to him on Back to the Future. "Yeah, but what if the rescue goes well, then we'd be safe in the future and then be able to come back."

"Ok, but by doing that, we," Duncan gestured himself, Jeremy, and towards the wall behind which was Lisa, "would leave the jail, go straight to the future, and never go to the gallows."

"But that's the whole point!" Jeremy said with bewilderment. Why wasn't this scientist getting it?

Duncan sighed a well-worn sigh, having had conversations like this with his staff on several meetings during the development of the Time Opener. Temporal mechanics was a strange set of theories already; trying to explain them while in the middle of a possible paradox already was virtually impossible. Plus, this was the first time those theories might even be put to the test.

"I'll put it another way; if my staff can be convinced that we could do your idea without consequence or risk of paradox, I'll open a portal right there in one minute," he said, looking at his watch and noting the time as five-oh-eight A.M. Both of them watched the empty space, but after a couple of minutes, nothing happened. Jeremy frowned and Duncan smiled with sympathetic amusement. Suddenly, the jail door opened, and both turned to face the entryway.

"You, Negro," Constable Smith called out. "Come here!"

Duncan glanced at Jeremy, and then walked cautiously towards the man.

"What's the matter?" Duncan asked.

"You have been declared the property of the town of Salem," Smith reported. "As such, you are thereby held accountable for murdering your previous master." He held up a small piece of parchment with writing on it. "This is an order to place you in the pillory until such time as you are retrieved for execution for your crimes as a witch," he said with veiled pleasure. "Also ordered is for ten good lashings for your attempt to lie and deceive the court."

Duncan's heart sank; he was stunned as the Constable reseated his gun in his arms, held in such a way that was easy to lift and fire if he needed to. He was reminded of the burning sting of his one lashing; he could not begin to imagine getting through ten of them. Duncan closed his eyes, took a slow breath, and went deep inside himself to find the strength and courage to handle this unexpected punishment. He opened his eyes, and looked over at Jeremy, who he was sure was fully ready to fight on his behalf. As expected, Jeremy had started to walk forward.

"Don't," Duncan said, holding up a firm hand. "I can do this. It will be okay," he tried to assure the young man. He appreciated the boys' sensibility, but he did not want him harmed unnecessarily. Jeremy paused, and finally obeyed with reluctance.

"Good luck, Duncan," Jeremy said after a few moments. Smith took Duncan by the chains, and Jeremy watched this, feeling helpless in an increasingly out-of-control situation.

As soon as the door shut, a voice called out from behind him, startling him.

"Foolish boy," the old man from the night before shuffled forward, pointing a finger at him. "You still managed to be declared guilty of witchcraft!"

"Who are you?" Jeremy shot back, puzzled by the mysterious stranger. If the man was so interested in Jeremy's safety, the least he could have done was tell him his name.

"Corey," the man rasped. "Giles Corey. What was their evidence?"

Jeremy looked the old man up and down, taking in his appearance. He had to be a senior citizen; he had a scraggly white beard and a head that was sparsely covered with jagged white hairs.

"They said we were possessing some girls, and then this guy said—"

"Aha!" Corey blurted. "Those curs-ed children have been the bane of these towns. It would be better if they were put on trial!"

"You almost sound like you don't believe in witches," Jeremy noticed, a bit surprised.

"Witches?" Giles Corey repeated, and then chuckled bitterly. "There is not a man or woman in this jail who I would call a witch."

"But I thought everyone here believed in witches," Jeremy said.

"My boy," Corey said, turning to face him, so that Jeremy could see his whole face in the low afternoon light. "I am eighty-one years in my life, and I have never seen so much as a flick of magic or sorcery," he snapped his fingers on his left hand, squinting at Jeremy. "I have no reason to believe in such things. As it goes, I am no witch, yet here I am."

"Have you had your trial yet?"

"Not yet. I have been in this terrible jail for four months; let it be four years and I shall still not give them the satisfaction of a plea!" Corey said with powerful energy. Jeremy was impressed that he seemed so vibrant, even for his age.

"What do you mean?" Jeremy asked.

"Do you know nothing?" Corey looked at him with wide eyes. "Why, if I enter a plea, they would lay claim to my lands as payment! I have afforded that land to the husbands of my daughters in my will, and I cannot allow it to be forfeit for the lies of awful children and their horrible families!"

Jeremy tried to picture what it was like to be this old and still have his vigorous, determined defiance. He marveled at the man while hoping that tomorrow's rescue would be successful.

Cyrus walked into the tavern, stepping out of the orange sunlight of dusk and into the candle-and-firelight of the drinking room. Christopher glanced up from beside his bar, and offered a smile as he noticed Cyrus' entrance. He abandoned some work repairing a damaged chair and headed over towards Cyrus to greet him.

"Good evening, Cyrus," the friends clasping forearms. He broke a teasing smile, saying "Have you returned for yet another night of gluttony?"

"Gluttony?" Cyrus feigned offense at the accusation. "Please, Christopher, may I remind you that it was a drinking race that old Gedney challenged me to?"

Christopher laughed heartily at that, remembering the events of the previous evening. "Very well, I grant you that point. In truth, he very much wanted to buy you a round for embarrassing Reverend Mather during court. Old Cotton and Barty Gedney have never seen eye to eye on spectral evidence," he finished with an amused guffaw.

"Yes, I had heard of their disagreements," Cyrus sighed, trying not to seem too conflicted about the matter.

"What did you do with that batch of lobsters you paid for with your winnings?" Christopher asked.

"I gave some to those who are doomed," Cyrus replied honestly. He had already decided to stick to the story he had given Herrick at the jail, and he was prepared to stand for it. As it happened, the surly Franklin Peters swung around on his stool, an angry scowl on his face. Cyrus was not surprised by his presence, nor by the fact that he still held a firm grip on his stein of ale.

"You fed those—, those—" Peters stammered with heavy slur, then finally found a word and finished with, "witches!"

"Yes sir, I did such a thing," Cyrus replied evenly, hoping his respectful tone would be enough to settle the drunken man.

"Why would you do this," Franklin said unsteadily, and then his eyes focused on a thought, "unless you were conspiring with them to do wicked deeds!"

Cyrus had been steadily annoyed by this man, but now he was dangerously close to naming Cyrus a witch. Cyrus let his emotions run.

"DO NOT ACCUSE ME, OLD MAN!" he bellowed and stepped close to Franklin so that their noses nearly touched. He hoped his extreme agitation would be enough to be convincing. "You are a wretched man who spends his day inebriated and unkempt," he sneered, and he stepped back and gestured at the man's disheveled outfit. The whole tavern of men was silent, and all eyes were set on the confrontation. "The things I do *I* have to reckon with *God* at the end of each day!" He looked around the room, and continued to let his anger run its course so that now he was addressing the whole lot.

"Those who have been found guilty by the law shall pay their penalty before man and God! I elected an act of forgiveness, for the good of *my soul*, according to the teachings of the Bible!" Cyrus returned to stand in front of Franklin, who stood slack-jawed as he listened to Cyrus speak. "I will not permit you to slander my name and my deeds for your own pitiful, contemptible sad ends!"

He breathed loudly through his nostrils, certain that it could be heard across the room. After a few moments, Christopher Reilly stepped forward and gently touched Cyrus by the elbow, almost afraid to bring his wrath upon him. Cyrus allowed his friend to guide him back from the confrontation; Franklin slowly closed his mouth, took a swig of his ale, and then raised his stein in the air.

"Forgive me," Franklin said groggily. Cyrus made sure to let his apology linger for a few moments before tersely accepting it by nodding his head. Franklin turned back to the bar and Cyrus turned towards the door. As his eyes passed over the men of the tavern, a few raised their drinks in respect to Cyrus. Christopher stopped walking and turned to face Cyrus.

"Are you quite all right?" he asked Cyrus in a concerned, hushed voice. Cyrus took the opportunity to tug his waistcoat and tend to his frock.

"I am sure all is well," he replied, meeting Christopher's eyes. "I believe I made my point well."

"With all who are here," Christopher noted. He decided to change the subject. "What was your reason for coming by the tavern, to be sure?

"I wished to have an ale and to bid farewell, as I should be returning to Falmouth on the morrow," Cyrus said. "We expect to leave Salem well before dawn, as I will likely find much work to do at the smithy."

"Have you settled with mum yet?" Christopher asked.

"Just now. May I have a loaf of bread and some ale for the morning drive?" Cyrus requested, pulling out his money.

"Of course," Christopher said, and left to gather Cyrus' requested purchases. Upon returning, he handed the bread and two bottles of the dark brown beer.

"Tell me, Cyrus," Christopher said just as Cyrus was about to leave. "They are to be hanged some time tomorrow, between the eighth and eleventh hours of the day. Why do you not want to stay and witness it?"

"My friend," Cyrus said. "I have seen my grandfather and my father die, and I have seen the battle dead from the occasional Indian attack. I do not feel the desire or need to be witness to the death of any man, regardless of the justice."

Seven, Duncan counted.

With his head and hands painfully stuck in the holes of the pillory and himself thus forced to stand bent over, he grimaced in silence at the latest whip lashing. His back seared white-hot; it was a pain unlike any he had never before experienced. He concentrated on all the men and women of this era, and those before and after it, who suffered at the lashings for their various perceived crimes. Tears of pain, frustration, and fury streamed down his face as he swallowed each attempt to cry out, but just as importantly, to not feel hatred for this unjust punishment.

A new crack-smack was vaguely heard by his ears, accompanied by another stab of pain that crossed his back and the previous spots the whip had landed.

Eight.

Saturday, August 23 1692

CHAPTER XXXII

The wagon was loaded with all the supplies. Brent, Aaron and Cyrus had mostly finished their planning before nine o'clock, at which point they went to sleep in shifts. Aaron drew the first shift, followed shortly by Brent, and finally Cyrus. This was to ensure that Aaron awoke as early as was necessary for them to set the plan in motion. Now it was around five A.M. and they were already almost out of town.

"Ugh," Aaron said, "I have an itch on my nose!"

"Don't scratch it," Brent reminded him. "This stuff isn't dry yet!"

"I am still unconvinced that this is necessary," Cyrus remarked with a yawn. The smooth features of his scalp were oddly surprising to see, even in the morning twilight; Brent had to stifle several amused smiles.

"I told you," Brent said brightly, "They might expect Indians, or even monsters of some kind. They won't expect this; it's all meant to shock them and make them hesitate to react. It's time to use their superstitions to our advantage."

The two had put up several arguments when Brent explained it to them, as well as during the actual preparation. Brent was forced to admit, however, that sleeping with the flour paste matting his hair down was uncomfortable, and made sleeping a bit less restful.

After half an hour, they reached the woods and made their trek to the horses. After feeding the horses (and settling them down from their fright at their bizarre costumes), Aaron provided all three men with some bread and ale. Brent nearly gagged at the first taste of the ale; it was as bitter as the beer he was used to, but something about it seemed spoiled. Still, he realized that neither Aaron nor Cyrus had a problem with it, so he decided to grin and bear it.

They went over the plan a couple more times, this time pantomiming a few of the parts for practice. When they finished, the sky had softened to a dark pink. For what was probably the twentieth time, Brent checked to make sure the Opener was securely in his pocket. *This is our only way home*, he constantly reminded himself. As he checked his pockets, he also noted the small dagger in his left pocket, to be used to cut the ropes of the nooses. He had sharpened it himself last night to make sure it would sever the ropes quick and clean.

All they had to do now was wait until sunrise, and then the countdown would begin.

Lisa woke up, chilly and a bit nauseated. She sat up and looked around. The sun had already begun to rise, as evidenced by the generic glow that came from the window just out of her line of sight. She glanced around and noticed that Goody Proctor was already awake and watching her with a maternal smile. *Widow Proctor now,* Lisa reminded herself with a pang of guilt.

She looked further down the row of stalls, and saw the now-familiar pairs of dirty feet and simple, damaged shoes that lay shackled and protruding from the cells in the deep regions of the jail.

"How do you feel this morn, Child?" Proctor asked sweetly, in a soft voice so as not to awaken the others.

"I'm fine," she muttered, and gave a slight smile back to Widow Proctor. She turned to her own thoughts.

Lisa hugged herself, both to keep warm and to give herself a semblance of safety and comfort. She had been through an emotional quagmire since the verdict was read yesterday.

First was the shock of actually hearing her name called out, followed by the sentence of death. Part of Lisa was fine with that, seeing as Cyrus had promised a rescue. However, as soon as they returned to the jail, Lisa had discovered that one of the jail's residents, a woman named Ann Foster, had died that morning.

The seventy-two year-old woman had been sitting quietly, humming softly but not making sensible words, as Lisa had been told upon her return. Then, near the eleventh hour, she simply slumped sideways, falling to her right and then rolling to a sprawl. It was the third such death this year, according to Wilmot Redd and Elizabeth Proctor; the first two they reported were two women named Sarah Osborne and Lydia Dustin. Lisa remembered that during their group gathering the previous morning, Ann Foster had introduced herself bashfully and then said little else before

Lisa left for trial.

It had disgusted Lisa how frail, dirty, and haggard the jailers had allowed these women to get, and it infuriated her. However, she also realized that the rescue that was supposed to be happening for her and the guys also made her feel guilty for leaving these nice women and the little girl without a way out of this situation. For the rest of the evening, she had simply sat curled up in her cell with her knees tucked tight in her chest. She had cried for the death of Ann. She then felt anger and frustration at the jailers for letting the woman die, and for mistreating her. She felt helpless and hopeless because there was nothing she could do to make them be more humane. This led to the frustration she felt towards the women for refusing to try to escape; most of them stuck by their feelings that even if they were not witches, their jailing was punishment for some unknown crimes that God wanted them to pay retribution for.

Then she worried about the hanging; what if they weren't able to rescue them? Would she die, strangled in a past she had never cared to know about before? However, wrangling with this questions only reminded her that she was being selfish; what about all these women in here, who didn't have a chance of rescue or help? Lisa felt like a horrible person for leaving them, especially the tragic four-year-old Dorcas, who no longer really knew her family and whose future couldn't be anything but bleak. And by the time Lisa reached these thoughts, it brought her back to the first set, and the emotional cycle would begin anew.

However, she had now had some sleep, and while she still felt pangs of remorse at abandoning these women to this horrible treatment, she allowed herself the luxury, for a few minutes, of the hope that in a few hours, she would be able to enjoy a very long shower and a large cheeseburger.

It was not long, though, before she slipped into fretting over the hanging, the rescue, and the guilt. After a bit of sitting silently, Elizabeth Proctor made to scoot towards her.

"Lisa," she said. It was the first time the woman had addressed her by her name. Lisa looked up at her. Miss Proctor continued, "I want to pray with you. May we?"

Wilmot and a few of other women had begun to walk towards her; it gave her the chills, having a horror-movie feel to it. It felt very real and final; she could very truly die in the next couple of hours.

All the women knelt and brought their hands together in classic prayer pose, and Lisa realized that she too should kneel. Jingling with a noise that seemed somehow suddenly louder, Lisa knelt down. It felt weird to do so; she was pretty sure that in her entire life in going to a Baptist church, she had never knelt to pray. However, she dutifully and respectfully joined the eight women, in a flattened circle, and Elizabeth began a prayer.

"Dearest Lord, it is I, Elizabeth Proctor. I humbly bow my head before Thee, in the hopes and desire that you will receive our friend and sister, Lisa, into your loving arms, welcoming her into your Heaven."

Lisa felt oddly out of place for a moment when her

name had been mentioned, but she was quickly drawn back into Proctor's prayer. She sensed a deep compassion, and a bond, that apparently Elizabeth had also noticed had developed between them since Lisa's arrival.

After another minute of what Lisa felt like was a prayer that her preacher might have easily given, the circle of nine women said 'amen', and shifted to a sitting position. There seemed to still be a heavy sadness in the group; the loss of Martha to Tuesday's hanging and then Ann was a lot for these broken women to endure.

The conversations were sparse and quiet; Lisa had to fight off the concern that maybe something had gone wrong with the hanging. She began to wonder if they had forgotten about her. She had to remind herself that Jeremy would not let them do anything without making sure she was okay, but she also reminded herself that there really was nothing he could do in that case.

After what seemed like hours, the jail door opened.

Jeremy stepped around the end of the jail, led by Constable Smith. He looked intently for Duncan, and spotted him about twenty feet down the side of the jail. He was still trapped in the stocks, and his shirt was missing and he was slumping in a weakened fashion. Jeremy felt deep concern for the man he'd deeply distrusted only a couple of days ago.

"To the cart, and try nothing, boy," Smith snarled at him in his thick accent. Jeremy did as he was told, but went slowly as he continued to take in Duncan's appearance from afar.

"Be swift, lad!" Smith stuck out his foot and gave Jeremy a hard shove in the hindquarters, causing him to fall to the ground. With Smith laughing and heading towards Duncan, Jeremy stood and dusted himself off. His yellow polo was stained and dirty, and he gave up rather quickly, making his way to the oxcart. He climbed into the back and quickly took a seat so that he could watch Duncan. Lisa was in the cart also, and waved a quick wave as she too watched Smith and Duncan.

Smith kicked Duncan in the gut, and Jeremy had to stifle a yell. Duncan struggled to regain his footing, and Smith set about unlocking the pillory. While he did so, Jeremy could not help but notice there was some kind of litter that lay on the ground around the stocks.

Once the top half was lifted from the stocks, Duncan slumped to the ground. Jeremy and Lisa both could hear Smith yelling at him to get up and calling him a wicked lying slave.

"I wish we could help him," Lisa said.

"I know," Jeremy seethed. If it weren't for the musket at Smith's right side, and Constable Herrick tending to things with the horses, Jeremy would have already vaulted the side of the cart and laid out the red-haired law man.

After a few minutes, Duncan slowly got up, holding his arms unsteadily in front of him in a defensive posture. He gathered up his shirt and slowly pulled it on, twisting in obvious pain as he did. Jeremy was sure that he saw splashes of red on Duncan's shirt.

After another minute of staggering, his gait seemed to get a little more steady and sure-footed as he neared the cart. Reaching the wagon, Duncan finally climbed up, with Jeremy and Lisa helping to pull him on.

"Thank you," he wheezed. He stayed on his side, taking care not to roll onto his lacerated back.

"Are you okay?" Lisa asked with concern in a whisper.

Duncan grunted in response. "Please excuse me if I'm not the most neighborly," he said, interrupted occasionally with strong winces of pain as the oxcart bounced over bumps before turning around.

"What happened?" Lisa asked, looking up at Jeremy. "Why were you out on those things?"

Jeremy opened his mouth to reply but Duncan spoke up first.

"I have been declared 'property of the township'," he said. "So, for my tall tale about being from Port Royal, I got ten lashings and a night in the pillory."

"Oh, my God," Lisa gasped. "You mean you were out there all night?"

"Yep," Duncan said, finally sitting up and rubbing his wrists and neck. "And every time I began to nod off, my knees would buckle and I'd pull something in my neck. I got no sleep, and late last night some kids threw food at me."

"Duncan," Jeremy said, but couldn't think of anything to say. "I'm sorry," was all he could come up with, and he felt lame for coming up short.

"Don't worry about it," Duncan said with eyes closed,

massaging his neck and shoulders with both shackled hands. The oxcart turned around, and began to go back down the road towards the jail, which the constables had referred to as 'Prison Lane'.

"I'll be fine," he grunted in discomfort a moment later.

Salem looked a lot different in broad daylight of sixteen ninety-two than it did in twenty-ten. There were fewer buildings, but not as sparse as a ghost town that Brent had been imagining. There were people, but they mostly were standing, not just walking randomly, like in the movies. There was a rustic, almost friendly and welcoming look to a town that for several decades was known for its reclusive rejection of all things not Puritan.

The trio sat in silence for most of the ride, taking in the sights of the town on their last trek through Sixteen Ninety-Two Salem. Lisa reflected on the sadness and guilt she had wrestled with all the previous night, and Duncan simply tried to not feel pain. Jeremy kept a close watch on both, but neither seemed to want anything, so Jeremy sat cross-legged and soaked up everything he could about his last hour in historic Salem. He had seen much of the town when they were taken back and forth during the trial, but now there was an odd calm to the world. The only interruptions of the serenity he sensed were the few dozen citizens who lined the streets and occasionally threw things at the cart. It seemed that many people were simply bad throwers, as most of the rotted vegetables they threw either flew right over the cart and landed beyond it, or smashed against the side, barely getting on the three prisoners. Lisa tried to dodge things, but never really needed to; Duncan seemed either oblivious to it or simply did not care. Jeremy had to stifle a teasing laugh at the townsfolk; with the possibility of going home so close, he didn't want to do anything to mess it up.

Thinking about how the town looked in comparison with the future, he noticed that the buildings seemed older and grayer, and the lots seemed to alternate between reasonably well-kept half-acres of farm and completely undeveloped thickets. Jeremy did some mental mapping, trying to compare what he knew of Twenty-Ten Salem with what he currently saw around him. It was difficult, considering that there were nearly no real familiar landmarks after three hundred years. As if on cue, he caught sight of the old Corwin Witch House coming up to their right. *It's probably just 'Judge Corwin's house' here,* Jeremy noted to himself. Still, he could not help but notice that the color was different than the charcoal-grey he was familiar with; here, it was grey, but much lighter, with patches here and there that brown, as if those spots were never covered with paint stain. Perhaps the job had been done lazily or possibly in a hurry, and had never been followed up on. As they passed the Corwin house, Jeremy had an insight, and looked back to imagine where Paolo's restaurant would stand in the future, the night this whole adventure began. In spite of the dark situation, Jeremy could not help feeling a bit geeked out at the moment.

They were reaching the outskirts of town. After another several hundred yards, the cart took the fork in the road to the right, taking them out of town. *I bet we're on Boston Street now,* he realized. He could see the bridge that crossed over a small river that Jeremy did not recall from the future. He frowned, his mental map suddenly disoriented. Lisa's voice took him the rest of the way from his musings.

"So then, now, what is the plan?" Lisa asked. Jeremy shrugged.

"We don't know any specifics about the plan," Duncan said. Lisa did not like hearing that.

"Whatever it is, though, let me tell you I hope my part is small," Duncan commented through pained grunts. "Hopefully I'll have the strength to do whatever Brent needs us to do here in a few minutes. It's time to get the hell out of this place. And time."

Jeremy and Lisa couldn't agree more.

CHAPTER XXXIII
8:30 A.M.
Boundary of Salem Town
(a.k.a. Near Gallows Hill)

"Are you sure that they're going to be able to save us?" Lisa asked Duncan.

"No," he conceded, offering an ironic smile. The cart made a sharp left turn after crossing the bridge.

"Oh, I'm not feeling too good about this," Lisa said, tensing up and drawing her legs in to her chest. Jeremy scooted closer to her, and lifted his chains over her head so he could hug her. She let him.

"We gotta have faith that we'll get out of this," Jeremy said to her in her ear.

"I can't feel my faith right now," she said after a few moments, sniffling after the words.

"Neither can I," Jeremy said after a cold realization that he felt the same. His stomach was full of butterflies. "But we still have to try."

Lisa thought about that for a few moments. However, everything was colliding in her mind; the trial, the jail, the women, her guilt, the noose. *My God, I'm about to get hung!* Lisa thought with alarm. Suddenly, dread at the situation began to grip her insides. She wanted to jump off the cart and run wildly into the safety of the woods. She also desperately wanted Jeremy to hold her forever; there was safety and comfort in his hug. Unsure of what to do, she just sat still and loved her boyfriend, trying to squeeze every drop of love into this moment.

Too soon, the oxcart pulled to a stop.

Aaron placed his pocket sundial in a patch of sunlight upon the first sounds of people heading to witness the execution. He looked over at his companions; Cyrus stood forward of the group, facing the sounds and listening intently while Brent was applying the last bit of paint onto the horses' faces.

"It is nearly eight and thirty of the clock," he reported in a whispered voice.

Brent's stomach became churned at the update.

"Holy smokes," Brent said, feeling woozy. "We're going to get shot at." He took a couple of deep breaths, struggling to regain his composure.

"You have been shot at before," Cyrus pointed out casually; Brent had shared the story of his first visit to the past while they were preparing this rescue.

"Yeah, but that wasn't planned," Brent said. Part of him seemed to be rebelling against the idea of intentionally putting himself in danger. "This time, we're inviting them to shoot."

Aaron walked over to Brent, set a hand on his shoulder, and looked him full in the eye.

"My new friend, it is a good plan, and I believe it will succeed. You can do this."

Brent couldn't help but chuckle at the whole moment; perhaps it was the friendly concern and blue face staring back at him that had made the difference. However, somehow, Aaron's gesture helped. His confidence began to return, and he was able to fight back his anxiety.

"Thanks, man," Brent said with an appreciative smile after a few refreshing breaths. He then let the excitement of the possibility of victory start to thrill him, further driving his fears back. While he still had the nerve, he said, "Okay then, let's do this."

Aaron gathered his bow and proceeded to mount his horse, and then helped Brent mount behind him. Cyrus took his position at the reigns of the second horse, whose job was to pull the cart for the escape.

"Good luck," Cyrus said earnestly.

"Good luck to you," Aaron and Brent responded, each to the other two.

Brent once again checked on his tools in his pockets as they broke camp, and headed to their planned positions. Everything was in place; now it was time to save the day.

About a hundred yards away, the gallows tree stood out in this opening of thin woods. The majority of the trees surrounding it were thin and only about fifteen feet high; one might even have called them 'scraggly'. Behind the constable's oxcart was the tree line and the road they had just exited, and then the muddy slope of the hill, which descended to sea level. From there, the sloppy shore became a large pond that fed out to the North River off to their right. Across the pond it became a reeded marsh, which continued under the distant bridge they had just crossed. Jeremy realized that he could not place the bridge in his mental map; this pond must not exist in his own time. In fact, it was hard to even guess where they were exactly.

The hanging tree was ominous and foreboding to look at as they had approached it. Not only were the branches strong and large, but it was easy to tell which branch was used for the hangings. At least nine ropes remained tied to it, each of varying length, and some with frayed ends. Four of them looked freshly cut, so had not yet frayed much.

The tree sat on top of a low hill; high enough to be seen by town residents for a couple of miles, but lower than the other hill behind them, which Jeremy could only guess was the place the future Salem would call 'Gallows Hill', since it was highest hill in this area of Salem. He thought it strange that they were not going to Gallows Hill, until he vaguely remembered hearing someone mention that Gallows Hill wasn't where the real hangings had taken place. Now he knew for sure.

The cart halted under the branch, stopping in just the right position so that the end of the oxcart sat just below the old ropes.

Most of the magistrates had come and were having muted conversations with one another while standing to the side of the great tree. Jeremy noted that they were not wearing their court dress robes. Magistrate Gedney was dressed more similar to Doctor Griggs; Jonathan Hawthorne, the magistrate who seemed to be more of a prosecutor, looked more like a merchant now, as did Judge Corwin. Sewall, who had been clerk, stood beside them, resembling a young lawyer. Speaking with Sewall and Corwin was Reverend Mather. Beside the men were their horses, lashed to the spindly trees that made up the majority of these woods. Magistrate Stoughton apparently had decided not to attend, as did Judge Sewall, and the two quiet magistrates.

The constables dismounted from the driver seat of the cart, and the two dozen or so people who had come to witness their hanging had begun to settle into various spots, some standing as far as halfway down the muddy hill. Jeremy looked up into the sky, and realized that the sun had not come out today yet. The sky was a dreary dull gray-white, and the clouds had little form to them.

After a few moments, it occurred to Jeremy that neither constable had come back to handle the condemned. *Condemned*! His stomach ran ice cold at the word. *I could die here in a few moments!* Jeremy also began to fret, but as soon as he looked over at Lisa, he forced himself to maintain his composure. He then looked out into the wooded path that they arrived by, looking for some sign of their rescuers, but nothing looked out of place. *Where are those guys?* He wondered with annoyance. *There is such a thing as* too *close*. He sighed nervously as he continued to fight off his fears.

However, the man who had given the opening prayer at the main trial, Nicholas Noyes, appeared from amongst the magistrates and walked over towards the oxcart. Another man, a twenty-something fellow with a large black mustache who Jeremy had not seen before, walked alongside Noyes, carrying three noosed ropes.

"Up!" ordered Constable Smith from behind Jeremy, causing him and Lisa to jump in surprise.

Jeremy sneered at the man as he stood; he could not resist the opportunity.

"You know, there is one trick I could teach you," he whispered to the constable. "It involves soap and water."

Constable Smith glared hatefully at him, and was about to respond when Noyes and the other man reached the oxcart. Instead, his eyes darted back and forth between Jeremy and Noyes, weighing the moment. Finally, he decided against whatever he was thinking.

Jeremy helped Lisa stand, while Duncan stood, flinching at the silent screams of his untreated lashings. Jeremy's own single lashing still bothered him from time to time, so he knew his discomfort was a positive massage compared to Duncan's.

"Sherriff, if you will," Noyes extended an arm for his associate. Sherriff George Corwin nodded solemnly and climbed up onto the wagon, forcing the three to step back out of his way.

"Please promise me you'll keep your cool for just a few more minutes?" Duncan requested of Jeremy in whispers while the Sherriff tossed each noose over the branch.

"Bah," Jeremy dismissed the idea. "Besides, they wouldn't understand half the insults I'd toss at them anyway." Duncan smirked.

"Where do you think they are," Jeremy whispered, trying to sound casual.

"You know as much as I do, Jeremy," Duncan replied. "Still, if Brent's late, he's fired." Jeremy looked at Duncan's deadpan face, and could not decide if the scientist was joking or not.

The Sherriff finished his task, and turned to the prisoners.

"Come forward, one of you," he ordered with indifference. When none of them took the step forward, Constable Smith vaulted over the side and landed behind them. He grabbed Lisa from behind and pushed her forward. Lisa let out a surprised and frightened screech, fighting back.

"Do not fear, girl," Smith hissed in her ear, "'tis but only a bundle of string!"

"Hey!" Jeremy barked, grabbing the Irishman by the elbow with both shackled hands. Duncan's shoulders dropped slightly. "How about letting her go and putting that string around your own neck!"

Instead of continuing to struggle with Lisa, the constable paused for a moment, chuckling oddly, and then rounded on Jeremy and landed a powerful jab on Jeremy's lower jaw. The strike did not knock him off his feet, but it did stun him for a few moments, causing him to stumble around the oxcart for a moment. The crowd responded with laughter, mild applause and some jeering.

"That will be your last lesson, boy!" Smith said through his thick accent.

"You need to work on your definition of 'cool'," Duncan suggested quietly as he helped to steady the teetering young man. Jeremy nodded in agreement, but still felt like he had done the right thing.

While Lisa had been distracted by Jeremy's latest punishment, Smith had pulled her closer to the noose and held her in place as the Sherriff worked the noose around her neck. She struggled and thrashed her head about, but she was no match for the two seasoned lawmen; they had hanged several convicted witches this year alone.

Without words but with an iron glare, the Constable stepped back and set his hand under Jeremy's elbow. Jeremy frowned and reluctantly let himself be led forward. His breathing became rapid and his heart was racing as he watched the rope get forced over his head, and half of it cross his field of vision. He could feel the scratchy fibers irritate his neck, and he felt panic rising again. His throbbing jaw and a faint taste of metal distracted him from his anxieties; he suspected that he had some blood in his mouth. He reached up to adjust the noose, but his hand was smacked painfully by the Sherriff, who simply shook his head in the universal message of 'no'. He looked over at Lisa, who looked back at him.

"How's your jaw?" she whispered. Jeremy could hear the quiver in her voice.

"Still there, but maybe a little bigger now," his quipped; it felt like one side of his face was thick and larger now.

"I don't think they're coming," she mouthed at him with a subtle headshake. A tear rolled down her cheek and fell off her face; Jeremy desperately wanted to comfort her. He wanted to lift her spirits, but time was truly running out and he was at a loss.

Smith grabbed Duncan by the shirt, and snarled at him. Duncan felt his disgust at this man well up, and all the injustices that he had suffered since arriving in this historical place came to his mind. Desiring to unleash his anger, and he began to reach back. Smith saw this and let go, staring him fully in the eyes.

"Yer want to kill me, do yeh, Negro?" Smith teased in a whisper. "Perhaps I ought to have slipped in a few more lashes."

Duncan stared at the man, feeling every bit of the hatred he had fought the night before to avoid. He began to pull back his right hand, but then he made himself drop it. He forced himself to regain control; this was not the person he wanted to be, and hatred was not an emotion he wanted to be servant to. He made himself take a breath and lift his chin; he promised himself that he would deal with this tomorrow. He let Smith guide him to the noose.

After a few moments of helplessly looking into Lisa's eyes, Smith's remarks to Duncan drew Jeremy's attention to his right. Duncan looked as stoic as he had since his first met him two days ago, but now there seemed to be a real uncertainty and concern under his Vulcan-like demeanor. Jeremy closed his eyes.

Please God, he prayed silently, *don't let us die.*

"Hear ye all who bear witness," Sheriff George Corwin called out to the crowd. He was so loud it made the three prisoners jump. The whispered conversations subsided; Jeremy noticed at the cluster of magistrates had turned their attention to the hanging and each now stood with their hands clasped in front of their waists.

"These persons, so named as Lisa Carson, Jeremy Macer and the slave Duncan have all practiced the horrible crime of Witchcraft." The Sherriff spoke loudly and slowly for all to hear and understand. "In the trial held in the County of Essex on the twenty-first day of August, were indictments given, as they did plead not guilty, were they found guilty by the Jury. The sentence of death has been passed on these sorry souls." He paused a moment before continuing.

"Therefore, in the name of their majesties William and Mary, King and Queen over England and her realms, that on this day, Saturday the twenty-second of August, in the year of our Lord sixteen hundred and ninety-two, they are to be hanged by the neck until they be dead!"

There were incoherent cheers and more applause from the crowd at this, except from the magistrates. They simply stood quietly to witness the proceedings.

This is it, Jeremy thought with disappointment. He reached out his left hand with some jingling; Lisa noticed and reached out her right hand, clasping it in his. He loved her, and he would miss her.

The Sherriff turned to face the condemned, and opened his mouth as if to speak, when there rang out in the grey, overcast morning air a growing throb of galloping hoof beats. What the onlookers saw next was unbelievable, to say nothing of bizarre. Jeremy himself could hardly believe what he was seeing.

Everyone began to turn and face the opening of the Hanging Tree thicket. Beyond the tree line, along the path that brought them to the Hanging Tree, appeared two blue-headed men. They were both bald, and one had blue spikes rising from his scalp. They were dressed in flowing black robes, riding on the back of a large light-brown horse with blue splashes on its neck and face. At the speed the horse was galloping, their long black cloaks billowed behind them, giving them an almost mythical, frightening appearance. Immediately behind them emerged another bald, blue man dressed in black, driving a small wagon led by a black horse.

From the back of the horse with two riders, the blue-spiked man let out a throaty war cry.

The crowd began screaming as they scattered from the attacking blue wraiths.

CHAPTER XXXIV

It took a moment for everyone on the oxcart to register what was happening due to the spectacle their rescuers had made in their grand appearance. Nicholas Noyes stood on the ground next to the cart, apparently frozen in dreadful fright at the sight; alternately, the Sherriff had leaped over the side of the oxcart and was crouched near the horses, next to a largely uninterested Constable Herrick.

Duncan started to painfully laugh out loud. As soon as he gathered his wits again, Jeremy let out a whoop of excitement, relieved to see them appear.

"The Blue Man Group is saving the day?" he grinned in amusement at Duncan. Duncan shrugged, sharing his amused smile.

"One thing about Brent: he always thinks outside the box," Duncan said with a measure of pride in his employee.

The spectators had largely separated themselves, opening a clear pathway for the blue-faced horsemen to ride up towards the oxcart. The magistrates had also suffered some chaos; a few of them were cowering a bit behind the trunk of the tree or another magistrate. Only Corwin and Hathorne seemed to maintain their composure. Corwin stood rigid, watching the action play out, while Hathorne was yelling orders at the people and the executing officers. Staring down the approaching menace as the hoof beats grew louder, Nicholas Noyes finally reacted to Hathorne's commands. Seeing this, both Jeremy and Duncan reached up to pull off their nooses.

Before he could get it over his chin, he saw Duncan fall off the wagon, but not hit the ground. Duncan's fingers were clutching the rope and he was trying to hold himself up with his hands, but struggled while he was choking and suspended in midair. Jeremy was about to let go of his own noose when he felt a shove at his butt, and he lost his balance, just barely tightening his grip on his noose before he fell off the wagon and hung from the tree. Terror took over; the scratchy ropes now cut off his air supply as he writhed, his toes occasionally scraping against the edge of the oxcart that he desperately wanted to get back onto.

"Jeremy!" Lisa cried out, stepping forward to help her boyfriend; she was stopped by the restraint of the noose. Constable Smith had apparently not lost his composure at the sight of the blue apparitions. Lisa had seen him slam his upper body into Duncan, knocking him off the cart, and then kicking out with his left boot at Jeremy's backside, knocking him off. He then turned his attention to Lisa as she had yelled Jeremy's name, and took one step forward before Lisa reacted.

Everything that she had experienced since her arrival gripped her to the core, and she felt as angry as she ever had in her life; perhaps angrier. Realizing that there was something she could do, she scrunched her face in fury, and took a half step toward the charging constable.

"HA-YAH!" she bellowed unconsciously, channeling all her emotions into her right leg as it swung upward into Constable Smith's groin. She had kicked with so much power the man was lifted off the floor about an inch or so. Smith froze midstep, his face drained of all blood. He collapsed to the floor of the oxcart in the fetal position, tears forming at his simpering face.

"Asshole!" Lisa furiously called him through clenched teeth, and then she threw off her noose and tried to help the guys.

Brent gripped Aaron's waist as they rode; he had been growling and snarling at the townspeople, trying to frighten them with his bizarre appearance.

"Look!" Aaron called back to him. Brent looked up and saw Duncan and Jeremy dangling by the ropes around their necks, both holding their nooses and trying to get their footing on the oxcart.

Brent's heart jumped, knowing that only a few precious moments remained to save their lives. He pulled the iron rod out of his pants belt with his left hand, held the knife in his right hand, shifted his weight slightly, and then announced, "I'm jumping off now!"

"Good luck!" Aaron said, and slowed his horse just as they finally were about ten feet from the wagon. Brent clutched Aaron's belt at the back with his right hand and used it for a balance point to spin himself backwards off the horse. He landed with less grace than he had desired, and tumbled once. Successfully rolling onto his feet, he was pleased with the end result despite his general lack of physical prowess. He noticed Cyrus was still racing the get-away wagon towards him, and only had a few dozen more yards left to go.

Aaron continued on with his own part of the plan, which was to distract and frighten everyone else. He had the reigns in one hand, and he pulled out his own iron bar, and then pulled out Brent's cell phone. He kicked his horse, and began charging towards the magistrates, and as he pulled close, he widened his eyes and aimed the phone at the men. Some of them cringed, and Aaron hit the button that Brent had showed him. A horrendous sound burst out of the small mysterious device (Brent had called it a 'band named Metallica'). The magistrates and several men nearby cringed and cowered as Aaron directed the horse to rear near several of them. After a few moments, Cotton Mather had managed to overcome his surprise and fright enough to have the presence of mind to pull out a pistol, and took aim. Aaron just barely caught sight of the pistol and remembered the iron bar. He swung it, and though he missed, the pistol flew out of Mather's hand and landed a few feet from him on the ground. Aaron gave a ferocious roar and snarl towards Mather, both as part of the whole act, and a little bit out of surprise at Brent's magic (which he had insisted was 'science'). Cotton Mather cringed at his appearance and sounds, and Aaron took the chance to turn the horse around and charge back towards the oxcart.

Back at the oxcart, Brent ran forward, charging the man who stood at the floor of the cart. Nicholas Noyes trembled, and Brent once again did his impression of a raptor, he quickly made wild and crazed faces, roaring and hissing as loud and fierce as he could. He used his momentum to leap up onto the cart next to Lisa, who was doing her best to help pull Jeremy aboard.

"They're choking! Help!" Lisa said, her voice betraying her panic. Brent went to reach up and cut their ropes, and suddenly realized the knife was no longer in his hands. He glanced at the ground where he had fallen off the horse, and the knife lay there in the dirty grass.

"Hurry!" Lisa yelled, pulling at Jeremy, who was turning purple. Duncan's thrashing was already slowing down dangerously. Only one idea came to mind to solve the problem.

"Stand back!" Brent told Lisa, and he reached into his pocket, pulled out the Time Opener, and pressed the activate button. The tip burned with hot energy and flame. People began to scream in fright and call for God at the sight of the Time Opener's fire.

"Hold!" ordered a man behind him. Brent turned and saw the Sherriff aiming a musket directly at him.

Annoyed and impatient with these people, Brent swung at the musket barrel with the iron bar in his left hand. It connected with a metallic clang, and Brent yanked as soon as the barrel and bar met. The musket was pulled out of the Sherriff's stunned hands, and Brent quickly turned back to the hanging men. He jabbed at the ropes right above the noose knot, and suddenly Jeremy fell hard onto the ground a few feet below. Lisa jumped down from the cart and helped loosen his noose just as Cyrus arrived with the wagon. Brent could hear Jeremy hacking and coughing as air returned to his lungs. Finally, Brent severed Duncan's rope, who then fell to the ground as well. He deactivated the Opener, leapt down, and made sure Duncan was breathing.

"Help me load him up!" Brent ordered, and Lisa and a weak Jeremy both help him lift the scientist onto the back of the wagon. Brent began to feel better as they were loading him on because Duncan had begun to help lift himself up.

Everyone else jumped onto the back of the wagon, and Cyrus lashed the reigns, directing the horse back into action. Unfortunately, there was more weight for him to pull, and the wagon took off, but much slower than it had arrived.

Aaron's horse was galloping up, and he pulled alongside the wagon, trying to see how to move on with the next stage of the plan. So far, they had been lucky, and no one had been fired upon. Brent stood up and bellowed.

"*You are foolish men! There are no such things as witches!*" he bellowed, faking his best Irish accent, but somehow he felt like he sounded more like a very poorly done Swedish accent. He had debated the choice of words with Aaron and Cyrus the night before; Aaron did not like the idea of the announcement at all, and while Cyrus liked it, he wanted something less incendiary. However, once Brent had convinced them to wear the blue paint all over their heads, he found that they would pretty much agree to almost all the rest of his suggestions.

By now, four of the officials had regained their wits enough to begin to pursue them.

"We aren't going fast enough!" Jeremy wheezed, feeling a bit concerned as about for men mounted horses and began to chase them.

"We know!" Brent said, annoyed with himself for not figuring the extra weight into his plan. He handed Jeremy the iron bar.

"Here! It's magnetized! If they get a musket close to you, use this to yank it out of their hands!" Brent explained to him. Duncan was finally sitting up and getting back to normal. Brent looked ahead; there was only about a dozen yards to go before they got out of the clearing of the thicket.

"Aaron!" Brent held out Aaron's bow and quiver. Aaron reached out and accepted it.

"Can you do it on horseback?" Their original plan had been for Aaron to fire from the wagon; after they changed the plan, it had been forgotten to check that detail.

"I shall try my best!" Aaron called back as he swung the quiver onto his shoulder, and shifted his weight on the horse's back. The horse slowed a bit, and Aaron urged him to keep pace.

Just as they took the corner, Brent took out his first pack of noise makers, and pulled the lighter out and lit them. He tossed them out, and they landed almost perfectly in the middle of the entrance to the clearing. With almost perfect timing, the set of firecrackers went off in a series of loud and sharp pops, frightening the horses and surprising the riders, slowing them down.

"Firecrackers!" Lisa said with surprised impress.

"Here, toss this in the road when I tell you to!" Brent said, handing her a small sack that seemed to be full of sand. He then turned and used the lighter to light the fabric that plugged some kind of fluid inside of a bottle. They looked behind them; the riders had just emerged from the thicket, braving the dangers of the noisemakers.

"Is that a Molotov cocktail?" Jeremy asked, pointing at the bottle.

"It will be if it works," Brent responded, and he lobbed the bottle as hard as he could towards their pursuers. A musket shot rang out. Everyone froze, taking a moment to check themselves to see if they had been hit. Then, they each exchanged glances to make sure no one else got hit. Another shot rang out.

"How much farther?" Brent called to Cyrus.

"Less than about four hundred feet!" Cyrus estimated. He continued to guide the horse over the uneven, winding road.

"Can I throw this yet?" Lisa asked. Brent shook his head. Then he pulled out his last two packs of firecrackers, and looked at Jeremy.

"It is *not* a Molotov cocktail," Brent said, pointing past the horsemen. The bottle lay on the ground, a small fire had spread around it, but the bottle had never exploded. "Going to have to scare 'em again!" He lit the firecrackers and threw them so that each one landed in separate wheel ruts in the road. Again, the rapid pops of the several individual noisemakers filled the air, and the horses reared, forcing their riders to have to regain control before they could continue the pursuit.

"We are almost at the trees!" Cyrus announced, continuing to work his horse as hard as he could.

"Great!" Brent yelled, exhilarated that their rescue plan was almost a success.

"Brent!" Aaron called out, holding three specially-prepared arrows out to him.

Brent took the arrows, and used the lighter to light two of the arrows. Then he tapped Lisa on the shoulder.

"Get ready!" He pointed to the middle of the road. "Just throw it down there, right in the center!" He looked behind him, to see how far they were from the trees they had prepared. "On the count of three. One…two… three!" he nodded, and she tossed the sack in the middle of the road. It landed near a spot where the dirt appeared to have been recently disturbed.

"It should be close enough!" Aaron remarked to the unasked question, and reached out a hand for an arrow. Brent handed one to him, and Aaron turned back, took careful aim, and released his arrow. However, instead of hitting the sack, it hit a one-foot-thick tree on one side of the road, which then exploded in a loud, muffled 'bang'. Everyone watched as the tree shifted near the top; the trunk was surrounded with a gray-and-brown dust cloud.

Meanwhile, Brent handed Aaron the second arrow, and he fired it in the same fashion, but at another tree on the other side of the road. Just before it exploded, Jeremy noticed that there were several of the sacks tied around it; he was pretty sure he had seen signs that the trees had been chopped into with an axe, too.

Aaron's second arrow landed on its mark as well, causing the tree to shift as well. By now, the first tree was falling, and the second tree fell within seconds of the first. Aaron took the third lit arrow, and fired it at the sack Lisa had dropped. It exploded, but there was a fourth 'bang' that followed, tossing brown dust high into the air and obscuring any view beyond the felled trees. The road was completely blocked; no one would be able to pursue them further.

It was finally over; they had escaped.

The party took no chances, and they raced along the highway, pushing the horses to the limit. After about ten minutes, they took the left turn, passing the general store that had the name of a man called Humphrey Case on its door. No one was out, which everyone agreed was for the best; no one could witness that the Blue Men had taken this road as their way of escape. The sun finally broke through the clouds, and shone down on them.

The final part of the plan had been that they make the trek back to the pond that would someday be called Cedar Pond. It was up to Aaron and Cyrus to identify that point in the road at which they needed to break off, since it was their wagon that had been damaged. Within half an hour, they had successfully spotted that point. They veered off into the woods, managing to wend their way half way into the foliage towards the pond before they had to leave the horses tied to trees. They made the rest of the way on foot.

"So, magnetizing the iron rods?" Duncan asked Brent. "I didn't see that coming."

"Just before we left Boston to come back here yesterday, I tied a couple of iron rods to the two wagon axles, and then used some wires to build an electromagnet coil," Brent explained, trying to choose his words so that Jeremy and Lisa could be a part of the conversation. "I then magnetized several bars. I had this really cool idea to have like nine or ten dangling from ropes on the trees, so that as the cops chased us, their muskets would get pulled off target." Brent pantomimed the action he imagined, drawing amused smiles from everyone.

"Sweet," Jeremy commented, impressed at all the stuff they had done. He jumped up onto a fallen log and walked along its slippery surface.

"So did you guys shave your heads to do this?" Lisa asked them, indicating their smooth blue scalps.

"No," Aaron chuckled, and both Cyrus and Brent said no and shook their shiny blue heads.

"We had to be unrecognizable," Brent began, and then Cyrus took over.

"Brent convinced us to put a flour paste in our hair to glue it down flat on our heads," Cyrus said with a bemused, blue smile.

"And the spikes on your head?" Duncan asked with a raised eyebrow.

"Eh, what can I say," Brent shrugged, stepping casually

on a jagged stump, and then bouncing off it. "I wanted to do something different." Everyone chuckled at his remark.

They approached the clearing that surrounded the pond. Brent saw where their footprints still were from the other day.

"I figure you can wash the paint off here, and change clothes. As long as you guys wash your hair and faces really well, there should be no reason anyone should link you to us," Brent reminded them as they got closer to the muddy beach.

"Well, I hate to almost get hanged and run, but," Jeremy interjected, "as cool as time travel is, I think this was quite enough for me."

"Really?" Lisa asked, tilting her head in surprise. "You, Mister 'This Is So Cool'?"

"Well," he shrugged, "enough for *today*."

"I don't know about any of you," Lisa said, "But I do not want to be here any more than I have to. No offense," she said, turning to Aaron and Cyrus. Both men bowed the heads briefly in respect.

"I think we agree that we understand," Cyrus said with a sympathetic smile.

"I want to thank you for everything you did to save us," Duncan said, stepping forward and extending his hand. Aaron took it first, and then Cyrus had his turn. "I know it took a lot to put yourselves at risk, and I cannot thank you enough."

"Yeah," Jeremy said, shaking hands with his historic friends. "I'm glad to have met you guys. I hope you enjoyed it in the future."

"We did not," Aaron admitted with a smile, "but you were quite hospitable, nonetheless." Cyrus shook Jeremy's hand.

"Do tell your friend Elizabeth that I quite enjoyed our conversations," he said, a twinkle appearing in his eye for a brief moment.

"I'll do that, I promise," Jeremy said. He was really going to miss them.

Lisa stepped forward, taking her turn to bid them farewell. She took Aaron's hand with both of hers, and leaned up and kissed him politely on his blue cheek.

"Thank you so much," she said, and hugged him as she was overwhelmed with relief and appreciation. She then turned and did the same for Cyrus.

"It was our pleasure," Cyrus said.

"You are our friends," Aaron pointed out. "There was no other option."

"It was sweet just the same," Lisa said, stepping back and smiling. "I hope you and your wife have a healthy baby."

"Thank you very kindly," Aaron smiled, suddenly stricken with the desire to go home. He had put it off to help, but now it was time to go.

"What are you going to name it?" Lisa asked.

Aaron looked at Cyrus, and then at Lisa sheepishly. "We have decided that, if a boy, we shall call him John, and if a girl, she would be Marie," he said.

"Those are wonderful names," Lisa said. "Tell your wife

we all wish you the best!"

"Yeah," Jeremy said. "Good luck!" Duncan and Brent also offered their well-wishing for his fatherhood.

Aaron reached into his pocket, suddenly remembering that he had Brent's cell phone, and handed it to him. Brent took it, and then sighed reluctantly as he put it in his pocket.

"Thanks a bunch guys," Brent said. "I mean it. For putting up with me, and for helping us."

Aaron demurred, and Brent stepped over to Cyrus.

"I want to apologize for hitting you," Brent said. "I— you were looking out for us. Thanks."

"You hit well," Cyrus said, rubbing his jaw. "Do not forget, too, that you also were looking out for your friends. I would be honored to have gained such loyalty."

Brent suddenly felt self-conscious, and changed the subject, pulling out the time device.

"Ready to go?"

He began to set the time as Jeremy, Lisa, and Duncan all voiced their readiness.

"Hey, wait," Jeremy said. Everyone looked at him. "Did you say this is Cedar Pond?"

"Yeah, I guess so," Brent said. "Why?"

"My house is somewhere around here," Jeremy said. "At least, it will be in a few hundred years."

"And in a few minutes," Lisa pointed out.

"I'm just saying, why don't we all go to my house and go from there?" He suggested. Everyone considered it for a moment, and agreed.

"What time are you setting for us?" Duncan asked Brent.

"What time do you suggest?" Brent asked in reply.

"Six A.M."

Brent did as he was instructed. He activated the Time Opener, and it spit its fire and electrical discharges. He bent down, started the rift, and pulled upward to just above head level. The suspended line of blue and yellow energy burst open, revealing a dark, twilight sky. On the outside of the rift was sixteen-ninety two nature, with birds chirping and other things buzzing, and on the inside of the rift was quiet, with the occasional distant hum of a semi driving along I-95.

Brent stepped aside to let everyone through. Lisa went first, and the lower side of the rift severed some of the chains of her foot shackles. Jeremy stepped through, noticing Lisa's success with the rift, and used it to destroy his chains.

"Hurry up, please," Duncan said. Brent stood aside to allow Duncan through, but Duncan frowned and set his hand on Brent's shoulder, directing him through the rift first. Finally, as the rift showed signs of destabilizing, Duncan stepped through, severing his chains and then stepping back from the rift.

The rift began to close, and within seconds, Aaron and Cyrus, and the world of sixteen ninety two were gone from their view. Duncan, Brent, Lisa, and Jeremy all stood for a moment in the cool, dark, July night air, reveling in the moment. At long last, they were home, and safe.

EPILOGUE - 1692

Noon
Saturday, August 23, 1692
Jonathan Corwin's House

Everyone stood around the sitting room in the house of Jonathan Corwin, talking quietly in small groups as they waited this emergency meeting to come to order. All the magistrates had been summoned, including those who had not attended the attempted hanging. The only person who was not a member of the town judgeship was Cotton Mather, who had been ordered to sit in the meeting.

Outside the Corwin House, Sheriff George Corwin waited alongside Noyes and the Constables James Smith and Joseph Herrick. They had been directed to await the conclusion of the meeting of the magistrates, curious and anxious to learn how the town leaders would handle the crisis of the witches and blue-skinned men who rescued them from the noose.

Earlier, the four men who gave chase to the witches returned after the trees had fallen and so obstructed the road that led from the town to the Hanging Tree. Hathorne had taken authority immediately, ordering all the citizens to record their names on a parchment. Once that was done, he then required all men and women present (there had come only five women) to swear their oath not to reveal the events they had just witnessed, until further instruction was given. Each had solemnly sworn before God not to discuss or speak on the failed hanging, even in the privacy of their homes.

Jonathan Corwin entered the sitting room, his noble features seemed more sharp and forbidding than usual, perhaps the result of the escape that had occurred. He carried parchment and ink, and handed them to Sewall the Clerk. He then paused at the center of the entryway of the room, taking a moment to make eye contact with each man in attendance. Finally, he spoke.

"How could this escape happen?" he asked. He waited to allow the men to consider their answers.

"Honorable Corwin—" Cotton Mather began.

"Enough!" Magistrate Gedney barked, his angry face suggesting a loss of patience in anything Mather had to say. "It was *you* who convinced us to rush this trial, and to bring them to hang with haste!"

Several of the other men in the room nodded or uttered their agreement with Gedney.

"I tell you to have not done so would have been the equal of this ill-fated day!" Mather argued back. Corwin watched silently as the two men debated.

"Indeed! If we had followed our own course," Gedney said angrily and red-faced, "they would be in the jail this minute, and we would not have been forced to suffer those unnatural beings and their magic! The men were *blue*!"

"Hear hear!" a few of the men seconded. Embattled, Cotton Mather turned to Corwin, hoping for some support.

"The matter at the moment is not who is blameworthy," Corwin said evenly. His lips drew into a taut line. "The matter is how we must proceed, inasmuch as we cannot allow this—" Corwin paused, seeking the right word, and then said, "*disgrace* to become known."

Each man mulled his words, although Mather and Gedney seemed more distracted with exchanges of despising glances. Finally, Wait Still Winthrop, the Governor's Council who was sitting in on behalf of the absent Lieutenant Governor and Magistrate William Stoughton, spoke up.

"This must be made such that it never happened," Winthrop said.

"What do you suggest?" Hathorne inquired, suspicious of the slender man's point.

"I suggest that we remove any evidence that anything official has happened over the past three days, aside from regular town and county business," Winthrop said. Every man gasped at the suggestion.

"Destroy court records and legal documents?" Corwin said, unable to believe that such a thought had been expressed; and by the representative of the King and Queen, no less!

"Everything," Winthrop stated. "Burn everything you have that relates to the presence of these people. I will not carry news of this day to Governor Phips, or even London, and in doing so bring the King's shame onto me, this Colony, and this town."

"What of the people who have been witness this day?" Gedney asked.

"They must be compensated for their eternal silence,"

Cotton Mather said, dumbfounded at the prospects of quieting the gossip of many dozens of men.

"It can be no less than unanimous. This is the agreement of the magistrates?" Corwin asked, requiring a clear answer from every man. No one dissented. "We shall burn and destroy the documents and statements of records of the examination, trial, and indictments. The felled trees must also be removed and destroyed. We shall use the town treasury to bribe each who was witness to-day. The expense will be pretended to be for a town harbor ship which will unfortunately be lost in sinking. What of informing Stoughton?"

"I will return to Boston after noon today, and I will inform him," Mather offered.

"I shall accompany you," Winthrop said, settling the matter.

Corwin closed the meeting, declaring that the people who were named Jeremy Macer, Lisa Carson, and their slave Duncan, never existed, except in stories told over ales. They would become myth or fable, for the magistrates knew they would never be able to extinguish the rumors except by ignoring them.

No record would survive, no evidence would remain; no, not even spectral evidence would prove that any such individuals had ever trod on soil in the town of Salem.

After the meeting, the Sherriff, Executor Noyes, and the Constables were informed on the decision of the magistrates. They were sworn to secrecy on the matter, and then ordered to arrest any man who spoke of the matters of this past week since the hangings on Tuesday. All four men nodded their understanding, and broke their meeting to execute their duties.

Over the next few days, all who stood present to the non-hanging received a compensation of one pound, six shillings.

Mather returned to Boston as promised, and together with Wait Still Winthrop, informed the lieutenant governor of things that had come to pass. Stoughton, for his part, managed to retain his dignified control, in spite of the gravity of the news.

To the good fortune of the town leaders, the events of that week quickly faded from the general public memory. By dusk of Monday, whispers around town had turned to the latest gossip, none of which, thankfully, included talk of witches.

Life in Salem returned to its own version of normal.

The fire-glow of the hole through which their friends had just disappeared faded, and Aaron and Cyrus proceeded to set about cleansing themselves of their disguise. They disrobed and used the pond to wash; soon, the blue was only in the water, and both men had pink skin on their faces and full manes of hair on their heads. After their swim, they emerged from the water, and went to put on fresh clothing. Something near the wagon caught Cyrus' eye.

"Hallo, what is this?" he said, walking over and picking up the strange bag.

"What is it?" Aaron asked, pulling on his trousers.

Cyrus showed him a bag made of brown paper, which was crumpled but filled with something loose and heavy. Cyrus brought it over to Aaron, unfurling the top of the bag and looking inside. He showed it to his friend.

"Dear Lord," Aaron said, swooning a bit at the unexpected discovery.

"There is a note inside," Cyrus said. He pulled it out and unfolded the beautifully white paper, which had perfectly parallel blue lines, one red line that ran across the blue lines, and three perfect holes. He read the words written on the paper:

Guys-

I just wanted to thank you again for everything you did for us. It took me a few months to save up enough to try to pay you back the money you spent on us. I don't know how much this is worth in your time, but I hope it covers it. Good luck!

Sincerely yours,
Brent
p.s. – you wouldn't believe how hard I had to work to convince Duncan to let me send this to you!

Cyrus reached into the bag, and pulled out a handful of golden and silver chains, golden rings, and a few tarnished silver spoons.

The two men began to laugh, as the stress of their hardship over the past few days unloaded in the form of pure, joyous laughter. It helped that they now had more than twice the wealth they had earned from Aaron's skins and furs.

They finished dressing, and took a few minutes to give a prayer of thanks to God for their successful adventure, and for their friends' safe return home, as well as for the gift from Brent.

They disposed of the remaining evidence and fed the horses, and then finally got on the road to begin their journey home. They were a bit anxious as they made first part of the drive to Boston, occasionally looking behind them to make sure that they were not followed. After paying the Boston merchant from whom Aaron had borrowed the horses and wagon, they recovered their own horses and wagon, and began their return trek back to Falmouth. By this point, they felt reasonably safe from being associated with the escape, and so were able to travel the remainder of the day with relatively good spirits.

It was dark by the time they had arrived at the outskirts of Falmouth, and Aaron stopped at the smithy. Cyrus removed his supplies and his share of the precious metal from Brent's sack, bid his friend good night, and went into blacksmith home that was adjoined to its workshop.

Aaron lingered for a few moments more, and then set his path towards the home of his mother-in-law to greet his wife.

Friday, September 19, 1692
Field Beside the Town Jail

Giles Corey, who had defied the town magistrates for months by refusing to enter a plea either of guilt or innocence for the accusation of his role as a witch, lay naked under a wooden board. Atop of him were several dozen heavy stones. This punishment, called 'peine forte et dure'*, was intended to make him yield and finally enter a plea. Giles had no intention of yielding. He resolved himself to not even make sounds of pain or suffering during his ordeal.*

This was not the first time they had tortured him to get him to enter a plea. Previously, he had been made to stand all day with his arms outstretched, held in the pillories on two separate days, and even had his feet tied to his neck until his nose bled.

Today was the third day of his latest torture; he had been given some bread and water throughout, but he had had little sleep. However, he knew he hated Sherriff George Corwin. Earlier that day, Corwin had asked him for a plea. Giles had but one reply: in anger and defiance, he cried out "More weight!"

More weight was added. Corwin then climbed up onto the unsteady, large rocks that pressed Giles, and he looked down upon the old man. The great weight caused Giles to feel a terrible pain in his head, as well as in his body, so that his tongue and eyes bulged out of his head. Corwin, pitying the man without sympathy, lifted his cane and used it to force Giles' tongue back into his mouth. Giles had to keep reminding himself that if he failed, his sons would never receive his land. He had to endure this.

Finally, after the sun had passed beyond his sight and now lay to the west, Giles felt something change inside him. It was time, and he knew it. He laughed a pathetic and shallow laugh, followed by coughing due to the heavy wood and stones that lain on him for two days; Sherriff Corwin heard this and came over to look at him.

"How do you plead, guilty or innocent?" Corwin asked quietly.

"I curse you for this," Giles Corey said in a whisper amidst painful and forced laughter. A tear rolled down his right cheek. He then raised his voice to a bitter croak.

"More weight!"

Corwin stepped back, glanced at the men who lifted the stones, and signaled them to begin to lift another stone. He looked back at Corey, and with a disappointed frown, ordered the men to leave the large stone where it lay.

Giles Corey was dead.

Monday, September 22, 1692
The Hanging Tree in the Common Land

Martha Corey, widow of Giles, Mary Eastey, Ann Pudeator, Alice Parker, Mary Parker, Wilmot Redd, Margaret Scott, and a man named Samuel Wardwell all stood shoulder to shoulder along the length of the oxcart.

Nicholas Noyes finished his now-familiar prayer for the condemn-ed. Mary Eastey, whose sister, Rebecca Nurse, was one of the first to be hanged, began a prayer.

"My God," she said, her head bowed, "I beg of your kindness and mercy as my life is taken this day. I seek mercy for each of these souls who will soon be in your glorious presence. Yet, my Father in Heaven, I beg that you give sight to those who condemn us; I pray that the witch hunt will end. Only your glory and splendor can bring an end to this."

The whole lot of the condemned said Amen as she did. Noyes looked at them for a moment, and then gave a signal to the constable, who started the horses to pull the cart. One by one, they fell off the oxcart and dangled by the ropes around their necks, twisting and writhing, their hands tied by rope behind their backs. Several of them gagged and hacked as their movements inadvertently tightened the nooses, hastening their suffocation. A couple of them actually had not moved at all after falling off the wagon, for in their fall, their necks had been broken, and they were immediately dead.

As the last of the supposed witches finally stopped wriggling and expired, Nicholas Noyes walked along each of them, prodding their feet with his pistol. Finally certain that the orders given in their Death Warrant had been met and satisfied, he turned to the few spectators who remained.

"What a sad thing it is to see eight firebrands of Hell hanging there."

Noyes mounted his horse, and with the constables behind him, he left the Hanging Tree, leaving the so-called firebrands to sway lifelessly in the light wind.

The four-year-old Dorcas Good was released from jail on the tenth day of December, sixteen hundred ninety two; nine months after she was imprisoned alongside her mother and Aunt Mary. Because of her many impressionable months of near-isolation from her family in the putrid conditions of the cell, she had a very difficult time adjusting back to life outside of shackles.

Within a few months, Dorcas began to suffer emotional breakdowns, leading to a period of insanity. Estranged from her father, she was taken to Boston and treated in an orphanage. She was separated from other children for days at a time, all while receiving the best available medical treatment for her mental condition.

Fortunately, by the end of the year, her father had begun to confront his role in her imprisonment and his wife's death. To make amends as best he could, William Good began to make more frequent trips to Boston to spend time with his daughter, in spite of her calamity. Within weeks, his weekly visits increased to become daily, and Dorcas began to recover from her insanity.

Before her birthday in sixteen ninety four, she returned home with her father. Finally recovered and in a right state of mind, Dorcas began to rediscover her childhood, and as Salem put its witch-hunt infamy behind it, Dorcas too was able to put her past behind her.

Within weeks of the September hangings, Cotton Mather and his father, Increase Mather, each published their treatises that argued against the use of spectral evidence in the trial of suspected witches. Increase Mather argued in his, which was published on October third, "It were better that ten suspected witches should escape than that one innocent person should be condemned."

This created more debates, particularly between Cotton and Bartholomew Gedney. However, it soon became apparent that Sir William Phips, governor of Massachusetts Bay Colony, was convinced by the Mathers' arguments. On October eighth, Governor Phips submitted his order that all cases tried could no longer use spectral evidence.

Elizabeth Proctor, who had barely escaped execution at the time of her husband's hanging, remained in the jail for the remainder of sixteen ninety two. During that time, she had been pregnant, and gave birth to her son, John, on the twenty-seventh of January. In the many months of her imprisonment, she tried to keep herself joyful in her spirit and in her religion. Although she had lost her husband, her family, and her lands while in prison, she was released after the birth of her son. In time, she would remarry and regain the esteemed status she held before the horrible accusations.

Late in summer of sixteen ninety three, Aaron and Cyrus again made their annual trip. This time, they left Anna home because their infant son, John Quincy, was still not yet of a travelling age. They stopped at the Marble Wharf, and made their visit with Britson without event.

While at the pub, both Aaron and Cyrus at the grated bar, talking to Christopher Reilly.

"Christopher," Aaron said jovially. "I cannot help but notice that this town carries a different mood from last year. What has changed?"

Christopher suddenly looked unsettled.

"It is Salem, the same as it has been in all my time in New England," Reilly replied. He busied his hands and tried to avoid further detail.

"Yes, but whatever became of all the witches?" Aaron asked, genuinely curious. He knew of Governor Phips' orders and the subsequent settling of things, but he wondered from personal perspective.

Christopher looked at him, and then made a decision, and stepped over to Aaron and Cyrus, leaning down and dropping his voice.

"My friends, this is a matter we do not speak of," he said. "It is an embarrassing time that every man, woman and elder would like to forget, and so we elect not to speak of it at all. Please, let us speak of other things."

Raising his eyebrow, Aaron exchanged a knowing look with Cyrus. He lifted his stein, called for a toast for the town and people of Salem, and everyone shared the toast and drank merrily. As he drank, he recalled Jeremy's remark about the passing of the witch trials, and Aaron quietly reveled in his pride at having been a part of it, in some way.

EPILOGUE - 2010
6 A.M., Friday, July 2, 2010
Cedar Pond

All four stood for a few moments, not talking or moving, just standing. Finally, Brent spoke.

"Well, that was some adventure," he remarked.

"Okay, so I guess we should head over to my house," Jeremy volunteered, ready to go home. He suddenly became acutely aware that he was famished.

"We can't," Duncan said. "It's too early."

"What do you mean? Nobody's home," Jeremy said, not following Duncan's point.

"Yes, you are," Lisa said, catching on and snapping her fingers. She turned to Brent and Duncan. "This is still Friday morning, right?"

Duncan winced as he nodded, and Brent replied "Yep". Jeremy finally realized that they were right; at the moment, he was somewhere in front of them, asleep in bed. It was a weird thing to realize.

"So what are we going to do?" Jeremy asked.

Brent reached into his pocket and pulled out his phone. "Let's call Andrew and David, so they—crap, that won't work either!" Brent frowned at the time overlap, and Duncan nodded in agreement with his conclusion.

"I want food," Duncan declared with another wince, apparently still trying to deal with the pain from the lashings. "I'll buy."

"If I could get to my money, we could take the bus to a little food place nearby," Jeremy said, trying to figure out how to get in the house without waking anyone, including himself, up.

"I've got some," Brent offered. He pulled his wallet out of his side pack, and double-checked. "Eight bucks."

Instead of an actual response, Duncan started to chuckle, and then laugh.

"What?" Brent asked, his blue eyebrows knitted in peeved confusion. Lisa started to giggle too; Jeremy saw what they were laughing at, and began to laugh too.

"Sorry," Duncan wheezed between laughs. "It's just trying to take you seriously in that blue face paint." He finished with more laughter.

Realizing that he might in fact look silly in his disguise, he joined in the laughter. All four of the time travelers laughed for almost a minute before the moment passed. Finally, Brent waded into the water and dunked his head in, scrubbing at the blue until it started to come off. The spikes loosened to reveal black curly hair, and within a few minutes, after rubbing his face with his black cloak, he looked almost back to normal, with a few blue smears and smudges here and there.

"So what is this place you mentioned?" Duncan asked while Brent was still cleaning his hair.

"It's called Bob's," Jeremy said. "I'm pretty sure they open real early."

"Do they sell pancakes?" Duncan asked. "I'm not

usually that into them, but today I am craving pancakes."

Jeremy guessed that they did, and when Brent was finished removing his disguise, the foursome started walking to the bus stop, following Jeremy and Lisa's lead.

Within minutes, they got onto Joyce Road, walked the length to Lynnfield Street, and very quickly they stood at the bus stop. However, the daily bus routes had just begun, so they had to wait almost twenty minutes before a bus pulled by.

The restaurant was in fact open, and did indeed serve breakfast items, which pleased everyone. The waitress was astonished that everyone at the table ordered almost two meals each.

"Before we eat," Duncan said, reflecting on the past few days, "Let's say Grace."

Everyone bowed their heads respectfully.

"Lord," Duncan began, "thank you for the journey we just traveled, and thank you for seeing us home safely. As we eat, let us remember the wonderful things our world has that we would not have had in other times, and let us remember those who suffered through the Witch Trials, and died." He waited a few beats, and then finished with, "Amen."

"Amen," everyone repeated, and picked up their forks. Jeremy was about to take a long swig from his tall glass of milk when he heard Lisa sniffle. He looked over at her, and her eyes were watery.

"What's wrong," Jeremy asked.

"Nothing," Lisa lied. She did not want to go into it.

"Come on," Jeremy pressed. Duncan reached over and set his hand on Jeremy's elbow, silently suggesting to let him handle it.

"Lisa," Duncan said to her, "Things that happened in the past may have happened a long time ago, but they did happen. And they were sad, terrible things."

"I know," Lisa sniffed. "I can't help but feel like we should have done something for them." She seemed to have her tears under control again, but then broke down completely. Jeremy put his arm around her, and she fell into his shoulder and sobbed for a few moments. The waitress walked by awkwardly, and Duncan and Brent both wordlessly implied that things were fine and under control; the waitress shuffled away, concerned and curious about the odd group she had as customers this morning.

After a minute or so, Lisa sat back up, snatched a napkin out of the dispenser, daubed at her eyes, and then looked angry.

"I mean, everyone was nice to me in there," she said without preamble. Everyone listened and waited patiently, allowing Lisa time to say what she wanted to say. "Every single one," she said pointedly. "And the poor little girl! She's only four years old and she was in there for *months*! Who does that? Seriously!" she gestured her befuddlement, looking at each of her companions incredulously.

"I wish there was something we could do," Duncan said, sensitive to her feelings. "But if there is something to be remembered, it's that if we were to right every wrong in the past, we would have nothing to learn from. It would be an endless cycle of preventing ourselves from making mistakes."

"I'm sorry, Doctor Duncan," Lisa sniffed dismissively but respectfully, "But I'm not really interested in the 'meaningful time travel' stuff. That's him," she pointed at Jeremy, and then blew her nose with a new napkin. "I just can't believe that we left them to die."

They sat in silence for another minute, no one really knowing what to say to help Lisa deal with this.

"But you're probably right," she conceded, "There probably wasn't anything we could do. I just can't help but feel rotten."

"I'm sorry," Duncan said, looking her in the eyes to make sure she knew he meant it.

"Thank you," she said. Jeremy squeezed her, and whispered into her ear, "I love you. I'm sorry too." He kissed her on the hair. She appreciated that. Sometimes Jeremy didn't say the right things, or maybe he didn't think about her feelings from her point of view when she wanted him to, but he always tried, and in a way, that was what she needed.

Everyone ate a good, filling meal; it was so nice to have food in their bellies, and the three former prisoners agreed that the food smelled a whole lot better after spending three days and nights in a place that was, in effect, a giant outhouse.

They sat in the diner until well after eight. Jeremy saw himself driving his car, apparently on his way to meet with

Doctor Arvind, and earned shushes for his thrill. Once Original-Jeremy had driven past, Duncan suggested that they go ahead and leave, and make their way around the neighborhood and wait for their Original selves to get through the morning uninterrupted.

A weird side-effect of time travel, they discovered, was that Jeremy was receiving Original-Lisa's text messages, which actually helped them keep up with what was happening. Duncan had to remind Jeremy not to answer it when it began to ring, at the time Original-Lisa had called Original-Jeremy to come pick her up.

They had decided to wait at Whitney Park, which was at the end of Whitney Drive. As soon as they heard a honk and a squeal of tires, they all started towards Jeremy's house.

"Interesting," Duncan remarked.

"What's that?" Brent asked.

"I don't remember David honking the horn," Duncan said. "But that's definitely the Aspen's horn."

By the time they made it to Jeremy's house, he saw his neighbor out in the back yard, still tending to things there. He got everyone to sneak up to his house without her seeing them, and they got inside.

"How's your back?" Jeremy asked Duncan once everyone had settled into a chair. They all had cooed in delight at the modern comfort they had not experienced in half a week.

"It hurts like hell," Duncan said, sitting awkwardly.

"What's wrong with your back?" Brent asked, puzzled.

453

"He got whipped while out on the stocks last night," Jeremy answered.

"What?!" Brent said, standing up from Jeremy's couch. "I thought you had pulled a muscle during the get-away or something!"

"Nope," Duncan said patiently.

"Do we need to get you to a doctor?" Lisa asked.

"Yes," Duncan said, "But I wanted to wait until we got David and Andrew back first. As a matter of fact," Duncan said, looking at the wall clock, "We can probably go ahead and call them in a minute."

Andrew stood up in the sunny parking lot, pausing to rub his sore shin where Jeremy had kicked him. David was still bent over, coughing a couple of times as he tried to catch his wind again after Lisa's assault. The time rift had just closed, with Duncan and the other two behind it.

"David, man, you okay?" Andrew asked, and hobbled over a few steps to check on him.

"Yeah, man," David wheezed. "Man, she can hit!" He stood up, and his face scrunched in pain as he stretched out the spasms and sore muscles of his abdomen.

Andrew's phone began to ring. Andrew looked at David, surprised that it was ringing. *It was probably Becky*, he considered. He pulled out his phone; it made even less sense.

"It's Brent's number!" Andrew remarked, showing it to David. "I don't get it." He answered the call; Duncan's voice spoke. Andrew did a double-take.

"Duncan?"

David heard that, and then squinted one eye and he looked up into the sky, trying to sort that out.

Duncan told them that he would explain it later, and then told Andrew to come get them from Jeremy's house. Luckily, the address was still in the GPS. Fifteen minutes later, they were pulling into Jeremy's driveway.

"Wow," David marveled as they took in everyone's appearance.

Jeremy had taken the chance to shower, and then Lisa took her turn. She did not want to put those clothes back on ever again, but she kept the jeans and put on one of Jeremy's shirts. At least she felt cleaner. She would need at least a bath and another shower before she could feel like she had fully washed sixteen-ninety-two off her.

Although Duncan wanted to take up Jeremy's offer for a shower, he felt that he should have his wounds looked at first. He let Brent shower too, and then had everyone ride with him to the hospital.

The hospital was a major pain. First they waited for hours, and when Duncan finally got looked at, there were concerns of racially-motivated crime. However, the staff relented when Duncan denied repeatedly that anything had happened, and that he would refuse to press any charges anyway. The doctors directed the nurses to clean the wounds thoroughly and apply what seemed like an acre of bandages to his back. He learned that he needed fifty-seven stitches overall, and that while many of the welts were strong the skin had not broken. The doctors also prescribed him a series of painkillers, steroids, and antibiotics, since he had shown signs of infection in several places.

It was dark by the time they left the hospital. After getting the medicines Duncan needed from the nearby pharmacy, they headed back to Jeremy's house.

"I'll need you two to come to Edison with us," Duncan said, downing his first dose of medicine. He was almost ecstatic to be able to use modern amenities again.

"Why?" Jeremy and Lisa both asked, taken aback.

"Because I need you to sign some paperwork, and we need to prepare a report on this event," Duncan said.

"A report?"

"Don't seem so surprised. You can't expect technology like this to be built by some lone scientist in his garage, using his family fortune for funding," Duncan said, a teasing twinkle in his eye. Lisa didn't get the reference, but Jeremy bashfully chuckled in amusement, as did the other scientists. "This device was built with serious money and with the highest secrecy classification. You'll need to sign oaths of non-disclosure, too."

"Aw man!" Jeremy complained half-seriously. "You mean I can't talk about this with *anyone*?"

"Who would you tell?" Andrew asked with curiosity, flipping through one of the National Geographic magazines on the table.

"Doctor Arvind, for one," Jeremy said.

"Yeah, I was afraid you'd say that," Duncan said with a sigh. "With him, you can mention it once, but only to admit that you...you know. Anyway, we'll follow up and make sure he also knows that this is not to be discussed."

The next morning, everyone loaded up in the SUV (after Andrew, Brent and Jeremy had gone to retrieve his car from the parking lot downtown) and headed to New Jersey. Jeremy and Lisa were given a tour of the time-travel facility, and met the rest of Duncan's staff.

After signing what seemed like a textbook's worth of papers, Jeremy and Lisa were ready to go home again. The next day would be the Fourth of July, so Duncan invited them to stay at his home, where his wife was more than happy to be a hostess. On Sunday, the four drove up to New York and watched some of the grandest fireworks displays the young couple had ever experienced. Afterward, Duncan and his wife kindly took them home, and then returned to Edison.

"Maybe things will get back to normal now," Jeremy commented as the Duncans drove off, Lisa walking beside him with an arm in his.

"Maybe," she said. "I don't know how long it will be for me, though."

"Do you want to talk about any of it?" he asked.

"No," she said, looking at the ground as they walked.

"Well," Jeremy said after a few moments, "if you ever do, I hope you'll talk to me. I'll always listen."

"Actually, I don't think I can talk to you," she said playfully. "I just signed a bunch of things that say I can't talk to anyone about it, you know," she winked at him.

"Nice try," Jeremy said with a half-smile. They

continued walking down his street, just enjoying the evening air, and hearing distant booms and cracks of unofficial leftover July Fourth celebrations. Jeremy realized that he had traveled through time, just as he had always dreamed, but having Lisa next to him, in his arms and in his heart, was all he could ever wish for. He squeezed her tight and the two walked, enjoying the night and each other.

Lisa tried to put the experience of the examination behind her, but there were times that she could not deal with the emotions that memory provoked. She could not seek professional help, but she didn't think it was something that was critical to her mental health, but she knew that keeping it inside wouldn't work, either. She wanted to talk to Jeremy about it, but she didn't feel like he would understand, so she never mentioned it. It came up from time to time during the occasional big argument between them, and she always left him befuddled as to how to understand her.

However, a month and a half later, in late August, it was different.

"Hey," Jeremy remarked as they walked through the mall one particular day, "it's August twenty-third! We almost got hanged three hundred and –" he paused to work the math, and then finished with "eighteen years ago!"

"Shh!" Lisa said testily, holding her finger to her lips.

"What?" he said. "These people don't have a clue."

"Still," she said. "I don't want to bring it up."

She was testy and moody for the next hour and a half as

they wandered around the mall. Finally, as they were leaving, Jeremy asked, "What's with you? Every time I mention…*that time*…you get all upset and then we don't get along for the rest of the day!

"I told you I don't want to talk about it!" She said as she opened her car door, getting into the drivers' side. Jeremy frowned and then climbed into her car.

"I don't get it," he said. "We did the same stuff! I got beat up a bit more, but that's it! It's actually a pretty cool experience, once you think about it. Why do you get all bent out of shape at the mere mention of it?"

"Because!" was all she said, angrily jamming the key into the ignition.

"That's not an answer!" Jeremy barked back. "I want to know why you do this!"

"Because!" she said again, this time fighting tears. "Because!" she said once again, as the memories boiled to the surface. It had been so embarrassing and demeaning, and she had not shared it with anyone, and now it was this broken thing in her heart and in her mind that she couldn't get rid of.

Her sudden shift to tears caught Jeremy off guard, and he waited to see if she would explain more than 'because'.

"What did they do when they examined you?" she asked. He told her, shrugging as if it was no big deal.

"That's about as much as what happens when you go to the doctor anyway," he said. "There's nothing special about that. Didn't that happen to you?"

"Basically," she said quietly. She could see he still

459

didn't get it. "But what you don't understand is that I had no idea what was going on. And on top of that, that creep Smith watched me undress, and was looking at me the whole time." The memory made her skin crawl again. Even now, she wanted to vomit.

Jeremy felt the urge to track him down and kick his butt; however, Jeremy also knew the guy was dead, and that he'd have to accept that as punishment enough. He felt bad now; he didn't think about her experience much.

"To have those nasty people touching me was—," she tried to think of a word to describe it, but only came up with a shiver and a mild gag. She then told him about the rest of the details of the examination. Jeremy listened closely, trying to remember that what Lisa needed right now was someone to understand her pain, not to try and help her solve the feelings.

When she had finished, Jeremy sat quietly. He felt a bit silly; he was disappointed in himself for not trying to be there at the time, back when they were in the cart and she really needed him. He told her as much.

"I know you care, and I know you love me," Lisa said. "And I realize that if I hadn't told you, you wouldn't have known," she continued. "It just would have been nice if you had been as interested in what was wrong with me as you were with being in time travel."

Jeremy felt peeved at that, but he made himself squash the feeling, since he knew she was right. He had been preoccupied back in the past, and he could have paid better attention to things. He apologized out loud, and internally he promised to work on being more attentive.

Lisa felt much better after sharing her experience with him. She realized that she was not completely sure why she had not done so before; however, it was done now, and they could move on. They exchanged 'I love you's, and Jeremy hugged her for a long time.

Later that evening, they sat on the couch, watching TV. Jeremy had just sat back down with some chips, and he leaned back after a few bites. Lisa nestled herself comfortably into his arms, and pulled her knees up to her chest. As she sat there, in love with her boyfriend, a thought occurred to her.

Things were back to normal; everything was going to be okay.

Troy Duncan stood in his bedroom in front of his wife. She sat quietly, more speechless than patient, as he finished telling her about his adventure. It was necessary; she knew only a little about his professional work, but now that he was home and would eventually take his shirt off around her, he needed to explain the bandage and the his injuries. She had already noticed the injuries on his neck and wrists.

"My God, Baby," she whispered after two minutes of solid silence. "I don't know what to say."

"You don't have to say anything," Duncan said to his wife. "I just needed to tell you before you see it."

She told him to take off his shirt. He complied. She got off the bed and walked around it, and gently traced her finger around the edges of the bandage. Duncan made himself not wince instinctively; although she touched him where he was not injured, her very touch made his skin feel extremely sensitive.

"Show me," she demanded with concern. Duncan pointed to where the bandage should be removed from, and she slowly peeled it off his back. He felt tiny stings of pain and discomfort in spite of the medication, as the bandage poked him in spots and stuck to the welts in others.

He heard her gasp behind him, and then heard her start to cry. He turned and wrapped his arms around her as tears fell from her eyes.

"Shh, baby," he said to her. "It's all right."

"No it's not!" she exclaimed, pulling back from him. "I mean, you were whipped, Troy!"

"I know that," he said softly. "And it hurt," he added. "Everywhere."

She looked up at him. Without words, he pointed four fingers at his chest. She realized what he meant, and her head tilted slightly, new tears welling in her eyes. He stood quietly and allowed her to process everything.

Eventually, she wiped them away and blew her nose. Finally, she walked over to him, held his face with both hands, and looked him in the eyes.

"Are you okay?" she asked. He knew she did not mean his back injuries.

"I don't know," he said. "I have not really had to confront my skin color since I was in college. I had to fight with all I had to not succumb to hatred." His hands had balled into fists.

"Why not? Why don't you hate them with every fiber of your being," she said passionately, clearly trying to hate them for him.

"Because," Troy Duncan said, "if I give in, if I let myself hate them, then what have I gained? How would I be any better than them, or anyone who came before us?" He frowned briefly, hoping she would understand. Then he said, "It would undo everything we have ever fought or suffered for."

She did not say anything after that. She helped redress his bandages, and they spent the evening out at dinner. After the dinner, they strolled in a park, enjoying the warm summer evening.

They walked by the small flower gardens in the city park, and his wife stopped to enjoy the arrangement. As they stood and quietly looked at the garden, she turned to him.

"Troy?" she said.

"Hmm?" he asked absently, and then turned to look into her eyes.

"I'm proud of you," she said.

Duncan smiled, and embraced her with all his appreciation. Something released inside him, and he felt like his emotions from this experience were going to be much easier to handle.

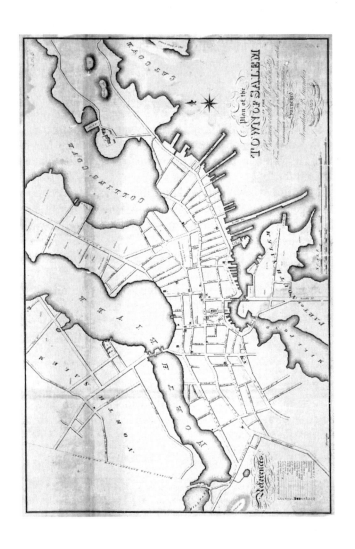